Studies on American Poetry
美国诗歌研究

李正栓 陈岩 著

北京大学出版社
PEKING UNIVERSITY PRESS

图书在版编目(CIP)数据

美国诗歌研究/李正栓,陈岩著. —北京：北京大学出版社,2007.1
（文学论丛）
ISBN 978-7-301-11593-0

Ⅰ. 美…　Ⅱ. ①李…②陈…　Ⅲ. 诗歌—文学研究—美国—英文
Ⅳ. I712.072

中国版本图书馆 CIP 数据核字(2007)第 013261 号

书　　　名：	美国诗歌研究
著作责任者：	李正栓　陈　岩　著
责 任 编 辑：	刘　爽
标 准 书 号：	ISBN 978-7-301-11593-0/I·0892
出 版 发 行：	北京大学出版社
地　　　址：	北京市海淀区成府路 205 号　100871
网　　　址：	http://www.pup.cn　电子信箱：zpup@pup.pku.edu.cn
电　　　话：	邮购部 62752015　发行部 62750672　编辑部 62755217
	出版部 62754962
印　　刷　者：	北京大学印刷厂
经　　销　者：	新华书店
	787 毫米×1092 毫米　16 开本　25.25 印张　426 千字
	2007 年 1 月第 1 版　2007 年 12 月第 2 次印刷
定　　　价：	44.50 元

未经许可,不得以任何方式复制或抄袭本书之部分或全部内容。
版权所有,侵权必究
举报电话：(010)62752024　电子信箱：fd@pup.pku.edu.cn

本书得到"河北省中青年社科专家五十人工程"资助

特此致谢

总　　序

近两年,河北省组织实施了"河北中青年社科专家五十人工程",并计划利用几年的时间编写出版"河北中青年社科专家五十人工程"文库。目前即将出版的有《商品流通领域研究》、《富民经济论》、《马克思主义哲学在中国的理论嬗变》等六部书稿,还有十部书稿计划陆续出版,内容涉及哲学、政治学、经济学、法学、管理学、英美文学等许多学科,涵盖了许多前沿性问题,仅从书的名字即可知其意,都是运用马克思主义理论为指导,紧密联系当前经济社会发展的实际,努力进行理论创新的结果,对现实具有较强的指导意义。不难看出,河北的中青年社科专家年富力强、视野开阔、治学严谨,具有适应时代要求的综合素质,在他们身上体现了河北社科理论队伍人才辈出、社科事业兴旺发达的繁荣局面和美好前景。

我们知道,要使党和国家的事业不停顿,首先是理论上不停顿。马克思主义自诞生以来,之所以能够始终保持旺盛的生命力,一直成为无产阶级认识世界和改造世界的锐利武器,就是因为它善于根据发展变化的实际不断进行理论创新。党的十一届三中全会以来,我们确定了改革开放的路线,不断加深了对社会主义发展规律的认识,1992年邓小平同志南方谈话以后我们对社会主义本质有了全新的认识,党的十四大对邓小平同志建设有中国特色社会主义理论作出系统的阐述,党的十五大确立了邓小平理论在全党的指导地位,党的十六大把"三个代表"重要思想写进了党章,确立为党的指导思想,实践证明,我们党在理论创新上取得的每一个成果,都极大地推动了中国特色社会主义的发展进程。党的十六届三中、四中全会进一步提出了许多新的理论观点,特别是科学发展观、加强党的执政能力建设、构建社会主义和谐社会等一系列理论创新,必将推动我国经济社会和党的建设事业的新发展。

在新世纪新阶段,我国面临着实现社会主义现代化、完成祖国统一、维护世界和平和促进共同发展三大历史任务。我国的改革发展正处在关键时期,社会的经济成分、组织形式、就业方式、利益关系和分配方式日益呈现出多样化趋势,有许多新事物、新情况、新问题、新矛盾需要我们去研究、探索和回答,这既为繁荣发展哲学社会科学提供了良好的机遇,也对广大社科理论工作者提出了新的考验。马克思主义哲学是唯一科学的世界观和方法论,是无产阶级的精神武器,是我们认识当代世界纷繁复杂问题的指针。无论从事何种学科的研究,都必须掌握正确的思想方法,必须学好马克思主义哲学,以深厚的马克思主义理论素养,打牢深入研究各种社会问题的根底。毛泽东同志在1938年党的六届六中全会上说过:"在担负主要领导责任的观点上说,如果我们党有一百个至二百个系统地而不是零碎地、实际地而不是空洞地学会了马克思列宁主义的同志,就会大大地提高我们党的战斗力量,并加速我们战胜日本帝国主义的工作。"在1955年3月召开的中国共产党全国代表会议上提出"我劝同志们要学哲学"。学习哲学,有助于人们树立辩证唯物主义和历史唯物主义的世界观,掌握科学的方法论。当然,在新的历史条件下,马克思主义哲学作为马克思主义的重要组成部分,也要坚持与时俱进,要加以丰富和发展。例如关于辩证法和认识论的对象需要进一步明确,在谈到辩证唯物主义的对象时,指的只是世界观的对象,而认识论的对象是什么,这不太明确。又如辩证唯物主义的内容有待补充,结构需要更加严密。列宁在《哲学笔记》中提出的建构体系的原则是逻辑与历史的一致,这在20世纪二三十年代是得到公认的。但是,二三十年代的苏联哲学家主要不是根据这一原则,而是根据经典作家的一些论述来建构辩证唯物主义与历史唯物主义的体系的。再如辩证唯物主义的一些具体内容需要根据时代的发展变化和科学的进步加以修正,如宇宙起源和演变的理论、物质的构成与内部结构的理论、世界形势的变化发展等等,都需要适应时代发展变化的要求,不断地进行发展创新,哲学社会科学工作者要勇于肩负起这一责任。哲学如此,其他各门学科也都有许多问题需要进一步研究和发展。

　　中青年理论工作者在当前我国经济社会发展中大有可为。以"三个代表"重要思想为指导,树立和贯彻落实科学发展观和努力构建社会主义和谐社会的提出,为他们提供了不断创新的广阔舞台。中青年社科理论工作者要抓住这一有利时机,刻苦钻研,扎实工作,不断创造出更大的成绩。要认真学习马克思主义经典著作,学习当代马克思主义中国化的新成果邓小平理论和"三个代表"重要思想。要以老一代学者为榜样,树立崇高的历史使命感和社会责任感,甘于清贫、耐住寂寞、潜心研究。要坚持理论联系实际的良好学风,坚持把马克思主义基本原理与具体实践相结合,注重研究全局性、前瞻性、战略性的重大课题,促进理论创新、制度

总序
Preface to the Series

创新、科技创新的蓬勃进行。要坚持从自己所处的省情市情出发,围绕本地区经济社会发展的实际,多开展应用对策研究,研究本地贯彻落实科学发展观的重大理论和现实问题,有条件的可发展有地方特色和区域优势的基础理论研究。要自觉地改造自己的主观世界,把做人做事做学问结合起来、统一起来。

在文库出版之际,我表示衷心的祝贺,也希望河北省哲学社会科学战线涌现更多的优秀人才,创造更多的优秀成果。

黄栌森
2005年4月

前　　言

早在 20 世纪 90 年代，我就为全校非英语专业的学生开设了"英美诗歌欣赏"选修课，选修这门课的人由少到多，最后一个班曾经达到了 230 人。教务处对这门课给予了充分肯定，同学们也对这门课表现出了浓厚的兴趣，至今那些同学已经毕业多年，但他们对这门课仍然念念不忘。现在，我同时为英语专业和非英语专业的学生开设英国和美国诗歌课，陈岩老师也多年为英语专业本科生开设美国文学史，我们在共同的教学活动中，形成了一些共识。

我们认为，诗歌是一门能给人裨益的课程，是培养人们修养的良好素材。大学生们非常喜欢诗歌，只是有时感觉有点难。教师虽然能讲授一些诗歌，但毕竟课时有限，所讲诗歌难免会少一些，不能满足学生们的要求。因此，我们觉得加强学生自主性学习很有意义。于是，我们进行了一种研究，目的是为了使这种研究成果方便读者学习诗歌。我们做了这样一种尝试：对美国重要诗人的重要作品进行研究，但又不同于学术论文，在很大程度上是对诗歌进行注解、诠释、解读和评论，并附译文。因此，这是一种立体的、综合性的研究。与当初出发点有所不同的是，读者对象有所扩大，读者对象不再仅仅是选修课的学生和英语专业的学生了。

本书对美国历史上从殖民时期到 20 世纪初的 20 位著名诗人的 90 首诗歌进行了研究，包括：对诗人的生平和创作风格进行简要介绍；对所选诗歌在词汇、诗行或语篇层次上进行详细解释；概括作品的段落大意和主题思想；对每首作品的创作技巧、思想内容进行分析和评论；对每一首诗进行了翻译。

作为一种新型的、综合的研究成果，本书的选材不同于教材，它容量大，题材广，包括常规教材选用的内容，又远远超出了教材的容量。我们之所以这样做，是因为我们想对美国诗歌有一个比较完整、系统的研究。这一研究成果不仅涉及美国文学中的诗歌文化，也可以从中窥见美国历史的发展、民族心理的形成、民族精神的成长，以及美国人的世界观、人生观。可以说，这一成果，以诗歌研究的形式，研究了美国人对爱情和友谊的态度与追求、对农业的态度、对工业的思考、对伦理的考察、对奴隶制的批判、对战争的评论，对人生的思考与分析。

本书行文使用英文，以便使读者以原语进行思考，我们用自己的理解和语言对所选诗歌进行了解读，把自己的理解以注释和评论的形式呈现给读者。为了保证语言的正确性，我们不仅严格要求自己，还聘请了美国诗歌教授、专家卡特博士（Dr. Richard T. Carter）对英文部分进行审读。

本成果的另一特色是中文译文，这是我多年翻译实践的积累和我翻译观点形成的见证。我坚持以诗译诗，力争最大程度地再现原作的风姿和风貌，尽量保持原作的形式。但有些时侯，中国古典诗歌形式对我的影响不可抵制，便采用了中国诗歌形式来表达原作的内容，形式虽变，我仍然强调对原作内容的忠实。这一研究成果之所以要加进中文翻译，是因为对美国诗歌研究不仅仅是英语专业广大教师和学生的事情，也是我国外国文学研究工作者应该重视的一个领域。美国文学的历史虽然不长，其发展对我国诗歌的发展也是有借鉴作用的，比如他们多种多样的诗歌形式和内容。美国诗歌发展中也有我国诗歌对他们影响的见证，比如，美国意象派诗歌的形成非常受惠于翻译家们和诗人们对中国古典诗歌的译介。美国诗人庞德大量翻译了李白的诗歌，尽管改写译很多，中国诗歌意象密集的特点成为他们模仿的对象。在美国，有一大批美国籍的汉学家和华人后裔学者从事着中国诗词的翻译，这些翻译活动与研究对促进文化交流起到巨大的推动作用。我们通过中文译文了解美国的诗歌也是可取的。优秀文化可以互相借鉴，优秀成果应当共同分享。交流促进理解，理解促进友谊，友谊促进和谐，"太平世界，环球同此凉热"的远大目标可以实现。本书所用译文绝大部分是我多年积累的成果，有部分诗歌是我和其他学者共同研究并翻译的。

本书所选诗歌是我和陈岩教授共同确定的，陈教授侧重对原诗进行注解，我负责对所选诗歌进行翻译，我们共同对诗歌做出评论。

本书的阅读对象为以外国文学为研究对象的社会科学工作者、高校英语教师、英语专业研究生、英语专业本科生、自学考试本科段学生、成人高考本科段学生和其他英语诗歌爱好者。

在本书的成书过程中，我们得到省委宣传部的正确领导、热情指导和出版资助，省委宣传部理论处李社军处长和朱忠旗先生对本书的出版付出辛勤劳动。在此特表谢意。

前言
Preface

  本书是我们多年对美国诗歌进行思考的结果,然而,尽管我们努力使书中语言易读易懂,由于水平所限,难免有许多不周之处,望读者不吝赐教。

  在我们进行研究的过程中,曾参阅了国内外学者们的成果,在此一并致谢。

李正栓

2006 年元月

CONTENTS

Section One

American Poetry of the Colonial Period

2	I. Anne Bradstreet (1612–1672)
2	1. Life Story
2	2. On Anne Bradstreet's Poems
3	3. Selected Poems
3	(1) To My Dear and Loving Husband
5	(2) A Letter to Her husband, Absent upon Public Employment
9	(3) In Memory of My Dear Grandchild Elizabeth Bradstreet, Who Deceased August, 1665 Being a Year and a Half Old
12	II. Philip Freneau (1752–1832)
12	1. Life Story
12	2. Writing and Achievements
13	3. Selected Poems
13	(1) The Wild Honey Suckle
17	(2) The Indian Burying Ground

Section Two

American Poetry of Early Romantic Period

26	I. William Cullen Bryant (1794–1878)
26	1. Life Story

i

27	2. Selected Poems
27	(1) Thanatopsis
37	(2) To a Waterfowl
43	**II. Edgar Allan Poe (1809-1849)**
43	1. Life Story
43	2. Poe's Writings and Position in Literary History
44	3. Poe's Aesthetic Theory
44	4. Writing Features of Poe
45	5. Selected Poems
45	(1) To Helen
48	(2) The Raven
63	(3) Annabel Lee

Section Three

American Poetry of High Romantic Period

71	**I. Henry Wadsworth Longfellow (1807-1882)**
71	1. Life Story
71	2. Major Works
72	3. Features of Longfellow's Poetic Works
73	4. Selected Poems
73	(1) The Quadroon Girl
78	(2) A Psalm of Life
83	(3) Daybreak
85	(4) The Tide Rises, the Tide Falls
87	(5) The Village Blacksmith
93	**II. Walt Whitman (1819-1892)**
93	1. Life Story
94	2. Writing Features of Whitman
94	3. Selected Poems
94	(1) Youth, Day, Old Age and Night

96	(2) To Those Who've Failed
97	(3) The Bravest Soldiers
98	(4) Unseen Buds
100	(5) *from* A Song for Occupations
101	(6) To the United States
102	(7) I Sit and Look Out
105	(8) When Lilacs Last in the Dooryard Bloom'd
128	(9) There Was a Child Went Forth
134	(10) Cavalry Crossing a Ford
135	(11) O Captain, My Captain!
138	(12) Song of Myself (excerpted)
145	(13) I Hear America Singing

148   III. Emily Elizabeth Dickinson (1830–1886)

148	1. Life Story
148	2. Features of Emily Dickinson's Poems
149	3. Selected Poems
149	(1) Success (67)
151	(2) Wild Nights—Wild Nights! (249)
153	(3) "Hope" Is the Thing with Feathers (254)
155	(4) The Soul Selects Her Own Society (303)
157	(5) On a Columnar Self— (321)
160	(6) Some Keep the Sabbath Going to Church (324)
162	(7) Our Share of Night to Bear
163	(8) This Is My Letter to the World (441)
165	(9) I Died for Beauty (449)
167	(10) I Heard a Fly Buzz—When I Died— (465)
170	(11) I Like to See It Lap the Miles— (585)
173	(12) Because I Could Not Stop for Death (712)
177	(13) Alter? When the Hills Do (729)
178	(14) A Narrow Fellow in the Grass (986)
182	(15) Tell All the Truth But Tell It Slant— (1129)
184	(16) We Never Know How High (1176)
185	(17) He Ate and Drank the Precious Words (1587)
187	(18) I Never Saw a Moor
188	(19) To Make a Prairy
189	(20) The Sky Is Low—The Clouds Are Mean
190	(21) Apparently with No Surprise (1624)

Section Four

American Poetry of the Modernist Period

194	I. **Robert Frost (1874-1963)**
194	1. Life Story
195	2. Major Works of Frost
195	3. Writing Features of Robert Frost
197	4. Selected Poems
197	(1) The Road Not Taken
200	(2) Stopping by Woods on Snowy Evening
202	(3) After Apple-picking
208	(4) Fire and Ice
210	(5) Design
212	(6) Home Burial
226	(7) The Death of the Hired Man
241	(8) Mending Wall
247	(9) Birches
255	(10) Nothing Gold Can Stay
257	(11) Departmental
262	II. **Edwin Arlington Robinson (1869-1935)**
262	1. Life Story
263	2. Major Works of Robinson
263	3. Writing Features of Robinson
264	4. Selected Poems
264	(1) Richard Cory
267	(2) Miniver Cheevy
271	(3) The House on the Hill
275	III. **Stephen Crane (1871-1900)**
275	1. Life Story
276	2. Writing Features of Crane
276	3. Selected Poems
276	(1) Black Riders Came from the Sea

Contents

278	(2) A Man Said to the Universe
280	**IV. Ezra Pound (1885-1972)**
280	1. Life Story
281	2. Pound's Major Works
281	3. Selected Poems
281	(1) In a Station of the Metro
283	(2) A Pact
284	(3) A Virginal
288	**V. Hilda Doolittle (1886-1961)**
288	1. Life Story
288	2. Major Works of Hilda Doolittle
289	3. Selected Poems
289	(1) Oread
290	(2) Helen
294	**VI. William Carlos Williams (1883-1963)**
294	1. Life Story
294	2. Williams' Major Works
295	3. Selected Poems
295	(1) The Red Wheelbarrow
296	(2) This Is Just to Say
298	(3) Spring and All
302	**VII. T. S. Eliot (1888-1965)**
302	1. Life Story
303	2. Eliot's Major Works
303	3. Selected Poem
	The Love Song of J. Alfred Prufrock
326	**VIII. Carl Sandburg (1878-1967)**
326	1. Life Story
327	2. Characteristics of Sandburg's Poems
327	3. Selected Poems

327	(1) Chicago
332	(2) Fog
333	(3) Grass

336	**IX. Wallace Stevens (1879-1955)**
336	1. Life Story
336	2. Characteristics of Stevens' Poems
337	3. Stevens' Major Poems
337	4. Selected Poems
337	(1) Thirteen Ways of Looking at a Blackbird
344	(2) The Snow Man
346	(3) The Emperor of Ice-cream

349	**X. E.E. Cummings (1894-1962)**
349	1. Life Story
349	2. Characteristics of Cummings' Poems
350	3. Major Works of Cummings
350	4. Selected Poems
350	(1) L(a
352	(2) [R-P-O P-H-E-S-S-A-G-R]
354	(3) In Just —

Section Five

American Poetry of Contemporary Time

358	**I. Theodore Roethke (1908-1963)**
358	1. Life Story
358	2. Characteristics of Roethke's Poems
359	3. Major Works of Roethke
359	4. Selected Poems
359	(1) In a Dark Time
363	(2) My Papa's Waltz

II. Langston Hughes (1902-1967)

- 367   1. Life Story
- 367   2. Characteristics of Hughes' Works
- 368   3. Major Poems of Hughes
- 368   4. Selected Poems
  - 368   (1) The Negro Speaks of Rivers
  - 370   (2) Dreams
  - 371   (3) Words like Freedom
  - 372   (4) Warning

III. Robert Lowell (1917-1977)

- 374   1. Life Story
- 374   2. Characteristics of Lowell's Writings
- 375   3. Major Works of Lowell
- 375   4. Selected Poem
  - Katherine's Dream

381 **Bibliography**

Section One

American Poetry of the Colonial Period

I. Anne Bradstreet
(1612 – 1672)

1. Life Story

Anne Bradstreet was the first noteworthy woman writer in the early stage of American literary history. The collection of her poems, *The Tenth Muse Lately Sprung up in America*, which appeared in 1650, though in London, has always been regarded as one of the earliest publications by a settler of the New World. Many of her poems are personal in subject and often works meditating on domestic topics from a religious point of view. Her talent to capture the colonial experience in poetry established her place as one of America's most outstanding early writers.

As most early English settlers of the 17th century, Anne was born in England into a noble but very religious Puritanical family. In England, she was well educated and married to Simon Bradstreet at the age of 16. Two years later (1630) the whole family migrated to the Massachusetts Bay Colony and settled down there. Anne's father later became the governor of the colony, and her husband, the judge. But Anne kept working as a housewife, for she was by then a mother of 8 children. Life for early settlers was harsh and hard. However, Anne managed to spare time for reading classical works and poetry writing, mainly on the theme of domestic life in the new world. In 1647, a distant relative brought some of Anne Bradstreet's poems to England and had them published in 1650 under the title of *The Tenth Muse Lately Sprung up in America*, quite without Anne Bradstreet's knowledge, and these poems were soon well received in Britain. The poems in the first collection were also agreeable to the taste of American readers.

2. On Anne Bradstreet's Poems

Anne Bradstreet wrote in a traditional way to record the colonial experience, to express her apperception of private life, and to meditate over the Puritan doctrines. Besides, as an early poet, Anne Bradstreet frequently focused on the discussion on such natural facts as the four el-

Section One
American Poetry of the Colonial Period

ements (earth, air, fire, and water), the four humors (the four fluids of human body: blood, phlegm, choler, and melancholy), the four ages of man (In Western culture, the ancient time of human history was divided into four ages: Golden, Silver, Bronze, and Iron Ages), and the four seasons, collecting in what the author called "Quaternions." Anne Bradstreet was imperfect; however, she won a position in literary history for her genuine inspiration and force of character, as well as for the rarity as the first woman poet of the country.

3. Selected Poems

(1) To My Dear and Loving Husband

If ever two were one, then surely we.
If ever man were loved by wife, then thee;
If ever wife was happy in a man,
Compare with me ye women if you can.
5 I prize thy love more than whole mines of gold,
Or all the riches that the East doth hold.
My love is such that rivers cannot quench,
Nor ought but love from thee give recompense.
Thy love is such I can no way repay;
10 The heavens reward thee manifold, I pray.
Then while we live, in love let's so persever,
That when we live no more we may live ever.

Notes

Line 1 If ever two were one: If there had ever been two persons, a husband and a wife, living in perfect harmony in this world, they must be you and me.

Line 2 If there had ever been a husband who were sincerely loved by a wife, you are the lucky one.

Lines 3 – 4 I am the happiest woman in the world to be so loved by you. As a wife, none of any other women appears a match for me. I should be admired by them all.

Lines 5 – 6 I regard your (the husband's) love more valuable than all the gold or wealth. Love is abstract. Gold and wealth have value, while

our love is invaluable. It is something beyond measurement.
the East: the east hemisphere of the world, especially Asia.
Line 7 quench: put out (a fire). Usually a river's water can put out any fire. But our love is so strong that no water of any river, nor the water of all rivers, can put it out.
Line 8 recompense: repay; reward. My love for you can be rewarded by nothing else but your love for me.
Line 11 Then we should, when we are living, keep the love as it is now to the end of our life. persever = persevere
Line 12 live no more: after death. After death, our love, as our soul, will become eternal.

Comment on the poem

This poem was written between 1641 and 1643 but was not published until 1678, when the second edition of *The Tenth Muse Lately Sprung up in American* appeared in the New Continent.

Anne Bradstreet wrote on the everlasting theme of love to eulogize the true love between her husband and her. She strongly praised the sincerity of their love and felt grateful for all the love she had enjoyed from her husband. When they were alive, that love was so abundant and burning hot that "rivers cannot quench"; when they die, their death would just prove the love constant. The true love has overgrown the power of time and space.

The short poem is written in iambic pentameter, rhymed "aa, bb, cc, dd, ee, ff." In other words, we can say, this poem is written in couplet.

参考译文

致我亲爱的丈夫

如果有两人若一,那肯定是你和我。
如果有男人被妻子钟爱,那就是你;
如果有女人因男人而幸福,
女人们啊,你们跟我比。
我珍视你的爱情胜过整座整座的金矿,
胜过东方拥有的所有财富和宝藏。
我的爱是火,河水都不能把它扑灭。

Section One
American Poetry of the Colonial Period

也只有你的爱才能对它进行回报。
你的爱,我无论如何也难以报偿;
愿苍天成倍成倍地把你奖赏。
只要我们活着,咱们就一爱到底,
当我们辞世,我们也永远不分离。
(李正栓 译)

(2) A Letter to Her husband, Absent upon Public Employment

My head, my heart, mine eyes, my life, nay, more,
My joy, my magazine of earthly store,
If two be one, as surely thou and I,
How stayest thou there, whilst I at Ipswich lie?
5   So many steps, head from the heart to sever,
If but a neck, soon should we be together.
I, like the earth this season, mourn in black,
My sun is gone so far in zodiac,
Whom whilst I'joyed, nor storms, nor frost I felt,
10   His warmth such frigid colds did cause to melt.
My chilled limbs now numbed lie forlorn;
Return, return, sweet Sol, from Capricorn;
In this dead time, alas, what can I more
Than view those fruits which through thy heat I bore?
15   Which sweet contentment yield me for a space,
True living pictures of their father face.
O strange effect! Now thou art southward gone,
I weary grow, the tedious day so long;
But when thou northward to me shalt return,
20   I wish my sun may never set, but burn
Within the Cancer of my glowing breast,
The welcome house of him my dearest guest.
Where ever, ever stay, and go not thence,
Till natures sad decree shall call thee hence;
25   Flesh of thy flesh, bone of thy bone,
I here, thou there, yet both but one.

Notes

Line 1 nay, more: not only what I mentioned before, but also a lot of others.

Line 2 my magazine of earthly store: all of my possessions, here referring to "all my love to my husband."

Line 4 How stayest thou there: How should you stay there.

there: Europe. Anne wrote this poem when her husband was absent from her in Europe on business.

whilst I at Ipswich lie: While I have to stay in Ipswich.

Ipswich: It is a town outside of Boston, where Anne Bradstreet was in when she was writing this poem.

Line 5 So many steps: (We are separated from each other) for so far a distance.

head from heart to sever: Our separation is like the head being cut off the heart.

sever: divide or separate something by cutting; break.

Line 6 If but a neck: If it is not with a neck in between; neck here is used as an image, symbolizing something of a barrier.

Line 7 I, like the earth this season: I am just like the earth of this season (winter).

mourn in black: (The earth of this season) seems sorrowful or regretful as if it is very much depressed.

Line 8 My sun: my husband.

zodiac: the imaginary band of the sky containing the positions of the sun, the moon and the main planets, divided into 12 equal parts, named after 12 groups of stars. (黄道带：天空中的假想带，内含太阳、月亮及主要行星，分为12等分，称为十二宫，依十二星座而得名。)

In this line, zodiac refers to the immensity of distance.

Line 9 Whom I whilst I'joyed: While I enjoyed/loved whom (my husband)

Line 10 His warmth: the warmth of the sun, here it refers to the love from her husband.

such frigid colds did cause to melt: (his warmth) did cause such frigid colds to melt.

Line 11 now numbed lie forlorn: now (I am) lying here with all my limbs cold and numbed, completely incapable of thinking, and

Section One
American Poetry of the Colonial Period

lonely.
   forlorn: lonely and unhappy; uncared for.
Line 12 sweet Sol: the sun. Sol is god of Sun in ancient Rome.
   Capricorn: the sun's winter position, the tenth sign of the zodiac, the Goat.
Line 13 dead time: hard time; miserable time; here it means "winter"
   what can I more: what else can I do.
Line 14 view: look sincerely after.
   those fruits which through thy heat I bore: our children, whom were born through your heat. As a matter of fact, Anne Bradstreet was a mother of eight children.
Line 15 which: the children.
   yield: bear; provide.
Line 16 True living pictures of their father face: Their children's faces. Each child takes after the father, thus each appears, to the mother, as a vivid copy of the father.
Line 17 effect: the effect of her response to his absence.
Line 18 I weary grow: I have become exhausted.
Line 19 when thou northward to me shalt return: when you come northward and return to me.
Line 20 but burn: but love me with passions.
Line 21 the Cancer: the sun's summer position, the fourth sign of the zodiac, the Crab.
   my glowing breast: when my breast is filled with summer sun shine.
Line 22 The welcome house of him my dearest guest: (My heart) will become the house for welcoming my dearest guest, my husband, to return.
Line 23 ever, ever stay: stay forever.
   go not thence: never leave there.
Line 24 natures sad decree: death.
   decree: order given by a ruler or authority and having the force of a law.
Line 25 Flesh of thy flesh, bone of thy bone: I am your flesh and your bone.
Line 26 I here, thou there: though we are still far from each other.
   Yet both but one: we are actually existing as one person.

Comment on the poem

This is a rare-seen poem of an American wife's clinging passion for her husband who had been absent on business in Europe. With enormous metaphorical narrations, the speaker, or the woman poet in this case, expressed her passion that without the presence of him, her existence was quite similar to the state of "head from the heart to sever"; "The neck" was conceived as something blocking the union of head and heart. When the husband is away, "my sun is gone," "the tedious day so long"; however, once he "to me shalt return," "my sun may never set." To present the blazing feeling of love, the speaker takes advantage of some astronomical terms. Their love is vehement and constant, and neither the separation in life time nor that after death can ever affect it. In passion, Anne Bradstreet surpasses that of Sappho.

The poem rhymed every double lines (aa, bb, cc, dd ...) (couplet)

参考译文

致远任赴职的爱夫

我脑中、心中、眼里,甚至整个生命中,你无处不在。
你为我带来欢乐,让我倾情相爱。
若有两人合一,必是你我无疑,
可你怎能远走他乡,舍我孤独无依?
恰似头脑和心灵已被远远分离,
若不是被脖颈分开,我们早已在一起。
如同此时世间万物,我也忧郁叹哀,
只因我的太阳远处轨带。
他使我快乐,让我不再经历暴雨风霜,
他给我温暖,融化了心中的寒冷坚冰。
如今我却凄惨无力,最难将息;
归来吧,我的太阳,我的唯一。
在这冷清时节,怎堪回首往事,
曾记得——融融暖日,硕果累累。
一切美好回忆尽藏心头,
凝眸处,又现往昔音容。
此情切切!而今你别我南行,
终日慵倦,叹何时再相见。
待君北还团圆时,
但愿日不落,永远不我离。
日日照心田,

Section One
American Poetry of the Colonial Period

相伴两无厌。
只有相随无离别,
直到生死阴阳界;
我依然是君肉中肉,骨中骨,
纵离愁两处,你我永相依。
（周英莉 李正栓 译）

(3) In Memory of My Dear Grandchild Elizabeth Bradstreet, Who Deceased August, 1665 Being a Year and a Half Old

Farewell dear babe, my hearts too much content,
Farewell sweet babe, the pleasure of mine eye,
Farewell fair flower that for a space was lent,
Then ta'en away unto eternity.
5   Blest babe why should I once bewail thy fate,
Or sigh the days so soon were terminate;
Sith thou art settled in an everlasting state.
By nature trees do rot when they are grown.
And plums and apples thoroughly ripe do fall,
10 And corn and grass are in their season mown,
And time brings down what is both strong and tall.
But plants new set to be eradicate,
But buds new blown, to have so short a date,
Is by His hand alone that guides nature and fate.

Notes

Line 1 Farewell: have no more of somebody or something.
Line 2 the pleasure of mine eye: (the baby used to be) the pleasure of my life.
Line 3 fair flower: the baby.
    that for a space was lent: (the fair flower or the baby) who was allowed to live with me temporarily.
Line 4 ta'en away unto eternity: taken away, left me and went to the after life; died.

Line 5 bewail: mourn for; express my sorrow over (the death of the baby).

        thy fate: The baby's destiny of enjoying a very short life.

Line 6 the days: life of the baby.

        terminate: the word should be "terminated." For the sake of keeping the rhyme, Anne Bradstreet dropped a "d." so did "eradicate" in Line 12.

Line 7 Sith: since.

        everlasting state: heaven.

Line 8 rot: to decay or become damaged.

Line 9 thoroughly ripe: fully matured; fully developed.

Line 10 in their season: at the proper time; when they are ripe mown, being cut in large numbers.

Line 11 brings down: overthrow; cause to fall; kill.

Line 12 plants new set: the newly grown plants; the lasting of the plants.

Line 13 to have so short a date: to exist for such a short time.

Line 14 Is by His hand alone: it is just by God's hand that the nature and fate of human beings are guided.

Comment on the poem

    This poem is written in the form of a sonnet with the foot of iambic pentameter and the rhyme scheme of "ababccc," a variation of either Petrarchan or Shakespearan sonnet.

    Anne Bradstreet wrote this poem to mourn the death of her grandchild who was only a year and a half old. Usually, it is always very sad, melancholy for an old person to mourn over the death of a little baby. But this poem is rationally, but unconventionally written: Anne Bradstreet takes the untimely death of the baby just as an accidental event in nature.

    For a Puritan, human life consists of two sections: the present life in this world—this life, which is short and impermanent; and the afterlife, which is eternal with God. Thus, Anne Bradstreet persuaded herself not to be sad for the death of the loved child, since the baby has gone to the afterlife and is living with God. The baby is in a happier place, beyond pain, beyond hurt, sorrow and death.

    Anne Bradstreet wrote this piece of work to indicate her belief in the afterlife or to release herself from the sorrow brought by the death of a lovely child.

参考译文

悼爱孙
（于1665年8月一岁半时夭折）

别了，亲爱的孩子，我内心十分安详，
别了，可爱的宝贝，你是我眼中的欢乐。
别了，绚烂的花朵，你昙花般开放，
转瞬消失入寰，奔向了永恒。
上帝的宠儿，我不该为你的命运悲叹，
或惋惜你的尘缘过早中断；
因为你已升入天堂，安详而又恬淡。
参天树木自会腐朽，
飘香瓜果熟透自落。
谷物荒秽适时除刈，
时光吞噬强大之物。
万物初成即被消灭，
蓓蕾乍吐亦招催谢，
自然时运皆出主训。

（周英莉 译 李正栓 校）

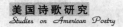

II. Philip Freneau
(1752 – 1832)

1. Life Story

Philip Freneau has always been regarded as "the Father of American Poetry."

Born on January 12, 1752 in New York City, Freneau was brought to New Jersey at 10 by his father, a ship builder and plantation owner. When he was studying law at the College of New Jersey (later Princeton University), he became a roommate of James Madison (1751 – 1836), later the fourth president of the United States, and his career as a poet also began during this period, though he had to do various jobs as a farmer, a journalist, or a sea captain, just for living.

As a poet, Freneau wrote truly and patriotically about his country. His first collection of poems, entitled *The American Village*, was published in 1772. When the Independent Revolution broke out, Freneau took great advantage of his poetic inspiration to devote all his patriotic talents to the revolutionary cause. As a result, a lot of poems were written for exposing the brutality of British colonialism and for encouraging the revolution. *The British Prison Ship*, *To the Memory of the Brave Americans* were both published in 1781.

From 1776 to 1778, Freneau was offered a position of secretary in the West Indies. There Freneau became interested in the romance of the past and the natural beauty of the American country. This brought to the country a large group of lyrical works; among them, "The Wild Honey Suckle" is considered the best.

Thus the poetic works of Freneau can be classified into two categories: poems of natural beauty and poems on American Revolution.

2. Writing and Achievements

Philip Freneau was called the "Poet of the American Revolution." Most of Freneau's poems are political satires or patriotic revolutionary verses with democratic ideas.

Section One
American Poetry of the Colonial Period

In his poems, Freneau tried to avoid imitation of English poets, but dedicated himself to describing American subject matter: American landscape, American images, his hatred toward the British colonists, and his resentment toward slavery.

Freneau's writings broke the bounds established by his forerunners. He wrote actively in a wide range about his contemporary life and displayed a fresh perception about nature.

3. Selected Poems

(1) The Wild Honey Suckle

Fair flower, that dost so comely grow,
Hid in this silent, dull retreat,
Untouched they honied blossom blow,
Unseen thy little branches greet:
5   No roving foot shall crush thee here,
No busy hand provoke a tear.

By Nature's self in white arrayed,
She bade thee shun the vulgar eye,
And planted here the guardian shade,
10 And sent soft waters murmuring by;
Thus quietly thy summer goes,
Thy days declining to repose.

Smit with those charms, that must decay,
I grieve to see your future doom;
15 They died—nor were those flowers more gay,
the flowers that did in Eden bloom;
Unpitying frosts, and Autumn's power
Shall leave no vestige of this flower.

From morning suns and evening dews,
20 At first thy little being came:
If nothing once, you nothing lose,
For when you die you are the same:
The space between, is but an hour,
The frail duration of a flower.

Notes

Line 1 dost: do.
   comely: attractively; showing a pleasing appearance.
Line 2 Hid: being planted in a remote spot.
   dull retreat: a plain, secluded place.
Line 5 roving foot: the treading feet of some loafing people.
Line 6 busy hand: aggressive people; unpitiful persons.
   provoke a tear: venture a picking of the flower; make the flower so angry as to cry with tears.

Stanza 1: The first stanza of the poem treats the advantages as well as the disadvantages of the flower's modest retirement—it is designed with beauty and well protected in solitude; whereas its beauty might be admired by few.

Line 7 By Nature's self: by nature itself.
   arrayed: dressed; arranged to appear in such a colour.
Line 8 She: Nature.
   thee: the flower.
   the vulgar eye: the very rude gazing (from human beings).
Line 9 the guardian shade: in the protection of God by being located under the bush.
Line 11 summer: the time when a flower is fully blooming and rapidly developing; the best time of life.
Line 12 declining: change from better to worse, from higher to lower state.

Stanza 2: The second stanza suggests that the honey suckle bears a special relationship with nature which has advised it to keep away from the "vulgar eye"; Nature has designed it in white—a color of simplicity and purity, and, it has sent the soft waters flowing gently by. However, in spite of all the nature's kindness, the flower cannot escape its doom. The best time of its life is fading, for death is waiting.

Line 13 Smit: (the poet being) deeply affected; together with.
   that must decay: that you (the wild honey suckle) must go to a lower, worse state; death is absolutely coming.
Line 15 They: the flowers in Eden.

Section One
American Poetry of the Colonial Period

nor were those flowers more gay: those flowers that did bloom in Eden were no luckier than others; the god of death comes to them too; nothing is so able as to escape the hand of death.

Line 16 the flowers that did in Eden bloom: the flowers bloomed in Eden (have to meet their death). This is a non-restrictive attributive clause modifies "They" in the above line.

Line 17 Unpitying frosts: (The flowers will die of the) merciless frosts.

Line 18 (Autumn's power) shall destroy any trace of the life of this wild honey suckle.

Stanza 3: The third stanza reveals the indifference of nature—the "unpitying frosts" are as much a part of nature as the "soft waters." Thus, the notion that nature has provided a "guardian shade" for the protection of the honey suckle is a sentimental fancy. It is relative, but death is absolute.

Lines 19 – 20 "morning suns" and "evening dews": symbols of nature's creative power.

Line 21 If nothing once: If (when you were born) you came from nothing. When you were created, you did not bring with you anything of your own.

you nothing lose: (when you die) you will lose nothing. Death just means turning back to nothing.

Line 23 The space between: the time between birth and death.

is but an hour: is merely a very short period of time (as the life of a flower).

Line 24 the frail duration: the very weak span of life (of a flower).

Stanza 4: In the fourth stanza, the poet sees his fate mirrored in that of the flower. Human beings, as any other creatures or flowers, are a part of nature. They originated from nature and will surely return to nature some day, thus their reduction to nature in the day ahead will constitute no real loss.

Comment on the poem

This is one of the most quoted works of Freneau. It was written in 1786 in regular 4 tetrameter stanzas, with 6 lines for each stanza and a rhyme scheme of "ababcc."

Before Freneau there had been some American poets who, however, wrote mostly on the religious theme and either in style or structurally they imitated English poets. Freneau, the first American-born poet, was one of the earliest who cast their eyes over the natural surroundings of the New Continent and American subject matter. As is displayed in this poem: Honey suckle, instead of rose or daffodil became the object of depiction; it is "wild" just to convey the fresh perception of the natural scenes on the new continent. The flowers, similar to the early Puritan settlers, used to believe they were the selects of God to be arranged on the abundant land, but now have to wake up from that fantasy and be more respectful to natural law. Time is constant but the time of a life is short; any favor is relative but change is absolute; with or without the awareness, nature develops: flowers were born, bloomed and declined to repose, and human beings would exist in exactly the same way. A philosophical meditation is indicated by the description of the fate of a trivial wild plant.

In this poem, the poet writes with the strong implication that, though in the work no one is presented in person, human beings may at times envy the flower. This is seen not because the "roving foot" would "crush"; nor that the "busy hand" would "provoke a tear"; nor because of the "vulgar eye," but because of the fact that the human being has the ability to foresee his death. Whereas, the flower, with its happy ignorance, lacks this consciousness and is completely unaware of its doom. Its innocence left it happier than the foreseeing human beings. Unfortunately, the human beings are quite unwilling to refuse this knowledge and that arouses all their sufferings.

参考译文

野忍冬花

美丽的花,长着这般标致的模样,
你隐藏的地方这么静寂而又阴暗,
无人触摸,甜蜜的花朵自由绽放,
也没人看见,小小花枝迎风招展:
这里没有闲荡者肆意把你践踏,
没有无情折枝的手让你垂泪花。

苍天安排你身着白素衫,
令你躲开粗俗者的眼光,
为你种了护卫绿荫一片,
还送来潺潺清水慢流淌;
你的盛夏悄然而去,

日渐西落也要休息。

百般娇艳终要凋零,
不忍见你未来劫难
伊甸鲜花欢乐娇容,
命运和你同病相怜,
霜冻无情,秋天力劲,
定将你摧,不留片痕。

从旭日朝晖到夜晚露滴,
小巧的你初露端倪,
既曾无得,更无损失,
生生死死,对你不变:
叹生死只是一瞬间,
怅繁花易落浮生短。
（李正栓　魏慧哲　译）

(2) The Indian Burying Ground

In spite of all the learned have said,
    I still my old opinion keep;
The posture, that we give the dead,
    Points out the souls eternal sleep.

5   Not so the ancients of these lands,
    The Indian, when from life released,
Again is seated with his friends,
    And shares again the joyous feast.

His imaged birds, and painted bowl,
10   And venison, for a journey dressed,
Bespeak the nature of the soul.
    Activity, that knows no rest.
His bow, for action ready bent,
    And arrows, with a head of stone,
15 Can only mean that life is spent,
    And not the old ideas gone.
Thou, stranger, that shalt come this way,
    No fraud upon the dead commit

Observe the swelling turf, and say
20   They do not lie, but here they sit.

Here still a lofty rock remains,
   On which the curious eye may trace
(Now wasted, half, by wearing rains)
   The fancies of a ruder race.

25 Here still an aged elm aspires,
   Beneath whose far-projecting shade
(And which the shepherd still admires)
   The children of the forest played!

There oft a restless Indian queen
30   (Pale Shebah, with her braided hair)
And many a barbarous form is seen
   To chide the man that lingers there.

By midnight moons, o'er moistening dews;
   In habit for the chase arrayed,
35 The hunter still the deer pursues,
   The hunter and the deer, a shade!

And long shall timorous fancy see,
   The painted chief, and pointed spear,
And Reasons self shall bow the knee
40   To shadows and delusions here.

Notes

Line 1 the learned: wise men; the knowledgeable persons.
Line 2 I still my old opinion keep: I still keep my old opinion.
Line 3 The posture: the attitude or position of the body.
    The posture, that we give the dead: the posture the dead body takes when it is being buried (usually on its back, as in the position when one is sleep on his back).
Line 4 Points out the souls eternal sleep: indicates the direction one's soul would take when it is leaving the body. Freneau believes

Section One
American Poetry of the Colonial Period

that Christian burial "points out" the belief that the soul is "asleep" until the resurrection.
eternal sleep: death.

Stanza 1: At the very beginning of the poem, Freneau, like all Christians, declared his insisting on the belief that the posture of the dead indicates the soul's eternal sleep.

Line 5 Not so the ancients of these lands: Not Indians, they believed differently.
Line 6 when from life released: when they are released from life.
  from life released: died.
Line 7 Again is seated with his friends: the corpse is buried in a sitting position, as if being together with his friends.
Line 8 And shares again the joyous feast: (The dead keeps the sitting position) as if he is feasting his friends.

Stanza 2: Freneau learned here how the American Indians buried their dead. Freneau made a note in his original manuscript that the North American Indians bury their dead in a sitting posture; decorating the corpse with wampum, the images of birds, quadrupeds, etc: And (if that of a warrior), with bows, arrows, tomahawks, and other military weapons.

Line 9 His imaged birds: the imaged birds used to decorate the dead person.
Line 10 venison: flesh of a deer used as meat.
  for a journey dressed: (the dead is) dressed in the way as if he is going for a new journey.
Line 11 Bespeak: be evidence of...; indicate.
Line 12 Activity, that knows no rest: shows the dead used to be a good hunter with unremitting activities. The soul is eternally active.

Stanza 3: The decorations of birds, bowl, venison and the dress for the journey all suggest that the dead person used to be a hunter, and by nature a very diligent one.

Lines 13 – 14 When the dead is in his grave, his weapons are made to keep the posture of triggering, too.
Lines 15 – 16 The death of a good hunter just indicates the exhaustion

of his life in this world, but not the ending of his belief.

Stanza 4: A further description of the decorated weapons of the dead warrior and a further indication that when a man is dead, his soul might live on.

Line 17 Thou, stranger, that shalt come this way: anyone, may be just a stranger, should come to this place to have a look of it by your own eyes, since the Indians really do the burying their dead as I had described.
Line 18 No fraud upon the dead commit: Do not disturb them; "them" here refers to the graves and their contents.
Line 19 Observe the swelling turf: look at the tomb of the dead yourself.
the swelling turf: a euphemism for tomb, when the tomb is covered with grass.
Indian graves typically look like low mounds, a few inches to as much as a foot in height, at least in the poet's part of the country.

Stanza 5: Anyone who comes here should not disturb the dead but just leave them in peace.

Line 21 Here still a lofty rock remains: a sacred rock still remains here.
Here: in the graveyard.
a lofty rock: a sacred rock; remains of ancient Indians.
Line 24 the ruder race: the Indian people; American Indians were often considered rude by European colonists. However, Freneau expressed this convention ironically by using the comparative degree of the adjective "ruder," with the strong suggestion that some other people (the European settlers) is already very rude.

Stanza 6: This stanza is a description of the petroglyphs on the face of the "lofty rock."

Line 25 an aged elm aspires: an old elm tree is flourishingly growing here.
Line 27 which: the shade of the old elm tree.
Line 28 children of the forest: children of nature, Indians in general. Europeans thought all Indians were "children."

Stanza 7: With the advancing of time, a lot of things were lost; howev-

Section One
American Poetry of the Colonial Period

er, something remains till today. The spreading of the aged elm tree can be taken as a symbol for the preserving of Indian tradition.

Line 29 oft a restless Indian queen: The "Queen" and the "barbarous forms" are ghosts that will chide those having no business there.
Line 30 Shebah: (=Sheba) the Queen of Sheba, a powerful Arabian country, paid a visit in homage to Solomon (I Kings x; II Chronicles ix) and became legendary in literature for her beauty and wisdom.
  The ghost, with her face pale, appears quite similar to the Queen of Shebah.
Line 32 To chide: to rebuke; to scold.

Stanza 8: About the Indian graveyard, there were ghosts who appear now and then to rebuke the loafing people.

Line 34 In habit for the chase arrayed: The hunters, even in the midnight, as they have been used to, dressed themselves as if ready for chasing the game.
Line 35 The hunter still the deer pursues: (In the midnight, over the wet dews) the hunter is still pursuing the deer.
Line 36 a shade: a shadow or ghost.

Stanza 9: Another picture the poet imagined of the primitive age when hunters chasing after the deer at midnight. He is iimagining their ghosts.

Line 37 And long shall timorous fancy see: At this place people will be fancied to stop and see for long time.
Line 38 The painted chief: the chieftain of the ancient Indian tribe who might be in the habit to have his face colorfully painted.
Line 39 And Reasons self: the Reason itself. Here by capitalizing the letter, "reason" is personified to parallel with the poet of wild imagination so as to show the analogy between the two.
Line 40 shadows: the imagined pictures of the Indian tribe.
  delusion: false opinion or belief; the pictures of Indians out of the poets imagination.
  Ghosts are still seen in imagination. Hence, "timorous fancy."

Stanza 10: The imagined pictures of the Indian people are so fantastic that everyone, as well as Reason, will be lost in the beauty of them. Reason knows there are no ghosts, but succumbs to the images awakened by the graves.

Comment on the poem

This is another of the two best lyrics of Freneau.

The poem was published in 1788 in his collection of essays and poems: *Miscellaneous Works*. In 1787, Freneau chanced to pay a visit to an Indian tribe and saw the strange way of the Indians burying a body. Freneau was greatly shocked and deeply impressed by their burying the dead in a sitting posture and that resulted in this poem of rich imagination.

The poem consists of 10 stanzas, written in the traditional iambic tetrameter quatrains, rhymed "abab."

The ten stanzas can be divided into two sections: From stanza 1 to the end of stanza 5, in it the poet described in detail what he had seen in an Indian tribe of their burying the dead in a sitting posture, their decorations, and their funerary customs.

The latter section consists of the last 5 stanzas. In this part, the poet takes great advantage of his poetic genius as to imagine, quite out of the lofty rock and an aged elm tree, the life of primitive Indians: How the tribe was governed; how diligently the hunters used to work. The poet, emotionally and mentally, is indulged in the pictures he himself had created.

Freneau points out differences between Christian and Indian in burial customs in order to set the stage for his vivid images of the Indians' spirits actively pursuing their old customs in the environs of their graveyard.

This poem has always been regarded as the first eulogistic poem about Indian custom and their bravery.

印第安人墓地

不管所有学者们怎么说，
我仍坚持不改初衷，

Section One
American Poetry of the Colonial Period

逝者的姿势仍然在摆着，
指引着灵魂睡眠般永恒。

当这片土地上古老的祖先，
印第安人走完生命的旅程，
逝者仍然安坐席间，
与朋友乐享欢宴的丰盛。

那鸟的肖像，那盛饭的画钵，
还摆放着鹿肉，整装待发模样，
昭示了那魂灵的本色：
辛劳一生，永不卸装。

弓似弯月待发射，
石造箭头已在弦，
死亡只是生命结，
执著信念仍续延。

陌生人请看这边，
说话莫把死人欺，
看看隆起的坟墓里，请直言：
逝者没躺着，他们是坐姿。

巨大石块仍犹在，
好奇之人细揣摩，
雨打表层半脱落，
此族更蛮奇思多。

榆树虽老悠然立，
层层绿荫为谁辟，
牧羊人们仍称赞，
林中孩童来耍玩。

常看见一个印第安女王，
（像塞巴，脸色苍白辫发飘。）
看见她许多原始野蛮状，
痛斥男人悠闲乐逍遥。

美国诗歌研究
Studies on American Poetry

午夜月伴滴滴露，
猎人惯着猎装行，
仍在追逐赶野鹿，
月下人鹿相随影。

迷恋的人们驻足长看，
花脸首领，利矛仍执，
面对印第安部落影幻，
理性若来亦俯首屈膝。
（李正栓　魏慧哲　译）

Section Two

American Poetry of Early Romantic Period

Ⅰ. William Cullen Bryant
(1794 – 1878)

1. Life Story

In the dawn of the 18th century when the term "Romanticism" was not in current yet, Bryant was recognized as the best poet that America had produced at that time. As a matter of fact, Bryant was the first American lyrical poet of distinction.

Bryant was born on a farm at Cummington, Massachusetts after the War of Indenpendence. As an ardent young man, he devoted himself to poetry writing and took nature and American landscape as a source for his poetic inspiration. Bryant's career as a poet began very early. At the age of 14, he published his first verse, *The Embargo* (1808); at 16, when his fellows were enjoying themselves in sports and games, Bryant was already a mature young man, meditating over the problems of life and death, which resulted in his greatest poem, "Thanatopsis," which was later published in the *North American Review* in 1817.

As the first lyrical poet of the country, Bryant took American landscape as the source of his poetic inspiration and thus made American subjects worthy of celebration. By this he enriched the treasure house of American poetry and established himself as one of the noteworthy writers in literary history. Besides, Bryant contributed greatly to the development of American newspaper. He has also been remembered as the first American translator of Homer's *Iliad and Odyssey*.

Bryant was sometimes called "the American Wordsworth." However, his poetic works, especially "Thanatopsis," either by theme or by style, with an austere and carefully controlled melancholy, suggested a strong resemblance to the works of the "Graveyard School." In Thanatopsis, Bryant developed a view of death which represents a sharp break from the Puritan attitude toward man's final destiny. He was inclined to idealize the life in countryside, but preach down city life; nevertheless, his description of the American landscape and the close observation of natural objects are quite original.

Technically, Bryant's theme and subject were rather conventional. Most of his poems were written in blank verse.

Section Two
American Poetry of Early Romantic Period

Among Bryant's major poetic works, besides "Thanatopsis," "To A Waterfowl" is also frequently appreciated. The work was composed in 1815, while he was on a journey on a cold winter day and felt desolated for not knowing what would become of him in the big world. Suddenly he saw a waterfowl flying across the sky and took comfort from the realization that the same God who guided the bird would surely guide him. This experience was rather movingly presented and the life of the waterfowl is vividly imagined in the writing.

2. Selected Poems

(1) Thanatopsis

    To him who, in the love of Nature, holds
    Communion with her visible forms, she speaks,
    A various language; for his gayer hours
    She has a voice of gladness, and a smile
5   And eloquence of beauty; and she glides
    Into his darker musings, with a mild
    And healing sympathy, that steals away
    Their sharpness, ere he is aware. When thoughts
    Of the last bitter hour come like a blight
10   Over thy spirit, and sad images
    Of the stern agony, and shroud, and pall,
    And breathless darkness, and the narrow house,
    Making thee to shudder, and grow sick at heart, —
    Go forth under the open sky, and list
15   To Natures teachings, while from all around
    Earth and her waters, and the depths of air
    Comes a still voice: —Yet a few days, and thee
    The all-beholding sun shall see no more
    In all his course; nor yet in the cold ground,
20   Where thy pale form was laid, with many tears,
    Nor in the embrace of ocean, shall exist
    Thy image. Earth, that nourished thee, shall claim,
    Thy growth, to be resolved to earth again;
    And, lost each human trace, surrendering up
25   Thine individual being, shalt thou go
    To mix forever with the elements;
    To be a brother to the insensible rock,

And to the sluggish clod, which the rude swain
Turns with his share, and treads upon. The oak
30   Shall send his roots abroad, and pierce thy mould.
Yet not to thy eternal resting place
Shalt thou retire alone nor couldst thou wish
Couch more magnificent. Thou shalt lie sown
With patriarchs of the infant world—with kings
35   The powerful of the earth the wise, the good,
Fair forms, and hoary seers of ages past,
All in one mighty sepulcher. The hills
Rock-ribbed and ancient as the sun, —the vales
Stretching in pensive quietness between;
40   The venerable woods—rivers that move
In majesty, and the complaining brooks
That make the meadows green; and poured round all
Old oceans gray and melancholy waste, —
Are but the solemn decorations all
45   Of the great tomb of man. The golden sun,
The planets, all the infinite host of heaven,
Are shining on the sad abodes of death,
Through the still lapse of ages. All that tread
The globe are but a handful to the tribes
50   That slumber in its bosom. Take the wings
Of morning and the Barcan desert pierce,
Or lose thyself in the continuous woods
Where rolls the Oregon, and hears no sound,
Save his own dashings—yet the dead are there:
55   And millions in those solitudes, since first
The flight of years began, have laid them down
In their last sleep—the dead reign there alone.
So shalt thou rest and what if thou shalt fall
Unnoticed by the living and no friend
60   Take note of thy departure? All that breathe
Will share thy destiny. The gay will laugh
When thou art gone, the solemn brood of care
Plod on, and each one as before will chase
His favorite phantom, yet all these shall leave
65   Their mirth and their employments, and shall come,
And make their bed with thee. As the long train
Of ages glide away, the sons of men,

Section Two
American Poetry of Early Romantic Period

    The youth in life's green spring, and he who goes
    In the full strength of years, matron, and maid,
70 The speechless babe, and the gray-headed men—
    Shall one by one be gathered to thy side,
    By those, who in their turn shall follow them.

    So live, that when thy summons comes to join
    The innumerable caravan, that moves
75 To the mysterious realm of shade, where each shall take
    His chamber in the silent halls of death,
    Thou go not, like the quarryk-slave at night,
    Scourged to his dungeon, but sustained and soothed
    By an unfaltering trust, approach thy grave,
80 Like one who wraps the drapery of his couch
    About him, and lies down to pleasant dreams.

Notes

Thanatopsis: The poem was written in 1811 but published in 1817. Thanatopsis, the title, means a meditation over death. (It is a compound Greek word made by "thanatos" meaning "death" while "opsis" meaning "think" or "look at.")

Lines 1 – 2 holds communion with: shares or exchanges thoughts or feelings with...
Line 2 visible forms: the objective existences in nature.
    she: Nature.
Line 3 A various language: different languages; language comprehensible in various ways.
    for his gayer hours: when he was merry and happy.
    his: the one who loves nature.
    gayer hours: merry occasion; happy time.
Line 5 eloquence of beauty: tremendous beauty.
    glides into: secretly approaches.
Line 6 darker musings: gloomy meditation.
Lines 6 – 7 a mild and healing sympathy: a sympathy showed by nature which is mild and which is curative to human's sadness and sorrow.
Line 7 that: the mild and healing sympathy.

steals away: gradually wears down; be gradually curative to...

Line 8 sharpness: the piecing painfulness caused by their meditation.

ere he is aware: before he (the person who loves nature) is able to realize (the great pain).

Line 9 the last bitter hour: the sorrowful moment when one's death arrives.

Lines 9 – 10 like a blight over thy spirit: (appears or arrives) like a disaster and seizes your spirit.

blight: disease that withers plants.

Line 11 the stern agony: the serious suffering of the mind and body.

Line 12 breathless darkness, and the narrow house: the state inside of a grave.

Line 13 shudder: shiver for fear of death.

grow sick at heart: greatly detest something or somebody.

Line 14 Go forth under the open sky: (at this moment when thoughts of death makes you shudder and sick at heart) you ought to go out into the natural surroundings.

list: listen.

Line 16 the depth of air: the highest level of heaven.

Line 17 a still voice: a quiet but steady sound.

Line 20 thy pale form: your dead body.

Lines 21 – 22 Nor in the embrace of ocean, shall exist thy image: nor will your figure take any shape in the embrace of ocean, referring to burial at sea.

Lines 22 – 23 shall claim thy growth: declare the ownership of your life.

Line 23 to be resolved to earth again: to return to the state before birth.

Line 24 lost each human trace: lost all the evidences of your having existed as a human being in this world.

Lines 24 – 25 surrendering up thine individual being: losing or giving up all the characteristics of you as a particular human being.

Lines 25 – 26 shalt thou go to mix forever with the elements: you shall be resolved forever with the other substances in nature.

Line 27 To be a brother to the insensible rock: to be resolved with the unconscious rock.

Line 28 to the sluggish clod: (you will be blended) with the hard earth.

Lines 28 – 29 which the rude swain turns with his share: the rough farmer would turn the hard soil up with his plough.

Line 29 treads upon: (the rude swain would) crush (the sluggish clod) with the feet.

Section Two
American Poetry of Early Romantic Period

Lines 29 – 30 The oak shall send his roots abroad: the oak tree would reach out its roots very far and may penetrate through your body.

Line 30 pierce thy mould: (the oak tree's roots would) go through your tomb.

Lines 31 – 32 Yet not to thine eternal resting place shalt thou retire alone—: However, you will not stay at your eternal resting place (the grave) quite by yourself.

Lines 32 – 33 nor couldst thou wish couch more magnificent: nor could you wish to have a more magnificent place for your grave.

Line 33 Couch: the natural surrounding around your tomb.

Line 34 patriarchs of the infant world: the prominent figures of the ancient time.

    the infant world: the early stage of human history.

Line 35 The powerful of the earth: the kings (who used to be the most powerful of this world).

Lines 35 – 36 the wise, the good fair forms: (you will lie down here side by side with) the bodies of those wise, noble people.

Lines 36 Fair forms: beauties.

    and hoary seers of ages past: the old prophets of the ancient time.

Line 37 All in one mighty sepulcher: (You will lie down with ...) all in one huge tomb.

    sepulcher: a burial place; tomb.

Lines 37 – 38 The hills rock-ribbed, and ancient as the sun: the hills which are with long thin raised rocky ranges and which are as old as the sun.

Lines 38 – 39 the vales stretching in pensive quietness between: the valleys which are stretching quietly through (the hills).

Line 40 The venerable woods: the old and thus respectable forests.

Lines 40 – 41 rivers that move in majesty: rivers that are flowing stately.

Line 42 poured round all...: reflected all...

Line 43 melancholy wastes: the desolate waste land.

Lines 44 – 45 Are but the solemn decorations all of the great tomb of man: (The hills, the vales, the woods, rivers, brooks, the old ocean's gray, the melancholy) are just the solemn ornaments to the great tomb of man!

Line 46 all the infinite host of heaven: all the numerous residents of the

universe.

Line 47 the sad abodes of death: the isolated tombs.

Line 48 Through the still lapse of ages: along with the quiet passing of the time.

Lines 48 – 49 All that tread the globe: all those people who now walk arrogantly on earth.
but a handful: are just a few compared to those who are sleeping peacefully in their tombs.

Lines 49 – 50 to the tribes that slumber in its bosom: among the people who are sleeping peacefully in their tombs.

Lines 50 – 51 Take the wings of morning: "The wings of the morning" is a metaphor for the sun. "Fly on the wings of morning and pierce the Barcan Desert and you will find the dead there."
pierce the Barcan wilderness: (the dead could) force a way into the Barcan desert.
The Barcan Desert is located in the northeast of Libya, Africa. It is here an image for the wildest area in the world. It indicates the fact that tombs can be found even in the wildest places on earth. Graves exist everywhere.

Line 52 lose thyself: get yourself lost physically.
the continuous woods: the large range of forests.

Line 53 Where: in the continuous woods.
rolls the Oregon: the Oregon River is flowing through.
Oregon in this poem is sometimes spelt as "Oregan." However, the same water is now more popularly known as the Columbia River, running in the southern part of Washington State, U.S.A.
In the three lines, very swiftly, the images leap from Africa, across the Atlantic Ocean to the west of American continent, refering to the high frequency of graves.

Lines 53 – 54 hears no sound save his own dashings: (in that continuous woods, people) cannot hear any other sound except the dashings of the Oregon River.

Line 54 yet the dead are there: Despite the remoteness we described above, people are still able to find graves around woods and rivers.

Lines 55 – 56 since first the flight of years began: since the very beginning of human world.
flight: action or process of flying through the air.

Lines 56 – 57 have laid them down in their last sleep: (Millions of peo-

Section Two
American Poetry of Early Romantic Period

ple) have ended their lives there in the last sleep (death).

Line 57 the dead reign there alone: in those places (tombs everywhere) the dead are absolutely the rulers.

Line 58 So shalt thou rest: Thus if you will die. "Rest" is the euphemistic speech for "die."

Lines 58 – 59 what if thou shalt fall unnoticed by the living: What will it matter if you die quietly and die without any friends come to record your will.

Line 60 Take note of thy departure: record your will.

Lines 60 – 61 All that breathe will share thy destiny: All the living people will absolutely meet the same end as you.

Lines 61 – 62 The gay will laugh when thou art gone: when you die, the optimistic people will still laugh as they used to.

Line 62 the solemn brood of care plod on: those care-laden people will go on living in anxiety.

Line 64 (chase) His favorite phantom: expect the imagined vision he enjoys.

phantom: illusion; unreal or imagined vision; image.

Lines 66 – 67 the long train of ages: the long sequence of historical "ages" of mankind.

Line 67 the sons of men: the descendants of the dead ancestors.

Line 68 The youth in life's green spring: young people in their life's full flowering.

Lines 68 – 69 who goes in the full strength of years: the mature adults.

matron: married woman; middle-aged or elderly married woman, esp. one with a dignified appearance.

Line 71 be gathered to thy side: be called by death; be attacked by death. Death attacks human beings without considering factors as age, sex, ability or possessions.

thy: God of death's

Line 72 those: people who had been gathering or sending the others to the God of death.

who in their turn shall follow them: who (those who had been gathering...) will become a member of the dead tribe.

Line 73 live: one should face life boldly.

Lines 73 – 74 when thy summons comes to join the innumerable caravan: when you are called to share the tremendous experience of all the people—death.

Line 74 caravan: covered cart or wagon used for living in, and able to be pulled by a horse. Here it means "a company of travellers."

Line 75 mysteriou realm of shade: the mysterious, gloomy kingdom; grave.
Line 77 Thou go not: (If you have to go to the realm of death) you should not go (like...)
the quarry-slave at night: the slave who has to go scourged and bleeding at night to his dungeon bed.
Line 78 Scourged to his dungeon: (the slave may be) driven by someone with a whip and be sent back to prison.
sustained and soothed: supported and comforted.
Line 79 an unfaltering trust: an unhesitating belief.
Lines 80 – 81 wraps the drapery of his couch about him: wraps himself with the heavy cover of his couch.
drapery: heavy cloth such as blankets or bed-clothing used as curtains.
Line 81 lies down to pleasant dreams: calmly lies down and waits for the arrival of death, as though waiting for ordinary sleep.

Comment on the poem

This poem is written in blank verse, namely, in unrhymed iambic pentameter, for the advantage to express with more freedom.

At the idea of death, the beauty of nature will make a person less pessimistic.

At the age of 16, when other kids were indulging in juvenile frivolity, Bryant already began to meditate over the significance of life and death. As a poet of the early 19th century, Bryant develops a view of death which represents a sharp break from the Puritan attitude toward man's final destiny. To the Puritans, death was seen as a preliminary to an afterlife. Bryant, however, treats death as part of nature, as the destiny of us all, and as the great equalizer in this world.

In Bryant's view, to those "who in the love of nature," nature offers all the kindness by presenting a smile and eloquence of beauty when one is in "gayer hours"; it shows sympathy and steals away their sharpness when one is in his darker musings. The death of a man means nothing but the returning to the origin, or a returning to nature. With this prospect, the reader may first be shocked, and soon after, he may shudder and grow sick at heart. However, if at that moment one just goes out to listen, a voice confirms that "Earth, that nourished thee, shall claim thy growth, to be resolved to earth again." Then he would become brother to rocks, clod, birds and to oak trees, he would lie side by side with patriarchs, with the wise, the good and the beauteous. Running around, is the all-beholding sun. In this kingdom, he is not the first, nor ought he be the last. Before the eternity of nature, a human being is rather frail and weak. Once he joins in the "one mighty sepulcher," he becomes a part of the hill, the vale, the woods, the river and he is tremendously stronger. Without a single exception, human beings will all share his destiny.

参考译文

死亡随想

如果你热爱自然，
与其间万象倾心交流，
就会领会她的多变的语言：
用欢快的声音、微笑和美
点缀着你的幸福时光；她
用温存和怜悯
抚平你的忧伤和哀思，
使你未曾体会过刺骨的痛楚。
当死亡的阴影笼罩了你的心灵，
当恐惧、寿衣、棺罩、
令人窒息的黑暗和狭窄的墓冢
令你不寒而栗，心里恶心，
去投入到大自然的怀抱吧，
去聆听她的谆谆教导，
每寸土地、每方水域、每缕空气，
都闪耀着她的智慧，而周围，
陆地上、水里、空中、
回荡着静静的声音——然而几天后，你，
能看见一切的太阳在他的行程中
再也看不见你；
也不会为躺在冰冷墓穴的你悲伤垂泣，
广阔的海洋也未留你丝毫踪影。
你将重新回归哺育你的大地；
零落成泥又化土，
形骸散尽融入自然，
相伴顽石再无转移。

日久沦作待垦之地,
遭人无情翻耕践踏。
橡树根须伸及四方,
终会刺穿你的安息之地。
你不会感到孤独寂寞,
也无须希冀你的床体面堂皇。
皆因比邻不乏风云人物,英雄豪杰
——国王权贵、有识之士,
倾城美女,古代先知,
同处一室无分别。
苍山幽谷,
密林长河,
呜咽山泉,
青青方草;
碧海深洋,
忧郁荒原,
——皆为其天然墓室,
肃穆又庄严。
金色太阳,宇宙天体,
斗转星移不离弃。
昔日风流人物,
今日无声也无息。
岁岁年年,
天涯海角,
人生长河不复还,
死神漠然永伴你。
芸芸众生,
古往今来,
终要托体同山永长眠。
人固一死,
何叹亲朋好友不再悲伤将你忘?
歌者亦歌,悲者亦悲,
各自须寻各自门,
然终有别离红尘时,
如约将你来相伴。
任时光流逝,
看人生百象,
良辰美景,

Section Two
American Poetry of Early Romantic Period

青春容颜，
新生婴儿，
迟暮之年，
——皆待死神来召唤，
生生不息共轮回。

故直面人生务须怕，
一朝踏上黄泉路，
匆匆过客皆相伴。
屏弃胸中怒与怨，
平心静气信念足。
恰似人生舞台已谢幕，
面带微笑归圆梦。
（周英莉　译　李正栓　校）

(2) To a Waterfowl

    Whither, midst falling dew,
While glow the heavens with the last steps of day,
Far, through their rosy depths, dost thou pursue
    Thy solitary way?

5   Vainly the fowlers eye
Might mark thy distant flight, to do thee wrong,
As, darkly seen against the crimson sky,
    Thy figure floats along.

    Seek'st thou the plashy brink
10 Of where weedy lake, or marge of river wide,
Or where the rocking billows rise and sink
    On the chafed ocean side?

    There is a Power, whose care
Teaches thy way along that pathless coast; —
15 The desert and illimitable air,
    Lone wandering, but not lost.

    All day thy wings have fann'd
At that far height, the cold thin atmosphere;

Yet stoop not, weary, to the welcome land,
20   Though the dark night is near.
   And soon that toil shall end,
Soon shalt thou find a summer home, and rest,
And scream among thy fellows; reeds shall bend,
   Soon, o'er thy sheltered nest.

25   Thou'rt gone, the abyss of heaven
Hath swallowed up thy form, yet, on my heart
Deeply hath sunk the lesson thou hast given,
   And shall not soon depart.

   He, who, from zone to zone,
30 Guides through the boundless sky thy certain flight,
In the long way that I must trace alone,
   Will lead my steps aright.

Notes

Waterfowl: A rather large American bird, probably a Canada goose. It often flies very steadily and quietly.

Line 1 Whither: to what place or state.
Line 2 While glow the heavens with the last steps of day: While the sky is glowing in the setting sun.
Line 3 their: the heaven's.
   rosy depths: the far, distant reach of the rosy sky.
   thou pursue: you exploringly fly.

Stanza 1: With the arrival of evening and in the setting sun and falling dew, where will the waterfowl, through the rosy clouds, fly to?

Line 5 Vainly the fowlers eye: the hunters eyes are faint (in the evening light); the goose is too far away to shoot.
Line 6 mark: get the sight of; see.
   to do thee wrong: to hurt or kill you.
Lines 7 – 8 As, darkly seen...: as can be seen (that your figure is smoothly flying against the background of the setting sun).

Section Two
American Poetry of Early Romantic Period

Stanza 2: In the rosy light of the setting sun, the hunter might see the bird, but it is too distant to be harmed. Thus it is able for the bird to fly easily and delightedly.

Line 9 Seek'st thou: Are you flying to look for...
  the plashy brink: a grassy lake bank with the soft padding of water.
Line 10 or marge of river wide: Or are you looking for a wide area along a river?
Line 11 Or where the rocking billows rise and sink: Or are you looking for the rolling waves which are rising and falling.
  billows: large waves.
Line 12 On the chafed ocean side: on the shore of the roaring ocean.
  chafe: become irritated or impatient;

Stanza 3: The poet is enquiring the destination of the fowl: Is it by the lake, along the river or at the ocean side?

Line 13 There is a Power: Somewhere in heaven there is a powerful hand.
Line 14 (whose care) Teaches thy way: (That powerful person or god) takes care of you and teaches you the direction of flight.
  along that pathless coast: teaches you the way of flying along the pathless coast.
Line 15 The desert and illimitable air: (That powerful person or god teaches you the way of flying in) the desert and that in the spacious sky.
Line16 Lone wandering, but not lost: (With the help of that god) though you are wandering all alone, you will not lose the way.

Stanza 4: The poet believes that a supernatural power is guiding and protecting the bird.

Line 17 thy wings have fann'd: your wings have been fluttering for a whole day.
Line 18 At that far height, the cold thin atmosphere: (you have been fluttering your wings all day) at that great height and in the very cold air.
Line 19 Yet stoop not, weary, to the welcome land: Despite all the exhaustion, do not attempt to come down to the ground.
  stoop: descend rapidly from a high flight.

Stanza 5: The evening is falling and the bird, though rather exhausted,

kept on flying.

Line 21 that toil shall end: the weary flying ought to come to an end.
Line 22 Soon shalt thou find…: You will soon find a place for your summer resort.
Line 23 scream among thy fellows: you will soon unite with the other birds.
Lines 24 – 25 reeds shall bend, soon, o'er thy sheltered nest: very soon you will find the reeds for making a shelter.

<u>Stanza 6</u>: Soon the weary flight will end and a shelter will be found.

Line 25 Thou'rt gone: You have gone; You have disappeared far into the sky.
Lines 25 – 26 the abyss of heaven hath swallowed up thy form: Your figure has disappeared in the boundless sky.
Line 28 And shall not soon depart: (the lessons you taught me) will remain in my heart for a long time.

<u>Stanza 7</u>: Though the bird has flown out of sight, the lessons it taught will stay in my heart forever.

Line 29 He: God. The one who designs the world, who guides the bird to fly in a map.
Line 30 thy: the bird's.
Line 31 the long way: the life time of a person.
       I: the poet.
Line 32 Will lead my steps aright: God who guides the bird will lead me to the right way as well.

<u>Stanza 8</u>: As the bird is led by God, my life should be guided by the same power too.

Comment on the poem

　　In the first three stanzas, there is no hint of any morals. However, in the fourth stanza, all of a sudden, a new figure as a god appears. The god has a supernatural power which directs the bird's flight. Bryant interrupted himself from describing a bird into teaching a lesson. Bryant may think it is not enough for a poem written just for the sake of its own, or just for the beauty of it, it should say something more than beauty; it should carry morals.

Section Two
AMERICAN POETRY OF EARLY ROMANTIC PERIOD

It rhymes "abab," while the length of each line is so different that you cannot find a regular foot. However, the two long lines in the middle of each stanza may refer to the balance in the floating of the bird. The first and the fourth lines, which are relatively shorter, look like two wings. The stanzaic form reminds one of a flying bird.

参考译文

致 水 鸟

露珠正在滴落，
白昼将退，天际遍洒柔辉，
天上玫瑰红一抹，
你要往何处孤独远飞？

猎鸟者也许已注意到
你振翅远飞却无法伤害你，
红霞满天，神秘轻罩，
看着你飘一般飞去。

你要寻觅杂草丛生
泥泞的湖滨、宽广河流的岸沿？
还是要寻觅波涛汹涌
海浪冲激的洋边？

有一种神力关心着你，
教你如何沿无路的海滨飞翔，
在沙漠和无以匹拟的长空里，——
你虽然独往却不迷失方向。

一整天，你拍翅飞翔，
忍受那高处寒冷稀薄的空气，
你已疲惫不堪，黑夜已临降，
可你却不肯屈栖欢迎你的大地。

这辛苦即将告一段落，
你很快会找到爱巢去歇息，

在同伴间欢鸣不已;你筑的巢窝
很快会让芦苇弯腰俯视。

你走啦。深邃的无际
已吞没了你的形象;但在我心里
已留下一个深深的教益,
它将永存我心底。

谁教你跨区飞翔,
指引你飞越无垠长空,
也会在我必须独自跋涉的征途上
指引我正确的航程。
(李正栓　译)

Section Two
American Poetry of Early Romantic Period

II. Edgar Allan Poe
(1809 – 1849)

1. Life Story

Edgar Allan Poe was the son of wandering players. Born in Boston on January 19, 1809, Poe was orphaned at the age of two. He was then adopted by John Allan, a tobacco exporter in Richmond, Virginia. With the help of the stepfather, Poe attended the University of Virginia at 17, but his gambling and drinking debts made Mr. Allan remove him from the university. After a bitter quarrel between the father and son, Poe ran away from home in 1827 to Boston. Then he entered West Point. But the discipline there was too harsh for Poe's nature and he was dismissed 8 months later for disobedience and failure in his duties. After that Poe had to make a living by writing or editing some magazines or journals.

Poe was that kind of artist who had literary genius but was always indulging himself in a bohemian life style. Thus, for a long time American literary criticism was reluctant to give a satisfactory account of Poe's works and failed to do justice to Poe's genius as well. After his death, for a long time, Poe remained the most controversial and most misunderstood literary figure in the history of American literature.

It was in Europe, 25 years after his death, especially in France, that Poe began to enjoy respect first. Then his fame returned to America. Consequently, Poe's new editions appeared; money was collected for an impressive tomb; and a large memorial meeting was held to solemnize one of the best poets American literary history had ever created.

2. Poe's Writings and Position in Literary History

Now the majority of critics in the United States, as well as those in the world, have recognized the real, unique importance of Poe as a great writer of fiction, a poet of first rank, and a critic of acumen and insight.

Today, though there are still arguments about Poe's poems and critical essays, there is no argument about his short stories, which are always regarded as the best in American literature.

Poe was the first American writer who formulated the technique of the short story. In pursuit of the totality of effect through compression, immediacy and finality, Poe invented the genre of the detective story and developed a new fiction of psychological analysis. Poe has thus often been considered as the father of the modern short story. Poe's short stories can generally be classified into stories of horror and detective stories.

As a critic, Poe was the first responsible American literary critic who wrote critical essays in American magazines to say much of American writing then was terrible. Poe was right, but he was bitterly attacked by most of his contemporaries on account of his ingenuity.

3. Poe's Aesthetic Theory

Both in his fictional and poetic works, Poe insists that artistic work should not be didactical. Poe's poetry, which is very small in quantity, truthfully embodies the following theoretical points:

(1) "Beauty is the sole purpose of the poem." Poetry must concern itself just with "supernal beauty," not with the narration of a story, nor even with the beauty of particular things.

(2) The immediate object of poetry is pleasure, not truth. The function of poetry is not to summarize, nor interpret earthly experience, but to create a mood in which the soul soars.

(3) Melancholy is the most legitimate of all the poetic tones. Sickness, abnormal love, death of a beautiful woman, are to him, unquestionably, the most poetical topics in the world.

(4) The length of writing, both of tales and poetry, should be about 100 lines, so that the reader can be well engaged in it without any interruption.

4. Writing Features of Poe

(1) Poe's writing style is traditional. He failed to carry the new idea into his style. So Poe is not creative on this point.

(2) Poe is not easy to read, just because of his ability to make good use of implications.

(3) Poe's diction and syntax is strict and this may also be responsible for his difficulties.

Section Two
American Poetry of Early Romantic Period

5. Selected Poems

(1) To Helen

    HELEN, thy beauty is to me
      Like those Nicean barks of yore,
    That gently, o'er a perfumed sea,
      The weary, way-worn wanderer bore
5   To his own native shore.

    On desperate seas long wont to roam,
      Thy hyacinth hair, thy classic face.
    Thy Naiad airs have brought me home
      To the glory that was Greece,
10 And the grandeur that was Rome.

    Lo! in yon brilliant window niche,
      How statue—like I see thee stand,
    The agate lamp within thy hand!
      Ah, Psyehe, from the regions which
15 Are Holy Land!

Notes

- Line 1 HELEN: the most beautiful woman in Greek myth; an image of beauty.
- Line 2 Nicean: of or pertaining to Nicea, an ancient city in Asia Minor. It is used here to cherish the memory of an ancient and remote place, and for the harmony of melody or for the nostalgical impression of ancient beauty.
  barks: boats; ships.
  of yore: of long time ago; long before.
- Line 3 a perfumed sea: the treasure house of art.
- Line 4 weary, way-worn wanderer: the story about Odysseus' exhausting long journey returning homeland after the Trojan War.
  Odysseus was an ancient Greek hero who planned the Trojan Horse Trick that ended the Trojan War. After the war, it took him ten years to go back home in Ithaca.
- Lines 4 – 5 bore to: was brought to.
- Line 5 native shore: homeland.

Stanza 1: The poet first mentioned Helen, the most famous beauty in Greek mythology. Then Poe compared himself to Odysseus, who wandered for ten years over the sea to get home. As Odysseus, Edgar Allan Poe was persistent in his chasing after fine arts with the sincere belief that art, or beauty and truth, is the ultimate aim, the home, for the wandering poet; while Helen, the embodiment of ancient beauty, is the guider to that dreamland.

Line 6 On desperate seas long wont to roam: "desperate sea" is used as transferred epithet. The real meaning of the line is "(I) have been desperate and accustomed to the wandering over the sea of art."
Line 7 Thy: Helen's.
hyacinth hair: "hyacinth" refers to the color between purple and blue. Helen's hair is in the beautiful color of hyacinth.
classic face: face with classic beauty.
Line 8 Naiad: (in Greek and Roman mythology and literature) daughter of Zeus. A water nymph or any of the less important goddesses, often presented as young girls living in trees, streams, or mountains.
airs: appearance and charm.
Line 9 (brought me home) To the glory of ancient Greece: (Helen's beauty brought me home) to the glory of ancient Greece, which is considered the origin of Western art and literature.
Line 10 grandeur: great achievements in literature and art; classical literature and art in history. (the beauty of Helen brought me home) to the great achievements of ancient Roman, which is another resource of Western culture.

Stanza 2: All the art and literature originated from one thing—beauty. Having taken Helen as the embodiment of beauty, the poet was confident that once he saw Helen, he was sure to be led by Helen to the home of beauty—fine art and pure literature. Poe insisted that Greece and Rome are the homes of beauty, the treasure houses of fine art and literature.

Line 11 Lo!: Look!
niche: a hollow place (recess) in the wall for holding a statue of god or goddess or other decorative object.
Lines 11 – 12 I see you stand in the delicate window niche like a statue.
Line 13 agate: hard, smooth and precious stone.

Line 14 Psyche: (in Greek mythology) goddess of the human soul, usually appearing in the form of a pretty young lady.
Line 15 Holy Land: Palestine and its chief city Jerusalem, which is a holy city for three principle religions—Christianity, Judaism, and Islam. In this poem, Poe strongly suggested that Greece and Rome are his "holy land."

Stanza 3: The speaker sees Helen standing in the bright niche and holding in her hand an agate lamp. She is quite similar to goddess Psyche from Greek Myth. Through his description of his passion to Helen, Poe expressed his pursuit and sincere devotion to beauty.

In the poem, three beauties in ancient Greek mythology—Helen, Naiad and Psyche—are mentioned just to show that beauty is something that existed; it is very holy but it is hard to reach.

Comment on the poem

This poem is believed to have been written when the poet was only fourteen, inspired, as Poe admitted, by the beauty of Mrs. Jane Stith Stanard, the young mother of a school fellow who was "the first purely ideal love of my soul." In this poem, the personal element of the young poet was almost completely sublimated in the idealization of the tradition of supernal beauty in art. The lady died in 1824. But she appeared in this poetic work in the figure of Helen, the well-known ancient beauty, with all the adoration of poet to her.

In the first stanza, Helen's beauty is compared to the Nicean barks—a suggestion of classical associations; what's more, "of yore," instead of "before" or "long ago," is applied to add the classical atmosphere to the poem. As the ancient ships had transported the ancient hero—Ulysses—home from Troy, so will the beauty of Helen lead the poet to the home of art. The second stanza starts with "On desperate seas." Actually, the transferred epithet is used just to show the poet's cordiality to the goddess of art. In classic myth, the flower Hyacinth preserved the memory of Apollo's love for the dead young Hyacinthus. (Hyacinthus is a very handsome young man of Greek myth and the object of Apollo's affections. Unfortunately, he was badly hurt by a discus when Apollo was gaming and dead soon. Very disappointed by that, Apollo changed him into the plant of hyacinth which had been taken as a symbol for affection). All of these, the hyacinth hair, the face of classic beauty and the expression of Naiad, are charming enough to lead me to the home of art—ancient Greece and ancient Rome.

In the third stanza, Helen is directly compared to goddess Psyche from the Holy land. Through his description of his passion to Helen, Poe expressed his pursuit and sincere devotion to beauty.

In the poem, three beauties in ancient Greek mythology—Helen, Naiad and Psyche—are mentioned just to show that beauty is something that existed; it is very holy but it is hard to reach.

参考译文

致 海 伦

海伦，对于我，你的美
正像古时奈西亚帆船，
载着疲惫的旅人
悠悠飘过芳香的海域，
驶向他故乡的海岸。

在长久习于汹涌的海面，
你那卷发及典雅的脸，
你海仙女的风姿使我熟记
古希腊的荣耀、
古罗马的庄严。

瞧！我见你玉立婷婷，
在光彩的壁龛里，
如玉雕神女，
手里还握着玛瑙油灯！
呵，你是赛琪，来自天国的圣地。

（李正栓　译）

(2) The Raven

Once upon a midnight dreary, while I pondered, weak and weary,
Over many a quaint and curious volume of forgotten lore—

Section Two
American Poetry of Early Romantic Period

    While I nodded, nearly napping, suddenly there came a tapping,
    As of some one gently rapping, rapping at my chamber door—
5 "This some visitor," I muttered, "tapping at my chamber door—
                Only this and nothing more,"

    Ah, distinctly I remember it was in the bleak December;
    And each separate dying ember wrought its ghost upon the floor.
    Eagerly I wished the morrow; —vainly I had sought to borrow
10 From my books surcease of sorrows—sorrow for the lost Lenore—
    For the rare and radiant maiden whom the angels name Lenore—
                Nameless here for evermore.

    And the silken, sad, uncertain rustling of each purple curtain
    Thrilled me—filled me with fantastic terrors never felt before;
15 So that now, to still the beating of my heart, I stood repeating
    "This some visitor entreating entrance at my chamber door—
    Some late visitor entreating entrance at my chamber door;—
                This it is and nothing more."

    Presently my soul grew stronger; hesitating then no longer,
20 " Sir," said I, "or Madam, truly your forgiveness I implore;
    But the fact is I was napping, and so gently you came rapping,
    And so faintly you came tapping, tapping at my chamber door,
    That I scarce was sure I heard you" —here I opened wide the door; —
                Darkness there, and nothing more.

25 Deep into that darkness peering, long I stood there wondering, fearing,
    Doubting, dreaming dreams no mortal ever dared to dream before;
    But the silence was unbroken, and the stillness gave no token,
    And the only word there spoken was the whispered word, "Lenore!"
    This I whispered, and an echo murmured back the word, "Lenore!"—
30   Merely this and nothing more.

    Back into the chamber turning, all my soul within me burning,
    Soon again I heard a tapping somewhat louder than before.
    "Surely," said I, "surely that is something at my window lattice;
    Let me see, then, what thereat is, and this mystery explore—
35 Let my heart be still a moment and this mystery explore; —
                'T is the wind and nothing more!"

Open here I flung the shutter, when, with many a flirt and flutter,
In there stepped a stately Raven of the saintly days of yore;
Not the least obeisance made he; not a minute stopped or stayed he;
40 But, with mien of lord or lady, perched above my chamber door—
Perched upon a bust of Pallas just above my chamber door—
      Perched, and sat, and nothing more.

Then this ebony bird beguiling my sad fancy into smiling,
By the grave and stern decorum of the countenance it wore,
45 "Though thy crest be shorn and shaven, thou," I said. "art sure no craven,
Ghastly grim and ancient Raven wandering from the Nightly shore—
Tell me what thy lordly name is on the Night's Plutonian shore!"
      Quoth the Raven "Nevermore."

Much I marveled this ungainly fowl to hear discourse so plainly,
50 Though its answer little meaning—little relevancy bore;
For we cannot help agreeing that no living human being,
Ever yet was blessed with seeing bird above his chamber door—
Bird or beast upon the sculptured bust above his chamber door,
      With such name as "Nevermore."

55 But the Raven, sitting lonely on the placid bust, spoke only
That one word, as if his soul in that one word did he outpour.
Nothing farther then he uttered—not a feather then he fluttered—
Till I scarcely more than muttered "Other friends have flown before—
On the morrow he will leave me, as my Hopes have flown before."
60   Then the bird said "Nevermore."

Startled at the stillness broken by reply so aptly spoken,
"Doubtless," said I. "what it utters is its only stock and store
Caught from some unhappy master whom unmerciful disaster
Followed fast and followed faster till his songs one burden bore—
65 Till the dirges of his Hope that melancholy burden bore—
      Of 'Never—nevermore.'"

But the Raven still beguiling my sad fancy into smiling,
Straight I wheeled a cushioned seat in front of bird, and bust and door;
Then, upon the velvet sinking, I betook myself to linking
70 Fancy unto fancy, thinking what this ominous bird of yore—
What this grim, ungainly, ghastly, gaunt, and ominous bird of yore

Meant in croaking "Nevermore."

Thus I sat engaged in guessing, but no syllable expressing
To the fowl whose fiery eyes now burned into my bosom's core;
75 This and more I sat divining, with my head at ease reclining
On the cushion's velvet lining that the lamp-light gloated o'er,
But whose velvet violet lining with the lamp-light gloating o'er,
    She shall press, ah, nevermore!

Then, methought, the air grew denser, perfumed from an unseen censer
80 Swung by angels whose foot-falls tinkled on the tufted floor.
"Wretch," I cried, thy God hath lent thee—by these angels he hath sent thee
Respite—respite and nepenthe from thy memories of Lenore;
Quaff, oh quaff this kind nepenthe and forget this lost "Lenore!"
    Quoth the Raven "Nevermore."

85 "Prophet!" said I, "thing of evil! —prophet still, if bird or devil! —
Whether Tempter sent, or whether tempest tossed thee here ashore,
Desolate yet all undaunted, on the desert land enchanted—
On this home by Horror haunted—tell me truly, I implore—
Is there—is there balm in Gilead? —tell me—tell me, I implore!"
90   Quoth the Raven "Nevermore."

"Prophet!" said I, "thing of evil! —prophet still, if bird or devil!
By that Heaven that bends above us—by that God we both adore—
Tell this soul with sorrow laden if, within the distant Aidenn,
It shall clasp a sainted maiden whom the angels name Lenore—
95 Clasp a rare and radiant maiden whom the angels name Lenore."
    Quoth the Raven "Nevermore."

"Be that word our sign of parting, bird or fiend!" I shrieked, upstarting—
"Get thee back into the tempest and the Night's Plutonian shore!
Leave no black plume as a token of that lie thy soul hath spoken!
100 Leave my loneliness unbroken! —quit the bust above my door!
Take thy beak from out my heart, and take thy form from off my door!"
    Quoth the Raven "Nevermore."

And the Raven, never flitting, still is sitting, still is sitting
On the pallid bust of Pallas just above my chamber door;
105 And his eyes have all the seeming of a demon's that is dreaming,
And the lamp-light o'er him streaming throws his shadow on the floor;
And my soul from out that shadow that lies floating on the floor

Shall be lifted—nevermore!

Notes

Line 1 a midnight dreary: When I feel dismal or gloomy at midnight.
weak and weary: when I was very sleepy and tired.
"dreary" and "weary" composed an internal rhyme; while "weak" and "weary" are alliteratively used.
Line 2 quaint: odd or old-fashioned.
lore: knowledge and traditions about a subject or possessed by a particular group of people.
Line 4 rapping: strike quickly and smartly.

Stanza 1: One midnight, while the poet was tired with reading and pondering, he heard the gentle knocks at his chamber door.

Line 6 "remember" and "December" composed another internal rhyme.
Line 7 separate dying ember: small pieces of burning woods that had cracked out of the stove. "ember" in this line suggests one more strong rhyme to "rember" and "December."
wrought its ghost upon the floor: scattered on the floor; left black marks on the floor.
Line 10 From my book: (I had been seeking) from my books (a way to cease my sorrow, but in vain).
surcease: *n.* cessation; the end; *v.* to cease from some action; to come to an end.
Line 11 the rare and radiant maiden: the bright girl.
Line 12 here: in the human world.

Stanza 2: In a cold night when the poet was alone, he was awakened by the tapping and realized that he had failed, by reading a book, to ease his sorrow for the lost Lenore.

Line 13 And the silken, sad...: The curtain is made of purple silk; it looks sad and shakes with uncertain rustlings.
Line 16 entreating entrance: appealing, begging, and asking earnestly to come into my chamber.
Line 18 This it is and nothing more: It is just like this—some visitor who comes late to me, and it could not be anything else.

Section Two
American Poetry of Early Romantic Period

<u>Stanza 3</u>: The poet felt frightened so he had to calm himself down by persuading that the tapping means a late visitor, and it could not be anything worse than that.

Line 19 Presently: Suddenly.
        hesitating then no longer: (My soul) is no longer hesitating.
Line 20 "Sir," said I, "or Madam": The poet is not quite certain about the personality of the visitor. He supposes the visitor must be a man or a woman.
        truly your forgiveness I implore: I truly implore your forgiveness.
Line 21 But the fact is: But the fact (for my failure in answering the door) is that I had been napping.
Line 23 That I scarce was sure I heard you: (You have tapped at my chamber so faintly) that I was not sure I could have heard you.
Line 24 there: out of the chamber door.

<u>Stanza 4</u>: The poet was suddenly excited as to apologize for not hearing the gentle rapping, but when the door is widely opened, he found nothing but darkness outside.

Line 26 mortal: human being.
Line 27 token: sign. Here it refers to the evidence for the appearance of something.

<u>Stanza 5</u>: The door was opened but it was all darkness and tranquility outside. The only sound echoing to the poet's ear was his murmuring of "Lenore." He began to wonder who might have done the tapping. But the more he wondered, the more frightened he became.

Line 31 all my soul within me burning: I am very excited (just because of fear and curiosity).
Line 34 what thereat is: What really is it over there.
        and this mystery explore: and (let me) explore this mystery.

<u>Stanza 6</u>: The poet returned to his chamber but the tapping appeared again and louder. He made up his mind to calm down and find out the truth.

Line 37 Open here I flung the shutter: So I forcefully threw the shutter

open.

with many a flirt and flutter: (The Raven) flew in quickly but not quite steadily. "flirt" and "flutter" are used alliteratively.

Line 38 In there stepped: (The Raven) rushed in. "There" is used for emphasis.

the saintly days: the holy old days.

Line 39 Not the least obeisance made he: He didn't make the least obeisance.

Line 40 mien: one's appearance, especially as an indication of mood.

Line 41 abust of Pallas: a chest sculpture of Pallas; a statue of Pallas. Pallas refers to Pallas Athena, the patron goddess of Athens in Greek mythology. Poe once expressed in *The philosophy of Composition*, "I made the bird alight on the bust of Pallas, also for the effect of contrast between the marble and the plumage—it being understood that the bust was absolutely suggested by the bird—the bust of Pallas being chosen, first as most in keeping with the scholarship of the lover, and, secondly, for the sonorousness of the word, Pallas, itself." Poe's conscious selection of Pallas Athena, goddess of wisdom, for the raven's perch, suggests the inclination of the poet to have the bitter truth revealed by an owl, Athena's traditional bird of wisdom.

Stanza 7: The poet opened the window and finally found that the tapping comes from a Raven perching on a bust of Pallas.

Line 43 ebony bird: black bird.

beguiling... into... : attract or deceive... into...

my sad fancy: my sad soul.

Line 44 the grave and stern decorum of the countenance: the serious and dignified appearance.

decorum: dignified and socially acceptable behavior.

Line 45 crest: feathers on a bird's head.

be shorn and shaven: be cut off.

art sure no craven: I am sure you are not a coward.

Line 46 grim: very serious; unpleasant.

Lines 46 – 47 Nightly shore and the Night's Plutonian shore: both refer to the infernal regions ruled by Pluto; hell. In Roman mythology, Pluto (Hades in Greek mythology) is the god of the infernal. It is believed that there are five rivers under there. That's why the word "shore" is used in the line.

Section Two
American Poetry of Early Romantic Period

Stanza 8: The poet was beguiled into smiling by the black bird and he asked its name and was replied with: "Nevermore," which becomes the repetitive refrain of several stanzas.

Line 49 Much I marveled this ungainly fowl to hear discourse so plainly: I was rather astonished to hear this ugly bird speak so clearly.

Stanza 9: The poet was astonished by the fact of a bird's talking, because neither had anybody ever experienced this nor was any bird named "Nevermore" before, despite the widely held belief that crows and ravens can mimic human speech if their tongues are "split" with a sharp tool.

Line 56 That one word: the word of "Nevermore."
　　　　as if his soul in that one word did he outpour: as if he had poured his soul into that word (Nevermore).
Line 57 Nothing farther then he uttered: then (except "Nevermore") he said nothing else.
　　　　not a feather then he fluttered: then he stopped fluttering his wings.
Line 58 I scarcely more than muttered: I expressed myself in a rather low voice.
　　　　have flown before: have left me before; died.
Line 59 he: the Raven.

Stanza 10: The bird's repetition of "Nevermore" accidentally corresponds with the poet's self-talk, as if the bird is ensuring him "I will never leave."

Line 61 reply: the Raven's reply as "Nevermore."
　　　　so aptly spoken: (the word "Nevermore" was) so appropriately spoken.
Line 62 its only stock and store: the only word the bird can collect.
Line 63 (That word "Nevermore") must be the one the bird unexpectedly picked up from its former unhappy master upon whom an unmerciful disaster is likely to fall.
Line 64 Followed fast and followed faster: (the disaster) is swiftly approaching.
　　　　till his songs one burden bore: till the master felt it (the repetition of "Nevermore") quite a burden.

Stanza 11: After his astonishment, the poet realized that the bird was repeating the only word it accidentally picked up from its depressed master and it, as a matter of fact, shared nothing about the poet's murmuring about Hope.

Line 68 Straight I wheeled a cushioned seat: right away the poet wheeled a padded chair.
　　　　in front of bird, and bust and door: (I turned...) in front of the bird, in front of the bust, and in front of the door.
Line 69 Then, upon the velvet sinking: Then I sank upon the velvet covered cushion seat.
Lines 69 - 70 linking fancy unto fancy: wildly imagining.
Lines 71 - 72 What this ... bird of yore mean by croaking "Nevermore."
　　　　The adjectives in Line 71 suggest the poet's complicated feeling towards the bird.

Stanza 12: The poet came nearer to the bird and began to fancy why the bird repeated that word.

Line 73 no syllable expressing: without uttering a single word.
Line 74 To the fowl: nothing was said to the fowl.
　　　　my bosom's core: deep in my heart.
Lines 75 - 76 Leisurely I put my head against the cushion's velvet lining with the lamp-light gloating over. I sat there and meditating over the meaning of that word and more else.
Lines 77 - 78 But on whose velvet violet lining with the lamp-light gloating over shall Lenore sit?
Line 78 She: Lenore.

Stanza 13: Thinking about that word reminds the poet of his lost Lenore.

Line 79 methought: I felt; I thought.
　　　　the air grew denser ... censer: the perfumed air from an unseen censer grew denser. The "denser" and "censer" in this line form an internal rhyme.
Line 80 Swung by...: the perfumed air from the censer was swung by...
Line 81 Wretch: very unfortunate or miserable person. In this line, the poet is calling himself so.

Section Two
American Poetry of Early Romantic Period

  thy God hath lent thee—by these angels he hath sent thee:
  Your God had sent the angels to take nepenthe to you so as to
  release you from your sorrow of the memory of Lenore.
Line 82 nepenthe: In classical mythology, a potion banishing sorrow, as
  in the *Odyssey*, IV, 419—430.

Stanza 14: The poet felt too much troubled by the memory of Lenore so he wanted some magic drug to release him from thinking about her.

Line 85 Prophet: the Raven.
  thing of evil: the poet implies the prophet is an evil thing.
  prophet still, if bird or devil!: but whether it is a bird or devil, it speaks like a prophet.
Line 86 Whether Tempter sent: whether it is sent by devil, or by the tempest to this world.
  Tempter: person who tempts; the devil.
Line 87 Desolate yet all undaunted: (The prophet is) desolate but still bold.
  on the desert land enchanted: on the enchanted deserted land.
Line 89 is there balm in Gilead?: Is there any magic drug in Gilead? This is quoted from *Jeremiah* viii: 22, a reference to an esteemed medicinal herb from Gilead, a place in Jordan.

Stanza 15: In stanza 14, the poet was inclined to release himself from the memory of Lenore. In the present stanza, he wants to find some magic drug to cure him.

Line 92 By that heaven that bends above us: for the sake of Heaven that is dominating us.
  by that God we both adore: for the sake of God whom we (the poet and the Raven) both worship.
Line 93 Tell this soul with sorrow laden: tell this soul which was laden with sorrow.
  this soul: my lost Lenore.
  ...if, within the distant Aidenn: if (my lost Lenore) is in the distant garden of Eden.
  Aidenn: variant spelling and pronunciation for "Eden."
Line 94 clasp: hold tightly with the arms; embrace.
  a sainted maiden: Lenore.

Stanza 16: The poet expressed his desire for meeting Lenore, but was boldly denied by a "Nevermore," and this brings the poem to the climax.

Line 97 Be that word our sign of parting, bird or fiend: Let that word (Nevermore) be the sign of our parting, whether you are just a bird or a demon. The poet doesn't want to see the Raven any more.
Line 98 Get thee back into: You should return to.
Line 99 black plume: black feather.
Line 100 Leave my loneliness unbroken: leave me alone and do not interfere.
Line 101 Take thy beak from out my heart: Take your mouth away from me.
thy form: your figure.

Stanza 17: The poet was so irritated by the bird's reply in the former stanza that he wanted to drive the bird away from him. However, the bird again responded with a "Nevermore."

Line 103 flitting: flying away; flying or moving lightly and quickly from one place to another.
Line 104 pallid: pale.
Line 105 have all the seeming of a demon's: have all the look of a devil's.
Line 106 And the lamp-light o'er him streaming: And the lamp-light pouring over him.
Lines 107-108 And my soul shall never be lifted from out that shadow that lies floating on the floor. My soul will never be released from that memory of Lenore.

Stanza 18: The Raven was rather innocent to the poet's reverie about "Lenore." However, the poet was obsessively in a mood of frustration.

Comment on the poem

The Raven was published in the *New York Evening Mirror* in 1845. Being regarded as the first poem with hazy conceptions in the West, it is the poem of which Poe himself felt quite proud and had been frequently taken by Poe as an example to illustrate his poetic art. Consisting of 18 stanzas, each with 6 lines, with the first five lines being trochaic octameter and the last line as trochaic tetrameter, this poem corresponds in every aspect with Poe's aesthetic standard for poetry: It took the lament over the death of a beautiful woman as its theme; with the 108 lines, it is readable at one sitting; it is pervaded with a sense of melancholy.

Although this poem was written in traditional feet and regular meters, Poe diverged from tradition with dramatic variation of the tone: mournful at the beginning (vainly I had sought to borrow from my books surcease of sorrow— sorrow for the lost Lenore. Lines 9 – 10); then trepid at some spots (the silken sad uncertain rustling of each purple curtain trilled me—filled me with fantastic terrors never felt before. Line 13 – 14); sometimes it showed a touch of humour (the usage of "Nevermore" as a pun), sometimes a mood of melancholy (the bird beguiling my sad fancy into smiling; other friends have flown away before. On the morrow he will leave me, as my Hopes have flown before) But finally, a very pessimistic illusion (my soul from out that shadow that lies floating on the floor shall be lifted—nevermore! Lines 107 – 108)

Once upon a dreary midnight, while the poet was pondering weak and weary, with the napping and tapping at his chamber door, the poet was led to a fantasy world of a dialogue between him and a raven. The whole scene might be a real one or just a dream but the mysterious Raven must be a symbolic character. It may be symbolic in various ways:

  a. The Raven symbolizes disaster and misfortune. Raven, the large bird like crow with black feathers, in Western countries, as well as it is in China, is conventionally regarded as an ominous fowl, a symbol of misfortune. Thus with the repetition of the "napping and tapping" the poet was filled "with fantastic terrors never felt before."

  b. The bird may symbolize the soul of the radiant maiden, the "lost Lenore." At the moment when the poet was in the darkness peering, wondering, expecting and whispering Lenore but was just responded with a "nothing more," the Raven, "with mien of lord or lady, perched above my chamber door." A conversation was held and the poet was so comforted with it. For twice, the poet felt the bird "beguiling my sad fancy into smiling."

  c. The bird may be taken as a symbol of the sub-consciousness of the poet. In the conversation the poet distinctly expressed his strong passion to Lenore. However, the only response from the Raven was "Nevermore." It seems what the poet had expressed is simply the view out of the "id," while the Raven's words are rather restrictive and seem out of "ego." The poet was too affectionate to Lenore to be restrictive, while the Raven was what warned him to be rational and that what had been lost would return "nevermore."

  d. The Raven is the symbol of modern reality. The poet was of the firm belief that in modern society human beings are apathetic creatures.

He was deeply resentful at the people's indifference towards his mourning to Lenore; therefore, he turned to the Raven for comfort. But quite to his disappointment, he was merely responded with a cold "nevermore."

As the most melodic poet in American literary history, Poe spent about four years for the creation of this piece of exquisite verse-narrative. In this poem, besides the regular meters and feet, the poet also employed many intricate musical expressions such as alliteration, internal rhyme, slant rhyme, end rhyme, perfect rhyme, imperfect rhyme, refrain and so on, so as to add variation, beauty and melody.

参考译文

乌 鸦

一次午夜时,我疲惫不堪困意浓,
稀奇古事挥不掉——
低头小憩时,忽闻窗外叩拍声,
好似有人轻轻把门敲——
心想必有来客访——
唯此无他响。

啊,我铭记那是在凄凉寒冬十二月;
死灰空留断魂烙。
欲把情愁付书海,
难忘佳丽魂已销——
举世无双窈窕女,安琪唤其叫勒诺——
香销玉逝无人叫。

丝帘哀怨簌簌响,
莫名恐惧心头涌;
屏息起身细思忖,
"过客欲求栖身所——
夜深探问把门敲,
唯此无他响。"

霎时心定意坚不狐疑,开口来问寻,

Section Two
American Poetry of Early Romantic Period

"先生/夫人请见谅,
意懒心倦正自烦,
叩门之音未听确,"
就此开门将客迎;
夜浓,无人影。

定足凝望,漫漫长夜心悬疑,
恰似幽梦初醒自难忘,
夜阑无声,静寂无形,
唯我低声唤勒诺;
凄然旷野映回声——
唯此无他响。

转身回屋,心有余悸难平息,
窗边又起叩击声,阵阵不绝耳。
"始知屋外不明之物在眼前,
欲将个中究竟细细探——
安神初定前去找,
唯风无他响。"

卷帘开窗,鼓翼振翅飞入一乌鸦,
神态自若如智者;
不卑不亢,快若迅雷栖我处,
风度无人肖——
飞旋落定如玉女神帕拉丝——
宜栖宜坐岿不动。

但见其神情肃穆现高贵,
顿使我悲郁情怀化笑颜,
"你貌若凡鸟而神自定,
让我想起古之神鹊黄泉落,
敢问你彼岸尊姓和大名,"
乌鹊答道"永不再会"。

其貌不扬一小鸟,吐字清晰令人奇,
纵然词不搭意难自圆,
世人罕有此经历,
有幸目睹它登门,

飞落室内神雕塑，
自唤名曰"永不再会"。

只见它静若雕像独端坐，
倾注灵魂于斯语，
唯此不言也不动——
我低声哀叹"亲朋皆逝我独留——
明日它亦弃我而去无望还。"
乌鸦即和"永不再会"。

惊闻接语称心又贴切，
始知其开口无他语，
必逢主人不幸遭磨难，
无奈常叹此一言，
长歌当哭忧愤起，
感慨"永不再会"。

而我已是悲思转笑颜，
侧身就座其栖息处，
慵倦陷沉思，
揣度这只亘古不祥鸟，
冷酷、笨拙、恐怖又憔悴，
缘和嘶叫"永不再会"。

我攒眉思忖不作响，
眼前它目光炯炯将我灼；
见我心驰神骛态依旧，
灯下安然斜靠丝绒衬，
而今物是人非，纵心念佳人，
已是永不再会。

暗炉幽香渐扑鼻，
疑为轻盈天使一路来，
"竟是我主送你到身边，
相赠忘忧物，解我心中千千结；
痛饮忘情水，换我痴情永相忘。"
却闻"永不再会"。

"无论你是鸟是魔,还是邪恶一先知,
不管你追随撒旦抑或屈从风暴,孤身一人不畏惧——
我如今身处荒原神恍惚——
在这闹鬼恐惧屋,恳切求尔语,
有否基列乳香将我医?"
却闻"永不再会"。

"无论你是鸟是魔,还是邪恶一先知,
看在我们头顶共青天,上帝同膜拜,
解我心中愁,在那远方乐土伊甸园,
我还能否相会梦中佳人名勒诺——
举世无双窈窕女,安琪唤其叫勒诺。"
却闻"永不再相会"。

"闭口休再提!"我心中怒火不可遏,
"你就此踏归黄泉路!
收回满口荒唐言!
使我莫烦扰!离我门上半身像!
与你不相干,快些飞离我!"
却闻"永不再会"。

只见乌鸦丝毫未动依自若,
栖我门上如玉帕拉丝,
魔鬼神情眼中露,
幽暗身形灯光映,
心中隐痛难抚平。
永远不再会!
(周英莉 译 李正栓 校)

(3) Annabel Lee

It was many and many a year ago,
   In a kingdom by the sea,
That a maiden there lived whom you may know
   By the name of ANNABEL LEE;
5 And this maiden she lived with no other thought
   Than to love and be loved by me.

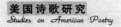

    I was a child and she was a child,
        In this kingdom by the sea;
    But we loved with a love that was more than love—
10   I and my ANNEBEL LEE;
    With a love that the winged seraphs of heaven
        Coveted her and me.

    And this was the reason that, long ago,
        In this kingdom by the sea,
15 A wind blew out of a cloud, chilling
        My beautiful ANNEBEL LEE;
    So that her highborn kinsmen came
        And bore her away from me,
    To shut her up in a sepulchre
20   In this kingdom by the sea.

    The angels, not half so happy in heaven,
        Went envying her and me—
    Yes! —that was the reason (as all men know,
        In this kingdom by the sea)
25 That the wind came out of the cloud by night,
        Chilling and killing my ANNABEL LEE.

    But our love it was stronger by far than the love
        Of those who were older than we—
        Of many far wiser than we—
30 And neither the angels in heaven above,
        Nor the demons down under the sea,
    Can ever dissever my soul from the soul
        Of the beautiful ANNABEL LEE:

    For the moon never beams without bringing me dreams
35   Of the beautiful ANNABEL LEE;
    And the stars never rise but I see the bright eyes
        Of the beautiful ANNABEL LEE;
    And so, all the night-tide, I lie down by the side
    Of my darling, my darling, my life and my bride,
40   In her sepulcher there by the sea—
        In her tomb by the sounding sea.

Section Two
American Poetry of Early Romantic Period

Notes

This is the last poetic work of Edgar Allan Poe. It is believed to be dedicated to the memory of Poe's wife, Virginia Clemm, who died in 1847 at the age of 26. The poem was first published on October 9, 1849 in the New York Tribune with the author's name as Ludwig.

Line 1 Many a year: many years.
Line 2 kingdom: a holy place in one's heart; the kingdom of love.
Line 3 a maiden: a pretty girl; a young lady.
Line 5 And this maiden she lived? The word "she" here is superfluously used for the sake of rhythm: to contribute an unstressed syllable to the anapestic foot.

Stanza 1: The pretty young girl Annabel Lee used to live in a kingdom by the seaside. Before her death, the only thing in her heart was to love or to be loved by me.

Line 7 The "child" does not mean that they fell in love with each other in childhood. Poe indicated that in the kingdom of love, they were both too young and naive to face the "highborn kinsmen." The scansion of this line begins with a caret at the very beginning, standing for the missing unstressed syllable.
Line 11 seraphs: (in the Bible) a member of the highest order of angels.
Line 12 Coveted: envied.

Stanza 2: Our love was so strong and beautiful that angels in heaven, who are with wings and living in heaven and likely to be freer and abler than any human beings, envied us. Seldom did any angels envy anything of the human world. If they did, there must be something spectacular in the object of their admiration.

Line 13 this: the winged seraphs' covetousness.
Line 15 chilling: the evil wind was so strong and cold and it blew my Annabel Lee ill.
Line 17 So that: because of that (the chilling wind).
  highborn kinsmen: God of death who also exists in heaven.
Line 18 bore: brought back; took away.
Line 19 sepulchre: Sepulcher; grand grave; tomb.

Stanza 3: My Annabel Lee was taken away from me. The faithful lovers were mercilessly separated by a superpower. Poe was indicating that Annabel Lee might be an angel from heaven, because she was "brought" back (not "taken away") to heaven and she had some "highborn kinsmen" up there.

Line 21 The angels, not half so happy in heaven: Because the angels in heaven were not half as happy as we were in this kingdom by the sea. "happy and heaven" is the figurative speech of alliteration to emphasize the angels in heaven are quite unhappy.
Line 23 reason: the reason for the angels' sending wind and bringing Annabel Lee from me.
Line 26 Chilling and killing: "Chilling" and "killing" are in end rhyme and feminine rhyme. They are used here to emphasis the cruelty of the "highborn kinsmen."

Stanza 4: The poet was quite clear about the reason of Annabel Lee's being taken away from him. The evil wind came out by night and Annabel Lee was taken away by night, that indicates that somebody may appear as angels in daytime, but as devils during night.

Line 27 it: a superfluous word. But our love is by far stronger than...
Lines 28 – 29 These two lines are attributive phrases modifying "love" in line 27, indicating that the poet was confident that the love between Annabel Lee and him is much stronger than the love of those people who were much older than they; and, their love is much stronger than the love of those who were believed much wiser.
"those who were older than we" refers to time or history. If their love is stronger than that of "those who were older than we," that simply implies their love must be the strongest and the most lasting in human history.
"many far wiser than we" refers to prominent figures in the world. If their love is stronger than that of the great persons' in the world, it must be the strongest and the most sensible in this world.
Line 31 demons: evil spirits.

Stanza 5: Though the evil wind and the highborn kinsmen are very powerful to take my beautiful Annabel Lee away from me, they are not so

Section Two
American Poetry of Early Romantic Period

powerful as to take her soul away from me. Our love is more powerful than death. After the death of one, our souls are still together.

Line 34 beams: sends out light; smiles brightly and happily.
Line 41 the sounding sea: the roaring sea.

<u>Stanza 6</u>: My Annabel Lee had gone to heaven. She reminds me of her bright face by the moon, so that I can see her in my dream; when I see the stars in the sky, I see her bright eyes, too. We are together and nothing can separate us, neither the human power nor the God of death is possible.

Comment of the poem

In *Annabel Lee*, when Poe was writing about the life and death of his wife, he did not use her real name, nor did he use the real background. Instead, he provided a false name and an imagined "kingdom by the sea." On the one hand, Poe did so to add some mythical or fabulous color to their love; on the other hand, Poe wanted to imply to us that such kind of true love could exist nowhere else but in a mythical kingdom of ancient time. Thus Poe showed his resentment of reality.

In the poem, Poe, instead of feeling sorry for himself, felt lost. The poem is not just a dirge. Much more than that, it is a mourning song for the death of a beautiful woman, which implies the death of beauty.

This last poem has always been regarded as the best of Poe's poems. It coincides on every side with Poe's poetic theories: consisting of 41 lines, it is quite readable at one sitting; it wears a sad and melancholy tone; it tells the story of the death of a beautiful woman; with the repetition of the /iː/ sound, it was so rhythmically written into a piece of "word music."

参考译文

安娜贝尔·李

很多很多年以前，
海边一个王国里，
君知住着一少女，
名叫安娜贝尔·李；
她在世上无杂念，

唯知与我相爱怜。

我们两人皆孩童，
住在海边王国里；
相爱程度比爱浓，
我和安娜贝尔·李；
天上六翼众天使，
垂涎我和我的李。

正是因为我们爱，
就在海边王国里，
云中吹出寒风来，
冻死我的漂亮李；
于是高贵亲属来，
从我手中掠她去，
墓穴把她关起来，
就在海边王国里。

天上天使并不悦，
开始妒忌她和我——
的确此因人人解，
（就在海边这王国。）
寒风乘夜云端起，
冻杀我的安娜·李。

但是我们爱更浓，
胜比我们年长者——
胜比几许智多星——
天上众多神天使，
海里无数怪妖精，
妄想拆散灵与魂！
我们生死不分离！

因为月辉带我梦，
梦见漂亮安娜·李；
除非见她明亮眸，
否则星辰难升起；
所以长夜邀我睡，

伴我生命伴新娘,
就在海边墓穴内,
滔滔海边她墓内。
(李正栓 译)

Section Three

American Poetry of High Romantic Period

Section Three
American Poetry of High Romantic Period

Ⅰ. Henry Wadsworth Longfellow
(1807 – 1882)

1. Life Story

Henry Wadsworth Longfellow was born in Portland, Maine, on February 27, 1807, into a well-to-do family. He was educated at Bowdoin College, where he was a fellow student with Nathaniel Hawthorne and Franklin Pierce, the 14th president of the United States (1853 – 1857).

After his graduation in 1825, Longfellow spent three years in Europe studying the culture and languages of Italy, Spain, and Germany. In 1836, Longfellow became professor of French and Spanish at Harvard, where he taught for 18 years and then he resigned in 1854 because he felt it interfered with his writing. Longfellow's most productive years were from 1843 to 1860. After 1854, Longfellow devoted himself completely to literary writing. Several long poems and collections of poems were published. But in his later time, he turned to religious and reflective poetry, and to translation. From 1864 to 1867, most of his time was spent in the translating of *The Divine Comedy by Dante* (1265 – 1321). His last collection of poems appeared in 1882, the year of his death. As a poet, Longfellow enjoyed the most popular reputation when he was alive, and his poetic works were regarded as the summit of the literary work of the 19th century. His poems were influential to most of his contemporary writers. However, his tremendous fame decreased rapidly soon after Longfellow's death and especially in the 20th century, Longfellow's fame as the most important American poet of the previous century had to be vacated to Walt Whitman.

2. Major Works

(1) *Voices of the Night* (1839), his first book of poetry, which contains "Hymn to the Night" and "A Psalm of Life."
(2) *Ballads and Other Poems* (1841), containing such favorites as "The Village Blacksmith."

(3) *Evangeline* (1847).
(4) "The Song of Hiawatha" (1855), a long poem that was based on American Indian legends.
(5) *Translation of Dante's Divine Comedy* (1865 – 1867).

3. Features of Longfellow's Poetic Works

Longfellow was the best-known American poet during the 19th century.

(1) Longfellow's long stay in Europe led to his mastery of several European languages and a broader knowledge of European literature than most other American literary figures, what's more, this enabled him to embody in his poetry chief romantic tendencies as humanitarian attitude, love of beauty, love of nature and love for the past; and it enabled him to introduce American themes to Europe: American Indians, anti-slavery ideas and the scenery of the New World. Longfellow was popular because of his high-mindedness, his spiritual aspiration, his refinement of thought, his refinement of manners, and the gentleness, sweetness and purity of his poetry.

(2) Longfellow was the first American poet to write narrative poems. "The Song of Hiawatha" is the first American epic in blank verse about the American Indians.

(3) Longfellow's style and subjects were conventional, especially in comparison with those of Whitman or more modern writers. He wrote in traditional regular meters and feet, in regular rhyming schemes. Longfellow did not appeal, as most of his contemporary writers did, for the breaking of American literature from European literature. Usually he wrote about American subjects, but always in European styles.

(4) Being a highly learned and cultivated man, and a professor of several languages, Longfellow composed all his works with accurately selected words and delicate expressions. The ideas he expressed are generally simple ones but he expressed them musically and powerfully.

(5) The child-like simplicity and detachment from the deep and important problems of contemporary life are perhaps the basic elements of Longfellow's appeal to the common audience; but on the other hand, they led to a fatal weakness in his work—lack of the depth and insight of a great artist such as Whitman. As a poet, Longfellow failed to reflect in his poetry what he felt personally, instead of what he attained from reading. He enriched his poems with second-hand knowledge.

However, in the late 19th century, Longfellow was doubtlessly the most popular American poet and a milestone in the development of American poetry.

4. Selected Poems

(1) The Quadroon Girl

The Slaver in the broad lagoon
    Lay moored with idle sail;
He waited for the rising moon
    And for the evening gale.

5 Under the shore his boat was tied,
    And all her listless crew
Watched the gray alligator slide
    Into the still bayou.

Odors of orange-flowers and spice
10   Reached them from time to time,
Like the airs that breathe from Paradise
    Upon a world of crime.
The Planter, under his roof of thatch,
    Smoked thoughtfully and slow;
15 The slaver's thumb was on the latch,
    He seemed in haste to go.

He said, "My ship at anchor rides
    In yonder broad lagoon;
I only wait the evening tides
20   And the rising of the moon."

Before them, with her face upraised,
    In timid attitude,
Like one half curious, half amazed,
    A Quadroon maiden stood.

25 Her eyes were large and full of light,
    Her arms and neck were bare;
No garment she wore save a kirtle bright,
    And her own long, raven hair.

And on her lips there played a smile
30 　　As holy, meek, and faint,
　As lights in some cathedral aisle,
　　　The features of a saint.

"The soil is barren, —the farm is old,"
　　The thoughtful planter said;
35　Then looked upon the Slaver's gold,
　　And then upon the maid.

His heart within him was at strife
　　With such accursed gains;
For he knew whose passions gave her life
40　　Whose blood ran in her veins.
But the voice of nature was too weak;
　　He took the glittering gold!
Then pale as death grew the maiden's cheek,
　　Her hands as icy cold.

45　The Slaver led her from the door,
　　He led her by the hand,
To be his slave and paramour
　　In a strange and distant land.

Notes

Quadroon: a person of quarter-negro blood; a person of cross-blood, especially of black and white.

Line 1 Slaver: the captain of a slave ship and a slave trader.
　　　　lagoon: a salt-water lake partly or completely separated from the open sea by sandbanks or coral reefs.
Line 2 Lay moored: (the slave ship has) lowered the anchor in the broad lagoon.
Line 3 He: "the slaver" in the first line.
Line 5 his: the slave-trader's.
Line 6 her: the ship's.

Section Three
American Poetry of High Romantic Period

Line 7 alligator: reptile of the crocodile family found especially in the rivers and lakes of tropical America and China. (短吻鳄)
Line 8 bayou: a creek flowing into a river or other body of water.
Line 10 them: the listless crew of the slave ship.
Line 12 a world of crime: the human world with slaves.
    The first 3 stanzas reveal an atmosphere of leisure and a tranquil background for the story.
Line 13 The Planter: the owner of a plantation.
Line 15 The slave trader is unfastening the door; he is leaving the planter's house. This implies a trade between them has failed.
    latch: a small iron bar used to fasten the door.
Line 17 He: the slave trader.
    My ship at anchor rides: My ship is staying at anchor.
    The slave-trader implies he didn't come to the planter deliberately for a trade; he was detained here just because of weather, so "make your decision, I'm not waiting longer than the turn of the tide."
    This may be the truth, however, it may yet be a way of bargain.
Lines 21 - 24 A Quadroon girl, with face uprising, and in timid attitude, is standing before the slave trader and the planter. She is innocent but very eager to learn what was happening.
Line 23 amazed: be filled with great surprise.
    In this stanza, the fourth line provides the subject and predicative for the whole.
Line 27 kirtle bright: a loose gown of woman's in bright color.
Line 28 raven hair: smooth black hair.
Line 30 As holy, meek, and faint: The smile is as holy, meek, and faint as...
Line 32 The features of a saint: This is a metaphor. (The girl has) all the features of a saint—a person with a holy or completely unselfish way of life.
Lines 25 - 33 The sincere description of the girl is provided and the girl impresses the readers with all her natural beauty, youth and goddess-like smile.
Lines 35 - 36 The shifts of the planter's sight implies an intended exchange of the girl for the gold.
Line 37 at strife: in a conflict.
Line 38 accursed: under a curse; hateful.
    gains: the gold planter would get by selling the girl.
Line 39 whose passion gave her life: (The planter knew) the girl's life was the fruit of someone's passionate love.
Line 40 whose blood ran in her veins: (the planter is clear) in the veins

of the girl whose blood is running.

Lines 39 – 40 (The planter hesitated because) he was aware of some facts about the girl.

Judging by the fact that the girl is a "quadroon" and the planter knows so much about the girl's bloodline, the correct inference indicates the girl's mother must be a black slave woman. And, in the slavery society, the girl must be the bastard child of the planter. The planter is her father! That explains the planter's hesitation over the trade.

Line 41 the voice of nature: the planter's conscious about the girl's natural concern with him (which is too weak to prevent him from the trade).

Line 42 He took the glittering gold: between the girl and the gold, the planter makes the choice of the latter.

Line 43 The girl's face becomes as pale as if she is dead.

Line 47 paramour: an unlawful lover of a married man or woman.

Line 48 The slaver will take the girl away in his ship to a new land.

Comment on the poem

Through the detailed presentation of the criminal situation about a white man exchanging his daughter for gold, Longfellow exposed the cruelty of the slavery system and showed his sympathy for the girl.

参考译文

有四分之一黑人血统的女孩

运奴船慵懒停泊
在广阔咸水湖中,
等待升起的明月,
等待晚间的疾风。

小船在岸边系着,
所有无聊的水手
瞅着灰色短吻鳄
溜进静静的河口。

橙花香料的香气

Section Three
American Poetry of High Romantic Period

不时向他们飘曳，
如同天堂的气息
浮动在罪恶世界。

园主站在茅檐下
心事重重把烟吸，
奴贩手摸门插销，
像是要匆忙离去。

他说："我的船停在
那边广阔湖水里，
只在等候晚潮来，
等待明月徐升起。"

女孩站在他们前
心生不安怯瑟瑟
头略仰看微扬脸，
又是好奇又惊愕。

眼睛又大又明亮，
裸露脖子和臂膀。
身上只穿鲜艳裙，
长发乌黑又滑顺。

她的双唇露笑容：
圣洁温顺又淡然，
好似教堂走廊中
圣人光辉在发散。

"农场已旧地贫瘠，"
园主若有所思说，
眼瞟奴贩手中币，
之后眼落少女身。

内心激烈在斗争，
交易肮脏良心灭，
他知少女源谁情，
知她流淌谁的血。

77

良知呼唤太弱微；
取过奴贩闪光币！
女孩顿时面如灰，
双手冰凉无生气。

奴贩领她出门口，
他手牵着她手走。
将在陌生遥远处，
她当奴隶和情妇。
（李正栓 周英莉 译）

(2) A Psalm of Life [1]

*"Life that shall send
A challenge to its end,
And when it comes, say 'welcome, friend.'"* [2]

**What the heart of the young man
　　　　said to the psalmist[3].**

Tell me not, in mournful numbers,
　Life is but an empty dream! —
For the soul is dead that slumbers
　And things are not what they seem.

5　Life is real! Life is earnest!
　　And the grave is not its goal;
　Dust thou art, to dust returnest,
　　Was not spoken of the soul.

　Not enjoyment, and not sorrow,
10　Is our destined end or way;
　But to act, that each to-morrow,
　　Find us farther than to-day.

　Art is long, and Time is fleeting,
　　And our hearts, though stout and brave,
15　Still, like muffled drums, are beating
　　Funeral marches to the grave.

Section Three
American Poetry of High Romantic Period

    In the world's broad field of battle,
        In the bivouac of Life,
    Be not like dumb, driven cattle!
20   Be a hero in the strife!

    Trust no Future, howe'er pleasant!
        Let the dead Past bury its dead!
    Act, —act in the living Present!
        Heart within, and God o'erhead!

25 Lives of great men all remind us
        We can make our lives sublime,
    And, departing, leave behind us
        Footprints on the sands of time;

    Footprints, that perhaps another,
30   Sailing o'er life's solemn main,
    forlorn and shipwrecked brother,
        Seeing, shall take heart again.

    Let us, then, be up and doing,
    With a heart for any fate;
35 Still achieving, still pursuing,
    Learn to labor and to wait.

Notes

1. Psalm: a song or poem in praise of God;
2. These lines are adapted from *Wishes to His Supposed Mistress* by Richard Crashaw.
3. Psalmist: composer of psalms.
   In Western culture, Psalmist usually refers to David, the composer of the most part of *The Book of Psalms*.

Line 1 in mournful numbers: in sorrowful words.
        numbers: verses; metrical feet; words.
Line 3 For the soul is dead that slumbers: for the soul that slumbers is dead.
Line 4 things are not what they seem: the truth of a matter may be quite

different from what it appears to be.

Line 7 Dust thou art, to dust returnest: (at birth) you were from the dust, and you will return to earth when you die. The line is quoted from *Genesis* 3: 19, when God is driving Adam and Eve out of the Garden of Eden, He says, "In the sweat of your brow you must make a living until you return to the ground, because out it you were taken; for dust you are and to dust you shall return." God's implication here is that Adam and Eve must suffer in the human world for the redemption of their eternal life. Therefore, their life in the mortal world is empty and worthless.

Line 8 was not spoken of the soul: (words of line 7) was not the accurate term for the soul. (The soul will not die with the body, it is eternal.)

Lines 9 – 10 Neither enjoyment nor sorrow is obliged to be the highest aim of our life.

Line 11 But to act: the crucial matter in our life is to take action, to practice what we have learned about this world.

Line 12 find us further than to-day: (if we take action), we make progress each day.

Line 13 Art is long, and Time is fleeting: though art can exist forever and it survives everything, time fleets and therefore, human life is limited.

Lines 14 – 16 Though our heart is strong and brave, still, it is beating like the muffled drums at a funeral towards the grave.

Line 15 muffled: wrapped or covered for protection or warmth.

In this line, the poet compares the beating of heart to that of a drum. The drum is muffled to soften its sound and make it more solemn. Similarly, our heart, with all the good care and solemnity, is eventually beating towards death.

The line is adapted from the Aphorisms of Hippocrates (469? – 375? B. C., famous Greek physician: the Father of Medicine).

Line 17 In the world's broad field of battle: the human world is compared to a battle field.

Line 18 bivouac: soldiers' camp. The human life is compared to a battle.

Line 19 dumb, driven cattle: animal recklessly driven by the tyrants but without any complaint.

Line 20 in the strife: in the battle of life.

Line 21 We should not expect too much about the visionary future, no matter how pleasant the future may appear.

Section Three
American Poetry of High Romantic Period

Line 22 We should not depend on the glory of the past, since it is already dead.

Line 24 We should act with courage and act with God over our heads.

Lines 25 – 26 Some great people have set examples for us that each one is quite able to achieve the highest honour in life.

Lines 27 – 28 And when we have to die, each should leave behind him the reputation as a hero.

Line 28 the sands of time: time, as measured by sand in an hourglass; history.

Line 29 The footprints left by us may enable another person (the "forlorn and shipwrecked brother" in Line 31) to follow.

Line 31 forlorn and shipwrecked brother: (the "another" in line 29 who may be a) depressed, unfortunate, helpless, lonely person.

Line 32 Seeing: when the "another" or "brother" sees the footprints left by me.

take heart: be encouraged.

The footprints left by me will probably encourage a follower (an unfortunate, helpless person) who is sailing over the ocean of life, to overcome his difficulties.

Line 33 be up and doing: be brave and active.

Line 34 a heart for any fate: the courage to face any destiny.

Line 35 Still: constantly.

Line 36 Learn to labor and to wait: learn to act and to be patient, for the human life consists of pursuing, acting and achieving. To accomplish them, hard labor is critical, while patience is the other necessity. This happened to coincide with John Milton's conclusion achieved when he was considering how his light is spent, "They also serve who only stand and wait."

Comment on the poem

"A Psalm of Life" was first published in *Voices of the Night* in the September edition of *New York Monthly* in 1839. It is very influential in China, because it is said to be the first English poem translated into Chinese.

The poem was written in 1838 when Longfellow was struck with great dismay: his wife died in 1835, and his courtship of a young woman was unrequited. However, despite all the frustrations, Longfellow tried to encourage himself by writing a piece of optimistic work.

The relationship of life and death is a constant theme for poets.

Longfellow expresses his pertinent interpretation to that by warning us that though life is hard and everybody must die, time flies and life is short, yet, human beings ought to be bold "to act," to face the reality straightly so as to make otherwise meaningless life significant.

The poem consists of 9 stanzas in trochaic tetrameters. It is rhymed "abab."

参考译文

生命礼赞

"生命挑战其目的,
这事发生时,就说:'朋友,欢迎。'"

这是那年轻人的心
对赞美诗作者说的话。

不要用哀婉的诗句对我说:
"人生只是梦幻一场!"——
因为昏睡的灵魂不再有生活,
而事物也不是表面的模样。

人生即真,不能虚度!
坟墓并非人生追求的目标;
你来自尘土,归于尘土,
这并非对灵魂的写照。

我们命运的终点或道路,
不是享乐,也不是忧伤;
只是行动,并且每一个今天
发现我们比前一个今天都有进展。

学艺须日久,时光飞如箭。
我们的心尽管坚强又勇敢,
依然像蒙住的鼓
敲打着葬礼的鼓点走向坟墓。
在世界辽阔的战场,

Section Three
American Poetry of High Romantic Period

在人生临时的营站,
不要像无言无语任人驱使的牛羊!
要在奋斗中做个英雄好汉!

别指望未来,不管它多么光明!
让死的过去把死的事物埋葬!
行动吧,在活生生的现实中行动!
赤心胸中存,上帝在天堂!

伟人的生平把我们提醒:
我们能使生命崇高无限,
即使辞世去也留身后美名,
在时间的沙滩上留下脚印串串。

或许另有人会看到这脚印,
他在人生肃穆的航行中
偶遭不幸:船沉后只剩孤独一人,
见这脚印便又有希望重生。

那么就让我们起来行动,
准备一个应对一切命运的胸怀,
成就总是有但永处追求中,
学会苦干还要学会等待。
(李正栓　译)

(3) Daybreak

A wind came up out of the sea,
And said, "O mists, make room for me."

It hailed the ships, and cried, "sail on,
Ye mariners, the night is gone."
5　　And hurried landward far away,
Crying, "Awake! it is the day."

It said unto the forest, "Shout!
Hang all your leafy banners out!"

It touched the wood-bird's folded wing,
10   And said, "O bird, awake and sing."

And o'er the farms,"O Chanticleer,
Your clarion blow; the day is near."

It whispered to the fields of corn,
"Bow down, and hail the coming morn."

15   It shouted through the belfry-tower,
"Awake, O bell! proclaim the hour."

It crossed the churchyard with a sigh,
And said, "Not yet! in quiet lie."

Notes

Line 1 came up out of: rose up from.
Line 2 make room for me: spare space for me.
Line 3 It: the wind.
   hailed: called to attract attention.
Line 4 Ye mariners: you sailors; the sailors.
Line 5 And hurried landward far away: (the wind) hurried towards land from far away.
Line 8 leafy banners: leaves are banners of the forest.
Line 11 o'er the farms: (the wind is flying) over the farms.
   Chanticleer: cock; rooster.
Line 12 Your clarion blow: blow your clarion.
Line 14 hail the coming morn: greet the coming morning.
Line 17 the belfry-tower: a tower with a bell on (top of) a church.
Line 18 Not yet: not be disturbed by me.
   in quiet lie: please lie in quiet. The wind encourages all but the dead, who must await a higher power.

Comment on the poem

This is a poem about nature. In the work, the wind, which travels up and down, far and near, is personified as a diligent worker, who is vigorous by himself, sympathetic to others and inspires the other members of nature to enjoy life, to fulfill their duty.

Section Three
American Poetry of High Romantic Period

参考译文

破 晓

一阵风从海上吹来,
它说:"雾啊,把路给我让开。"

它向轮船致敬并高喊:"水手们,
黑夜已经消亡,你们继续前进。"

之后它向远方的陆地急行军,
边走边喊:"快快醒来,已是天光大亮。"

它对森林说:"大声叫喊!
把你多叶的旗帜挂在外边。"

它触摸林鸟合起的翅膀,
说:"鸟儿啊,起来,唱。"

它来到农庄:"公鸡啊,
吹号吧,天马上就亮啦。"

它对玉米地低语轻声:
"弯下腰去,对要来的早晨要欢迎。"

它呼喊着想钟楼扫去:
"快醒来,钟啊,快给大家报时。"

它穿过教堂时还叹息,
说道,"别起来,请安静地歇息。"
(李正栓 译)

(4) The Tide Rises, the Tide Falls

The tide rises, the tide falls,
The twilight darkens, the curlew calls;

```
        Along the sea-sands damp and brown
        The traveller hastens toward the town,
5            And the tide rises, the tide falls.

        Darkness settles on roofs and walls,
        But the sea, the sea in the darkness calls;
        The little waves, with their soft, white hands,
        Efface the footprints in the sands,
10           And the tide rises, the tide falls.

        The morning breaks; the steeds in their stalls
        Stamp and neigh, as the hostler calls;
        The day returns, but nevermore
        Returns the traveller to the shore,
15           The tide rises, the tide falls.
```

Notes

Line 2 curlew: water bird with a long, thin beak that curves downward; a shore bird. （麻鹬）

Lines 3 – 4 The traveller is hurrying toward the town along the sea-sands which are damp and brown.
  The "sea-sands" gives a strong suggestion to "the sands of time," while the "traveller" indicates every individual in this world.

Line 6 Darkness settles on roofs and walls: evening has fallen over the roofs and the walls.

Line 7 the sea in the darkness calls: but in the darkness, the sea is still roaring.

Line 9 Efface: wipe out; eliminate.
  the footprints: the footprints of the travelers'. It is rather symbolic than realistic. The footprints indicate what a person had done and experienced in his life.

Line 12 Stamp and neigh, as the hostler calls: when the horse tender called them, the horses began to wriggle by stamping and crying.

Lines 13 – 14 Day and night circles, but a human can live only once. He has passed the shore, he is not likely to return any more.

Section Three
American Poetry of High Romantic Period

Comment on the poem

Longfellow is very good at finding unexpected meanings out of everyday experience. Thus in this poem, the simple language reveals a very profound philosophical theme: time and tide wait for no man. Time and tide are eternal but human life is limited. Time fades, tide effaces, but people are powerless before nature. The repetition of "The tide rises, the tide falls" for five times suggests the cyclic movement of nature and reflects the uncertainty of human life, appealing to people to cherish life.

The poem has only 3 stanzas in iambic tetrameter with a repeating refrain. It is rhymed "aabba."

参考译文

潮起潮又落

潮起潮又落，
黄昏渐黑，鹬鸟鸣叫；
沿着潮湿褐色的海滩
那旅人急匆匆往城镇赶，
潮起潮又落。

夜色往墙壁和房顶上降落，
但大海仍在黑暗中轰鸣；
微波用柔软白细的手
抹去沙滩上的脚印。
潮起潮又落。

东方已破晓，
厩里马儿踢又鸣，马夫在喊叫；
白昼复旧，那旅人却永远
不能回到海岸。
潮起潮又落。
（李正栓　译）

(5) The Village Blacksmith

Under a spreading chestnut-tree

          The village smithy stands;
      The smith, a mighty man is he,
          With large and sinewy hands;
5   And the muscles of his brawny arms
          Are strong as iron bands.
      His hair is crisp, and black, and long,
          His face is like the tan;
      His brow is wet with honest sweat,
10   He earns whate'er he can,
      And looks the whole world in the face,
          For he owes not any man.
      Week in, week out, from morn till night,
          You can hear his bellows blow;
15   You can hear him swing his heavy sledge,
          With measured beat and slow,
      Like a sexton ringing the village bell,
          When the evening sun is low.

      And children coming home from school
20   Look in at the open door;
      They love to see the flaming forge,
          And hear the bellows roar,
      And catch the burning sparks that fly
          Like chaff from a threshing-floor.

25   He goes on Sunday to the church,
          And sits among his boys;
      He hears the parson pray and preach,
          He hears his daughter's voice,
      Singing in the village choir,
30   And it makes his heart rejoice.

      It sounds to him like her mother's voice,
          Singing in Paradise!
      He needs must think of her once more,
          How in the grave she lies;
35   And with his hard, rough hand he wipes
          A tear out of his eyes.
      Toiling,—rejoicing,—sorrowing,
          Onward through life he goes;

Section Three
American Poetry of High Romantic Period

Each morning sees some task begin,
40   Each evening sees it close;
Something attempted, something done,
    Has earned a night's repose.
Thanks, thanks to thee, my worthy friend,
    For the lesson thou hast taught!
45 Thus at the flaming forge of life
    Our fortunes must be wrought;
Thus on its sounding anvil shaped
    Each burning deed and thought.

Notes

Line 1 spreading: flourishing.
Line 2 village smithy: village blacksmith shop.
Line 4 sinewy: having strong sinews; muscular.
Line 5 brawny: strong and muscular.
Line 6 iron bands: iron hoops or loops.
Line 7 crisp: (of hair) tightly curled.
Line 8 tan: (the skin) become brown by frequent exposure to the sun and the beat of the forge.
Line 9 with honest sweat: (his brow) sweats because he has been working honestly; "honest sweat" is a transferred epithet.
Line 11 looks... in the face: looks at something calmly and confidently; is completely at ease in front of others.
Line 12 owes not any man: is not in debt to anyone; is quite able to make the two ends meet.
Line 16 measured beat: the sledge beats rhythmical strokes in a steady speed.
Line 17 a simile; The village smith swings the hammer in a steady speed just like the village sexton rings the church bell.
Line 21 They: school chilren of the village.
Line 24 chaff: the outer covers of seeds (husks), separated from grain.
threshing-floor: the ground for separating the grain from chaff. The children enjoy themselves in catching burning sparks which are flying like chaff from a threshing-floor.
Line 27 parson: a priest of the church of England who is in charge of a Parish.
Line 38 Onward through life he goes: he goes onward through life.

Line 42 Has earned a night's repose: has obtained to him a sound sleep.
Line 43 worthy friend: respectful friend, the smith.
Line 45 at the flaming forge of life: the poet compares life to a burning furnace.
Line 46 Our fortunes must be wrought: our life must be tempered by all the heating and hammering on an anvil.
wrought: (old use) made; done.
Lines 47 – 48 Each burning deed and thought is shaped on this sounding anvil. The poet compares the bustling society to a sounding anvil.
burning deed: splendid achievements.

Comment on the poem

"The Village Blacksmith," appeared in *Ballads and Other Poems* in 1841, is one of the most famous poetic works of Longfellow, and that of American literary history as well.

As the representative poet of the 19th century, Longfellow is a master to sing his way into the consciousness of the readers. In "The Village Blacksmith," the popularity and significance originate, first, from the obvious scene of a village blacksmith shop under a "spreading chestnut tree" and the familiar figure of a masculine blacksmith, which appeal to everybody and which are able to evoke immediate response in the emotion of the readers; secondly, the popularity and significance of the poem come from the natural grace of easy rhyme, from clear meters, and, from melodic rhythms. With a vocabulary familiar to everyone as ballads or nursery songs, the poem is likely to be remained in the memory and accompany people through life; thirdly, a spirit of optimism and power of faith esteemed in the poem have been widely enjoyed by the readers. Therefore, with a calm and clear voice, Longfellow fits his subject exactly so as to illustrate the simple dreams of average humanity. The appealing words, as well as the impressing "spreading chestnut tree," have clung to the hearts of ordinary Americans and, similarly, won an enduring place in world literature.

The broad popularity and appreciation of this poem is also responded by the anecdote in 1876, when "spreading chestnut tree," which sat on Brattle Street in Cambridge, Massachusetts, fell victim to progress with the widening of the street, the children of Cambridge, some of whom probably "caught those burning sparks," gave their pennies to build a chair out of the tree and presented it to Longfellow as a gift on his 72nd birthday.

参考译文

乡村铁匠

乡村铁匠树下站，
栗树冠大又茂密，
他身高大魁梧汉，
手掌宽厚又有力，
臂膀肌肉很强健
坚实强壮如铁器。

浓密乌发长又卷，
面庞黝黑透健康；
辛勤汗水浸眉毛，
任劳任怨把钱赚，
直面人生坦荡荡，
自食其力不曾欠。

日出日落年复年，
铁炉风箱不间歇；
听他手轮大铁锤，
节奏平稳又合乐，
就像夕阳低悬时
司事敲响村内钟。

房门向着街里敞，
放学顽童往里瞧，
看熊熊烈焰的翻飞，
惊喜风箱的呼号，
火花飞溅如谷衣落场，
双双稚手难以捉到。
每逢礼拜去教堂，
坐在他的孩童间；
聆听牧师布道场，

倾听村内唱诗班
更听爱女声音美，
心中欣喜比蜜甜。

听似慈母声音回，
她在天国唱圣曲！
他要再忆母亲境，
母亲安卧坟墓里；
老茧硬手把泪擦，
双眼流出泪花花。

悲欢辛劳多少秋，
一生劳作无尽头。
每天清早劳作始，
每天夜晚活计终；
些事开始些事毕，
才能安睡夜幕中。

千恩万谢好朋友，
是你给上人生课：
生活恰似冶铁炉，
凡人造化从中炼；
伟业神思需锤塑，
繁华尘世比作砧。

（李正栓　周英莉译　21—24行为陈岩译文）

Section Three
American Poetry of High Romantic Period

II. Walt Whitman
(1819 – 1892)

1. Life Story

Walt Whitman was one of the great innovators in American literary history. He uses a style that was quite new and special in his *Leaves of Grass*.

The poetic style he devised is now called Free Verse — that is, poetry without a fixed beat or regular rhyme scheme.

Whitman was born and grew up in Brooklyn, New York. He received only five years of education but he read voraciously by himself. By nature, he was a man thirsty for experience. Thus, he tried a variety of jobs and picked up a first-hand knowledge of life and people in the United States.

In 1848, Whitman began to have some of his writings published. In the same year, he traveled widely to New Orleans, Chicago, and the Western frontier; the latter impressed him greatly and made him think a lot. People say that some of Whitman's experiences on this trip marked a turning point in his career. Soon after, Whitman began to write in a new style—free verse, for which he became famous. Whitman published the first edition of *Leaves of Grass* in 1855, containing only 12 of his best poems. The collection was soon enlarged the next year into 32 poems. Whitman wrote over 400 poems in his life. Before death, he collected most of them into his *Leaves of Grass* (383 poems in all).

Most of the poems in *Leaves of Grass* are about man and nature. Whitman was a lover of nature. However, a small number of very good poems deal with New York, the city that attracted him, and with the Civil War, in which Whitman served as a volunteered male nurse.

With the publication of *Leaves of Grass*, Whitman was praised by Emerson and a few other writers. But he was also bitterly attacked by the majority of his contemporary critics because of his unconventional style. Whitman wanted his poems to be for the common people. However, quite ironically, they were ignored by the general public during his life time. Yet with the arrival of the 20th century, Free Verse became the dominant form of poetic expression.

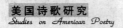

2. Writing Features of Whitman

Whitman was a singer for the ideals of equality and democracy and he celebrated human dignity. He was the one who kept a lifelong advocacy for the self-reliant spirit and the joy of common American labourers. In fact, his poems go beyond American subject to deal with the universal themes of nature, fertility, and mortality.

The frequent topics of Whitman's poetry are songs for himself, for the labour of the common American people, for natural creation, for the independence of the country, for love and friendship, and for the memorizing of President Lincoln.

One of the major principles of Whitman's technique is parallelism or a rhythm of thought in which the line is the rhythmical unit, as in the poetry of the English Bible.

Another feature of Whitman's versification is phonetic recurrence: the systematic repetition of words and phrases at the beginning of the line, in the middle or at the end.

Whitman believed that the voice of democracy should not be tied by traditional forms of verse. His influence on the poetic technique of other writers was small during the time he was writing *Leaves of Grass*. But today, elements of his style are apparent in the work of many poets.

3. Selected Poems

(1) Youth, Day, Old Age and Night

Youth, large, lusty, loving-youth full of grace, force, fascination,
Do you know that Old Age may come after you with equal grace, force, fascination?
Day full-blown and splendid-day of the immense sun, action, ambition, laughter,
The Night follows close with millions of suns, and sleep and restoring darkness.

Section Three
American Poetry of High Romantic Period

Notes

Line 1 large, lusty, loving: the three adjectives are alliteratively arranged to indicate the three paralleled states of youth.
lusty: full of strength; power; healthy.
fascination: the quality of charming powerfully. Force and fascination are also alliteratively used just to express the poet's pride of youth.
Youth: embodiment of strength, health and love; it brings fineness in movement and charm to a person.

Line 2 Old Age: the opposite to "youth."
The poet was reminding everybody that though youth can provide everything beautiful, it is short and fast vanishing; old age, another stage of human life, follows soon after, is as graceful, forceful and fascinating as youth.

Line 3 Day full-blown and splendid: (=day of full-blown and splendid time) It refers to youth, the best time of human life.
Day of the immense sun: time of early morning. The morning sun often looks larger. Youth is compared to the time of early morning of a day which must be very promising.
action, ambition, laughter: youth is the time for action, for ambition and the time for laughter.

Line 4 The Night: old age.
millions of suns: millions of stars. Astronomically, the sun is just one of the infinite number of stars.
sleep: death.
restoring: putting back into a former position; returning to nature.

Comment on the poem

Old age follows youth rather closely, and it comes with great knowledge and experience. The old age is followed by death and then everything returns to nature.

参考译文

青春、白日、老年与黑夜

青春,你志高、健壮、钟情,充满优雅、力量和魅力,你是否知道老年也会跟你一样充满优雅、力量和魅力?
白天盛开,阳光灿烂,充满骄阳、行动、雄心和欢笑,
夜晚随来,星辰百万,随夜入眠,暗色复还。
(李正栓　译)

(2) To Those Who've Failed

To those who've failed, in aspiration vast,
To unnamed soldiers fallen in front on the lead,
To calm, devoted engineers—to over-ardent travelers—
　　to pilots on their ships,
5　To many a lofty song and picture without recognition—
　　I'd rear a laurel-covered monument,
High, high above the rest—To all cut off before their time,
Possessed by some strange spirit of fire,
Quenched by an early death.

Notes

Line 1 aspiration vast: vast aspiration; a strong, important desire to do something.
Line 2 on the lead: doing something first or earlier than others.
　　　　To those soldiers who had died very early in the battlefield without leaving their names.
Line 3 calm, devoted engineers: the engineers who have been working calmly and devotedly.
　　　　over-ardent travelers: very sincere and eager travelers.
Line 5 lofty song and picture without recognition: some very qualified art works as songs and pictures, but the value and merit of them had not been accepted by society.
Line 6 rear: build; set up.
　　　　A laurel-covered monument: a monument covered with laurel, an ancient Greek and Roman emblem of victory or honour; I would like to build a monument of extreme honor to ...
　　　　All the "to-phrases" in the above lines function as adverbials of purpose to this line.
Line 7 High, high above the rest: (I would like to build my monument) much higher than any other monuments in the world.
　　　　To all: This "to-phrase" parallels the other "to-phrases" before

the subjective line.

cut off: sacrificed the lives.

their time: the proper length of their life time; the normal span of one's life. Here "their" refers to all the people "I'd build a monument to."

Line 8 Possessed by: (those people mentioned above—soldiers, travelers, pilots, etc. who had been) controlled by; fully absorbed in.

strange spirit of fire: the extremely great ambition or passion.

Line 9 Quenched: extinguished from this world (by early death).

Comment on the poem

I'd build a monument to those ambitious and passionate people who had sacrificed their lives for the pursuing of truth or for the fulfillment of responsibility.

参考译文

给那些失败的人们

对那些在热切期望中失败的人们，
对战场上冲锋时倒下的无名士兵们，
对专心致志的工程师们，对热衷旅行的人们，
对高昂的歌曲，对不被认可的图画，
我要竖立一座缠满桂枝的纪念碑，
比其他的碑要高出许多——还要献给所有早亡的人们，
他们被某种奇怪的强烈神灵附体，
却被早来的死亡熄灭。

(李正栓 译)

(3) The Bravest Soldiers

Brave, brave were the soldiers (high named today) who
   lived through the fight;
But the bravest pressed to the front and fell, unnamed, unknown.

Notes

Line 1 high named today: highly praised at present; highly rewarded by us.

live through the fight: survived the war.

Line 2 pressed to the front: (those soldiers who had been) forced to go to the battlefield.

fell: died; sacrificed their lives at the battlefield.

Now we offer great praise and award to those people who had survived the war, for we all believe they are brave soldiers. As a matter of fact, the bravest soldiers are those who had been forced to the front and died there without leaving their names to the monuments.

参考译文

最勇敢的士兵们

那些从战场上幸存下来的士兵们
今天被誉为很勇敢、很勇敢；
但是，那些被逼去战场的不知名的无人知晓地倒下去的才是最勇敢的人。

(李正栓 译)

(4) Unseen Buds

Unseen buds, infinite, hidden well,
Under the snow and ice, under the darkness, in every
  square or cubic inch,
Germinal, exquisite, in delicate lace, microscopic, unborn,
5 Like babes in wombs, latent, folded, compact, sleeping;
Billions of billions, and trillions of trillions of them waiting
(On earth and in the sea, —the universe—the stars there
  in the heavens,)
Urging slowly, surely forward, forming endless,
10 And waiting ever more, forever more behind.

Section Three
American Poetry of High Romantic Period

Notes

Line 1 infinite: without limits; in large quantity.
   hidden well: quite out of human sight.
Lines 2 - 3 in every square or cubic inch: in various shapes and tiny sizes.
Line 4 Germinal: in the earliest stage of development but with the intention of becoming a new organism.
   exquisite: very finely made or done; almost perfect.
Line 5 wombs: the female sex organ of a mammal where her young can develop.
   latent: existing, but not yet noticeable or fully developed.
   compact: firmly and closely packed together.
Line 6 billions of billions, and trillions of trillions of them: countless and in extremely large numbers.
Line 9 Urging: developing; forcing forward.

Comment on the poem

The unseen buds are in the very early stage of development but they have all been perfectly created. They are tiny and thin before the birth; they are like the baby in mother's womb, existing but not noticeable; they exist, closely packed and sleeping. They exist in tremendous number and waiting, waiting on earth, waiting in the sea, waiting in the universe, waiting on the stars in heaven with the strong potential for birth, for a complete life, for growing, and for great transformation. It reveals the power of nature: Nothing can obstruct though it is unseen at present.

The unseen buds are growing slowly but surely and waiting as they had been; they come into being in tremendous numbers and omnipresently exist. Still they will wait, just as they had waited very long before for the birth, for the appearance of a new life.

看不见的蓓蕾

无数的看不见的蓓蕾,深藏着,
在雪下,在冰底,在黑暗中,在每一
平方或立方英寸里,

幼芽、细腻、微小、精微、等着出生，
像子宫中的婴儿，潜伏着，弯着身，紧缩着，睡着，
数亿数亿的，数万亿数万亿的蓓蕾在等着
（在地上，在海中，在宇宙中，在天上的星星中）
慢慢地稳步地向前萌发，无止境地形成，
更热切地期待着，随后还有更多地在形成。
（李正栓 译）

(5) *from* A Song for Occupations

The president is there in the White House for you, it is not you
   Who are here for him,
The Secretaries act in their bureaus for you, not you here for them
The Congress convenes every Twelfth month for you,
5 Laws, courts, the forming of States, the charters of cities,
   The going and coming of commerce and mails, are all for you.

Notes

Line 3 act: work.
Line 4 convenes: meets or gathers; calls (a meeting).
Line 6 The going and coming of commerce: the dealing or management of a business.

Comment on the poem

   In this poem, "you" refers to every ordinary citizen of the country. The poet is reminding the citizens that they must be aware about the order of the society that all those high officials, including all the civil servants, congressmen, laws courts, the charters, are elected or created by the ordinary citizens and they must work for the sake of them, not vice versa.

参考译文

选自《职业之歌》

总统是为了你才在白宫，而不是

Section Three
American Poetry of High Romantic Period

你在这里是为了他,
部长们为了你才在办公室行动,而不是你为了他们才在这里。
国会为了你每十二个月召开一次,
法律、法庭、新州形成、城市立法,
商业交往,邮政穿梭,所有这一切都是为了你。
(李正栓 译)

(6) To the United States

To the States or any one of them, or any city of the States,
  Resist much, obey little,
Once unquestioning obedience, once fully enslaved,
Once fully enslaved, no nation, state, city of this earth, ever
5   After resumes its liberty.

Notes

Line 1 any one of them: any state.
Line 2 Resist much: stand straight and fight against much.
Line 3 Each time a state or a city is absolutely obedient, that indicates a time of enslavement.
Lines 4 – 5 ever after: One can never imagine to enjoy liberty after (being fully enslaved...)
  Once a single state or city is enslaved, it will not be a real state or real city in this world; nobody would be able to win real liberty.
Line 5 resumes: regains.

Comment on the poem

This is a piece of aporistic work. In short lines and plain words, the author warned: Either a country or a person, the only way to win liberty or freedom is through resistance against oppression and invasion. The more resistance and less obedience, the greater victory one is sure to obtain. The right response to any offensive action is never questioning, nor humbly obeying, but to pay the invader back in his own coins. This poem preaches distrust for an autocratic government and urges resistance to despotism.

参考译文

致美国

对于美国,其任何一个州,其任何一个城市,
要多抵抗,少服从,
一旦一味地顺从,便完全被奴役,
一旦完全被奴役,以后世界上任何民族,任何州,任何城市
都不能恢复自由。
(李正栓 译)

(7) I Sit and Look Out

I sit and look out upon all the sorrows of the world, and
   upon all oppression and shame,
I hear secret convulsive sobs from young men at anguish
   with themselves, remorseful after deeds done,
5 I see in low life the mother misused by her children,
   dying, neglected, gaunt, desperate,
I see the wife misused by her husband, I see the treacherous
   seducer of young women,
I mark the ranklings of jealousy and unrequited love attempted
10 to be hid, I see these sights on the earth,
I see the workings of battle, pestilence, tyranny, I see
   martyrs and prisoners,
I observe a famine at sea, I observe the sailors casting lots
   who shall be kill'd to preserve the lives of the rest,
15 I observe the slights and degradations cast by arrogant persons
   upon laborers, the poor, and upon negroes, and the like;
All these—all the meanness and agony without end I
   sitting look out upon,
See, hear, and am silent.

Notes

Lines 2-3 I sit here and look out at all the sorrows of human world,
    and look at all the oppression and shame of this world.

Section Three
American Poetry of High Romantic Period

Line 3 convulsive sobs: very sad, uncontrollable crying.
Lines 3 – 4 at anguish with: felt great pain or suffering of mind.
> I can hear the restrained sad crying from young people when they are regretful for all the sorrows of having done wrong.

Line 4 remorseful sorrow for having done wrong.
Line 5 low life lower society; the poor family.
> misused: mistreated; wrongly treated.

Line 6 gaunt: thin, as if ill or hungry.
> desperate: helpless.

Lines 5 – 6 I can see that in the poor families, the mother has often been mistreated by her children. They are neglected and helpless.
Line 7 treacherous: disloyal; deceitful.
Line 8 seducer: person persuades others to do something wrong.
Lines 7 – 8 I see the wife was mistreated by her husband; I see some men deceitful to seduce the innocent young women.
Line 9 ranklings: of the extreme degree; the worst.
> unrequited love: love of one person which was not reciprocated by the other sex.

Line 10 hid: kept in secret.
Lines 9 – 10 I see the great jealousy of (some young people) and the fruitless love of some other, though they tried to keep the failure a secret.
Line 11 workings: fighting.
> pestilence: a disease that causes death and spreads swiftly.

Line 12 martyrs: a person who by his death or sufferings proves the strength of his belief.
Lines 11 – 12 I see in the human world, some are fighting against the others; some are suffering from the deadly disease; some are cruelly ruling the people; some are sacrificing their lives for their belief; some had committed crime and had been imprisoned.
Line 13 cast lots: draw lots to try one's luck, to make the dicision.
Line 14 preserve: keep safe; keep alive; protect.
Lines 13 – 14 I see that over the sea, the sailors in starvation are drawing lots to decide which of them should be killed to provide food for the survival of the others.
Line 15 slights: insult.
> degradations: contempt.

Lines 15 – 16 I see very clearly some self-important persons are showing insults and contempt to the laborers, to the poor, to the Negroes and to all the people alike.

Lines 17 – 18 When I sit here, I can see all the unkindness and sufferings in this society. However, I can do nothing for a change of them except just looking at them happening, hearing them crying and staying in silence. I stay in self-reproach, but nothing more I can do. I fail in my responsibility to act.

Comment on the poem

Being a sympathetic person, Whitman felt rather sorrowful for all the unkindness existing in this world: the mother being misused, the treacherous seducer of young women, jealousy, battles, pestilence, tyranny, prison, slights, degradations, arrogance, and the astounding way of dealing with the famine at sea as well. He was shameful but he felt unable to do away with them. As a poet with strong social responsibility, Whitman accomplished his duty to expose, to condemn, to appeal for a reform, however, nothing further could be done except these. A sense of guilt made Whitman suffer but it could by no means be shaken off. Consequently, a strong implication of self-reproach is added to the last line.

参考译文

我坐着眺望

我坐着眺望世间的一切悲苦、
一切压迫和羞辱,
我听见年轻人因悔恨往事而痛苦时
暗中发出抽搐的呜咽,
我看见卑微的母亲为子女所折磨而奄奄待毙,
无人照应、消瘦如柴、濒临绝境,
我看见受丈夫虐待的妻子,我看见
诱骗青年妇女的奸诈之徒,
我注视着企图掩盖的嫉妒和单恋的痛苦,
我看见芸芸众生,
我看见战争、瘟疫、暴政,我看见
殉教者和囚徒,
我望见海上发生饥荒,水手们在拈阄决定
谁作牺牲来保全他人的性命,

我看见傲慢自大的人们加于劳动者、穷人、黑人
等人身上的轻蔑和侮辱，
我坐着眺望这一切——
一切无尽无休的丑行和痛苦，
我看着、听着，我默然。
（魏慧哲 译 李正栓 校）

(8) When Lilacs Last in the Dooryard Bloom'd

1

When lilacs last in the dooryard bloom'd,
And the great star early droop'd in the western sky in the night,
I mourn'd and yet shall mourn with ever-returning spring.
Ever-returning spring, trinity sure to me you bring,
5   Lilac blooming perennial and drooping star in the west,
And thought of him I love.

2

O powerful western fallen star!
O shades of night—O moody, tearful night!
O great star disappear'd—O the black murk that hides the star!
10   O cruel hands that hold me powerless—O helpless soul of me!
O harsh surrounding cloud that will not free my soul.

3

In the dooryard fronting an old farm-house near the white-wash'd palings,
Stand the lilac-bush tall-growing with heart-shaped leaves of rich green,
With many a pointed blossom rising delicate, with the perfume strong I love,
15   With every leaf a miracle—and from this bush in the dooryard,
With delicate-color'd blossoms and heart-shaped leaves of rich green,
A sprig with its flower I break.

4

It the swamp in secluded recesses,
A shy and hidden bird is warbling a song.
20   Solitary the thrush,
The hermit withdrawn to himself, avoiding the settlements,
Sings by himself a song.
Song of the bleeding throat,

Death's outlet song of life, (for well dear brother I know,
25 If thou wast not granted to sing thou would'st surely die.)

5

Over the breast of the spring, the land, amid cities,
Amid lanes and through old woods, where lately the violets
    peep'd from the ground, spotting the gray debris,
Amid the grass in the fields each side of the lanes, passing
    the endless grass,
Passing the yellow-spear'd wheat, every grain from its
    Shroud in the dark-brown fields uprisen,
30 Passing the apple-tree blows of white and pink in the orchards,
Carrying a corpse to where it shall rest in the grave,
Night and day journeys a coffin.

6

Coffin that passes through lanes and streets,
Through day and night with the great cloud darkening the land,
35 With the pomp of the inloop'd flags with the cities draped in black,
With the show of the States themselves as of
    crape-veil'd women standing,
With processions long and winding and the flambeaus of the night,
With the countless torches lit, with the silent sea of faces and
    the unbarred heads,
With the waiting depot, the arriving coffin, and the somber faces,
40 With dirges through the night, with the thousand voices
    rising strong and solemn,
With all the mournful voices of the dirges pour'd around the coffin,
The dim-lit churches and the shuddering organs—where
    amid these you journey,
With the tolling tolling bells' perpetual clang,
Here, coffin that slowly passes,
45 I give you my sprig of lilac

7

(Nor for you, for one alone,
Blossoms and branches green to coffins all I bring,
For fresh as the morning, thus would I chant a song for you
    O sane and sacred death.
All over bouquets of roses,

50 O death, I cover you over with roses and early lilies,
    But mostly and now the lilac that blooms the first,
    Copious I break, I break the sprigs from the bushes,
    With loaded arms I come, pouring for you,
    For you and the coffins all of you O death.)

                        8
55 O western orb sailing the heaven,
    Now I know what you must have meant as a month since I walk'd,
    As I walk'd in silence the transparent shadowy night,
    As I saw you had something to tell as you bent to me night after night,
    As you droop'd from the sky low down as if to my side,
        (while the other stars all look'd on,)
60 As we wander'd together the solemn night,
        (for something I know not what kept me from sleep,)
    As the night advanced, and I saw on the rim of the west
        how full you were of woe,
    As I stood on the rising ground in the breeze in the cool transparent night,
    As I watch'd where you pass'd and was lost in the
        netherward black of the night
    As my soul in its trouble dissatisfied sank, as where you sad orb,
65 Concluded, dropt in the night, and was gone.

                        9
    Sing on there in the swamp,
    O singer bashful and tender, I hear your notes, I hear your call,
    I hear, I come presently, I understand you,
    But a moment I linger, for the lustrous star has detain'd me,
70 The star my departing comrade holds and detains me.

                        10
    O how shall I warble myself for the dead one there I loved?
    And how shall I deck my song for the large sweet soul that has gone?
    And what shall my perfume be for the grave of him I love?

    Sea-winds blown from east and west,
75 Blown from the Eastern sea and blown from the Western sea,
        till there on the prairies meeting,
    These and with these and the breath of my chant,
    I'll perfume the grave of him I love.

11

O what shall I hang on the chamber walls?
And what shall the pictures be that I hang on the walls,
80   To adorn the burial-house of him I love?

Pictures of growing spring and farms and homes,
With the Fourth-month eve at sundown,
   and the gray smoke lucid and bright,
With floods of the yellow gold of the gorgeous, indolent,
   sinking sun, burning, expanding the air,
With the fresh sweet herbage under foot,
   and the pale green leaves of the trees prolific,
85 In the distance the flowing glaze, the breast of the river,
   with a wind-dapple here and there,
With ranging hills on the banks,
   with many a line against the sky, and shadows,
And the city at hand with dwellings so dense, and stacks of chimneys,
And all the scenes of life and the workshops,
   and the workmen homeward returning.

12

Lo, body and soul—this land,
90 My own Manhattan with spires,
   and the sparkling and hurrying tides, and the ships,
The varied and ample land, the south and the North in the light,
   Ohio's shores and flashing Missouri,
And ever the far-spreading prairies cover'd with grass and corn.

Lo, the most excellent sun so calm and haughty,
The violet and purple morn with just-felt breezes,
95 The gentle soft-born measureless light,
The miracle spreading bathing all, the fulfill'd noon,
The coming eve delicious, the welcome night and the stars,
Over my cities shining all, enveloping man and land.

13

Sing on, sing on you gray-brown bird,
100 Sing from the swamps, the recesses,
   pour your chant from the bushes,
Limitless out of the dusk, out of the cedars and pines.

Sing on dearest brother, warble your reedy song,
Loud human song, with voice of uttermost woe.

O liquid and free and tender!
105 O wild and loose to my soul—O wondrous singer!
You only I hear—yet the star holds me, (but will soon depart,)
Yet the lilac with mastering odor holds me.

14

Now while I sat in the day and look'd forth,
In the close of the day with its light and the fields of spring,
    and the farmers preparing their crops,
110 In the large unconscious scenery of my land
    with its lakes and forests,
In the heavenly aerial beauty,
    (after the perturb'd winds and the storms,)
Under the arching heavens of the afternoon swift passing,
    and the voices of children and women,
The many-moving sea-tides, and I saw the ships how they sail'd
And the summer approaching with richness,
    and the fields all busy with labor,
115 And the infinite separate houses, how they all went on,
    each with its meals and minutia of daily usages,
And the streets how their throbbings throbb'd,
    and the cities pent—lo, then and there,
Falling upon them all and among them all, enveloping me with the rest,
Appear'd the cloud, appear'd the long black trail,
And I knew death, its thought, and the sacred knowledge of death.

120 Then with the knowledge of death as walking one side of me,
And the thought of death close-walking the other side of me,
And I in the middle as with companions,
    and as holding the hands of companions,
I fled forth to the hiding receiving night that talks not,
Down to the shores of the water, the path by the swamp in the dimness,
125 To the solemn shadowy cedars and ghostly pines so still.

And the singer so shy to the rest receiv'd me,
The gray-brown bird I know receiv'd us comrades three,
And he sang the carol of death, and a verse for him I love.

From deep secluded recesses,
130 From the fragrant cedars and the ghostly pines so still,
Came the carol of the bird.

And the charm of the carol rapt me,
As I held as if by their hands my comrades in the night,
And the voice of my spirit tallied the song of the bird.

135 Come lovely and soothing death,
Undulate round the world, serenely arriving, arriving,
In the day, in the night, to all, to each,
Sooner or later delicate death.

Prais'd be the fathomless universe,
140 For life and joy, and for objects and knowledge curious,
And for love, sweet love—but praise! praise! praise!
For the sure-enwinding arms of cool-enfolding death.

Dark mother always gliding near with soft feet,
Have none chanted for thee a chant of fullest welcome?
145 Then I chant it for thee, I glorify thee above all,
I bring thee a song that when thou must indeed come,
    come unfalteringly.

Approach strong deliveress,
When it is so, when thou hast taken them I joyously sing the dead,
Lost in the loving floating ocean of thee,
150 Laved in the flood of thy bliss O death.

From me to thee glad serenades,
Dances for thee I propose saluting thee,
    adornments and feastings for thee.
And the sights of the open landscape
    and the high-spread sky are fitting,
And life and the fields, and the huge and thoughtful night.
155 The night in silence under many a star,
The ocean shore and the husky whispering wave
    whose voice I know,
And the soul turning to thee O vast and well-vail'd death,
And the body gratefully nestling close to thee.

Over the tree-tops I float thee a song,
160 *Over the rising and sinking waves,*
　　　over the myriad fields and the prairies wide,
Over the dense-pack'd cities all and the teeming wharves and ways,
I float this carol with joy, with joy to thee O death.

15

To the tally of my soul,
Loud and strong kept up the gray-brown bird,
165 With pure deliberate notes spreading filling the night.

Loud in the pines and cedars dim,
Clear in the freshness moist and the swamp—perfume,
And I with my comrades there in the night.

While my sight that was bound in my eyes unclosed,
170 As to long panoramas of visions.

And I saw askant the armies,
I saw as in noiseless dreams hundreds of battle-flags,
Borne through the smoke of the battles
　　　and pierc'd with missiles I saw them,
And carried hither and yon through the smoke,
　　　and torn and bloody,
175 And at last but a few shreds left on the staffs, (and all in silence,)
And the staffs all splinter'd and broken.

I saw battle-corpses, myriads of them,
And the white skeletons of young men, I saw them,
I saw the debris and debris of all the slain soldiers of the war,
180 But I saw they were not as was thought,
They themselves were fully at rest, they suffer'd not,
The living remain'd and suffer'd, the mother suffer'd,
And the wife and the child and the musing comrade suffer'd,
And the armies that remain'd suffer'd.

16

185 Passing the visions, passing the night,
Passing, unloosing the hold of my comrades' hands,
Passing the song of the hermit bird and the tallying song of my soul,

Victorious song, death's outlet song, yet varying ever-altering song,
As low and wailing, yet clear the notes,
  rising and falling, flooding the night,
190 Sadly sinking and fainting, as warning and warning,
  and yet again bursting with joy,
covering the earth and filling the spread of the heaven,
As that powerful psalm in the night I heard from recesses,
Passing, I leave thee lilac with heart-shaped leaves,
I leave thee there in the door-yard, blooming, returning with spring.

195 I cease from my song for thee,
From my gaze on thee in the west,
  fronting the west, communing with thee,
O comrade lustrous with silver face in the night.

Yet each to keep and all, retrievements out of the night,
The song, the wondrous chant of the gray-brown bird,
200 And the tallying chant, the echo arous'd in my soul,
With the lustrous and drooping star with the countenance full of woe,
With the holders holding my hand nearing the call of the bird,
Comrades mine and I in the midst,
  and their memory ever to keep, for the dead I loved so well,
For the sweetest, wisest soul of all my days
  and lands—and this for his dear sake,
205 Lilac and star and bird twined with the chant of my soul,
There in the fragrant pines and the cedars dusk and dim.

Notes

1

Line 1 lilacs last: the last lilacs; lilac is a type of tree with pinkish purple or white flowers giving a sweet smell. It, which may be Persian in its origin, had, in eastern symbolism, a connection with manly love.

Line 2 droop'd: drooped; bend or hang downwards through tiredness or weakness.

Line 4 trinity sure to me you bring: you surely bring me trinity. "Trinity" originally means "a group of three." In this poem, it indicates three images—first, the "lilac blooming perennial," which symbolizes something physical; second, the "drooping star in the west," which is symbolic of death; third, "thought of him I love," which is the meditation on death.

    The first part is the prelude to the whole work. With the trinity—the blooming lilac, the drooping star and the mourning of Lincoln as the central image, the poem was opened in a melancholy tone.

2

Line 7 fallen star: In the first stanza, the star was drooping, now it has fallen. Here "star" is the image of a "person," as the old saying goes, one falling star in the sky indicates the death of one person in the human world.

Line 8 "Shades" first implies the murdering of the president had left darkness in everybody's heart; meanwhile, it refers to the suspending situation of that night.
    moody: change often and quickly; displeased.
    President Lincoln was shot on April 13, 1865 while attending a performance at Ford's theatre for the sake of celebrating the final victory of the Civil War. After an ineffectual rescuer, Lincoln died on the 14. That's why the night between 13 and 14 is "moody" and "tearful" — that was a night causing most people sorrow.
    The three words "shades, moody and tearful" suggest all the agonies people suffered that night when worrying about the fate of Lincoln.

Line 9 murk: darkness. When it follows "dark," the two words show the emphasis of the despairing mood of the night.

    The repetition of the "O" strongly suggests not only the grief of American people that night, but also the grief from the sky. As a human being, I am too weak and helpless to stop the falling of the star.

3

Line 12 palings: fence or boundary made of pointed wood.
Line 13 leaves of rich green: leaves in dark green—when they are in the best time of life.
Line 14 with the perfume strong I love: (the lilac-bush was blooming) with the strong perfume that I love.
Line 17 sprig: small twig of a plant or bush with leaves.
    From the delicately blooming lilac-bush, the poet broke a sprig with its flower, which suggests the vigor of life.

In this part, the tone is shifted from melancholy to the description of various colors, the vigor of life.

4

Line 18 secluded recesses: lonely, remote places.
Line 19 A shy and hidden bird: the poet.
   warble: (a bird) sing in a continuous gentle trilling way.
Line 20 Solitary the thrush: the loneliness is rather serious that...
Line 21 avoiding the settlements: (the hermit—the poet himself) was avoiding the other people's interruption. The poet is describing the hermit thrush, a common, but elusive American bird.
Line 23 Song of bleeding throat: the continuous singing; the lasting songs. The throat was bleeding because of too much singing.
Line 24 Death's outlet song of life: I know death is the last song, the ending of all life.
Line 25 (I am clear) if the bird (the poet) was not allowed to sing he would surely die. The poet, in the image of a lonely bird, keeps himself alone and sings for the pitiful loss of a great life.

5

Line 27 peep'd from: peeped from; (the violets) are growing up, though without anybody's notice.
   spotting the gray debris: (just after the Civil War, the violets) are growing at and beautifying the ugly ruins of the war—the United States.
Line 32 "coffin" in this line is the subject to Part 5; "journeys" is the predicate verb, while all the above lines, led by prepositions or participles, are adverbial phrases to "journeys."

   The funeral train of Abraham Lincoln passed, amid multitudes of mourners, through Maryland, Pennsylvania, New Jersey, New York, Ohio, and Indiana on its way to Springfield, Illinois, where the martyred president was to be buried. (*The American Tradition in Literature*, 7th edition. p973)

In the poet's imagination, Lincoln's coffin was carried through the fields covered with flowers. The variety colors of the flowers strongly suggest the vigor of Lincoln's life, and the affection for him from different races.

6

Line 35 the pomp: splendid display or magnificence at a public event.

inloop'd flags: waving flags.

the cities draped in black: the cities are draped in the black cloth of mourning.

Line 36 of crape-veil'd women: "crape" is the black silk or cotton material worn as a sign of mourning. The poet personified the States as the grief-stricken women in black veil mourning Lincoln.

Line 38 silent sea of faces: numerous faces (of people) who are quietly waiting.

unbarred heads: liberated people (after the Civil War); open-minded people.

Line 39 the waiting depot: the railway or bus station where people are waiting (for the arrival of Lincoln's coffin). The figurative speech of transferred epithet is used in this phrase.

Line 40 dirges: song sung at a burial or for a dead person.

Line 42 you: Lincoln.

With many repetitions of the paralleled "with-phrases" (which show the common people's mourning for the martyred president) as the modifier, the poet presents the lilac sprig from his dooryard to Lincoln.

7

Line 46 (I present my lilac) not only for you, not for the president as a single person.

Line 47 I bring green blossoms and branches to all the coffins. Here the plural form of "coffin" indicates that besides to Lincoln, I bring flowers to some other people (all those dead in the Civil War).

Line 48 sane: sensible.

sacred death: very important sacrifice.

Line 52 copious: plentiful; abundant.

I break: I pick (the flowers).

Line 53 With loaded arms I come: I come to the coffins with colorful flowers in my arms.

The poet presents all his flowers not only for extolling Lincoln as a president, but also for the memorializing of all those who died in the Civil War. However, as among various flowers lilac blooms the first, Lincoln, among all the martyrs, is the most important.

8

Line 55 orb: globe; one of the planets. The "western orb" refers to the

falling star: alluding to the approach of death.
Line 59 look'd on: looked still; looked motionless.
Line 60 For some reasons I am not quite clear myself, I was kept sleepless, I therefore wandered during the night, solemnly.
Line 62 the rising ground: his standing on a hillside.
Line 63 lost in the netherward black: lost in the dense blackness of night.
Lines 64 - 65 When I saw that the star had fallen, had dropped into darkness and that your honored life had completely vanished from this world, my dissatisfied soul sank in its trouble. Concluded: you have fulfilled whatever task of your life.

9

Line 67 singer bashful and tender: the singer who is shy, self-conscious and delicate.
Line 68 In this the poet may have copied the famous saying, "I came, I saw, I conquered." in structure.
Line 69 But a moment I linger: but I am unwilling to leave, I want to stay longer.
the lustrous stars: the bright stars.
detain'd me: (=detained) prevented me from leaving.
Line 70 my departing comrade: Lincoln, the martyred president.
The poet presents his great sorrow and reluctance to leave Lincoln.

10

Line 72 deck my song: decorate or beautify my song.
Line 73 the large sweet soul: the great soul of Lincoln.
Lines 76 - 77 I'll have my loved people's grave perfumed with sea-winds, and, with my songs as well.

In the first stanza, having seen the president leaving for the other world, the poet was inquiring ways to express his sorrow.
In the second stanza, the poet recognizes that his songs must be the best means for bridging the physical and the spiritual worlds.

11

Line 78 chamber: grave.
Line 80 the burial-house: the grave.
Line 81 I would adorn the burial-house of the one I love with the pic-

tures of . . .

Line 82 the Fourth-month eve at sundown: (the picture of) evening sun setting in April.

Line 84 herbage: herbs, grass and other field plants.

Line 85 a wind-dapple: the surface of water waves in gentle wind.

To express my sincere love to the martyred president, I'd like to have his tomb adorned with pictures, but what kinds of them?

In the second stanza, the poet offers the ideal pictures he may choose: those presenting the beauty of nature and the vigor of human life.

12

Line 89 Look at this land, the liberated America, with your body and soul.

Line 90 My own Manhattan with spires: (Look at) the Manhattan Island with all its tall buildings.

Line 93 haughty: arrogant; proud and disdainful.

Line 94 just-felt breezes: very gentle, soft wind.

Line 96 The miracle: the sun; the sun light.

Line 97 Look at the delicious coming evening, look at the welcome night and look at the stars during the night.

The poet wants to decorate the grace with some scenery pictures of the country, which had just achieved the thorough liberation for all.

13

Line 99 gray-brown bird: the "hidden bird" in part 4.
   The poem returns to the image of a solitude bird expressing his grief with melancholy songs. The song of the hermit Thrush is very beautiful, and they sing mostly after sundown.

Line 104 liquid: (the song sounds) clear, pure and flowing.

14

Line 111 the heavenly aerial beauty: very noble picturesque; the country after the Civil War.
   the perturb'd winds: the chaotic state during the Civil War.

Line 115 minutia of daily usages: very small, daily rituals and routines.

Line 116 how their throbbings throbb'd: (I see) the beat of pulse of the streets; the poet had the streets and cities personified.

Line 118 the long black trail: the long black sign of death.

Line 122 I in the middle: I am between "the knowledge of death" and "the thought of death."

Line 124 the path by the swamp in the dimness: (I fled down to) the path by the swamp which lies in darkness.

Line 125 This refers to the bird in Part 13, which was singing in cedars and pines in dusk and the singing goes on for about two hours after full dark.

Line 127 comrades three: the three comrades—the knowledge of death, the thought of death and myself.

Line 134 tallied the song of the bird: corresponded, agreed with the song of bird. The bird and I share the attitude towards death. After meditating over the matter of death, the poet noticed the omnipresence and omnipotence of it.

Lines 135 – 162 are the words of the bird's song.

Line 135 soothing death: death that brings relief to people.

Line 136 Undulating round the world: waving, wandering in the human world.

Line 139 the fathomless universe: the boundless, mysterious universe.

Line 142 the sure-enwinding arms of cool-enfolding death: the arms of death are calm and sure to enclose everything.

Line 143 Dark mother: death.

Line 151 you (death) can hear I am singing the happy love songs for you.

serenades: a song sung in the open air at night, esp. to a woman by a lover.

The bird is singing for the praising of death. In its carol, death is lovely, soothing, delicate, and is a flood of bliss.

The bird is singing what the poet keeps in his mind: death is just the latter part of human life.

15

Lines 163 – 164 the gray-brown bird, loud and strong, is kept up to the storage of my soul.

Line 171 askant: (look at) with distrust or disapproval.

Line 175 shreds: strip of piece torn, cut or scraped from something; bits of flags remaining on broken staffs.

Line 182 The living remain'd: those who survived the war; parents and families and friends of the fallen.

Line 183 musing comrade: meditating comrades; those who are good at using their minds.

Death reminds the poet of the scenery of the battlefields: the flags, shreds of bodies, broken staffs, corpses, white skeletons.
To those who died in the battles, death means rest, however, who suffered most from the war are the survivors of the war.

16

Line 185 Passing: the visions (of Lincoln's funeral), as well as the night, had passed.
Line 186 unloosing: setting free.
Line 197 comrade lustrous with silver face in the night: the bright moon.
Line 198 retrievements out of the night: the rewards from night—the songs of birds, the stars.
retrievements: regaining of possession; correction.
Line 203 Comrades mine and I: (with) my comrades and I (in the midst).
Line 205 twined with: juxtaposed with; join closely with.

In the last part, the poet returns to the trinity image: the lilac, the star, and the song for the death of the loved one. Having relieved his sorrow over the death of Lincoln, he expressed his discovery of the reconciliation of life and death—death is the outlet song of life.

Comment on the poem

Concentrating on the theme of love and death—the passion of love bursting out because of the death of the respectable president, this poem presents the spiritual experience of the author.

Immediately after the prelude section, each line of the second section begins with an "O," a visual sign for the intensity of the grief. When the American people were all mourning, the poet plunged himself into the sea of lamenting crowds and his sorrow over the physical loss of the great person is interrupted by his discovery of the lilac bush in the front of the dooryard (part 3). With its "delicate-colored blossoms" and "heart-shaped leaves of rich green," the lilac reveals itself "every leaf a miracle," and as a strong suggestion of revival. The poet feels much reconciled when he laid the lilac onto the coffin: for the subliming of the soul out of mortal existence, for the rebirth of the dead through spiritual life. A bird's singing in the poem is another critical factor for the advance of Whitman. Whitman, as a poet, is quite similar with the hidden thrush on the point that "If thou wast not granted to sing thou would'st surely die." Whitman, having drowned himself in the mourning sea for over half the length of the poem, since recovers from lamentation and prepares for the singing of "Death's outlet song of life," for the constant spiritual existence of the world, for the immortality of life. The poet, with the help of the bird's songs, has realized that death is not the end but the beginning of eternity.

In the poem, various figurative speech, well-chosen idioms, as well as intricate symbols are skillfully used. The lilac, the bird, and the star are all metaphorically used as to add to the mourning atmosphere. The poem is written in free verse; however, many sections are structured on perfect antithesis, alliteration, and paralleling sentences, which seem too regular for Whitman but a tremendous solemnity just results from all the regularity.

When Lilacs Last in the Dooryard Bloom'd was finished in 1865 and first published in sequel to *Drum-Taps* (1865 – 1866). It was collected into the Memories of President Lincoln in 1867 when the 4th edition of *Leaves of Grass* was compiled.

参考译文

当紫丁香最近在庭院开放的时候

1

当紫丁香最近在庭院开放的时候，
那颗巨星早已陨落在西天的夜空，
我哀悼，且每逢春天都将哀悼。
一年一度的春光呦，你定会带给我三件东西，
每年开放的紫丁香、西天陨落的巨星
和对我爱的人的怀念。

2

啊，西天陨落的巨星！
啊，阴沉沉的夜空——忧悒而悲痛的夜空！
啊，巨星已消失——遮住星光的黑暗啊！
啊，使我无力的残酷的手——我无助的灵魂！
啊，环绕束缚我灵魂的无情的乌云！

3

Section Three
American Poetry of High Romantic Period

古老农舍的庭院里,白色栅栏旁,
一丛很高的碧绿心形叶子的紫丁香,
盛开着簇簇尖形精致的花,
散发阵阵令我陶醉的清香,
片片叶子都是奇迹——从这庭院的花丛中,
从娇嫩的花朵,心形的绿叶中,
我折下了一节花枝。

4

在与世隔绝的沼泽中,
一只羞涩的小鸟高啭呖呖,

这孤独的画眉,
避开尘世喧嚣的隐士,
在独自歌唱。

唱到啼血的歌,
死亡的生命之歌(亲爱的朋友,因为我清楚地知道,
倘若未经批准去唱,必将导致死亡。)

5

在春天的怀抱中,在大地上,在城市里,
乡间小路间,古老森林中,紫罗兰
刚刚探出地面,点缀灰白的岩块,
在小路两旁的草地上,穿越无边的草丛,
穿越金黄色的麦穗,
那麦粒在褐色的土地上的穗苞中膨胀,
穿越那盛开着红白花的苹果园,
一辆灵车在夜以继日地行驶,
把逝者运往安息的墓地。

6

灵车经过大街小巷,
经过乌云笼罩大地的日日夜夜,
庄严的旌旗随风飘荡,城市罩上黑衣,
各州如同蒙着黑纱的女人翘盼,
队列蜿蜒曲长,夜间灯火闪亮,
无数火炬齐照明,

解放了的人民千万张面庞汇成沉默的海洋,
车站等待的人群,缓缓而来的灵柩,人们悲痛的脸,
挽歌响彻夜空,歌声有力而庄严,
悲痛的挽歌汇聚灵柩周围,
烛光微弱的教堂,颤抖的琴声——你从中徐徐而过,
丧钟不停地鸣响,
从这里,灵车缓缓走过,
我献上那紫丁香花枝。

7

(这花枝不是献给你自己,也并非献给某个人
花枝献给所有的灵柩,
我清新如晨,将为你唱一支赞歌。
啊,明智而神圣的死亡,
到处都是玫瑰花束,
啊,死亡,我给你盖上玫瑰和早开的百合,
可是现在总是紫丁香首先盛开,
我从花簇中折下几枝,
怀抱满满的紫丁香花,我撒向你,
撒向所有灵柩和你——死亡。)

8

啊,西天云游的星星,
现在我明白了一个月前我漫步时你给我的暗示,
那时我在薄明的夜空下静静地散步,
你夜夜朝向我,像有话要说,
你低垂在夜空,好像就在我身边,
(其他星星只是在观望)
我们一起在幽暗的夜晚徜徉,
(因为不知什么搅得我夜夜难眠,)
那时夜深了,我看见西天边上的你,
满腔悲痛,
我站在高地上,凉风习习,夜空薄明,
我见你陨落,消失在夜幕里,
那时我失意的灵魂沉落痛苦中,
就如同你这忧愁的星星,
完成了使命,陨落,消失在夜空。

Section Three
American Poetry of High Romantic Period

9

在沼泽中歌唱吧,
害羞而温柔的歌手,
我听见了你的歌声,听到了你的召唤,
我听见了,我马上就来,我懂得你的歌声,
但我要停留片刻,因为那颗耀眼的星星留住了我,
那颗星星,我即将分别的朋友,挽留了我。

10

啊,我将如何为我爱的死者歌唱?
我将如何美化我的歌声来赞颂
逝去的伟大而美好的灵魂?
我将以何种馨香献给我敬爱的人的墓地?

东西两面的海风,
从东边海上吹来,从西边海上吹来,
直到会合在草原上,
我将以这些连同我赞歌的活力,
散发在我敬爱的人的墓地。

11

啊,我该把什么挂在灵堂的墙上?
我该把什么画儿挂在墙上,
来装饰我敬爱的人的灵堂?

选一幅农田农舍初春的画儿:
有四月的黄昏,
和袅袅炊烟,透明而光亮,
炫目艳丽的慵懒的落日万丈金光闪耀,穿越天空,
脚下有鲜美的芳草,
葱郁的树木上浅绿的叶子,
远处,河水的源头,平滑的水面,
微风拂过,激起层层涟漪,
两岸起伏连绵的山脉,在天空勾勒出条条轮廓阴影,
附近城市房屋簇拥,烟囱林立,
还有一座座工厂,归途中的工人,
一片生活的景象。

12

看啊,用肉体和灵魂,看看这片土地,
那尖顶林立的曼哈顿,
那波光粼粼,汹涌的海潮,那船只,
丰足多彩的土地,阳光普照的南北方,
俄亥俄河的两岸,闪烁的密苏里河,
还有那长满青草和谷物的广阔大草原。

看啊,绝伦的太阳是那么宁静、那么骄傲,
微风吹拂紫蓝色的清晨,
柔和晨光无限好,
正午太阳,普照大地,
随后是醉人的黄昏,夜晚和星星令人向往,
光芒照耀着我的城市,滋润人间大地。

13

唱吧,唱吧,灰褐色的鸟儿
从与世隔绝的沼泽中,
自丛林里飘出你的歌声,
穿越薄雾,穿越松柏林。

唱吧,亲爱的朋友,唱出你芦笛一样婉转的歌,
用满腔悲痛,大声唱出人间之歌。

啊,流畅,自由,温柔!
让我的灵魂毫无羁绊,——啊,令人惊奇的歌手!
我只愿听见你的歌——但那颗星星留住了我,
(但它不久也要离开)
那馥郁的紫丁香也把我留住了。

14

现在是白天,我坐着眺望,
日暮余晖,农夫在春天的田野上耕种,
大地上的湖泊、森林,
一幅广阔醉人的美景,
(狂风暴雨过后,)
出现绝美的空中美境,
午后时光匆匆,拱形苍穹下,

Section Three
American Poetry of High Romantic Period

传来妇女和孩子们的声音,
潮起潮落中,我看到了船儿在航行,
夏收渐近,农田一片繁忙,
无数分散的农舍,忙碌各自的生活,
为饮食与家用而奔忙,
街道的脉搏在跳动,城市在窒闷中喘息,
看啊,就在此时此地,
来了一片乌云,拖着一道长长的黑影,
降落在万物之上,万物之中,笼罩着我和一切,
我明白死亡,它的思想,以及死亡的神圣意义。

然后,死亡的意义走在我一边,
死亡的思想紧跟在另一边,
我夹在他们中间,
好像走在朋友当中,握着朋友的手,
我逃进沉默的黑夜,它隐藏、收留了我,
我来到水边,走过沼泽旁那条黑暗的小路,
来到那肃穆幽暗的柏树林还有阴森寂静的松树林。

那个害羞的歌者收留了我,
我认识的这只灰褐色的小鸟欢迎我们三个,
它唱起死亡的颂歌,还有悼念我敬爱的人的挽歌。

从与世隔绝的幽静深处,
从芬芳的柏树林和寂静阴森的松树林里,
传出了鸟儿的颂歌。

优美的颂歌令我痴迷,
黑暗中,我好像握着我的朋友的手,
我的心声应和着鸟儿的歌唱。

"来吧,可爱的,抚慰人心的死亡,
环绕世界波动,悄然来临,
在白天,在夜晚,每个人,所有的人,
死亡总会降临。"

"赞美着无边无际的宇宙,
为了生命和快乐,为了新奇的事物和知识,

为了爱,甜蜜的爱——只有赞美、赞美、赞美!
为了那冷静,包容一切的死亡的臂弯。"

"黑衣母亲总是悄然而至,
没有人为你唱支诚挚欢迎的赞歌吗?
那么我为你歌唱,赞美你在万物之上,
我带给你一首歌,但愿你注定要来的时候,
来得坚定。"

"来吧,强大的拯救者,
当你来到的时候,当你带走死者的时候,
我要愉快地为他们歌唱,
他们消失在你那浮动的爱的海洋里,
沐浴在你幸福的涨潮中。"

"我要为你唱快乐的小夜曲,
为你跳舞,向你致敬,
为你装饰,给你设宴。
广阔的风景和舒展的高空宜人,
还有生命和田野,以及伟大而令人深思的黑夜。"

"静寂的夜空,繁星点点,
海岸和我熟悉的海浪的沙沙私语,
灵魂正转向你,伟大而善于隐藏的死亡,
满怀感激的肉体也紧紧依偎着你。"

"飞越树梢,我献给你一首歌,
飞越起伏的波浪,飞越无边的田野和广阔的草原,
飞越拥挤的城市和熙熙攘攘的码头街道,
我欢快的把这首颂歌献给你,献给你,死亡。"

15

应和着我心灵的节拍,
灰褐色的小鸟嘹亮地唱不停,
歌声纯净,响彻夜空。

歌声穿透昏暗的松柏林,
在新鲜的雾气和沼泽的清香中清晰地飘荡,

而我和我的朋友夜晚就在这里。

被我的眼睛所束缚的视线打开了，
我看到了一系列的幻景。

我冷眼看着军队，
仿佛在静寂的梦里看到千百面战旗，
经历了战争的硝烟、导弹的穿击，
烟雾中到处飘移，扯破了，染上了鲜血，
最后旗杆上只剩了几片碎布，（一片沉寂，）
旗杆也裂成碎片。

我看到战场上无数的尸体，
我看到年轻人的白骨，
我看见所有阵亡战士的残骸，
但我看到的他们并非我想象的那样，
他们已经完全安息了，不再痛苦，
活着的人痛苦，死者的母亲痛苦，
妻子，孩子以及想念他们的同伴痛苦，
存活下来的战士痛苦。

16

经过这幻景，经过这黑夜，
我松开握着朋友的双手，
唱着隐居的鸟儿和我灵魂应和的歌，
胜利的歌，摆脱死亡的歌，永远变化的歌，
歌声低沉悲戚，清晰起伏，
淹没黑夜，
悲伤的歌声使人心低沉，令人昏厥，
就像警告，但转而迸发出喜悦的音符，
歌声覆盖大地，充塞天空，
犹如夜晚我在僻静处听到的嘹亮的圣歌，
走过时，我留给你这心形叶子的紫丁香花，
把你留在春天开满紫丁香花的庭院里。

我不再对你歌唱，
不再面向西方，不再凝视你，
也不再和你谈心，

啊,皎洁的月亮你的伙伴啊。

但是,我要将它们从黑夜中找回,一一留住,
那歌声,那灰褐色鸟儿奇妙的歌声,
那合拍的歌声,来自我心灵的回声,
还有那满脸悲伤的陨落的明星,
那听到鸟儿召唤而紧握我手的朋友,
我走在他们中间,
我将永远记住他们,为了我敬爱的死者,
为缅怀我一生在我的国土上见到的
最亲切、最博学的灵魂,——正是由此,
紫丁香、星星、鸟儿与我心灵的赞歌交织在一起,
留在芬芳的柏树林和朦胧昏暗的松树林。
(魏慧哲 译 李正栓 校)

(9) There Was a Child Went Forth

There was a child went forth every day,
And the first object he look'd upon, that object he became,
And that object became part of him for the
　　　day or a certain part of the day,
Or for many years or stretching cycles of years.

5　　The early lilacs became part of this child,
And grass and white and red morning-glories,
　　　and white and red clover, and the song of the phoebe-bird,
And the third-month lambs and the sow's pink-faint litter,
　　　and the mare's foal and the cow's calf,
And the noisy brood of the barnyard or by the mire
　　　of the pondside,
And the fish suspending themselves so curiously below there,
　　　and the beautiful curious liquid,
10　And the water-plants with their graceful flat heads,
　　　all became part of him.

The field-sprouts of Fourth-month and Fifth-month
　　　became part of him,
Winter-grain sprouts and those of the light-yellow corn,
　　　and the esculent roots of the garden.

Section Three
American Poetry of High Romantic Period

And the apple-trees cover'd with blossoms and the fruit afterward,
    and wood-berries and the commonest weeds by the road,
And the old drunkard staggering home from the outhouse of
    the tavern whence he had lately risen,
15 And the schoolmistress that pass'd on her way to the school,
And the friendly boys that pass'd, and the quarrelsome boys,
And the tidy and fresh-cheek'd girls, and the
    barefoot Negro boy and girl,
And all the changes of city and country wherever he went.

His own parents, he that had father'd him and she that had
    conceiv'd him in her womb and birth'd him,
20 They gave this child more of themselves than that,
They gave him afterward every day, they became part of him.

The mother at home quietly placing the dishes on the supper-table,
The mother with mild words, clean her cap and gown, a wholesome
    oder falling off her person and clothes as she walks by,
The father, strong, self-sufficient, manly, mean, anger'd, unjust,
25 The blow, the quick loud word, the tight bargain, the crafty lure,
The family usages, the language, the company,
    the furniture, the yearning and swelling heart,
Affection that will not be gainsay'd, the sense of what is real,
    the thought if after all it should prove unreal,
The doubts of day-time and the doubts of night-time,
    the curious whether and how,
Whether that which appears so is so, or is it all flashes and specks?
30 Men and women crowding fast in the streets, if they
    are not flashes and specks what are they?
The streets themselves and the facades of houses,
    and goods in the windows.
Vehicles, teams, the heavy— plank'd wharves,
    the huge crossing at the ferries,
The village on the highland seen from afar at sunset,
    the river between,
Shadows, aureola and mist, the light falling on roofs
    and gables of white or brown two miles off,
35 The schooner near by sleepily dropping down the tide,
    the little boat slack-tow'd astern,
The hurrying tumbling waves, quick-broken crests, slapping,

The strata of color'd clouds, the long bar of maroon-tint
　　away solitary by itself, the spread of purity it lies motionless in,
The horizon's edge, the flying sea-crow, the fragrance
　　of salt marsh and shore mud.
These became part of that child who went forth every day,
40　and who now goes, and will always go forth every day.

Notes

Line 1　went forth: went forward; developed.
Line 5　lilacs: It, may be Persian in its origin, had, in eastern symbolism, a connection with manly love.
Line 6　morning-glory: climbing plant with trumpet-shaped flowers that usu. close in the afternoon, often in the color of white and red, or white and blue. (牵牛花)
　　clover: small plant with (usually) three leaves on each stalk, and with purple, pink or white flowers, grown as food for cattle, etc. (三叶草)
　　phoebe-bird: bird in Northern America, with brownish-green back and faint yellow breast. (美洲翁鸟)
Line 7　third-month lambs: lambs born in March.
　　the sow's pink-faint litter: babies of one mother pig, which look pink and very weak.
　　foal: baby horse.
Line 8　brood: a family of young creatures (usu. birds) all produced by one mother at the same time. Here it refers to chickens or ducklings.
Line 9　the beautiful curious liquid: water.
Line 12　Winter-grain sprouts: sprouts of the plant which had just survived the severity of winter.
Line 14　the outhouse: the outside lavatory.
　　whence: where.
Line 23　clean her cap and gown: her cap and gown are clean.
Line 25　The blow, the quick loud word: This line suggests the intense relationship between a father and his son: the father gave the boy a blow, rebuked him; the boy argued with the father and tried to explain away.
Line 26　the yearning and swelling heart: the heart which is longing or missing of something.

Line 27 gainsay: deny.
the thought if after all it should prove unreal: the boy thought in fear if some day when he has grown up the standard he had admitted would be proved unreal.
Line 28 whether and how: Day or night, the boy's mind is filled with various questions and choices to be made.
Line 29 The boy begins to doubt whether everything is existing as it appears to be, or whether things are as what we think they are.
Line 30 fast: (people are) in quick succession; people are very close to each other.
The boy begins to realize the position of each human being in the universe: each is a passer-by and a traveler.
Line 32 teams: two or more animals pulling the same vehicle.
the huge crossing: the large group of people who are waiting for the ferry boat.
Line 33 the river between: the river between the villages.
aureola: a halo; the bright circle of light, as around the sun or moon in misty weather.
Line 35 schooner: fast sailing ship with 2 or sometimes more masts and sails. (纵帆船)
slack-tow'd astern: the schooner is towing a little boat behind.
Line 36 quick-broken crests: the top of waves which are quickly breaking.
Line 37 The strata of color'd clouds: various layers of clouds in different colors.
the spread of purity: (it) lies motionlessly in the pure and vast sky.

The boy becomes interested in something more mysterious—his fellow human beings and begins to meditate on the relationships between nature and man. Standing at the symbolic threshold of the outside world, the sea, the boy grown into a young man from a boy.

Comment on the poem

This poem suggests the natural process of a boy's growth. At the beginning, the boy was innocent and his world was limited within the village barnyard. Later, he grew older and sought into fields and streets. Finally, the boy learnt to meditate over the complexities of the world. He became mature.

参考译文

有一个孩子在成长

有一个孩子天天在成长,
第一眼看见什么,他就变成什么,
那一天或那一天的某时段,
或许多年,或几个年轮,
那被见之物就变成他的一部分。

早期的丁香成为这孩子的一部分,
还有草和红白两色的牵牛花,
还有红白两色的三叶草,还有东菲比霸鹟鸟的歌声,
还有三月出生的羔羊,还有同一头母猪生下的粉色群崽,
还有母马生下的马驹,还有母牛生下的小牛犊,
还有谷仓边或池塘边泥潭旁
唧唧喳喳的幼鸟,
还有旁边水里好奇地悬浮的鱼,
还有那漂亮好玩的液体,
还有长着优雅扁头的水中植物,
所有这一切都成为他的一部分。

四月五月的禾苗
成为他的一部分,
过冬的苗、浅黄的玉米苗,
还有可食用的花园草根都成为他的一部分。
开满鲜花的苹果树、花后结的果实,
木浆果和路边的最普通的草,
刚从酒馆外屋起身摇摇晃晃
回家的老醉鬼,
正往学校赶路的女教师,
过路的友好孩子们,吵闹不休的孩子们,
干净利索、小脸动人的女孩儿们,
赤脚的黑人男孩和女孩,
他所去过的城市和乡村发生的所有变化,都成为他的一部分。

他自己的父母,那个成为其父的他和那个

Section Three
American Poetry of High Romantic Period

在子宫孕育了并生育了他的她，
他们给了孩子他们自己的一部分，
比后来给的更多，他们成为他的一部分。

那个安详地在家中饭桌上摆放佳肴的母亲，
那个话语和蔼、穿戴干干净净方帽长袍的母亲，
那个经过之处就从身上衣服上散发馨香的母亲，
那个强壮、自给自足、男子汉气概、普通、易躁、不公正的父亲，
那偶然的打击、那大声叱喝、吝啬的讨价还价、狡诈的引诱，
家里的话语、语言、交往的人，
家具、求知和渴望的心，
那不能否认的情感，那种真实感，
白天的疑惑、夜晚的怀疑，
好奇的是否与怎样，
是否表里是一样，或只是幻觉与镜现？
街上男女挤成团，如果他们
不是幻觉与镜现，那么他们是什么？
街道和房正面，
还有橱窗里的货物，
各种交通工具、三五成群的人、厚木板铺成的码头，
渡口拥挤的人群，
夕阳西下时从高处看到的村庄，
还有村庄之间的河流，
影子、光环、雾、落在屋顶上的光
两英里以外的白色和棕色的山墙，
附近倦意懒散随潮移动的纵帆船，
船尾懒散拖着的小舟，
急冲急赶的波浪，很快消失的巨大的浪尖，
那层层的彩云，在远处孤独的
那长长的一抹栗色柔辉在纯洁辽阔的天空一动不动，
地平线的边缘，飞旋的海鸦，
盐泥和海岸泥土的芳香。
这一切都随孩子的成长成为他的一部分，
他现在每天在成长，以后每天也要总在成长。
（李正栓　译）

(10) Cavalry Crossing a Ford

A line in long array where they wind betwixt green islands,
They take a serpentine course, their arms flash in the sun
    —hark to the musical clank,
Behold the silvery river, in it the splashing horses loitering stop to drink,
Behold the brown-faced men, each group, each person,
    a picture, the negligent rest on the saddles,
5 Some emerge on the opposite bank, others
    are just entering the ford—while,
Scarlet and blue and snowy white,
The guidon flags flutter gaily in the wind.

Notes

Cavalry: soldiers fighting on horseback.
Line 1 A line of the ordered army is twistingly moving between the green islands.
    array: an ordered force or army.
Line 2 The line in which the army moved forward is like the trace of a snake. The soldiers' weapons are glittering in the sun light. Listen, the weapons are clacking to compose a music.
    serpentine: a metaphor; the line is zigzagging like a snake.
    clank: make a short loud sound as, like that of a heavy moving metal chain.
Line 3 Behold: look.
Line 4 the brown-faced men: the soldiers.
    negligent: careless in a pleasant way.
Line 7 guidon: flag of a military unit

Comment on the poem

    This poem is grouped under the *Drum-Taps* section in the 1881 edition of *Leaves of Grass*. With the description of the long array, the flash of weapons, the soldiers, the horses, the river, the river bank, the flags, the poem reminds its readers of a vivid scene of the American Civil War. However, all the motions described in the picture are recorded through a quick glance of the poet. With the "musical clanks" of weapons, the life and attraction of the picture are more likely to come out from the writer's imagination rather than from the picture itself.

参考译文

骑兵过河

长长的队伍迂回在绿色的岛屿之间，
蜿蜒地前进着，阳光中武器闪闪
——听，武器叮当成音乐，
看，那银光闪闪的河中马儿奔腾转步停下来饮水，
看，褐色面孔的人们，一群群，每个人，
都是一幅画，马鞍上还有大咧咧的人，
有一些人已出现在对面的河岸，其他人
才正走进河中——此时，
红色的、蓝色的、雪白的
队旗欢快地迎风飘扬。
（李正栓 译）

(11) O Captain, My Captain!

Captain! my Captain! Our fearful trip is done,
The ship has weather'd every rack, the prize we sought is won,
The port is near, the bells I hear, the people all exulting,
While follow eyes the steady keel, the vessel grim and daring;
5　But O heart! heart! heart!
　　O the bleeding drops of red,
　　　Where on the deck my Captain lies,
　　　　Fallen cold and dead.

O Captain! my Captain! Rise up and hear the bells;
10　Rise up—for you the flag is flung—for you the bugle trills,
For you bouquets and ribbon'd wreaths—for
　　　you the shores a—crowding,
For you they call, the swaying mass, their eager faces turning;
Here Captain! dear father!
15　This arm beneath your head!
　　It is some dream that on the deck,
　　　You've fallen cold and dead.

My Captain does not answer, his lips are pale and still,
My father does not feel my arm, he has no pulse nor will,
20 The ship is anchor'd safe and sound, its voyage closed and done,
From fearful trip the victor ship comes in
    with object won;
      Exult, O shores, and ring, O bells,
        But I with mournful tread,
          Walk the deck my Captain lies,
25   Fallen cold and dead.

Notes

Line 1 fearful trip: the American Civil War which lasted from 1861 to 1865. President Lincoln was shot on April 14, 1865, 5 days after the termination of the war.

Line 2 rack: a ruined or disorganized state.

    weather'd every rack: experienced all the hardships.

    the prize: the triumph of the Civil War; the abolishment of slavery all over the country.

Line 4 While our country has just striven out of the war and intending to the stability; while all our people are looking at the new government for better achievements.

    keel: the ship the "captain" is in and which is the symbol of the newly liberated country. "Keel" here symbolizes the source of stability.

    vessel: the ship, the country.

Stanza 1: The poet metaphorically compares the country as a ship, and the president, a captain. The country, with the piloting of the president, has just survived the war and won the liberty for all the people.

Line 10 for you: the flag is flinging for you; the bugle is trilling for you; bouquets and ribbon'd wreathed are for you; the shores are crowded for you; people are calling for you; the swaying mass's faces are eagerly turning for you.

Line 14 dear father: the poet worships the president as father of the country.

Line 15 This arm beneath your head: the poet supposes the seriously

Section Three
American Poetry of High Romantic Period

wounded president was lying in his arms.
Line 16 dream: something unbelievable.

Stanza 2: The "captain" has seen the breaking of the dawn, when all the honours are accessible, he falls in front of his people. This enhances the strength of the tragic scenery.

Line 18 still: motionless.
Line 19 nor will: (he was) unconscious.
Line 22 with object won: when it (the victory ship) has reached the destination; when it (the ship) has fulfilled the task.
Line 24 with mournful tread: heavily, (I) set down my feet; I'm rather depressed.
Line 25 Walk the deck: walked on the deck.

Stanza 3: With all the calling and ringing of the bells, the captain is unable to come to. The helplessness drives the poet to great despair.

Comment on the poem

The poem consists of 3 stanzas, with each stanza containing 8 lines and follows a rhyme scheme of "aabbcded." The first 4 lines of each stanza are almost in heptameter, while each of the latter 4 lines is alternatively in trimeter or tetrameter. The metrical foot within every stanza also varies freely from iambus to trochee. The shifts of the methods parallel the ups and downs of the poet's passion and the freedom of expression, which avails the poet to make the work coherently whole.

The stanzaic form looks like a ship, with the word "captain" at the head of each stanza. The stanzaic form was deliberately chosen and designed.

参考译文

啊,船长!我的船长!

啊,船长!我的船长!可怕的航程已完成;
这船历尽风险,企求的目标已达成。
港口在望,钟声响,人们在欢欣。
千万双眼睛注视着船——平稳,勇敢,坚定。

但是痛心啊！痛心！痛心！
瞧一滴滴鲜红的血！
甲板上躺着我的船长，
他倒下去，冰冷，永别。

啊！船长！我的船长！起来吧，倾听钟声；
起来吧，号角为您长鸣，旌旗为您高悬；
迎着您，多少花束花圈——候着您，千万人蜂拥岸边；
他们向您高呼，拥来挤去，仰起殷切的脸；
啊，船长！亲爱的父亲！
我的手臂托着您的头！
莫非是一场梦：在甲板上
您倒下去，冰冷，永别。

我的船长不作声，嘴唇惨白，毫不动弹；
我的父亲没感到我的手臂，没有脉搏，没有遗言；
船舶抛锚停下，平安抵达；航程终了；
历尽艰险返航，夺得胜利目标。
啊！岸上钟声齐鸣，啊！，人们一片欢腾！
但是，我在甲板上，在船长身旁，
心悲切，步履沉重：
因为他倒下去，冰冷，永别。

（杨霖 译）

(12) Song of Myself

(excerpted)

1

I celebrate my self, and sing myself,
And what I assume you shall assume,
For very atom belonging to me as good belongs to you.

I loafe and invite my soul,
5   I lean and loafe at my ease observing a spear of summer grass.

My tongue, every atom of my blood, form'd from this soil, this air,
Born here of parents born here from parents the same,
    and their parents the same,
I, now thirty-seven years old in perfect health begin,

Section Three
American Poetry of High Romantic Period

    Hoping to cease not till death.
10 Creeds and schools in abeyance,
    Retiring back a while sufficed at what they are, but never forgotten,
    I harbor for good or bad, I permit to speak at every hazard,
    Nature without check with original energy.

6

    A child said *What is the grass*? fetching it to me with full hands;
15 How could I answer the child? I do not know what it is any more than he.

    I guess it must be the flag of my disposition, out of hopeful green stuff woven.

    Or I guess it is the handkerchief of the Lord,
    A scented gift and remembrancer designedly dropt,
    Bearing the owner's name someway in the corners,
        that we may see and remark, and say Whose?
20 Or I guess the grass is itself a child, the produced babe of the vegetation.

    Or I guess it is a uniform hieroglyphic,
    And it means, Sprouting alike in broad zones and narrow zones,
    Growing among black folks as among white,
    Kanuck, Tuckahoe, Congressman, Cuff, I give them the same,
        I receive them the same.

25 And now it seems to me the beautiful uncut hair of graves.

    Tenderly will I use you curling grass,
    It may be you transpire from the breasts of young men,
    It may be if I had known them I would have loved them,
    It may be you are from old people, or from offspring
        taken soon out of their mothers' laps,
30 And here you are the mothers' laps.
    The grass is very dark to be from the white heads of old mothers,
    Darker than the colorless beards of old man,
    Dark to come from under the faint red roofs of mouths.

    O I perceive after all so many uttering tongues,
35 And I perceive they do not come from the roofs of mouths for nothing.
    I wish I could translate the hints about the dead young men and women,
    And the hints about old men and mothers, and the

offspring taken soon out of their laps.

What do you think has become of the young and old men?
And what do you think has become of the women and children?

40 They are alive and well somewhere,
The smallest sprout shows there is really no death,
And if ever there was it led forward life, and does not
    wait at the end to arrest it,
And ceas'd the moment life appear'd.

All goes onward and outward, nothing collapses,
45 And to die is different from what any one supposed, and luckier.

Notes

Line 1 celebrate: praise; honor.
Line 2 assume: admit; perceive.
    What words I have used to praise myself would do the same to you.
Line 3 Each of us is a part of nature, thus, we have the same structure.
Line 4 loafe: (=loaf) wander; move freely.
    While I am loafing, I invited my soul to go together, since both are free.
Line 5 I lean and loafe: In my wandering, I stopped and stooped (being attracted by something)
    a spear of: a narrow piece of (grass leave).
Line 6 form'd from: (be) created from.
    this air: ... was created or originated from this air.
Line 7 I was born here; my parents were born here.
    from parents the same: ... from the parents who were born from the same soil and used to take the same air.
Line 8 begin: so I begin.
    I am now strong and healthy, I begin to hope my singing of myself will not stop till my death.
Line 10 Creeds: religious doctrines.
    schools: theory of a particular group of scholars.
    in abeyance: the condition of not being in use or in force.
    When I am singing myself and wandering, I'd like to leave all

Section Three
American Poetry of High Romantic Period

the creeds and schools aside, to have them retire back.
Line 11 sufficed: (I felt) I have had quite enough of creeds or schools.
they: the creeds and schools.
but never forgotten: in spite of my unwillingness to all the creeds and schools, I would never have them forgotten.
Line 12 harbor: *v.* accept; admit (whatever of nature).
I permit to speak: I permit nature to speak.
at every hazard: whenever; in any case.
Line 13 check: considering.
original energy: the real intention (of nature).
Lines 12 – 13 I am willing to accept whatever nature provides, good or bad, without considering the real intention of it.
Line 16 it: grass.
In Lines 16, 17, 21, 22, the subjective "it" all refers to "grass."
disposition: a general tendency of character, behavior, feeling.
... out of hopeful green stuff woven: (the flag of my disposition) was woven out of the hopeful green material.
Line 18 A scented gift and remembrancer: (I guess) the grass may be the handkerchief of the lord which might be a pleasantly smelt gift or souvenir.
designedly dropt: intentionally dropped somewhere for others to pick up. (In old times, a handkerchief is often used as a keepsake between lovers.)
Line 19 Bearing the owner's name someway in the corners: the handkerchief, if dropped as a keepsake, may have the owner's name written or embroidered somewhere in the corner of it.
say Whose: ask whose handkerchief it is.
Line 20 the produced babe of the vegetation: the baby grown out of plants.
Line 21 a uniform hieroglyphic: a kind of particular letters as those of the oriental countries.
Line 22 Sprouting alike: growing from a seed in the same way.
broad zones and narrow zones: (in) rich place or barren soil.
Line 24 The grass grows among Kanuck, Tuckahoe, Congressman, Cuff.
Kanuck: French Canadian.
Tuckahoe: a Virginian who lived on the poor land in the tidewater region and ate "tuckahoe," a brown fungus.
Cuff: black people.

In this line, Congressman indicates the people of high position, while the others are representatives of the lower society.

Line 24 I give them the same, I receive them the same: The grass is not snobbish. It provides equally to all the people mentioned above, and, it takes from them the same kindness.

Line 25 And now it seems to me the grass appears in the form of the uncut hair of graves.

Line 27 You may have grown from the breasts of young men.
transpire: grow out; derive.

Line 28 Quite probably if I had known those young men, I would have loved them.

Line 29 The grass may have grown from old people, or from the new born children.

Line 30 And here you are the mother's laps: And here the grass, which takes good care to them, roles as mothers' laps to the dead children.

Line 31 This grass is in dark green, so it seems not possible to have grown out of the white heads of old mothers.

Line 32 The grass is darker than the colorless beards of old men, thus it could not have grown out of the old men.

Line 33 Dark to come from under the faint red roofs of mouths: the color of the grass is in such a dark green color that it is really difficult to make an exact description of it.
the faint red roofs: the upper jaw of a human mouth.

Line 34 perceive: notice; be aware of.

Lines 34 – 35 After having listened to so much gossip about it, I finally realized that the grass does not grow out of nothing; each of them is significantly growing, as a matter of fact.

Line 36 I wish I am able to comprehend the symbolic meaning of grass from the dead young men and women, from the old men and mothers, from the offspring.

Line 38 has become of: has happened to ... (after death).

Line 40 They: the young and old men, the women and children.

Line 41 The smallest sprout: the smallest buds, the new shoots of plant may suggest that there is actually no such things as death in this world—every death in this world is doubtlessly the prediction of a new birth.

Line 42 if ever there was: if ever there was such a thing as "death," it leads forward to a new life.

arrest: stop; bring to an end.
Line 43 At the moment the life ceased, a new life begins.
Line 44 All: all the new lives.
Line 45 luckier: to die is luckier than anyone had supposed.

Comment on the poem

"Song of Myself," consisting of 1345 lines, is the longest poem in *Leaves of Grass*. The poet takes for granted the self as the most crucial element of the world and thus sets forth two of his principal beliefs: first, a theory of universality; second, all things are equal in value.

In Part 1 of the selected sections, the author unfolds the theme of "a leaf of grass is no less than the journey-work of the stars" by cordially celebrating himself. Meanwhile, he "extols the ideals of equality and democracy and celebrates the dignity, the self-reliant spirit and the joy of the common man."

In Part 6, the poet's attitude towards life and death is pertinently presented: "The smallest sprout show there is really no death"; "ceased the moment life appeared," and "to die is different from what any one supposed, and luckier."

参考译文

自我之歌
（节选）

1

我赞美自我，歌唱自我，
我承担的你也将承担，
因为属于我的每一个原子也同样属于你。

我邀请我的灵魂一起遨游，
我俯身悠然观察着一片夏日的草叶。
我的舌头、我血液的每个原子，是在这片土壤、这种空气里形成的，
是这里的父母生下的，父母的父母也是在这里生下的，他们的父母也一样，
我，现在三十七岁，身体健康，开始行动
希望永远如此歌唱自我，直到死去。

信条和学派暂且不论，

后退一步,明了它们当前的情况已足,但也绝不是忘怀,
不论善恶我都能接受,我允许随意发表意见,
顺乎自然,保持原始的活力。

6

一个孩子双手捧着满满的青草问我,
"草是什么?"
我能怎样回答他呢?我知道的并不比他多。

我猜想它是我性格的旗帜,
由象征希望的绿色物质组成。

或者我猜想它是主的手帕,
是特意抛下的清香的礼物和纪念,
某个角落写着主人的名字,
以便我们看到谈论,问,"是谁的呀?"
或者我猜想青草本身就是孩子,
是植物生产的婴儿。

我又猜想它是统一的象形文字,
它意味着,
不管遇到宽阔还是狭窄的地域都要发芽,
在黑人和白人中间同样生长,
开纳克人、塔卡河人、
国会议员、囚犯,我给予他们一样,
对待他们也一视同仁。

现在我觉得它像是坟墓上未修剪的美发。

我将轻柔地对你,卷曲的青草,
你也可能从青年男子的胸膛上长出,
如果我认得他们,或许我早已爱上他们,
或许你从老年人,
或即将离开母亲怀抱的婴孩身上长出,
在这里你就是母亲的怀抱。

青草比古老母亲苍苍白发颜色要深,
比老头们花白的胡子要深,

Section Three
American Poetry of High Romantic Period

因为它来自淡红色的上颚。

啊,多少人说完后我便去感悟,
我感悟它来自淡红色的上颚,是有所图。

我希望我能翻译死去的年轻男女的暗示,
还有老人、
母亲和即将离开母亲怀抱的婴孩的暗示。

你认为那些年轻人和老年人变成了什么?
你认为那些妇女和孩子变成了什么?

他们在某个地方活得很好,
最小的嫩芽表明世上真的没有死亡,
即便是有,它也是引导生命向前,
并不会等到最后阻止生命,
生命一旦出现,死亡立刻消失。

万物都在向上,前进,没有事物在衰竭,
死亡并不是人们想象的那样,而是更幸运。

(魏慧哲　李正栓　译)

(13) I Hear America Singing

I hear America singing, the varied carols I hear,
Those of mechanics, each one singing his as it
　　　should be blithe and strong,
The carpenter singing his as he measures his plank or beam,
The mason singing his as he makes ready for work, or leaves off work,
5　The boatman singing what belongs to him in his boat, the
　　　deckhand singing on the steamboat deck,
The shoemaker singing as he sits on his bench,
　　　the hatter singing as he stands,
The wood-cutters's song, the ploughboy's on his way in
　　　the morning, or at noon intermission or at sundown,
The delicious singing of the mother, or of the young wife at
　　　work, or of the girl sewing or washing,
Each singing what belongs to him or her and to none else,
10　The day what belongs to the day—at night the party

  of young fellows, robust, friendly,
Singing with open mouths their strong melodious songs.

Notes

Line 1 the varied carols I hear: I hear merry songs in different words by different people.
Line 2 Those of mechanics: (I can hear) those songs of mechanics.
  each one singing his: each mechanic is singing his joyful songs. (In the following lines, "the carpenter singing, the mason singing, the boatman singing, the deckhand singing, the shoemaker singing, the hatter singing, the each singing" are all structured in the same form.)
Line 4 makes ready for work: when he is preparing for his work.
  leaves off work: when he has finished his work.
Line 5 what belongs to him in his boat: his harvest; fish he had caught.
  the deckhand: person who does cleaning or other unskilled work on a ship.
Line 6 the hatter: the hat maker.
Line 7 The wood-cutter's song: the song the wood-cutter is singing.
  the ploughboy's: the song the young farmer (is singing).
  noon intermission: a pause of work at noon.
Line 8 The delicious singing of the mother: I can hear the beautiful/sweet songs of the mother.
Line 9 Each: each of the persons mentioned in the above lines.
Line 10 The day what belongs to the day: The day is singing the songs that belong to the day.
Lines 10 – 11 at night ... friendly: at night, groups of young people, strong and friendly, are singing, with open mouths, the vigorously tuneful songs.

Comment on the poem

  The poem presents to the readers a picture. While traveling around the country, Whitman, seemingly, was listening to a concert performed by his entire fellow Americans. The long catalogue of the "songs" from various professions of laboring people brings readers to the acme of optimism. The readers may be impressed that God seems extremely lavish when he led people to the New World, where everybody feels sufficient and everyone is apt to enjoy his/her life. It's paradise where everybody sings.

参考译文

我听见美利坚在歌唱

我听见美利坚在歌唱,听见各种颂歌在回响:
机械工在唱,每个人都心情愉快、歌声嘹亮;
木匠在唱,边唱歌边把木板和大梁来丈量;
泥瓦匠在唱,上工前后都在唱;
船夫在唱船上事,水手歌唱在汽艇甲板上;
鞋匠坐着凳子把歌唱,帽匠站在店铺里唱;
伐木工、农村青年清晨走路、中午间休、黄昏回家都在唱;
母亲在甜唱,少妇在边工作边唱,少女在边缝洗边唱;
每个人都在唱自己关心而不属于别人的事;
白天唱着白天的事,夜里身强力壮互相友好的青年人
张口大唱,歌声悦耳、雄壮嘹亮。
(李正栓 译)

Ⅲ. Emily Elizabeth Dickinson
(1830 – 1886)

1. Life Story

Emily Dickinson, born in Amherst, Massachusetts on Dec. 10, 1830, was the best poetess America ever created. She was a daughter of a prominent lawyer and politician. She did not receive much formal education but read widely at home. Actually, during the narrow span of her lifetime, she kept staying at home except for a few short trips to Boston or Philadelphia.

Emily Dickinson was a witty woman, sensitive, full of humanity and with a genius for poetry. While she was living in almost total seclusion, she wrote in secret whatever she was able to feel, to see, to hear and whatever she was able to imagine. She wrote whenever and wherever. Although she guarded her poems even from her family, 1,775 poems were discovered and published after her death. However, as the only noteworthy woman poet in American literature of the 19th century, she had only seven of her poems published during her lifetime, and it was not until the beginning of the 20th century that her genius was widely recognized.

2. Features of Emily Dickinson's Poems

In subject matter Emily Dickinson was very similar to the great romantic poets of her time. Her poems are short, many of them being based on a single image or symbol. But within her little lyrics she wrote about some of the most important things in life: love, nature, morality and immortality. She wrote about success, which she thought she never achieved; and she wrote about failure, which she considered her constant companion. She wrote of these things so brilliantly that she is now ranked as one of America's greatest poets.

Poetry is for Dickinson a means to attain pleasure, a way to preach her doctrine, and a medium to express her world outlook, an outlet for her despair and a remedy to pacify her soul. Her life experience fostered her belief as an existentialist as well as a great poet.

Despite her seclusion of life, Emily Dickinson covered a wide range of subjects in poetry. Her favorite subjects are love, death or natural beauty. In her writing she wrote about life and death, expecting to understand the meaning of life by understanding the meaning of death.

Living in the 19th century, a comparatively religious era, Emily Dickinson did not belong to any organized religion. However, she wrote of God, man and nature; she probed into the spiritual unrest of man and often doubted about the existence and benevolence of God, because she felt that wild nature was her church and she was able to converse directly with God there.

Emily Dickinson was a poet who could express feelings of deepest poignancy in terms of the true and wise saying, often in an aphoristic style. Her gemlike poems are all very short, but fresh and original, marked by the vigor of her images, the daring of her thought and the beauty of her expression.

Emily Dickinson wrote in the conventional metrical form, though she did not always strictly observe the rules of versification.

Emily Dickinson defamiliarised conventional poetic form, deliberately overusing capitalization and dashes, to make her poems looking strange. In some way, she is very much similar to the style of John Donne.

3. Selected Poems

(1) Success (67)

Success is counted sweetest
By those who ne'er succeed.
To comprehend a nectar
Requires sorest need.

5   Not one of all the purple host
Who took the flag today
Can tell the definition,
So clear, of victory,

As he, defeated, dying,
10 On whose forbidden ear
The distant strains of triumph

Breaks, agonized and clear.

Notes

Line 3 comprehend: obtain; fully understand.
       nectar: sweet liquid collected by bees from flowers; sweet, good-tasting drink. In Greek and Roman mythology nectar is the food for all the gods and goddesses in the Olympian mountains. In this poem, it refers to "success" which is always hardly gained.
Line 4 sorest need: great desire; immediate requirement.

Stanza 1: People who had never succeeded would consider success as the sweetest, because all the obtaining of success originates from one's immediate requirement for it.

Line 5 the purple host: people of very high rank; the noble people. This comes from the fact that purple is the color of robes worn by Roman emperors and Catholic cardinals.
Line 6 Who took the flag: powerful people; people in high positions.
Line 7 tell: explain; understand.

Stanza 2: None of those in high positions can interpret the real meaning of success, since none of them can really understand "success."

Line 9 As he, defeated, dying: as for that person who had been defeated, who was dying.
Line 10 whose: the defeated, dying person's.
       forbidden ear: senseless ears.
Line 11 strains: notes of music.
Line 12 Breaks: (the strains) sound off and on; intermittently.
       agonized: causing great pain.
       clear: significant.

Stanza 3: To people who have failed, who have been badly wounded and dying, the music of victory, though sounds far from them, is heartbreaking, painstaking and significant.

Comment on the poem

    Everybody requires a successful life. However, who is able to understand the meaning of "success"? It is not those who were born into the high society, nor those who had easily taken the critical positions. It is those people who had been striving with every effort and had been badly wounded but never gratified that are able to catch, in their last breath, the music of victory. This poem is a song for the common people.

参考译文

成　　功（67）

从未成功的人认为，
成功的滋味最甜美。
有强烈的渴求
才能知道甘露的美味。

今天在紫色人群中
所有举旗的人
没有一个能像他如此清楚地
给胜利一个定义。

他，战败，将死，
耳朵震伤欲聋，
猛然听见胜利的呼叫，
清晰响亮却充满苦痛。
（李正栓　译）

(2) Wild Nights—Wild Nights! (249)

Wild Nights—wild Nights!
Were I with thee
Wild Nights should be
Our Luxury!
5　Futile—the Winds—
To a Heart in port
Done with the Compass—
Done with the chart!

Studies on American Poetry

Rowing in Eden—
10　Ah, the Sea!
Might I but moor—Tonight—
In thee!

Notes

Line 1 Wild Nights: the wild stormy nights; nights with tempest. It may also suggest that the love is wild or the inner world of the poet is wild during this kind of nights.

Line 2 Were I with thee: If I were with thee (the person who inspired the poem).
thee: a lover.

Stanza 1: A tempest is conventionally considered as a turbulent weather, however, if I were together with you, my lover, the wild nights become greatest pleasure to me.

Line 5 Futile: unnecessary; useless.
Line 6 a Heart in port: a person in safety.
Line 7 Done with: completely finished; absolutely unnecessary.
　　compass: device for finding direction.
Line 8 chart: detailed map used to help navigation at sea, showing coasts, rocks, the depth of the sea etc.

Stanza 2: (If one has true love in heart, it is just like a ship in port) to a heart in safety, compass or chart, even the winds become quite unnecessary.

Line 9 Rowing in Eden: When tonight I am rowing my boat over the sea of love.
　　Eden: the garden of Eden. It refers to the ideal world of love.
Line 10 the Sea: the sea of love.
Line 11 moor: fasten a boat to the bed of the sea; be in the protection of ...
Line 12 thee: her lover.

Stanza 3: The poet is enquiring if she is able to win the passionate and eternal love that night.

Section Three
American Poetry of High Romantic Period

Despite the fact that Emily Dickinson lived as a spinster all her life, she is good at writing about the wild consummated love, "*Wild Nights—Wild Nights*" is a proper evidence. In the work, the poet, by alluding the woman and man in love to the images of a boat and a port, very smartly delivered to the readers the real passion deeply buried in her heart and the tragedy of her being "in port"—unable to find what she so deeply desires: "wild nights" of passionate love.

参考译文

暴风雨夜——暴风雨夜！(249)

暴风雨夜——暴风雨夜！
我若与您同在，
这样的夜
应是一种奢侈。

风啊，你无能为力——
因为心已在港口回避
罗盘已不起作用——
海图也不必再用！

泛舟游于伊甸园——
啊，大海！
但愿今夜——我能——
停泊在你的胸怀！
（李正栓　译）

(3) "Hope" Is the Thing with Feathers (254)

"Hope" is the thing with feathers—
That perches in the soul—
And sings the tune without the words—
And never stops—at all—

5 And sweetest—in the Gale—is heard—
And sore must be the storm—
That could abash the little Bird

That kept so many warm—

I've heard it in the chillest land—
10   And on the strangest sea—
Yet, never, in extremity,
It asked a crumb—of Me.

Notes

Line 1 The poet uses her genius to compare the abstract "hope" to a concrete appearance — a bird, which can fly far and high.
Line 2 perches: (a bird) comes to rest from flying; goes into the stated position.

Stanza 1: "Hope" is compared to a bird which stays in the soul and sings constantly there.

Line 5 the Gale: the blow of a strong wind.
Line 6 And sore must be the storm—: The storm must be a grievous one.
Line 7 That: It leads an attributive clause which modifies "the storm." abash: cause to feel uncomfortable or ashamed in the presence of others.
In this line, we should notice "could," which indicates what we are talking about here is just a possibility. If the storm could probably abash the songs of bird...
Line 8 That: another attributive clause which modifies "Bird" in Line 7. so many: many people; (the bird, the song of hope) used to keep many people warm.

Stanza 2: In the strong wind, the song of hope is sounded the sweetest. It must be a very harsh and grievous storm if it could possibly eliminate the songs of hope which had kept many people warm.

Line 9 it: the bird's singing; the song of hope.
the chillest land: the severest state; (I have heard the songs of hope in) the most difficult situation.
Line 10 on the strangest sea: (I have heard the songs of hope) in the most unexpected places.

Line 12 It: hope.
    crumb: very small amount of reward.

Stanza 3: "Hope" helps us in all the severe conditions but never requires any reward from us. Hope only gives, but never intends to take anything from people.

参考译文

"希望"是个长着羽毛的东西(254)

"希望"是个长着羽毛的东西——
它栖息在灵魂之中——
唱着没有歌词的旋律——
永远唱个不停——

大风中——能听到——最美的歌声——
暴风雨肯定最让人心痛——
令那只小鸟惊惧
它却曾使多人感到暖意——

在最寒冷的陆地,我听到它——
在最陌生的海上,我听到它——
在即便是绝境中,
连面包碎屑它也不向我索取。
(李正栓 译)

(4) The Soul Selects Her Own Society (303)

The Soul selects her own society—
Then—shuts the Door—
To her divine Majority—
Present no more—

5   Unmoved—she notes the Chariots—pausing—
At her low gate—
Unmoved—and Emperor be kneeling

Upon her Mat—

I've known her—from an ample nation—
10 Choose one—
Then—close the Valves of her attention—
Like Stone—

Notes

Line 1 society: principle of life she had chosen.
Line 4 Present no more: the soul presents nor more.

<u>Stanza 1</u>: The soul, after the choice of her own society, shuts her door to her divine majority (and) no more presents.

Line 5 She was unmoved when she notes …
    Chariots: (together with "Emperor" in the 7th line) are symbols for authorities, powers or temptations.

<u>Stanza 2</u>: She (the soul) was unmoved when she notes the Chariots pausing at her low gate; she was also unmoved when she sees an Emperor fell on his knees to her.

Line 9 her: the soul.
    an ample nation: a great population.
Line 11 Valves: structure in the heart or in a blood-vessel allowing the blood to flow in one direction only. (心脏或血管的瓣膜) In this line, it refers to "mind."

<u>Stanza 3</u>: I know that once the soul has chosen one belief from an abundant nation, she would then close the valves of her heart like stone (and would never open it to any others).

Comment on the poem

The soul is so autocentered that she accepts only what she chooses and she is so tough-willed as to defy the divine majority. The soul is so self-asserted that she despises all kinds of authorities, powers and temptations represented by the Chariots and the Emperor. In this poem, the Soul symbolizes a persistent individual, living upon self-reliance and un-

Section Three
American Poetry of High Romantic Period

able to reconcile herself with those she dislikes. She insists on the supreme importance of the self in choosing ways of existence and refuses to conform to the existing social conventions.

The poet is very careful in selecting words to express her points. She takes for granted the self as the center of the world. The self confronts a large crowd which she despises, but the self reveals a remarkable personality of self-maintenance and self-assertion. By emphasizing the importance of individuality, the poet seems to imply that one is soulless if she is apt to yield to the majority without her own ideas and that she would lose her own identity in existence if she discards the principle of choosing and distinguishing.

参考译文

灵魂选择自己的友伴 (303)

灵魂选择自己的友伴——
之后——把门紧关——
对神圣的大多数——
它再也不出现——

发现车辆——驻轮不前——她不为所动——
尽管就在她低矮的门前——
发现皇帝下跪——她不为所动——
尽管就在草席上边——

从一个大民族中——我知道了她——
你也选一个吧——
之后——关闭关注的阀门——
像一块石头——
（李正栓　译）

(5) On a Columnar Self—(321)

On a Columnar Self—
How ample to rely
In Tumult—or Extremity—
How good the Certainty

5   That Lever cannot pry—
      And Wedge cannot divide
      Conviction—That Granitic Base—
      Though None be on our Side—

      Suffice Us—for a Crowd—
10   Ourself—and Rectitude—
      And that Assembly—not far off
      From furthest Spirit—God—

Notes

Line 1 Columnar: a word derived from "column," a solid upright pillar that can bear immense weight and pressure. "A columnar self" presents to the readers the living image of a self-reliant person. In the first line of the poem, a suggestion of self-reliance is already strongly presented.

Line 2 ample: more than enough; abundant; large in size; spacious; extensive.

Line 3 Tumult: disturbance or confusion; turmoil.
    Extremity: the limit of something; the furthest point; great misfortune.

Line 4 How good the Certainty: How good to rely on the Certainty.

Line 5 Lever (杠杆): bar or other device turning on a fixed point which lifts or opens something with one end when pressure applies to the other end.
    pry: inquire too curiously or rudely.

Line 6 Wedge: piece of wood or metal that is thick at one end and narrow at the other to a sharp edge, used to split wood or rock, to widen an opening or to keep things apart.

Lines 1-6 How ample it is to rely on a Columnar self in tumult or extremity; how good it is to rely on the certainty which lever cannot pry and wedge cannot divide.

Line 7 Conviction: firm opinion or belief.
    Granitic Base: The conviction based on granite, a kind of hard, gray stone, which is often taken as an image for stability or constancy.
    The conviction, which is so firm and persistent that no lever can

Section Three
American Poetry of High Romantic Period

remove it and no wedge can split it, is the granite base for the Columnar self.

Line 8 None: none of the convictions, the firm believes; none of the other people.

None be on our Side: none of the convictions appear at the surface; not deliberately.

Line 9 Suffice: feel enough, adequate; feel satisfied.

Us: those with columnar selves.

a Crowd: the conventional society; those with columnar selves.

Lines 7 - 9 Conviction, as the granite base, will suffice us in the conventional society, in spite of all the absurdity, foolishness or hostilities the world may present to us.

Line 10 Rectitude: honesty; moral correctness.

Line 11 Assembly: heaven.

Ourself and rectitude and that assembly are all not far off from the furthest spirit—God.

Despite the fact that the poet admits that the "Us," the rectitude, and the assembly are all not far off from the furthest spirit—God, what she still intends to tell is that, when she stands almost by herself, with her integrity, her "columnar self" confronting a large crowd which she despises, she is quite confident to resist the challenge of a crowd who may equally contain the spirit of God. By this, Emily Dickinson extends her courage to a will to defy God. In her mind, the human integrity is essentially built on the strong conviction of oneself.

参考译文

在同一圆柱上（321）

在同一圆柱上——
这样便足矣：要么依赖混乱
要么依赖非常手段——
确定无疑又该多好

杠杆不能刺探
楔子不能分开
深信不移——那花岗岩底座——

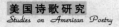

尽管没人在我们这一边——

让我们满足——为了一大群——
为我们自己——也为了正义——
还为上帝这最远处神灵的——不远处——
那一干人群——
（李正栓 译）

(6) Some Keep the Sabbath Going to Church (324)

Some keep the Sabbath going to Church—
I keep it, staying at Home—
With a Bobolink for a Chorister—
And an Orchard, for a Dome—

5 Some keep the Sabbath in Surplice—
I just wear my Wings—
And instead of tolling the Bell, for Church,
Our little Sexton-sings.

God preaches, a noted Clergyman—
10 And the sermon is never long,
So instead of getting to Heaven, at last—
I'm going, all along.

Notes

Line 1 Sabbath: day of the week intended for rest and worship of God (Saturday for Jews and Sunday for Christians).
Line 3 Bobolink: a type of small North American singing bird; the singing of this bird.
Chorister: a member of a group of people who sing together in a church (choir).
Line 4 Dome: rounded top of a church.

Stanza 1: On Sabbath day, most people go to church, but I do not; instead, I stay at home, listening to the singing of bobolink as psalms, taking my orchard for a shrine.

Section Three
American Poetry of High Romantic Period

Line 5 keep the Sabbath in Surplice: hold very formal religious ceremonies.

Line 6 my Wings: the poet compares herself to a bird which sings in an orchard while fluttering the wings; or to a winged angel, more likely.

In any literature, "bird" is taken as the embodiment of freedom.

Line 8 Our little Sexton: sexton is a person with the job of taking care of a church building, ringing bells and digging graves. Here the poetess alludes to the little bird as her sexton to her. In her church of nature, the little bird is the only one who preaches with its singing.

Stanza 2: When I am staying at home on Sabbath day, hearing the spontaneous singing of the bobolink bird, I feel closer to God.

Line 9 God preaches: God is like a well-known Clergyman and He preaches directly to me.

Line 10 sermon: talk usually based on a sentence from the Bible and given as part of a church service.

Line 11 People go to church on Sabbath for the sake of going to heaven after death so as to have their happy afterlife. However, since I don't go to church, I might not have the chance to go to heaven after death.

Line 12 I am willing to live the mortal life in this natural way.

Stanza 3: I believe when I am staying at home on Sabbath day, I am able to get directly in touch with God. I am here already enjoying the bliss of heaven in the natural world.

参考译文

有些人过安息日去教堂 (324)

有些人过安息日去教堂——
我也过安息日,只不过是在家里——
让食米鸟代替唱诗班歌唱——
让果园成为礼拜的圣地——

有些人过安息日穿白色法衣——
我只穿飞行章——
我不为做礼拜鸣响寺钟,
只把司事的小曲歌唱——

上帝布道,是著名的牧师——
布道文从不冗长,
于是,即便不去天堂——
最终,我也胜似前往。
(李正栓 译)

(7) Our Share of Night to Bear

Our share of night to bear,
    Our share of morning,
Our blank in bliss to fill,
    Our blank in scorning.

5   Here a star, and there a star,
    Some lose their way.
Here a mist, and there a mist,
    Afterwards—day!

Notes

Line 1 share: chance.
    share of night: part in difficult state. "Night" is the image of difficulty.
    to bear: to carry; to suffer.
Line 2 share of morning: part, role in happiness. "Morning" is the image of happiness.
Line 3 blank: absence; missing.
    bliss: thorough happiness as if one were in heaven.
    to fill: to result in.
Line 4 scorning: strong, usually angry feeling of disrespect; strong contempt.

Stanza 1: Our chance in an awkward predicament may promise a great prospect of happiness; while our absence in happiness may possibly result in our absence in a strong contempt.

Line 5 star: a symbol for good luck.
Line 6 Some: somebody.
Line 7 mist: thin fog; difficulties.

<u>Stanza 2</u>: If in our life we have the good luck too frequently, some of us would miss the way. However, if we account difficulties very often and are able to overcome them, we will be more confident for a bright future.

参考译文

我们要忍受黑夜

我们要忍受黑夜，
我们也要向往黎明，
我们要用幸福把空白填写，
我们也用蔑视填空。
此处吉星高照，彼处福星悬空，
有人却把方向迷失。
此处薄雾弥漫，彼处浓云形成，
云雾散去后——灿烂白日。
（李正栓 译）

(8) This Is My Letter to the World (441)

This is my letter to the World
That never wrote to Me—
The simple News that Nature told—
With tender Majesty

5 Her Message is committed
To Hands I cannot see—
For love of Her—Sweet—countrymen—
Judge tenderly—of Me

Notes

Line 2 That: the world.
　　　　wrote to Me: offered me anything knowledgeable.
Line 3 The simple News: all the simple knowledge about the universe.

Stanza 1: This is a letter I wrote to the world, the world of men, which provided nothing knowledgeable to me before. If I have learned something about this world, it is Nature which, very tenderly and solemnly, has passed me all the message.

Line 5 Her Message: Nature's message; all the mysteries in nature.
Lines 5 - 6 is committed to: is promised to a certain cause or position.
Line 6 Hands I cannot see: people I don't know; the reader.
Line 7 Her: nature.
　　　　Sweet: my dearest people.
　　　　countrymen: my fellows.

Stanza 2: I have honestly passed all my realization of nature to the people I do not quite know. So for the sake of our love to nature, I plead with all—either intimates or nodding acquaintances—for a tender judgment to me. As a poet, Emily Dickinson takes poetry as a medium to attain pleasure, to preach her doctrine, to express her comprehension of the world, but she is unable to know whom her readers are. Thus she pleads with them for a fair judgment.

参考译文

这是我写给世界的信 (441)

这是我写给世界的信，
它却从不把我理会——
是大自然通报了简单的信息——
充满了温柔与权威

她把信息交到
我看不见的手里——

Section Three
American Poetry of High Romantic Period

为了爱她——亲爱的——同胞们——
评判我——要充满柔情蜜意
（李正栓 译）

(9) I Died for Beauty (449)

I died for beauty, but was scarce
  Adjusted in the tomb,
When one who died for truth was lain
  In an adjoining room.

5 He questioned softly why I failed?
  "For beauty," I replied.
"And I for truth—themself are one;
  We brethren are," he said.

And so, as kinsmen met a-night,
10 We talked between the rooms,
Until the moss had reached our lips,
And covered up our names.

Notes

Line 1 beauty: the poet's comprehension of "beauty," including both natural beauty and the beauty of art. In this poem, the word refers more to the latter.
  scarce: hardly, barely.
Line 3 When: then quite unexpectedly or to my surprise (I discovered something)
  lain: laid.
Line 4 adjoining room: the next room (tomb).

Stanza 1: I died pursuing the beauty of art and immediately as I became accustomed to the new circumstance of a tomb, I was told that there was another who died for truth and arrived in the next room.

Line 5 failed: died; sacrificed myself.
Line 7 I for truth: I died for truth.
  themself: beauty and truth themselves.

The English Romantic poet John Keats wrote in *Ode On a Grecian Urn* the famous lines: "Beauty is truth, truth beauty—that is all ye know on earth and all ye need to know."

In this poem, Emily Dickinson shares Keats' belief that beauty and truth are closely related: they are one. Therefore, she deliberately misspells the "themselves": "Them" in the plural form because "beauty and truth are two things"; "Self" is in a single form because beauty and truth indicate one thing.

Line 8 We brethren are: We are brothers.

Stanza 2: I died for beauty and he died for truth. Since "beauty is truth, and truth beauty," we are as close as brothers, or like twins.

Line 9 a-night: at night

Line 11 moss: very small gray or yellow flowerless plant growing in thick masses on damp surfaces of trees or stones. An old English saying goes as "An rolling stone gathers no moss." Therefore, "moss had reached our lips" strongly suggests that the two of them must have been motionless and had kept talking for a very long time.

Line 12 (the moss has) covered up our names: we have naturally united into one; we have been completely forgotten by the human world.

Stanza 3: The two of us are like kinsmen who met at night, and we talked in separated rooms for a very long time until we have harmoniously united into one and have been completely forgotten by the human world.

This is the poem conveying Emily Dickinson's aesthetic view that beauty and truth are closely related.

参考译文

我为美而死 (449)

我为美而死,但还不怎么
适应坟墓里的生活,
这时一位为真理而死的人

Section Three
AMERICAN POETRY OF HIGH ROMANTIC PERIOD

被安放在隔壁墓室里。

他柔声问我我为什么失败而亡;
"为了美",我回答说,
"我为了真理——美和真是一样,
我们俩是兄弟,"他说。

就这样,像近亲在夜里相遇,
我们隔墙而谈,
直到青苔把我们的嘴封闭,
将我们的名字埋掩。
（李正栓　译）

(10) I Heard a Fly Buzz—When I Died—(465)

I heard a Fly buzz—when I died—
The Stillness in the Room
Was like the Stillness in the Air—
Between the Heaves of Storm—

5   The Eyes around — had wrung them dry—
And Breaths were gathering firm
For that last Onset—when the King
Be witnessed—in the Room—

I willed my Keepsakes—Signed away
10 What portion of me be
Assignable—and then it was
There interposed a Fly—

With Blue—Uncertain stumbling Buzz—
Between the light—and me—
15 And then the Windows failed—and then
I could not see to see—

Line 1 buzz: the continuous humming sound made by an insect as a bee,

167

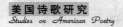

a fly or a wasp.
Line 4 Heaves: regular rises and falls of something.
Heaves of Storm: the rise and fall of the storm.

Stanza 1: When I was dying, I heard the buzz of a fly which reminded me of the stillness in the air.

Line 5 The Eyes around: the people who are around and watching me.
had wrung them dry: Those people (relatives and friends) had cried a lot so there were no more tears (in their eyes).
Line 6 And Breaths were gathering firm: People around me were holding their breath.
Line 7 last Onset: the arrival of death.
Onset: the vigorous beginning of something unpleasant.
the King: the god of death.
Line 8 Be witnessed: be seen; arrived.

Stanza 2: Before the absolute power of death, I was helpless, so were my relatives and friends. They could do nothing more than gathering around me, tearless and breathless, and watching the arrival of death to me.

Line 9 willed: wished; having made the arrangement for something to be left to others after my death.
Keepsakes: something usually small, given to be kept in memory of the giver.
Signed away: formally gave up.
Line 10 What portion of me be (assignable): (I formally gave up) what used to be part of me; (I gave off) all the material wealth which can be abandoned after death (with the implication that there is something like soul or spirit which is not assignable).
be: which was.
Line 11 Assignable: can be signed in a will; can be given to somebody as a share.
Lines 11 - 12 it was there interposed a fly: there was a fly appeared there; my assignment was interrupted by the appearance of a fly.
Line 12 interposed: put in between; came in between.

Stanza 3: When I was abandoning this material world, a fly comes to

Section Three
American Poetry of High Romantic Period

me.

Line 13 With Blue—Uncertain stumbling Buzz—: the fly is a "blue bottle" with shining blue abdomen. There is an old American folk-song, "The Bluetail Fly," which the poet probably had heard. These flies are attracted to carrion and will lay their eggs on a corpse.

- stumbling Buzz: in my weakening ears, the buzz is fading; I am losing my sense of hearing.

Line 15 the Windows failed: my eyes closed.
Line 16 I could not see to see—I could not see what I am seeing. I am losing my sense of eyes.

Comment on the poem

This poem is the description of the moment of death. The poetess made use of a very strange image of a fly to symbolize her last touch with the human world and, moreover, the perspective of a decaying corpse. The fly appeared as something which is able to fly between the two worlds of life and death.

Besides, the word "fly" is very cleverly used in the work. On the one hand, it refers to that insect; one the other hand, it may indicate "free flying": Before death, the "fly" was buzzing around, I hear it; after death, it may lead me to go far and forever, I am flying.

The fly is inconsequential, of little importance—implying perhaps that death is the same.

参考译文

我死时——听到一只苍蝇嗡嗡叫——（465）

我死时——听到一只苍蝇嗡嗡叫——
室内的寂静
像空气窒息了——
像风暴的间停——

周围的眼睛——已把眼泪哭干——
呼吸正在恢复平静
为了那最后的一击——有人看见，
死神——就在房中——

我立遗嘱——把我的纪念品分掉——
在想我的哪一部分
可以分赠——这时一只苍蝇嗡叫
打扰了我的事情——

嗡叫凄惨——声音飘忽,逐渐微弱——
回响在光——和我——之间——
随后,心的窗户关闭——在后来——
再也看不见先前所见——
(李正栓 译)

(11) I Like to See It Lap the Miles——(585)

    I like to see it lap the Miles—
    And lick the Valleys up—
    And stop to feed itself at Tanks—
    And then — prodigious step

5   Around a Pile of Mountains—
    And supercilious peer
    In Shanties—by the sides of Roads—
    And then a Quarry pare

    To fit it's Ribs
10 And crawl between
    Complaining all the while
    In horrid—hooting stanza—
    Then chase itself down Hill—

    And neigh like Boanerges—
15 Then—prompter than a Star

    Stop—docile and omnipotent
    At it's own stable door—

Section Three
American Poetry of High Romantic Period

Notes

Line 1 it: a train.
   lap the Miles: rapidly run for miles.
Line 2 lick the Valleys up: (the train) tenderly but closely goes through the valleys.
Line 3 feed itself at Tanks: fill itself up with water at tanks.
Line 4 prodigious step: (the train would move on with) enormous steps; (the train moved forward in) great speed.

Stanza 1: I enjoy the scene of a train gently passing through valleys. It may halt to fill itself with water and then go on rushing in greater speed.

Line 5 Around a Pile of Mountains: (the train moves) around a lot of mountains.
Line 6 And supercilious peer: And (the train) cast an arrogant look at the (shanties).
Line 7 In Shanties—by the sides of Roads: (The train would cast a ... look at) the poorly built huts, sheds or cabins appearing along the railways.
Line 8 And then a Quarry pare: And then (the train) glimpsed a quarry by the road sides.

Stanza 2: The train is able to run quickly and looks arrogantly at all the others along the railroads.

Line 9 To fit it's Ribs: (The train) is in the right size to run along the valley.
   fit: to be of the right size.
   it's: =its; the valley's.
   Ribs: the two sides; the slopes along the railroads; the ties that support the track resemble ribs.
Line 10 And crawl between: And (sometimes the train have to) climb (the slopes) between the valleys.
Line 11 Complaining all the while: (when climbing, the train was) complaining all the time.
Line 12 In horrid—hooting stanza: (the train) runs with a frightful sound that is quite similar to the noise from a factory. All the crawling, complaining comprise, as if, a stanza of a poetry.

The sounds of a train is compared to the comprising of a poem.
horrid: frightful; horrible.
hooting: sound made by a vehicle's horn, factory siren, etc.

Line 13 Then chase itself down Hill— : Then (the train) rushes swiftly down the hillside.

Stanza 3: With its speed and sounds, the train is in harmony with nature when it is running round the hills.

Line 14 And neigh like Boanerges: (The train would) cry loudly like Boanerges.
Boanerges: sons of thunder (Mark III, 17); a surname meaning "son of thunder," given by Christ to James and John. By extension, the word refers to any vociferous preacher or orator.

Line 15 prompter than a Star: (the train runs) swifter than the falling of a star.

Line 16 Stop: (the train) stops.
omnipotent: all-powerful.

Line 17 At it's own stable door: (The train stops) at the railway station. The train is here compared to a horse so it takes the station as a stable.

Stanza 4: The train presents great speed and noise when running, but it appears docile and dignified when motionless.

Comment on the poem

This poem is an interesting study of how Dickinson makes the train part of nature by animalizing it. A train, the product of industrial revolution, is animalized to be a harmonious part of nature. In the poet's eyes, when the train is running, it laps, licks and feeds itself like an animal; moreover, the train appears a passionate figure: it peers, crawls, complains; it even comprises poems; it is wild and swift when in motion, while it is still, it looks a majestic member of the world.

参考译文

我喜欢看它舔食一哩又一哩——(585)

我喜欢看它舔食一哩又一哩——

Section Three
American Poetry of High Romantic Period

喜欢看它舔食一谷又一谷——
喜欢看它停在水塔下把自己喂足——
之后——又迈步飞跃向前去

绕过一堆又一堆的山峦——
傲视道路两旁——
一间又一间的棚屋——
然后爬过石槽

这石槽是照它身材穿凿
它爬行其间
边爬边抱怨
声音可怖——语气不满——
之后又急冲下山——

鸣声似雷——
之后,神速如星

然后停下——温顺又崇高
停在自己的厩棚门口——
(李正栓 译)

(12) Because I Could Not Stop for Death (712)

Because I could not stop for death—
He kindly stopped for me—
The Carriage held but just Ourselves—
And Immortality.

5 We slowly drove—He knew no haste
And I had put away
My labor and my leisure too,
For His Civility—

We passed the School, where Children strove
10 At Recess—in the Ring—
We passed the Field of Gazing Grain—
We passed the Setting Sun—

Or rather—He passed Us—
The Dews drew quivering and chill—
15　For only Gossamer, my Gown—
My Tippet—only Tulle—

We paused before a House that seemed
A Swelling of the Ground—
The Roof was scarcely visible—
20　The Cornice—in the Ground—

Since then—'tis Centuries—and yet
Feels shorter than the Day
I first surmised the Horses' Heads
Were toward Eternity.

Notes

Line 2　He: death; angel of death. In this poem the angel of death is personified.
　　　　The angel of death is here presented as a very polite gentleman. The word "kindly" relaxes the solemn tone of this poem about death.
Line 3　Carriage: vehicle pulled by horses for carrying people; in this line, "Carriage" refers to hearse, a car to carry a body in a coffin to the funeral before being put in the grave.
　　　　Ourselves: the angel of death and the poet.
Line 4　Immortality: state of living forever (Here it is also personified); immortality appears in the same carriage with "death" and the poetess.

Stanza 1: The angel of death, in the image of a kind person, comes in a carriage for the sake of Immortality and the poet.

Line 5　He: god of death. God of death isn't in a hurry when doing his duty.
Line 6　put away: left over; gave up.
Line 8　Civility: politeness; respect.

Stanza 2: To show my politeness to god of death, I gave up my work

Section Three
American Poetry of High Romantic Period

and my enjoyment of life as well; I give up my life.

Line 10 Recess: play period during school session.
　　　　in the Ring: in the playground; standing in ring when playing games.
Line 11 Gazing Grain: the grain which is gazing upwards. The figurative speech of personification is skillfully used here to remind the reader that we, as human being, are just passers-by in this world; comparatively, the grain in the fields, growing year after year, is able to gaze upwards one generation after another.

Stanza 3: The journey of our carriage implies the experience of human life: school implies time for childhood; the fields of gazing grain, for youth and adulthood; while the setting sun, for old age.

Line 13 He: the setting sun.
Line 14 The Dews: the appearance of "the dews" implies the falling of night.
　　　　drew quivering and chill: brought me a sense of fear.
Line 15 (I felt chilly and frightened) because I was dressed only with Gossamer and Gown.
　　　　Gossamer: fine, 'silky substance of webs made by small spiders; very thin, silky materials, usually for woman's dresses. Here it refers to the shroud on the dead body.
Line 16 Tippet: long piece of fur, etc., worn by a woman round the neck and shoulder, with the end hanging down in front.
　　　　Tulle: soft fine silky net—like material used especially for veils and dresses.

Stanza 4: Probably we may say the sun sets before we reach the destination—the night falls, death arrives. I felt a fear and chilly after death, for my shroud is thin and my scarf too light. Despite the description of "death," the usual gloomy and horrifying atmosphere is lightened by the poetess with the elegantly fluttering clothing she describes.

Line 17 House: grave.
Line 20 Cornice: ornamental moulding in plaster, round the walls of a room, just below the ceiling.

Stanza 5: This stanza shifts to the description of the tomb. With the words as "House, swelling (which conveys a suggestive similarity to 'vault') roof," especially "cornice," the grave is described as a magnificent building.

Line 21 then: the arrival of my death.
Line 23 surmised: supposed; guessed.

Stanza 6: Several centuries had passed since the arrival of death upon me. However, I felt it is shorter than a day. On that day I suddenly realized that death is the starting point for eternity, and the carriage is heading towards it.

Comment on the poem

The poem is discussing death, a very gloomy subject, but it is done with a rather light tone. The tone is light just because the author does not take death as a catastrophe; instead, she treats the angel of death as a very polite gentleman, as a long-missing guest: giving up her work and leisure, putting on her fine silky dresses, she accompanies death in the same carriage to eternity. All the beauty of this work lies in the poetess' open-minded attitude towards death.

参考译文

因为我不能停下来等待死神——(712)

因为我不能停下来等待死神——
他却好心好意地停车来接我——
车内只有我和他——
不对,还有"永恒"。

我们驱车慢行——他不慌不忙
而我呢,我不再劳作
也不再闲暇,
以报答他的礼貌——

我们经过学校,孩子们正追逐喧闹,
恰是课间——操场欢腾——
我们经过望着我们的谷田——
我们经过西下的太阳——

Section Three
American Poetry of High Romantic Period

或可说——是太阳经过我们——
露水带来了凉意和寒战——
因为我衣薄如纱——
我肩只披绢——

我们在一幢房子前停车，
它似是地面隆起——
房顶几乎看不见——
屋檐——在地中——

自那以后——几百年过去了——然而
却感觉比那一天还短，
那一天我猜测拉车的马
头朝向永恒而去。
（李正栓　译）

(13) Alter? When the Hills Do (729)

Alter? When the hills do.
　　Falter? When the sun
Question if his glory
　　Be the perfect one.

5　Surfeit? When the daffodil
　　Doth of the dew:
Even as herself, O friend!
　　I will of you!

Notes

Line 1　Alter: become different; change. This is an abbreviated sentence for "Are you asking me whether my love for you will alter?"

Line 2　Falter: move or act hesitantly, usually because of fear or indecision. Another abbreviated sentence for "Are you asking me whether I am hesitating in loving you?"

Stanza 1: If you ask whether I'll alter, the reply from me is that my love for you will alter only when the hills change their shape; if you ask whether I am hesitating in loving you, my response is I would only when the sun doubts its power. (In fact, the sun's power is constant and thus I would never falter.)

Line 5 Surfeit: to be filled with too much of something; feel tired of something. This is the third abbreviated sentence for "Are you asking whether I am tired of your love?"
Line 7 herself: the daffodil in the 4th line.
O friend: my lover; my sweetheart.

<u>Stanza 2</u>: I would never feel tired of your love. I would only when the daffodil feels tired of the dews. But everybody knows that will never happen.

This is a eulogy for sincere love.

参考译文

变心？等到山无陵（729）

变心？等到山无陵。
迟疑？等到太阳
自问他的光荣
是否最完美和最有力量。

厌倦？等到水仙花
厌倦露珠时。
爱友啊，水仙只要厌露珠
我才把你来厌恶！
（李正栓　译）

(14) A Narrow Fellow in the Grass（986）

A narrow Fellow in the Grass
Occasionally rides—
You may have met Him—did you not
His notice sudden is—

Section Three
American Poetry of High Romantic Period

5   The Grass divides as with a Comb—
     A spotted shaft is seen—
     And then it closes at your feet
     And opens further on—

     He likes a Boggy Acre
10   A Floor too cool for Corn—
     Yet, when a Boy, and Barefoot—
     I more than once at Noon

     Have passed, I thought, a Whiplash
     Unbraiding in the Sun
15   When stooping to secure it
     It wrinkled, and was gone—

     Several of Nature's people
     I know, and they know me—
     I feel for them a transport
20   Of cordiality—

     But never met this Fellow
     Attended, or alone
     Without a tighter breathing
     And Zero at the Bone—

Notes

Line 1 A narrow Fellow: a snake; but the poet never directly mentions the word "snake" throughout the work. The concealment of the word is purposely designed to add mystery and subtlety to the description.

Line 2 Occasionally rides: (the narrow thing) sometimes appears, zigzags, moves (in the grass).

Line 3 did you not: haven't you ever met one of it (snake)?

Line 4 notice: appearance; he often appears suddenly.

Stanza 1: Whether you have seen them or not, in nature there are the narrow things of abrupt and surprising appearances.

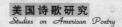

Line 5 (when a narrow thing passes) the grass is tidily divided in the middle as if by a comb.

Line 6 shaft: a long, slender bar or rod. Here it refers to the snake, which is "spotted."

Line 7 it: the grass.
　　　closes: the grass comes together again.

Line 8 opens further on: (when the narrow fellow has run off, its trace disappears at your feet but) the opening appears in the grass still further in front of you.

Stanza 2: When the narrow thing passes, the grass is often tidily divided as if by a comb and very abruptly, the division would disappear at your feet as it runs off from you.

Line 9 Boggy Acre: soft and wet place.

Line 10 A Floor: a place ("the boggy acre" in the above line).
　　　　too cool for Corn: (the boggy acre is a place) too cold to plant corn. But the narrow fellow likes it because I frequently met him there.

Line 11 when a Boy: when I was a boy.
　　　　Barefoot: when I was barefoot.

Line 12 I more than once at Noon: I met with the narrow fellow more than once at the boggy acre at noon.

Line 13 a Whiplash: when I met with it, I didn't recognize it at once, so I mistook it for a whip.

Line 14 Unbraiding: uncoiling; staying straight.

Line 15 to secure: to pick up; to get hold of.

Line 16 wrinkled: coiled up; twisted.

Stanza 3: The description of her meeting the coachwhip, a yellow snake with black spots, noted for its great speed. The scales on its tail give it the appearance of a braided leather whip, hence the name.

Line 17 Nature's people: various animals in nature.

Line 20 cordiality: sincerity and friendship.

Stanza 4: I feel sharing a friendship with those familiar Nature's people. We stay in harmony with each other.

Line 22 Attended: accompanied by others.

Section Three
American Poetry of High Romantic Period

Line 23 a tighter breathing: too frightened to breathe freely.
Line 24 Zero at the Bone: a sense of chill, of being frightened at the deepest part.

Stanza 5: But whenever I met with this narrow fellow, whether I was with any companion or alone, I could not help the cold shivers running down my spine.

Comment on the poem

This is a short poem in which the poet defamiliarised what she was describing. What is "the narrow fellow"? The poet did not tell. Instead, detailed description of it is generously offered— its appearance, zigzags and moves in the grass; its tidily dividing of grass in the middle as if by a comb, and the memory of meeting it in childhood; the dictions is accurate and the presentation is vividly done. The poet feels sharing a friendship with these familiar Nature's people and feels quite able to stay in harmony with it.

参考译文

草地里有一个瘦长的家伙（986）

草地里有一个瘦长的家伙
他有时奔驰——
你可能见到过——或许没见过，
他突然的预报是——

草地被分开，好像梳子拢过——
带斑点的细杆出现——
之后他接近您脚下——
然后又继续向前——

他喜湿地泥沼，
谷物难以适应其寒冷——
但当我还是孩子时，赤着双脚——
在中午时分，我不止一次

见到他，我以为是鞭绳

散落在阳光中，
我弯腰去捡，
他却扭曲着离去了——

大自然中不少的居民
我知道，他们也认识我——
我为他们感到激动，
那是一种亲情——

但从来未遇到这个家伙，
不管是与人结伴还是一人独行，
无不感到呼吸急促，
还感到一种彻骨的寒冷——
（李正栓 译）

(15) Tell All the Truth But Tell It Slant—(1129)

Tell all the Truth but tell it slant—
Success in Circuit lies
Too bright for our infirm Delight
The truth's superb surprise

5   As Lightning to the Children eased
With explanation kind
The Truth must dazzle gradually
Or every man be blind—

Notes

Line 1 slant: not straight up and down; mildly; tactfully.
Line 2 Circuit: circling the truth, circumlocution.
Line 3 Too bright for: (the power of the truth is) too bright for...;
     too much to bear.
     infirm Delight: the state when we believe we are in a great joy.
     People are likely to believe they are in happiness, but the truth
     may be rather shocking, rather cruel, or simply on the contrary;
     that's why the "Delight" is "infirm."
     Here the poet is implying that human beings are too often in-

Section Three
American Poetry of High Romantic Period

dulged in fantasy to face reality.
Line 4 superb: perfect in form, quality, wonderful.

Stanza 1: The superb surprise of truth is too much for us who are not quite ready for it. Thus if one has to tell the truth, tell it indirectly.

Line 5 As Lightning to the Children: the truth to people may be like lightning to children. A simile is used in this line for a further explanation. The superb surprise of a truth is compared to "Lightning," which suggests something rather astonishing and shocking.
eased: comforted.
With kind explanation, (the shock of lightning to children) can be comforted.
Line 7 dazzle: be blinded with too much light.
The truth must be presented little by little.
Line 8 Or: otherwise.

Stanza 2: Truth should be presented gradually as the fear of lightning to children be eased with tender explanation; otherwise, someone would be unexpectedly hurt by the cruelty of truth.

Comment on the poem

The idea Emily Dickinson wants to convey in this poem is that, though everybody is a part of nature and honesty is important, people need careful strategy when communicating with others, since people sometimes enjoy a fantastic world rather than a real one. The true face of reality, as lightning, if coming directly, may be disastrous to someone. What's more important, when people are accustomed to a certain atmosphere, it is not easy for them to accept anything new. It takes time for people to adjust the eyes for any new light.

参考译文

要讲出全部真理,但不要直言——(1129)

要讲出全部真理,但不要直言——

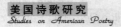

成功之道在于迂回。
对真理超人的惊喜，
脆弱的喜悦难胜任过分的辉煌。

正像用好故事解除孩子们
对闪电的恐惧，
真理要逐渐展现，
否则会令人目眩——
（李正栓　译）

(16) We Never Know How High (1176)

We never know how high we are
　　Till we are called to rise;
And then, if we are true to plan,
　　Our stature touch the skies.

5　The heroism we recite
　　Would be a daily thing,
Did not ourselves the cubits warp
　　For fear to be a king.

Notes

Line 1 how high: what capacity, ambitions we have.
Line 2 we are called to rise: we are encouraged to complete a plan.
Line 3 then: when we have been encouraged.
　　　　true to plan: have done what we can; faithful to ourselves.
Line 4 stature: a person's natural height; one's potential capacity.

Stanza 1: We are not always aware of ourselves. Actually we do not know what capacities we have unless we are encouraged by others to do something to prove them. While once we are encouraged to do something and to attempt persistently, we find ourselves much more competent than we can imagine. We were created with the capacity to touch the sky (extremely high).

Line 5 we recite: (what) we repeatedly mentioned; (what) we used to

Section Three
American Poetry of High Romantic Period

  admire very much.
Line 6 a daily thing: something easy to get; trifles.
Line 7 cubits: a measure of length, originally the length of the forearm—from the elbow to the tip of the middle finger; it is about 18 to 22 inches.
  warp: cause to turn or twist out of shape.
Line 8 For fear to: because of the anxiety that.
  king: an image for a very important person; a very high social position.

<u>Stanza 2</u>: Once we have realized how capable we are, the heroic deeds we used to admire are no longer an empty illusion. We distort the heights we could actually achieve out of our fear to take responsibility.

This poem reveals a remarkable personality of self-confidence and self-assertion.

参考译文

我们从来不知有多高 (1176)

我们从来不知我们有多高，
直到有人要我们起飞；
那时，如果把计划中的事做完；
我们的身材就能摸到天

口头常提的英雄主义
会是司空见惯的小事，
我们没有因为怕当上国王
就把自己的腕尺拧弯。
（李正栓　译）

(17) He Ate and Drank the Precious Words (1587)

He ate and drank the precious words,
  His spirit grew robust;
He knew no more that he was poor,
  Nor that his frame was dust.

5   He danced along the dingy days,
        And this bequest of wings
    Was but a book. What liberty
        A loosened spirit brings!

Notes

Line 1 He: any person.
       the precious words: knowledge, the *Bible*.
Line 2 robust: strong; healthy.
Line 3 He knew no more: He no longer felt.
Line 4 Nor that: he no longer felt ... either.
       his frame: the human or animal body.
       This line suggests an allusion to the *Bible*. "For dust thou art, and unto dust shalt thou return." (*Genesis*, III. p19)

Stanza 1: Once a person has read the *Bible*, he becomes healthy and strong in spirit. He no longer feels he is humble, nor does he feel life empty.

Line 5 danced: moved or went freely and gracefully.
       dingy: dirty and faded.
       dingy days: unpleasant time.
Line 6 bequest of wings: knowledge as wings which are left to us as property by our ancestors.
Line 8 a loosened spirit: well-learned, freed mind; liberated thought.
       The relaxation of mind would bring you to a world of liberty.

Stanza 2: (If one has a profound knowledge) he would feel easier in difficulties and would be able to face frustrations with grace. All his strength and grace, which, as wings added to a person, are derived from the knowledge of the world. Thus we cannot help admiring the well-learned mind bringing great liberty to the human being!

This poem is a song of knowledge.

Section Three
AMERICAN POETRY OF HIGH ROMANTIC PERIOD

参考译文

他吃喝了珍贵的文字 (1587)

他吃喝了珍贵的文字，
精力变得充沛；
他再也不知什么是贫穷，
再也不想他体格是泥土做成。

在黑暗的日子里他欢舞，
这飞行章赠物
只是一本书。解放了的精神
带来何等的自由！
（李正栓　译）

(18) I Never Saw a Moor

I never saw a Moor—
I never saw the Sea—
Yet know I how the Heather looks
And what a Billow be.

5   I never spoke with God
Nor visited in Heaven—
Yet certain am I of the spot
As if the Checks were given—

Notes

Line 3 Yet know I how the Heather looks: Yet I know how the Heather looks.
    Heather（石南属植物）: low evergreen plant or shrub with small purple or white bell-shaped flowers, common on moorland.
Line 4 Billow: large, rolling wave.

Stanza 1: Although I had never had the chance to see a moor or the sea, I know what the wild plant looks like, and how the wave rolls.

Line 7 the spot: the heaven.
Line 8 the Checks: the exact description of heaven.

Stanza 2: Although I never had the chance to speak with God, nor did I have the chance to visit heaven, I am quite certain about everything in heaven as if someone had described it to me. This is a poem singing for the power of imagination.

参考译文

我从未见过荒野

我从未见过荒野——
也从未见过大海——
但我知道石楠花的模样
也知道巨浪的形状。

我从未跟上帝对话,
也从未去过天国——
但我知道天堂的样子
仿佛有人已经描述过——
（李正栓　译）

(19) To Make a Prairy

To make a prairy it takes a clover and a bee—
One clover and a bee
And revery.
The revery alone will do,
5　If bees are few.

Notes

Line 1　prairy: prairie; wide area of level grassland.
　　　　 clover: any of various types of small, usually 3 leafed plants with pink, purple or white flowers, often grown as food for cattle.

Section Three
American Poetry of High Romantic Period

Line 3 revery: reverie. (A state or occasion of) pleasant thoughts and dreams while awake; imagination.

Comment on the poem

It takes a clover and a bee to make a prairie. However, without any clover or bees, a person may also have the landscape of a prairie quite out of his imagination.

This is a song of imagination. The poet suggests that a human being's imagination can be as reliable as experience.

参考译文

要制造草原

要制造草原,需要苜蓿和蜜蜂——
一株苜蓿、一只蜂,
还需要想象。
如果蜜蜂不多,
想象本身就够了。
（李正栓　译）

(20) The Sky Is Low— The Clouds Are Mean

The sky is low — the Clouds are mean.
A Travelling Flake of Snow
Across a Barn or through a Rut
Debates if it will go—
5   A narrow Wind complains all Day
How some one treated him.
Nature, like Us is sometimes caught
Without her Diadem.

Notes

Line 1 mean: gloomy; (the sky) gray; poor in appearance.
Line 2 A Travelling Flake of Snow: a flying flake.
Line 3 The flake is hesitating whether it should fly across the barn or fly

through a rut.
Line 4 Debates: considers; argues with itself.
Lines 2 – 4 A flying flake is doubting which direction to take.
Line 5 A narrow Wind: A narrow-minded wind.
Line 6 How some one treated him: How badly, how indifferently the others had treated him.
Line 7 Us: Human beings.
Line 8 Diadem: crown worn as a sign of royal power; dignity.

Comment on the poem

The poet intends to confirm that nature—the sky, clouds and wind—is quite similar to human beings: It is not constantly clear, soft, gentle, or respectable. Instead, it hesitates, complains; it may feel depressed for a while and it becomes passionate the next. In a word, it is just these similarities between human and nature bring the two closer.

参考译文

天低——云黑

天低——云黑。
一片行走的雪花，
穿谷仓，越车辙，
该走还是该歇——
微风成天抱怨
有人曾把他虐待。
像我们人类一样,有时发现
大自然也不戴头冠。
（李正栓　译）

(21) Apparently with No Surprise (1624)

Apparently with no surprise
To any happy Flower
The Frost beheads it at its play—
In accidental power—
5 　The blonde Assassin passes on—
The Sun proceeds unmoved

Section Three
American Poetry of High Romantic Period

To measure off another Day
For an Approving God.

Notes

Line 3 it: the flower.
　　　　its: the frost's; or, the flower's, more likely.
　　　　at its play: when the flower is playing; do something playfully, very easily.
Line 4 (The frost hurts the flower when it is playing) quite by accident.
Line 5 blonde: *n.* the golden-haired girl; *adj.* pretty.
　　　　Assassin: a person who murders for political reason or reward. Here it refers to "frost" which has done harm to flowers.
Line 6 proceeds unmoved: doesn't respond properly.
Line 7 to measure off: to go on its (the sun's) movement.
Line 8 For an Approving God: God approves the changing of the seasons, even though the flowers die.

Comment on the poem

　　The frost, as an image for the demonic power in nature, may accidentally destroy the flower, an image for noble spirits. However, the sun is indifferent to all the harms the cruel frost had done just for the sake of pleasing God.

　　Emily Dickinson intends to reveal that god is indifferent and sometimes showed His power in evil force, which may appear under pretty decoration and exist as a natural part of this world. Flowers grow but frost destroys them all by nature when autumn arrives. God's continual renewal of the world is wise and just, though it entails suffering and death.

参考译文

显然不惊讶（1624）

显然不惊讶：
对任何幸福的花朵，
严霜轻易地将它斩首——

不用故意去杀——
这白色杀手继续前进——
太阳直行,无动于衷,
去为悦人的上帝
裁制另一天。
（李正栓　译）

Section Four

American Poetry of the Modernist Period

I. Robert Frost
(1874 – 1963)

1. Life Story

In the 20th century, Robert Lee Frost was perhaps the most beloved poet in America and the most successful American poet widely accepted all over the world. He was the Pulitzer Prize winner on four occasions; he received honorary degrees from about 40 colleges and universities; and the American government presented him a gold medal in 1960 for his contribution to American culture. His works have been translated into most foreign languages and are being continually enjoyed by the readers of the world. Actually, during his life time, Frost won almost all the great honors a poet can receive in this world, except the Nobel Prize. In 1961, when Frost was 87, he was honored to read one of his poems, "The Gift Outright", at the inauguration of President John F. Kennedy. In 1963, Frost received the Bollingen Prize just before his death on January 29 at the age of 88.

Frost, though his parents were New Englanders, was born in California. His father, a graduate of Harvard and a newspaper reporter, died when Frost was 11, and his mother brought Frost and his sisters back to New Hampshire, where he was educated and managed to graduate from high school at the top of his class.

Frost began his writing of poems very early and got a good reputation for it. But after school, he had to run a farm left by his grandfather to support the family. In spite of many years' work in the field, Frost, though a sincere lover of nature and country life, was always an inept farmer, but a voracious reader, and he kept writing poems all those days. However, Frost's path to recognition was unfortunately quite a long one: most of his poetic works were refused by publishing houses in the United States and, therefore, he decided to sell the farm and venture everything on a literary career. In 1912, he sailed for England, together with his wife, five children and a full case of manuscripts of his poems.

The year after his arrival in England, Frost's first book of poetry, *A Boy's Will* (1913) was published. It was Ezra Pound, who felt he heard a fresh voice in Frost, who brought him to the attention of influential critics and introduced him to British publishers. In 1914, his second volume of poems, *North of Boston* (1914) came out in England, but Frost and his large family were forced to return to the United States because of the First World War. Upon his arrival, Frost was most surprised to find a warm welcome from American people and American publishers. Anyway, Frost still chose to live on his own farm. Now his poems were able to make him enough money to hire assistants to run the farm well.

Although his fame grew with the appearance of a succession of books and papers, Frost continued to write in his own style, not influenced by his friend Ezra Pound as so many other writers of the time were. He considered the farm his home and its activities remained the focus of his poetic works.

2. Major Works of Frost

Frost was a very diligent writer all his life. Besides what we mentioned above, Frost provided to the world a rather large number of poetic works, including:

(1) *Mountain Interval* (1916), containing such characteristic poems as "The Road Not Taken" and "Birches."
(2) *New Hampshire* (1923), which won Frost the first of his four Pulitzer Prizes includes "Stopping by Woods on a Snowy Evening."
(3) *West-Running Brook* (1928).
(4) The second Pulitzer Prize was gained by his *Collected Poems* (1930).
(5) *Further Range* (1935), which won him the Pulitzer Prize for the third time.
(6) *Witness Tree* (1942), which brought him the fourth Pulitzer Prize.

3. Writing Features of Robert Frost

(1) Frost's themes: Frost was a serious poet. Though he is generally considered a regional poet whose subject matters mainly focus on the landscape and people of New England, he wrote many poems that investigate the basic themes of human life. He wrote about the daily life of ordinary people—farmers, shepherds; small rural events, fence mending, apple picking, good and evil, all the matters of life and death.

Some were not frequent poetical subjects for his time, but he insisted on them, not as ways to escape from modern society, but as ways to understand life better.

(2) Frost's style: Frost had long been well known as a poet who can hardly be classified with the old or the new. Unlike most of his contemporaries in the early 20th century, Frost did not break with the older poetic tradition, nor did he make many experiments with form. Instead, Frost learned from tradition and made the colloquial New England speech into a poetic expression. Hence Frost's poems are full of life, truth, and wisdom. Compared with his contemporaries, his poems are filled with more energy and loaded with more pleasure, while those of the latter are often too obscure to be understood by the average reader.

(3) Combination of tradition and modernism. Frost combined the traditional sonnet, rhyming couplets, and blank verse with a clear American local speech rhythm. In verse form, he took advantage of tradition and of the experiments of his contemporaries; he wrote in both metrical forms and free verse, sometimes he wrote in a form that borrows freely from both—a form that might be called semi-free and semi-conventional. Thus his poems are careful, loving explorations of reality. Many of his poems are fragrant with natural beauty.

(4) Deceptive simplicity. Frost wrote in a simple form with profound ideas. Most of his poems are short and direct on the informational level, with simple diction. However, it would be a mistake to imagine that Frost is easy to understand just because he is easy to read. As a matter of fact, Frost's poems were very carefully constructed, yet he made them seem effortless by using colloquial language and familiar, conventional rhythms. The profound ideas are often delivered under the disguise of plain language and simple form, for what Frost did is to take symbols from the limited human world and the pastoral landscape to refer to the great space beyond the rustic scene.

Most of Frost's major poems were written before 1930, although he kept on writing all the way through the 1950s and into the 1960s. In the last twenty years of his life, he devoted himself mostly to the poetry of religious themes. In the 1940's, he wrote some long poems in blank verse— "A Masque of Reason" (1945), "Steeple Bush" (1947), and "A Masque of Mercy" (1947), all are dramatic dialogues—discussions of religious insights and contemporary society.

Section Four
American Poetry of the Modernist Period

4. Selected Poems

(1) The Road Not Taken

Two roads diverged in a yellow wood,
And sorry I could not travel both
And be one traveler, long I stood
And looked down one as far as I could
5   To where it bent in the undergrowth;

Then took the other, as just as fair,
And having perhaps the better claim,
Because it was grassy and wanted wear;
Though as for that the passing there
10 Had worn them really about the same.

And both that morning equally lay
In leaves no step had trodden black.
Oh, I kept the first for another day!
Yet knowing how way leads on to way,
15 I doubted if I should ever come back.

I shall be telling this with a sigh
Somewhere ages and ages hence:
Two roads diverged in a wood, and I—
I took the one less traveled by,
20 And that has made all the difference.

Notes

Line 1 diverged: went out in different directions.
       yellow wood: an implication of the season—autumn.
Line 4 looked down one: looked along one of the two roads.
Line 5 bent: turned away; disappeared.

Stanza 1: The poem begins as if when the poet was walking in a wood in late autumn at a fork in the road. He was choosing which road he should follow. Actually, it is concerned with the important decisions which one must make in life: one must give up one desirable thing in order to possess the other.

Line 6 the other: (the traveler is determined to take) the other road of the two.
as just as fair: (the second road looks) in the same condition as the first one. My choice of the second road is as reasonable as the choice of the first.
Line 7 the better claim: a better reason (for taking the second road).
Line 8 wanted wear: (My reason for taking the other road is) because that road did not look quite worn out; it appeared more isolated, less used.
Line 9 as for that: concerning the condition of the second road.
the passing there: the frequency of people passing that road; people's footprints on that road.
Line 10 worn them really about the same: the two roads have been trodden in almost the same degree, neither is better than the other, actually.
them: the two roads.

Stanza 2: After the judgment and hesitation, the traveler makes up his mind to take the road which looks grassy and wants wear. This is often believed to be the symbol of the poet's choice of a solitary life—taking poetry writing as his life profession.

Line 11 both: both roads.
Line 12 In leaves no step had trodden black: (that morning both roads were covered by) the fallen leaves of trees which had not been trodden black by anybody.
Line 13 the first: the first road.
for another day: for next choice.
Line 14 way leads on to way: one road may branch into several minor ways. It may diverge into many branches. In human life, one choice leads to more further choices.
Line 15 come back: return to the first road (to keep my promise of taking it for the next choice).

Stanza 3: The two roads are equally pretty, so as soon as he made the choice of the one, the poet felt pitiful for abandoning the other. He is quite aware that his intention of "next choice" will be nothing than an empty promise.

Line 16 telling this with a sigh: He regrets his decision. His regret doesn't lie in his choice of the first road, but in that he was unable to take both.

this: the poet's choice of one road and abandonment of the other.

Line 20 all the difference: the difference of my life from that of the others'.

Stanza 4: The poet was imagining many years later when he is recalling the choice he made today, he would respond with nothing else but a sigh, for it would be too hard for anyone, after many more experiences in life, to make any comment on the choice made early in life.

Comment on the poem

Robert Frost is a master at pulling a thread out of what looks like quite a simple theme. This poem, as many of Frost's poems, begins with the observation of nature, as if the poet is a traveler sightseeing in nature. By the end, all the simple words condense into a serious, philosophical proposition: When anyone in life is confronted with making a choice, in order to possess something worthwhile, he has to give up something which seems as lovely and valuable as the chosen one. Then, whatever follows, he must accept the consequence of his choice for it is not possible for him to return to the beginning and have another chance to choose differently. Frost is asserting that nature is fair and honest to everyone. Thus all the varieties of human destiny result from each person's spontaneous capability of making choices.

This is also a symbolic poem. The "yellow wood" may symbolize sophisticated society, in which most people are likely to follow a profitable but easier way; each "road" symbolizes a possibility in life; the "traveller" is the embodiment of every individual in the human world; the road which is "grassy and wanted wear" refers to a solitary life style; while "way leads to way" implies the complicated circumstances of the human world. Through the description of "A Road Not Taken," the poet presents to the reader his experience of taking a road. With simple words and profound connotation, Robert Frost teaches. However, in the form of a natural poem, he teaches delightfully.

The poem is very regularly structured with 4 classic 5-line stanzas, with the rhyme scheme "abaab" and in conversational rhythm.

美国诗歌研究
Studies on American Poetry

参考译文

一条未走的路

两条路岔开在黄叶秋林，
遗憾我不可能同时都走，
遗憾我只是孤身一人，
我伫立远眺想看到路遥终尽，
只见那路拐进矮树林里头。

于是我选了另一条，同样不错，
或许我更有理由选择它，
因为这路上长满了野草未经踩磨；
尽管这条路经人走过
与第一条路同样足迹乱杂。

那天早晨，两条路同时摆在我面前，
树叶埋住台阶，还没被踩黑；
第一条留待日后再去选！
但又知道，路尽路始紧接连，
我怀疑我是否还能再回归。

很久很久以后在某处，
我会叹息着把这事情讲：
两条路岔开在一林，我未跬蹰——
选择了一条人们较少走的路，
而这选择竟决定了人间与天上。
（李正栓　译）

(2) Stopping by Woods on Snowy Evening

Whose woods these are I think I know.
His house is in the village, though;
He will not see me stopping here
To watch his woods fill up with snow.

5　My little horse must think it queer

Section Four
American Poetry of the Modernist Period

    To stop without a farmhouse near
    Between the woods and frozen lake
    The darkest evening of the year.

    He gives his harness bells a shake
10 To ask if there is some mistake.
    The only other sound's the sweep
    Of easy winds and downy flake.

    The woods are lovely, dark and deep.
    But I have promises to keep,
15 And miles to go before I sleep—
    And miles to go before I sleep.

Notes

Line 1 woods: This image frequently appears in Frost's poems, symbolizing the mystery of nature, death or catastrophe.
Line 2 His: the owner of the woods.
Line 4 snow: Another frequent image in Frost's poems. It usually symbolizes something of purity and loftiness.
Line 9 He: my little horse.
Line 10 To ask: the horse asks me (whether there is a mistake). The little horse is personified.
Line 12 downy flake: the soft and finely patterned snow flakes.
Line 13 dark and deep: The phrase is alliterated to enhance the mysterious atmosphere of woods in darkness. The woods, while covered by snow, appear lovely; but as a matter of fact, they are filled with mysteries.
Line 14 promises: one's responsibility or duty in the world.
Line 15 miles: long distance; heavy duty in life.
        sleep: rest during night; end of life.

Comment on the poem

    The poem presents a picture of tranquility: On a winter evening, a sleigh driver stopped by a wood while everything is covered with snow. The poet is enjoying a momentary relaxation on the onerous journey of life. The woods are lovely, but dark and deep. The man is alone with nature in a peaceful scene; however, the scene of tranquility, though appearing in peace and harmony, is not without the temptation of death. The speaker, as the poet himself, for a while was rather attracted by the mystery of death. Fortunately, his former promises reminded him of his responsibility in the world and he was thus detached from the dark woods, which may quite possibly be taken as a mysterious seduction to suicide. The repetition of the last two lines indicates the speaker's sense of responsibility or simply his helplessness in front of nature.

The poem is written regularly in iambic tetrameter with 4 lines in 4 stanzas, with the rhyme scheme as "aaba, bbcb, ccdc, dddd."

参考译文

雪夜停林边

这是谁家的树林我想我知道,
尽管他家住在村子里;
他看不见我在这儿停住并观瞧
他的林中雪栖树枝落满地。

我那匹小马肯定认为很古怪,
在这一年中最灰暗的黄昏,
湖面冰封,近无人家,林木雪盖,
停在这儿是什么原因?

它摇动缰铃,似乎在问:
你停在这里,有没有搞错?
此外别无任何的声音,
只有清风徐来,雪花飘落。

树林幽深,景色迷人,
不过,我有约要赴,
须走路程遥远才能投宿,
须走路程遥远才能投宿。
　　　　　（李正栓 译）

(3) **After Apple-picking**

My long two-pointed ladder's sticking through a tree

Toward heaven still,
And there's a barrel that I didn't fill
Beside it, and there may be two or three
5 Apples I didn't pick upon some bough.
But I am done with apple-picking now.
Essence of winter sleep is on the night,
The scent of apples: I am drowsing off.
I cannot rub the strangeness from my sight
10 I got from looking through a pane of glass
I skimmed this morning from the drinking trough
And I held against the world of hoary grass.
It melted, and I let it fall and break.
But I was well
15 Upon my way to sleep before it fell,
And I could tell
What form my dreaming was about to take.
Magnified apples appear and disappear,
Stem end and blossom end,
20 And every fleck of russet showing clear.
My instep arch not only keeps the ache,
It keeps the pressure of a ladder-round.
I feel the ladder sway as the boughs bend
And I keep hearing from the cellar bin
25 The rumbling sound
Of load on load of apples coming in.
For I have had too much
Of apple-picking: I am overtired
Of the great harvest I myself desired.
30 There were ten thousand thousand fruit to touch,
Cherish in hand, lift down, and not let fall.
For all
That struck the earth,
No matter if not bruised or spiked with stubble,
35 Went surely to the cider-apple heap
As of no worth.
One can see what will trouble
This sleep of mine, whatever sleep it is.
Were he not gone,
40 The woodchuck could say whether it's like his
Long sleep, as I describe its coming on,

Or just come human sleep.

Notes

Line 1 two-pointed ladder: the ladder with two pointed up-ends.
Lines 1 – 2 sticking through a tree toward heaven still: ... is still pointing through a tree towards heaven.
Line 2 heaven: the sky; or with the implication of "paradise."
Line 4 it: the ladder. The barrel is beside the ladder.
Line 6 I am done with: I have kept picking apples for such a long that I'm rather tired of it; I have finished the picking of apples for the day.
Line 7 I am entirely exhausted by the picking that I feel I am grabbed by a winter sleep.
    on the night: (the sleep is) approaching; the night air is pervaded with the intention of a sound sleep.
Line 8 The scent of apples: in the nice smell of the fresh apples.
    drowsing off: falling into a light sleep; dozing off.
Line 9 rub...from...: delete; drive... away...
    strangeness: a sense of surprise; the approaching of drowsing.
Line 10 I got from: my sub-conscious or dream begins with (the scene of looking through a pane of glass, actually, through a piece of transparent ice).
Line 11 skimmed: (the piece of ice) I took/picked up from the surface of water in the drinking trough this morning.
    drinking trough: long narrow boxlike object for holding water or food for domestic animals.
Line 12 I held against: I held the piece of ice to my eyes so as to look through it at the hoary grass.
    hoary grass: old, dry and decaying grass in gray color, covered with frost.
Line 13 It: the ice.
Lines 14 – 15 But I was already quite asleep before the ice's falling to the ground.
Lines 16 – 18 Because of my toil of picking apples all day, when I am napping now, apples appear and disappear in my dream in exaggerated shapes.
Line 19 Stem end and blossom end: (in my dream) apples come with their top end or the bottom end towards me.

Section Four
American Poetry of the Modernist Period

Line 20 every fleck of russet showing clear: Because of one whole days picking, I am now able to distinguish the brown spots on different apple peels.

Line 21 instep arch: the curved part of the upper surface of one's foot.
not only keeps the ache: not only keeps worrying me with the pain.

Line 22 It keeps the pressure of a ladder-round: (In my sleep,) I can still feel the pain caused by the pressure of the ladder stick as if I am going on with picking.
In Lines 21–22, "keep" is repeated to imply both the physical pressure the poet suffered and the psychological pressure as well.

Lines 21–23 In these lines, while resting in a dream, the poet could not help feeling his picking.

Line 24 the cellar bin: the underground room for storing fruits.

Line 25 rumbling sound: deep, heavy, continuous sound; the sound of pouring apples into the cellar bins.

Line 26 load on load of apples: apples of one truck-load after another.
coming in: coming to my ears (while I am dreaming); coming into the bins.
In Lines 24–28, the sound of pouring apples remains to the poet's ears in the dream.

Lines 29–30 I longed for a big harvest every year. But now when I have got it, I feel tired of it just because of too many apples to pick.

Line 31 Cherish in hand: When I am picking, I have to protect or tend the apples lovingly.
lift down: very carefully to put down the apples; most people would use "pull down." By using "life down," Frost magnifies the care of his picking.

Line 32 For all: for all the apples.

Line 33 struck the earth: (apples) fall accidentally down to the ground.

Line 34 if not bruised: whether or not (the apple) is injured on the skin.
spiked with stubble: injured by the short stiff remains of the twigs under the trees.

Line 35 Went surely to the cider-apple heap: (While the apples are being picked, they are classified. Thus, the fallen apples, whether injured or not,) will sure be sorted out for cider.
cider-apple heap: heap of apples sorted out for making cider—an alcoholic drink made from apple juice. Most cider is drunk as

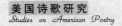

plain sweet juice, only a minority is fermented in America.

Line 36 As of no worth: (apples sorted out for making hard cider) are believed to be worthless.

Lines 37 – 38 Everyone can easily observe that whatever sleep it is, it will sure be troubled by image of apples. I can't have a peaceful rest, because I am overtired.

Line 39 Were he not gone: If I had a woodchuck with me.

Line 40 it: my sleep.

Lines 40 – 41 like his long sleep: like the woodchuck's hibernation.

Line 41 as I describe its coming on: as I have described that the long sleep, an image for death, is ushering in.

Line 42 Or just one human sleep: Or (my sleep is) just a short nap after hard work.

Comment on the poem

This is one of Frost's narrative poems on the New England pastoral landscape. The poet takes advantage of the stream-of-consciousness skill to convey what the narrator feels after his apple-picking for a whole day. However, the picking of apples can be taken as the symbolic annotation to the writer's persisting pursuit of a lofty ideal. Consequently, instead of concentrating on the bumper harvest of the labor, in the poet's monologue, emphasis lies more on his succulent apperception of life, and on the objective claim after picking. Therefore the picking of apples may refer to his career of poetry writing, which brought him a great reputation, but has exhausted him to the extreme as well.

The poet presents a paradoxical image by "I am overtired / Of the great harvest I myself desired" (Lines 28 – 29). This is the conflict between ideal and reality: everyone longs for achievements; however, people are by nature to take achievements for granted if once they swarm in. Yet despite the exhausting toil, the poet deals with every apple very attentively, as an immense evidence of his devotion to a poet's career.

The structure of this poem obtains frequent commendation. In the monologue of an apple picker, a world of half reality and half illusion is presented. Due to the whole day's toil, the apple-picker is speaking while half sleeping and half waking; the balance of the poem is maintained by the contrast of paralleled scenes: the scene of picking and that of storing, the scene of laboring and that of resting, the scene of waking and that of sleeping, the scene of normal existence and that of the distorted one seen through ice, the scene of reason and that of the dream.

Section Four
American Poetry of the Modernist Period

Reality and illusion are combined and mixed to express what the poet had felt, heard, seen and apprehended. The sentences of the work are not regular. Some are short, but some may run for over 5 lines, and consequently, a blending of them directs to the ambiguity of the contrasting scenes.

The rhyme scheme of this poem varies freely. Among the 42 lines 20 rhymes appeared, none of which was regularly designed. This also adds to the creation of a true, but at the same time, illusory atmosphere.

Frost seems versed in dramatic techniques. Many of his poems possess a dramatic quality, especially in the use of monologue which has a long tradition from the Renaissance poets, through Robert Browning and Alfred Tennyson, to many others.

参考译文

摘苹果之后

长梯穿过树顶,露出尖尖的两端,
刺向沉寂的苍穹。
梯子旁边,有一只木桶
还没有装满。也许还有三两个苹果
我未摘下,仍挂枝头。
不过现在我已经把这活干完了。
夜晚散发着冬日里睡眠的气息:
苹果馨香四溢,我瞌睡不止。
我揉揉眼睛,却揉不掉眼前的怪异,
这异象来自今天早晨:我从饮水槽里揭起一层冰,
就像是一块窗玻璃,我隔窗望去,
那是一个衰草的世界。
冰溶了,我任它掉下、摔碎,
但没等它落地,我早就
渐入梦乡。
我还说得出
我的梦会是怎样一个形状。
硕大的苹果时隐时现,
一头是枝,一头是花,

黄褐色的斑点,一目了然。
我的脚板不仅酸痛,
还得使劲撑住梯子档的分量。
我感到那梯子随着弯倒的树枝在摇晃,
耳边只听到隆隆的声音
从储藏室传出。
一桶又一桶苹果往里送。
摘苹果的活儿
我干得太多了,我盼望有个大丰收,
可这我累得我精疲力竭。
有千万只苹果要摘,
捧在手心,轻拿轻放,别掉在地上。
因为所有一切
只要一掉在地上,
即使没碰伤,也没让草梗扎破,
就只好堆在一边,做苹果酒,
好像一钱也不值。
你看啊,搅我睡觉的是些什么,
先不说,这是不是睡觉。
如果土拨鼠没有走开,
听我说睡梦怎样来到我身边
那它会说,这倒与它的冬眠相似,
或者说,这不过是人类的冬眠。

(田洁　杨丽　译　李正栓　校)

(4) Fire and Ice

Some say the world will end in fire,
Some say in ice.
From what I've tasted of desire
I hold with those who favor fire.
5　But if it had to perish twice,
I think I know enough of hate
To say that for destruction ice
Is also great
And would suffice.

Section Four
American Poetry of the Modernist Period

Notes

Line 2 Some say in ice: Some say the world will be destroyed by ice.
Line 3 tasted of desire: understanding or knowledge about "desire."
Line 4 hold with: approve of; agree with.
   who favor fire: people who believe the world will be destroyed in fire.
Line 5 perish: die; be destroyed; ended.
Line 6 know enough of hate: know a lot about hatred between people.
Line 7 To say: If we talk about.
   that for destruction: the power of destruction.
Line 8 (ice) Is also great: Ice is as destructive as fire.
Line 9 suffice: be enough; be adequate (to destroy the world); surpass...in degree.

Comment on the poem

At the beginning of the 20th century, the human world was involved in World War I. After the feverish fantasy of the initial period, when human faith became increasingly shaky, the intellectuals began to meditate on warfare, to introspect the meanness in human nature. Some of them tried to predict the tragic ending of the human world: either in fire—the Earth being burned up by the sun, or in ice—the Ice Age will soon return to Earth as some scientists had strongly suggested. Under these circumstances, Robert Frost wrote this poem in 1920 to declare his opinion.

In this poem, Robert Frost, of course not scientifically but humanistically, first reveals his identical view with those "in fire," for he is inclined to believe, that fire, as the symbol of desire, is destructive. However, at the same time, Frost was worried about the power of "ice," the symbol of hatred, which is believed to be as dangerous as "desire" in ruining the world.

参考译文

火 与 冰

有人说世界将毁于火，

另有人说世界会毁于冰。
根据我对欲望的体验，
我赞成前者的预言。
但如果我必须毁灭两次，
我想我对仇恨颇有了解，
可以说，冰也具很大破坏性
毁灭世界力量足矣。
（李正栓　译）

(5) Design

I found a dimpled spider, fat and white,
On a white heal-all, holding up a moth
Like a white piece of rigid satin cloth—
Assorted characters of death and blight
5 Mixed ready to begin the morning right,
Like the ingredients of a witches' broth—
A snow-drop spider, a flower like a froth,
And dead wings carried like a paper kite.

What had that flower to do with being white,
10 The wayside blue and innocent heal-all?
What brought the kindred spider to that height,
Then steered the white moth thither in the night?
What but design of darkness to appall? —
If design govern in a thing so small.

Notes

Line 1 a dimpled spider: a spider with hollow belly; a spider with a smiling, triumphant air.
Line 2 heal-all: plant that is believed to cure every disease.
　　　holding up: holding in the spider's mouth; catching.
Line 3 Like a …: the moth which is like a…
　　　rigid: stiff; not easily bending or yielding.
　　　satin: silk material that is shiny and smooth on one side.
Line 4 characters of death and blight: the spider, moth, and flower.
Line 5 Mixed ready to begin the morning right: (the characters and the

blight) are mixed to wake up right in the morning.
Line 6 ingredients: the characters of death and blight which had been mixed ready to cook the broth.
Line 7 A snow-drop spider: the spider is as white as a snow-drop—a type of small white flower which appears in the early spring, often when snow is still on the ground.

Stanza1: The poet vividly presents the shocking scene of a white spider devouring a white moth on a white flower.
Line 11 the kindred spider: the spider which shares a common source, or closely related with the moth; the spider and the moth are from the same family.
Line 12 steered: guided; brought.
Line 13 appall: feel with horror or dismay; deeply shocked.
Line 14 a thing so small: the matter of a spider's eating a moth.

Stanza 2: The spider and the moth are all parts of God's creation and they share a lot in common. Thus it is a horrible scene if one of them cruelly devours the other. However, the most frightening fact, in addition to the malicious killing, is that "a thing so small" has been "governed" by God.

Comment on the poem

While Frost devoted most of his writings to the beauty of New England, he did not fail to see the terror and tragedy in nature. *Design* is one of the few which generates a sense of horror.

As a naturalist poet, Robert Frost was sometimes rather baffled by the ambiguous intentions of nature: It creates all the species in the universe, including spider, moth and flower. However, God behaves very indifferently when one of the species is being cruelly swallowed by the other. The three figures of the this poem—spider, moth, and the flower, are all creations of the cosmos, and they are all designed in the color white. Nevertheless, they are respectively the embodiment of innocence (heal-all), the embodiment of evil (spider) and the embodiment of victim (moth).

Frost is a lover of nature, but at the same time, he is agnostic about nature. He is able to feel the power of a somewhat dominant hand over this world. Yet, he also admits that though the power is pervasively influential, it is inexplicable. This may result in the tragic implication that no one in this world is completely safe; each may exist as the other's prey.

The poem was written in 1922 and collected in *New Hampshire*. The rhyme scheme varies in different stanzas: The "abba" rhyme repeats itself once in the first stanza. In the second stanza, the rhyme scheme goes as "aca, acc" just to show the uncertainty and sorrow of the scenes.

参考译文

天　意

我发现一只雄赳赳的蜘蛛，又肥又白，
趴在一株万能花上，抓着一只蛾，
一只白色的像绷紧的锦缎般的蛾——
各色死亡的特征和祸害
混合在一处即将在一早醒来
就像那女巫毒液中的原料般组合
一只如雪的蜘蛛，一株泡沫般的白色花朵，
还有那死亡之翼，如纸鸢般撑开。

那又怎样，那朵花通体是白色，与路边
那蓝色的无辜的万能花又有何干？
是什么将你的宗亲蜘蛛带到那般高处
然后指挥着白蛾在夜晚到那里来？
如果天意连这等小事都要来裁判，
除了黑暗的天意，还会是什么使我们愕然？

（杨丽　田洁　译　李正栓　校）

(6) Home Burial

He saw her from the bottom of the stairs
Before she saw him. She was starting down,
Looking back over her shoulder at some fear.
She took a doubtful step and then undid it
5　To raise herself and look again. He spoke
Advancing toward her: "What is it you see
From up there always— for I want to know."
She turned and sank upon her skirts at that,

And her face changed from terrified to dull.
10 He said to gain time: "What is it you see,"
Mounting until she cowered under him.
"I will find out now—you must tell me, dear."
She, in her place, refused him any help
With the least stiffening of her neck and silence.
15 She let him look, sure that he wouldn't see,
Blind creature; and a while he didn't see.
But at last he murmured, "Oh," and again, "Oh."

"What is it—what?" she said.
             "Just that I see."
"You don't," she challenged. "Tell me what it is."

20 "The wonder is I didn't see at once.
I never noticed it from here before.
I must be wonted to it—that's the reason.
The little graveyard where my people are!
So small the window frames the whole of it.
25 Not so much larger than a bedroom, is it?
There are three stones of slate and one of marble,
Broad-shouldered little slabs there in the sunlight
On the sidehill. We haven't to mind those.
But I understand: it is not the stones,
30 But the child's mound—"

             "Don't, don't, don't, don't," she cried.

She withdrew, shrinking from beneath his arm
That rested on the banister, and slid downstairs;
And turned on him with such a daunting look,
He said twice over before he knew himself:
35 "Can't a man speak of his own child he's lost?"

"Not you! —Oh, where's my hat? Oh, I don't need it!
I must get out of here. I must get air. —
I don't know rightly whether any man can."

"Amy! Don't go to someone else this time.
40 Listen to me." "I won't come down the stairs."

He sat and fixed his chin between his fists.
"There's something I should like to ask you, dear."
"You don't know how to ask it."

    "help me, then."
Her fingers moved the latch for all reply.

45 "My words are nearly always an offense.
I don't know how to speak of anything
So as to please you. But I might be taught,
I should suppose. I can't say I see how.
A man must partly give up being a man
50 With womenfolk. We could have some arrangement
By which I'd bind myself to keep hands off
Anything special you're a-mind to name.
Though I don't like such things' twixt those that love.
Two that don't love can't live together without them,
55 But two that do can't live together with them."
She moved the latch a little. "Don't—don't go.
Don't carry it to someone else this time.
Tell me about it if it's something human.
Let me into your grief. I'm not so much
60 Unlike other folks as your standing there
Apart would make me out. Give me my chance.
I do think, though, you overdo it a little.
What was it brought you up to think it the thing
To take your mother—loss of a first child
65 So inconsolably—in the face of love.
You'd think his memory might be satisfied—"

"There you go sneering now!"

    "I'm not, I'm not!
You make me angry. I'll come down to you.
God, what a woman! And it's come to this,
70 A man can't speak of his own child that's dead."
"You can't because you don't know how to speak.
If you had any feelings, you that dug
With your own hand—how could you? —his little grave;
I saw you from that very window there,

```
 75    Making the gravel leap and leap in air,
       Leap up, like that, like that, and land so lightly
       And roll back down the mound beside the hole.
       I thought, Who is that man? I didn't know you.
       And I crept down the stairs and up the stairs
 80    to look again, and still your spade kept lifting.
       Then you came in. I heard your rumbling voice
       Out in the kitchen, and I don't know why,
       But I went near to see with my own eyes.
       You could sit there with the stains on your shoes
 85    Of the fresh earth from your own baby's grave
       And talk about your everyday concerns.
       You had stood the spade up against the wall
       Outside there in the entry, for I saw it."

       "I shall laugh the worst laugh I ever laughed.
 90    I'm cursed. God, if I don't believe I'm cursed."

       "I can repeat the very words you were saying.
       'Three foggy mornings and one rainy day
       Will rot the best birch fence a man can build.'
       Think of it, talk like that at such a time!
 95    What had how long it takes a birch to rot
       To do with what was in the darkened parlor.
       You couldn't care! The nearest friends can go
       With anyone to death, comes so far short
       They might as well not try to go at all.
100    No, from the time when one is sick to death,
       One is alone, and he dies more alone.
       Friends make pretense of following to the grave,
       But before one is in it, their minds are turned
       And making the best of their way back to life
105    And living people, and things they understand.
       But the world's evil. I won't have grief so
       If I can change it. Oh, I won't, I won't!"

       "There, you have said it all and you feel better.
       You won't go now. You're crying. Close the door.
110    The heart's gone out of it: why keep it up?
       Amy! There's someone coming down the road!"
```

"You—oh, you think the talk is all. I must go—
Somewhere out of this house. How can I make you—"

"If—you—do!" She was opening the door wider.
115 "Where do you mean to go? First tell me that.
I'll follow and bring you back by force. I will! —" .

Notes

The family burial ground near the farmhouse can still be seen in remoter parts of New England and other areas. (see Perkins, *The American Tradition in Literature*, p1269)

Line 1 He: the husband, who has just returned from his burying of the baby.

Line 2 starting down: intending to go downstairs.

Line 4 undid it: hesitated (in taking a step to go downstairs).

Lines 6 – 7 for I want to know what it is you can always see from up there.

Line 8 sank upon her skirts: sat down.

Line 9 her face changed from terrified to dull: The wife was a very reserved woman. She was first rather terrified by the death of their baby, and then when she saw the husband coming back so soon from the burying she felt very disappointed with him but felt hard to complain directly, thus her facial expression was dull. Dull in resignation, he will never understand.

Line 11 Mounting: going upstairs and nearer to the wife.
cowered: retreated or moved backwards in fear or distress.

Line 12 I will find out now—: I must now find out what you have seen up there about my burying of the baby.

Line 13 in her place: motionlessly; without saying anything.

Line 14 With the least stiffening of her neck and silence: With the last strength, she tried to hold her neck up but still kept silence.

Line 15 sure that he wouldn't see: She knew the husband so well that she was sure he would not understand where all her sorrow lies.

Line 18 What is it—what?: What do you think may be the reason for my sorrow?

Section Four
American Poetry of the Modernist Period

Just that I see: The husband believed he had just found out what the sorrow was.

Line 19 The wife challenged the husband that he had not found out the truth and he should tell her what her sorrow is if he had.

Line 20 wonder: feeling of surprise.

Line 21 it: the scene of the graveyard.

here: upstairs and looking through the window.

Line 22 be wonted to it: be used to the scenery of the little graveyard through the window.

Line 25 Not so much larger than a bedroom: the graveyard outside the window is very small.

Line 26 Looking through the window we can see tombstones on the hillside, three of them are made of thick stones and one is made of marble.

Line 28 those: those tombstones on the hillside.

Lines 29 - 30 But I understand: it is not the stones, but the child's mound—: But I can quite understand what had caused all your sorrow is not those tombstones there but the small tomb of our child.

Line 30 The wife could not bear the direct mentioning of their child.

Line 32 banister: the handrail of a stair and the upright poles supporting it.

Line 33 a daunting look: a discouraging, frightening look. The wife was very disappointed to her husband for his mentioning the child in such an easy tone.

Line 38 I don't quite know whether any man is able to mention his lost baby in your tone.

Line 43 You don't know how to ask it: You don't know how to comfort the others.

help me, then: If you think I don't understand, please give me a chance and help me to do better. The husband is pleading.

Line 44 The wife did not answer. As a response, she just moved the latch, an implication for leaving.

Line 45 The husband complains that whatever he said seems an offense to the wife; they had seldom agreed with each other on any events.

Line 47 Though I am always wrong, I am modest and probably able to be taught to do things right.

Line 50 arrangement: agreement.

Line 51 which: the arrangement.

bind myself to keep hands off: keep the memory of preventing me from unhappy topic; promise not to speak of...

Line 52 Anything special: the annoyances of a family.
you're a-mind to name: You're willing to declare.

Line 53 such things: the "arrangement" in Line 50.
those that love: those people who love each other; the husband and wife in general.

Line 54 them: the "arrangement" in Line 50.

Line 55 two that do: the two people who love each other; the husband and wife who have love between them.

Line 58 if it's something human: if it is something of human life or nature.

Line 59 Let me into your grief: Let me share something of your sorrow and know the reason of your present resentment.

Lines 59 – 61 I am not so much...make me out: I am your husband, so I am a necessary figure in the whole matter and I am the one who can't be kept off by your standing far away from me.

Line 61 Give me my chance: please allow me to know the matter and share your sorrow as well.

Line 62 you overdo it a little: you have been too fussy about the way of burying the dead boy.

Lines 63 – 65 The husband tried to say something to comfort the wife.
As a mother, you believe, in the face of love, the loss of your first child is an unpardonable mistake. However, it is just because you were brought up to think so, however, it is not necessarily the truth.

Line 65 inconsolably: (=inconsolable) can't be comforted; unpardonable.

Line 66 his memory might be satisfied—: Our baby might have felt quite satisfied for his quick leaving after birth. The Christians all believe in the "after life" —a selected human being will enjoy eternal life after death of the body.

The "—" at the end of the line strongly implies that the husband's comforting words were interrupted by the wife.
his: our boy's.

Line 73 how could you?: how could you muddle through the digging of the little grave? How could you dig the baby's grave yourself? In Western tradition, graves like this should be dug by friends or other family members less close to the tragedy, such as the father's brother.

Line 75 gravel: small stones; hard, rough earth.

Section Four
American Poetry of the Modernist Period

leap and leap in air: (I saw that) you had been too light-hearted as to have thrown the earth into the air when you were digging the grave.

Line 76 Leap up: when the husband was digging, the gravel leapt again and again. That implies the wife felt the husband had been working too leisurely and with a rather light heart. That's what she could not bear.

land so lightly: the gravel.

Line 79 crept down the stairs and up the stairs: She goes up and down the stairs because she could not keep her eyes off the scene, much as she would like to.

Line 80 spade kept lifting: another evidence for the man's lightheartedness—when digging a grave for the baby, the man had lifted the spade too high.

Line 81 rumbling voice: deep heavy continuous voice. The wife felt a man whose first child had just died should not speak in such a deep and loud voice. Instead, he should keep silence for a long while or whisper when he had to say anything. That's why she said, "You don't know how to speak." (Line 71)

Lines 84 – 85 These two lines imply another complaint of the wife. She felt if he were a considerate husband, he would have cleaned the fresh earth off his shoes in case she would see it and cause her sorrow.

Line 86 talk about your everyday concerns: another cause for the wife's detestation. She had insisted on long silence equaling to greater sorrow, thus the husband is also expected to stay in solemnity. Anyway, he is supposed to have been too eager to talk and that indicates his indifference and neglecting of all her sufferings.

Lines 87 – 88 had stood the spade up against the wall: One more mistake the husband made to irritate the wife. If the husband were a considerate person, he would have kept that sad spade completely away from her. At least he should not have stood the spade in the entry to arouse her new sorrow.

Lines 89 – 90 The husband felt he was badly misunderstood by the wife. However, while she was in deep grief, he couldn't find a chance to express himself or apologize. He himself must take all the absurdity.

Lines 92 – 93 Three foggy mornings and one rainy day: the bad weather of a period or the shifting of time.

the best birch fence: things of good value.

        The sentence strongly implies that time might be the best cure for any injuries. This is probably the husband's comforting words to the wife but, obviously, it is not well accepted by the latter. It seems the wife was thoroughly indulged in her sorrow and was too sentimental to face reality, but the husband appeared quite reasonable.

Line 94 such a time: at the time when we were talking about the death of the first child.

Line 96 the darkened parlor: the parlor where the coffin is in. The baby was not buried, and was still in the parlor, in its coffin. Only the grave was dug. The wife and husband are speaking of the recent past.

Line 97 The nearest friends: the most reliable person. The wife was complaining the husband who used to express himself as the best friend but when in trouble, he appeared as quite a different person. She felt disappointed with all his words and his behaviors as well.

        go: going to the graveside.

Line 98 comes so far short: is so far short of the reality of death.

Line 99 They might as well not try to go at all: The friends who had said to be willing to die together with the dead person might not try to go with this child, because the child was too small.

Line 102 make pretense: make themselves appear to be going with the dying in order to deceive others; making believe.

Line 103 their minds are turned: they changed their minds to other matters, to the things of their ordinary life.

Line 104 making the best of their way: make the best excuse.

Line 105 They make the best excuse for the changing of minds and not without great efforts, they made the best excuse by beautifying the human world and all the things they understand.

Line 106 But the world's evil: However beautified, the present world is considered by the wife an evil one.

Line 108 have said it all: you have expressed all your sorrows.

Line 110 The heart's gone out of it: You have cried so much as your heart had been seriously hurt and it has gone out of you. You have to make a change by stopping thinking about the matter of the baby any more.

        why keep it up?: It is not necessary to keep the sad story about the child always in your mind; you have cried more than enough. The husband is still trying to ease the wife's sufferings.

Section Four
American Poetry of the Modernist Period

Line 112 you think the talk is all: The wife denied the husband's view as time is curable and talk is able to relieve everybody. As a mother, she believed that the harm brought by the loss of their first child will keep staying and smoldering in her heart, and will never be relieved by any talks.

go—: This "go" has double meanings. On the one hand, it equals the meaning of "go" in Line 97, which means to die together with the one you loved; on the other hand, it refers to the wife's present intention of leaving the house and her husband. The wife might at first burst out with an expression of her resentment. However, she soon made a swift change of the idea. Therefore, after the dash, "Somewhere out of this house" took the place of the might be "with our child."

Line 114 If—you—do!: If you must go or leave this house and leave me then there will be consequences. The dashes present the husband's determination. So is the function of the dash at the end of the last line.

Comment on the poem

This poem presents a dramatic dialogue.

A baby died. The father dug a grave for him just behind the house. But the views over the death of the baby of the father and the mother differed: The woman was in deep sorrow and she simply could not control it. While the man, though he is also sorrowful, thought more about his wife, so he controlled himself and made efforts to comfort her. However, that resulted in the wife's misunderstanding of him and their marriage came into trouble.

The wife believed the husband had been too quick in burying the baby by himself. She complained the husband had come back from burying too soon, and, he had been too careless for the death of their first child. While the husband found other ways to express his inner sufferings and he just felt that the wife had carried the matter too far.

Their relationship has gone sour. They are very different people. Men and woman are different. The death of the baby is only one of the most harmful reasons for their annoyance. Frost shows us that the poem is a dramatic one. Frost was in the habit to choose the short, sharp movements for best expression, thus in this piece of work, he made use of a momentary attention towards a family affair, to present the conflicts between the couple. By plotting the dramatic dialogue, Frost successfully depicts their vivid characters: the wife, an over-sentimental woman who is frail in nature but a little arrogant and nonconformist in appearance; the husband, a comparatively more reasonable man, not without humor, appeared more considerate.

This poem is written in very loose blank verse, loose iambic. Since the poem is composed of thorough conversation, it is in the colloquial language of a couple of farmers. If it was done in very strict iambic, the poem will lose colloquial sense, lose its truthfulness.

参考译文

家 冢

从楼梯的底部,他看到她。
她还没有看到他。她正准备下楼,
带着一丝恐惧,扭过肩膀向后张望。
她迟疑着迈了一步,而后犹豫着
挺起身又向外望。他走近她
问道:"你总是在那上边
看什么——,我想知道。"
她听见问话,转过身,在旁边坐下,
脸色由惊恐转为麻木。
他迫不及待地问"你看到了什么?"
他登上楼,直到她蜷缩在他的身下。
"现在我要知道——你必须告诉我,亲爱的。"
她,呆在那里,用她微微僵直的脖子和沉默
拒绝他的帮助。
她让他观察,确信他不会明白。
盲目的家伙,看了一会儿,他仍不明白。
但最后,他低声说"噢",又一声"噢"

"是什么——,什么呀?"她问。
"就是我看到的那样。"
"你不知道,"她质疑说,"告诉我是什么。"

"奇怪的是我没能立刻看到。
以前我也从没从这里注意过什么,
我必须习惯它——,那就是原因。

Section Four
American Poetry of the Modernist Period

是那块墓地,那是我的家人们被埋葬的地方!
从那么小一扇窗户里,就可以尽收眼底。
还不及一间卧室大,不是吗?
有三块石板,一块大理石,
肩宽的厚板堆在那里,在阳光下,
在山坡上。我们不必在意那些。
但我明白:它不是些石头,
而是孩子的坟——"

"不要说啦,不要说啦,"她哭喊着,
从他的臂弯下缩出来,
那只臂靠在扶栏上向下滑落;
她转向他,脸上带着令人畏缩的表情,
他说了两遍,自己却不知不觉:
"一个男人不能提到他失去的孩子吗?"

"你不能说!——,噢,我的帽子在哪儿?
噢,我用不着它!
我必须离开这儿。我必须呼吸空气。——
我真不知道是不是任何一个男人都可以这样。"

"艾米!这时候不能去别人那里。
听我说。""我不会下楼的。"
他坐下来,用拳头托着下巴。
"有些事,我想问你,亲爱的"

"你不知道怎样问。"

"那么,帮帮我。"
她的手指移动门闩,作为对他的回答。

"我的话几乎总会伤你。
我不知道如何说些事
去取悦于你。但是我想
你可以教我。我不能说我知道怎样。
一个男人和女人们在一起时
必须部分放弃做个男人。我们可以达成协议,
有了它,我可以约束我自己不去讲

那些你不愿提及的特殊事。
虽然我不喜欢此类事情横在夫妻间，
两个不相爱的人没有这些事是不能共同生活的，
但两个相爱的人却因为
这些事而不能生活在一起。
她又挪动了些门闩。"别——，别走。
千万别在这时候把它带给别人。
告诉我吧，如果你是宽容的。
让我分担你的悲伤。我并非
不同于其他人，你远远地站着
会让我冲向你。给我个机会，
我真的认为，你在这件事上你有点过火。
是那些伴随你长大的观念使你认为
失去第一个孩子的母亲是
如此的罪无可恕。——蒙爱之恩泽，
你应该想到对孩子的记忆可以得到满足——"
"你在那儿嘲笑！"

"不是的，我不是在嘲笑！
"你惹火我了，我要下来。
上帝，这是什么女人！竟然成了这样，
一个男人不能提他自己的死去的孩子。"

"你不能，因为你不知道怎样提。
如果你有任何感情，你
亲手去挖他的小坟——，你怎么会这样？
我就从那扇窗户看到，
你让碎石在空中乱溅，
像那样，像那样溅起，轻轻地着地
滚回到洞边的土堆。
我想，那个男人是谁啊？我不认识你。
我缓缓地，在楼梯那儿，上下走动，
又来看，你的锹仍旧扬着。
然后，你进来了。我听到你隆隆的声音
从厨房里传出，我不知道为什么，
但我走近，亲眼看到。
你可以坐在那儿，鞋上粘着污垢，
那是你自己孩子的坟墓上的新土，

Section Four
American Poetry of the Modernist Period

说着日常的琐事。
你把锹靠墙立着
就在门口外,我看到了。"

"这真是荒谬至极。
我被误解了,上帝,我是否可以不信我被误解了。"

"让我来复述你当时说的话:
'三个有雾的早晨,一个下雨天,
就可以腐蚀一个人能建起的最坚固的桦树篱笆。'
想想啊,在这种时候说这样的话!
多长时间可以毁掉桦树,
与在暗坟中的孩子有何相干。
你不会在意的!最要好的朋友会
愿意为你而和什么人一起死。孩子在世不长
更没人想要和他一起。
不,从一个人从病到死的那一刻起,
他就是孤单的,他死时更孤单。
朋友们装腔作势地跟去坟墓,
还没死者入土,他们就改变了想法
找出最好的借口重返生活
和那些仍旧活着的人们,
还有那些他们理解的事情。
但是这个世界是邪恶的。
如果我可以改变这一切,
我就不会如此悲伤。
噢,我就不会如此悲伤,我不会!"

"好了,你说完了,感觉好点了吧。
你现在不能走。你还在哭呢。关上门。
你已经因此伤透了心,为什么总提这事呢?
艾米!有人顺着公路走过来了!"

"你——,噢,你以为这就完了。我必须走——
到这房子外的任何地方去。
我怎样才能让你——"

"如果你——真那样做——!"她把门开大了些。

225

"你到底要去哪？先告诉我。
我会跟着你，强制你回来，我会的！——"
（杨丽　田洁译　李正栓校）

(7) The Death of the Hired Man

Mary sat musing on the lamp-flame at the table,
Waiting for Warren. When she heard his step,
She ran on tiptoe down the darkened passage
To meet him in the doorway with the news
5　And put him on his guard. "Silas is back."
She pushed him outward with her through the door
And shut it after her. "Be kind." she said.
She took the market things from Warren's arms
And set them on the porch, then drew him down
10　To sit beside her on the wooden steps.
"When was I ever anything but kind to him?
But I'll not have the fellow back," he said.
"I told him so last haying, didn't I?
If he left then, I said, that ended it.
15　What good is he? Who else will harbor him
At his age for the little he can do?
What help he is there's no depending on.
Off he goes always when I need him most
He thinks he ought to earn a little pay,
20　Enough at least to buy tobacco with,
So he won't have to beg and be beholden.
'All right,' I say, 'I can't afford to pay
Any fixed wages, though I wish I could.'
'someone else can.' 'Then someone else will have to.'
25　I shouldn't mind his bettering himself
If that was what it was. You can be certain,
When he begins like that, there's someone at him
Trying to coax him off with pocket money—
In haying time, when any help is scarce,
30　In winter he comes back to us. I'm done."
"Sh! not so loud: he'll hear you," Mary said.
"I want him to: he'll have to soon or late."
"He's worn out. He's asleep beside the stove.
When I came up from Rowe's I found him here,

35   Huddled against the barn door fast asleep,
       A miserable sight, and frightening, too—
       You needn't smile—I didn't recognize him—
       I wasn't looking for him—and he's changed.
       Wait till you see."
                 "Where did you say he'd been?"
40   "He didn't say. I dragged him to the house,
       And gave him tea and tried to make him smoke.
       I tried to make him talk about his travels.
       Nothing would do: he just kept nodding off."
       "What did he say? Did he say anything?"
45   "But little."
              "Anything ? Mary, confess
       He said he'd come to ditch the meadow for me."
       "Warren!"
             "But did he? I just want to know."
       "Of course he did. What would you have him say?
       Surely you wouldn't grudge the poor old man
50   Some humble way to save his self-respect.
       He added, if you really care to know,
       He meant to clear the upper pasture, too.
       That sounds like something you have heard before?
       Warren, I wish you could have heard the way
55   He jumbled everything. I stopped to look
       Two or three times—he, made me feel so queer—
       To see if he was talking in his sleep.
       He ran on Harold Wilson—you remember—
       The boy you had in haying four years since.
60   He's finished school, and teaching in his college.
       Silas declares you'll have to get him back.
       He says they two will make a team for work:
       Between them they will lay this farm as smooth!
       The way he mixed that in with other things.
65   He thinks young Wilson a likely lad, though daft"
       On education—you know how they fought
       All through July under the blazing sun,
       Silas up on the cart to build the load,
       Harold along beside to pitch it on.
70   "Yes, I took care to keep well out of earshot."
       "Well, those days trouble Silas like a dream.

You wouldn't think they would. How some things linger!
Harold's young college-boy's assurance piqued him.
After so many years he still keeps finding
75　Good arguments he sees he might have used.
I sympathize. I know just how it feels
To think of the right thing to say too late.
Harold's associated in his mind with Latin.
He asked me what I thought of Harold's saying
80　He studied Latin, like the violin,
Because he liked it—that an argument!
He said he couldn't make the boy believe
He could find water with a hazel prong—
Which showed how much good school had ever done him.
85　He wanted to go over that. But most of all
He thinks if he could have another chance
to teach him how to build a load of hay—"

"I know, that's Silas' one accomplishment.
He bundles every forkful in its place,
90　And tags and numbers it for future reference,
So he can find and easily dislodge it
In the unloading. Silas does that well.
He takes it out in bunches like big birds' nests.
You never see him standing on the hay
95　He's trying lift, straining to lift himself."

"He thinks if he could teach him that, he'd be
Some good perhaps to someone in the world.
He hates to see a boy the fool of books.
Poor Silas, so concerned for other folk,
100　And nothing to look backward to with pride,
And nothing to look forward to with hope,
So now and never any different."

Part of a moon was falling down the west,
Dragging the whole sky with it to the hills.
105　Its light poured softly in her lap. She saw it
And spread her apron to it. She put out her hand
Among the harplike morning-glory strings,
Taut with the dew from garden bed to eaves,

                As if she played unheard some tenderness
110   That wrought on him beside her in the night.
        "Warren," she said, "he has come home to die:
        You needn't be afraid he'll leave you this time."
        "Home," he mocked gently. "Yes, what else but home?"
        It all depends on what you mean by home.
115   Of course he's nothing to us, any more
        Than was the hound that came a stranger to us
        Out of the woods, worn out upon the trail.
        "Home is the place where, when you have to go there,
        They have to take you in."
                        "I should have called it
120   Something you somehow haven't to deserve."

        Warren leaned out and took a step or two,
        Picked up a little stick, and brought it back
        And broke it in his hand and tossed it by.
        "Silas has better claim on us you think
125   Than on his brother? Thirteen little miles
        As the road winds would bring him to his door.
        Silas has walked that far no doubt today.
        Why doesn't he go there? His brother's rich,
        A somebody—director in the bank."

130   "He never told us that"
                        "We know it though."
        "I think his brother ought to help, of course.
        I'll see to that if there is need. He ought of right
        to take him in, and might be willing to—
        He may be better than appearances.
135   But have some pity on Silas, Do you think
        If he had any pride in claiming kin
        Or anything he looked for from his brother,
        He'd keep so still about him all this time?"
        "I wonder what's between them."
                        "I can tell you.
140   Silas is what he is—we wouldn't mind him—
        But just the kind that kinsfolk can't abide.
        He never did a thing so very bad.
        He don't know why he isn't quite as good

          As anybody. Worthless though he is,
145   He won't be made ashamed to please his brother."

      "I can't think Si ever hurt anyone."
      "No, but he hurt my heart the way he lay
      And rolled his old head on that sharp-edged chair-back.
      He wouldn't let me put him on the lounge.
150   You must go in and see what you can do.
      I made the bed up for him there tonight.
      You'll be surprised at him—how much he's broken.
      His working days are done; I'm sure of it."

      "I'd not be in a hurry to say that."
155   "I haven't been. Go, look, see for yourself.
      But, Warren, please remember how it is:
      He's come to help you ditch the meadow.
      He has a plan. You mustn't laugh at him.
      He may not speak of it, and then he may.
160   I'll sit and see if that small sailing cloud
      Will hit or miss the moon."

                  It hit the moon.
      Then there were three there, making a dim row,
      The moon, the little silver cloud, and she.
      Warren returned—too soon, it seemed to her,
165   Slipped to her side, caught up her hand and waited.
      "Warren?" she questioned.
                  "Dead," was all he answered.

Notes

Line 1 Mary: the hostess of the family.
       musing on: thinking in a deep or concentrated way, quite igno-
       ring what is happening around one.
Line 2 Warren: the host of the family, husband of Mary.
Line 3 ran on tiptoe down: ran downstairs very gingerly.
Line 4 the news: the news about their hired man's returning to them.
Line 5 put him on his guard: make him preparing for a surprise (of the
       hired man's returning)

Section Four
American Poetry of the Modernist Period

Silas: name of their late hired man.

Line 7 Be kind: the wife expected the husband to be friendly and thoughtful to the newly returned hired man.

Line 11 When was I ever anything but kind to him?: When heard of the returning of the old hired man, the husband was rather angry as to ask the wife resentfully whether he used to be extremely kind to that person.

Line 12 the fellow: their old hired man.

Line 13 I told him so: I told the hired man that he was not allowed to come back to me when we were making hay last time.
last haying: (when Silas was intending to leave us for a supposed better pay in) the busy season of making hay last year.

Line 15 Who else will harbor him: I don't think anybody else would be so kind as to hire him or accept him.
harbor: give shelter to; hire.

Line 17 What help he is there's no depending on: Nobody is able to depend on whatever help he may offer (because he is aged and weak); He was not at all a reliable person and now too aged and frail...

Line 18 Whenever I needed him most, he left us.

Line 21 be beholden: having to feel grateful to...

Line 24 Then someone else will have to: If you say someone else can afford to pay you fixed wage, you'd better go to him.

Line 25 bettering himself: improve his life by himself.

Line 26 If that was what it was: if he was able to afford himself a better life.

Line 28 coax him off with pocket money: gently persuade him to leave us with a small sum of money.

Line 29 In haying time, when any help is scarce: (He left us) in haying time when it is very difficult to find any other hands for help.

Line 30 In winter: when it is cold and we have nothing to do in the field, when we don't need any help (he always returns to us).
I'm done: I have finished all the haying work; I have had enough of a hired man like him.

Line 32 I want him to: I want him to hear my comment upon him.
he'll have to soon or late: He'll have to hear or know my comment on him soon or late.

Line 35 Huddled against the barn door: crowded his body tightly together into a smaller space and lay against the barn door.

Line 39 Wait till you see: Wait for a while and soon you'll see all his changes.

Line 42 his travels: "travels" is here a euphemism for "tramping life." This word strongly suggests that Mary was a very considerate woman and she offers quarters for the other's self-respect even to a much inferior person.

Line 43 Nothing would do: I failed in trying to coax him to talk about his recent life.

Line 46 He said he'd come to ditch the meadow for me: (=Did he say he'd come to ditch the meadow for me) It is probably what Silas had promised before he left this family last time. Warren mentioned the sentence as a satire. That's why in the next line Mary pleaded with Warren to take Silas' excuse for granted and forgive him once more just for the sake of the self-respect of an old man.

Line 47 But did he? I just want to know: But I just want to know if he said he had come to ditch the meadow for me again this time.

Line 48 What would you have him say: What else can you expect him to say (as an excuse for coming back to us)?

Line 50 Some humble way: Poor and nonsensical as it was, Silas needed some humble way—an excuse, to save his self-respect.

Line 55 He jumbled everything: When he was speaking, he was actually unable to express himself clearly, for he is too old.

Line 58 He ran on Harold Wilson—: He kept talking about Harold Wilson, the boy appears in the next line. By making himself occupied in the talking about another person, Silas was trying to prevent others from asking something about his sufferings.

Line 61 to get him back: to get Harold Wilson, a younger hired man, back to our farm.

Line 63 Between them: With the efficient work of the two of them. lay this farm as smooth: do the farm work efficiently and well.

Line 64 The way he mixed that in with other things: when Silas was talking about his workmate Wilson, he was confused, mixing different events.

Line 65 a likely lad: a likable young man.

Lines 65 – 66 daft on education: (Harold Wilson was) crazy about getting education.

Lien 66 how they fought: how Silas and Harold had argued together.

Line 68 to build the load: to have the hay piled up.

Line 69 Harold along beside to pitch it on: Harold would run around the cart to throw the hay on it.

Line 70 to keep well out of earshot: Warren recalled the scene when just years ago Silas and Harold's diligent work was always accompanied with the endless debate between them, he had to stand far apart to keep from being drawn into the argument.
Line 71 trouble Silas like a dream: Now Silas is old and weak, he has lost his youth forever. The memory of his diligent work on our farm often returns to his mind but as a dream.
Line 72 You wouldn't think they would: As a host, you are unable to share with Silas the same memory of that time as a dream. "They" refers to "those days."
How some things linger!: Sometimes some trivial things appear very important to somebody. They are rather unwilling to get them out of memory.
Line 73 assurance: confident belief in one's own abilities and powers.
Line 74 After so many years he still keeps finding: Harold's associated in his mind with Latin; for many years Silas kept Harold in his mind just because of their arguments on studying Latin.
Line 79 He asked me: Silas asked me.
Line 80 Harold once expressed that he studied Latin quite out of interest, just as he had studied the violin.
Line 81 that an argument!: Silas believed Harold's words that he studied Latin just out of interest were not the truth but a way of expressing his arguments. The truth Silas would be inclined to take is that Latin might be the course Harold had to study for graduation.
Line 83 He could find water with a hazel prong: hazel prong refers to a forked twig of a hazel tree. Some people insisted on a superstitious belief that one can discover underground water just by pointing a hazel prong to the ground and moving forward. The twig would bend down on the spot with the source of water.
Line 84 Which: his inability to convince Harold of this ability to find water with a hazel prong.
how much good school had ever done him: what a profound knowledge he had got. Here lies an irony, a sarcasm.
Line 85 go over that: repeat that old argument.
Line 87 to teach him: to teach Harold Wilson.
Line 88 that: Silas' skill of building a load of hay.
Line 89 bundles every forkful in its place: When making hay, Silas used to be an expert who was able to fork each bundle of hay to the accurate place.

Line 90 tags and numbers it: has the bundles labeled and numbered; piling the bundles in good order. A metaphor.
  future reference: the identification of the bundles of hay in future.
Line 91 dislodge it: take out a certain bundle of hay; move or force a bundle of hay from a previously fixed position.
Line 95 straining to lift himself: (Silas) never tried to lift himself because he was accidentally standing on the hay he was lifting.
Lines 96 – 97 Silas believed by teaching Harold Wilson the best way to make hay, he would have contributed to this world.
Line 98 a boy the fool of books: a boy who is just a bookworm, who learns everything from a book but knows very little about physical labor.
Line 99 Poor Silas, so concerned for other folk: Despite all his poverty, he was still worrying about the matter of others and, on the other hand, did not cease to laugh at the inferior.
Line 100 nothing to look backward to with pride: A poor man like Silas has nothing in his memory to be proud of.
Line 101 nothing to look forward to with hope: The future for a poor man like Silas appears hopeless.
Line 102 So now and never any different: As a matter of fact, his life of the past, present and future are all similarly filled with sufferings.
Line 106 spread her apron to it: Mary spread her apron to the moonlight.
Line 107 the harplike morning-glory strings: the strings which are holding the climbing plant are like those of a harp's.
Line 108 Taut with the dew: (the strings are) tightly stretched because of the weight of the wet dew.
Line 109 played unheard some tenderness: played (with those strings) a tune of tenderness but without the appreciation of any others.
Line 110 That wrought on him: The husband was a little touched by her tune of tenderness.
Line 113 mocked gently: laughed at her a little ironically.
  what else but home: I know Silas had taken our farm as nothing else but a home.
Line 114 It all depends on what you mean by home: The real meaning of "home" depends on how one wants to understand it.
Lines 116 – 117 (any more) Than was the hound that came a stranger to us out of the woods: Silas to us means no more than a strange

Section Four
American Poetry of the Modernist Period

hunting dog just ran out of the woods. We don't have a close link with him.

Line 117 worn out upon the trail: (the hound was) dirty and exhausted on the rough country road.

Lines 118 – 119 Home is the place where, when you have to go there, they have to take you in: This has become a common proverb in America. Attention should be paid to the two "have to's," which suggest Silas' helplessness and Warren's unwillingness.

Line 119 it: a home.

Line 124 claim on us: believe to have the right to require us to do something for him.

Line 126 his door: Silas' brother's door.

Lines 132 – 133 He ought of right to take him in: Silas's brother has the duty to take good care of Silas.

Lines 135 – 136 Do you think: If he had any pride in claiming kin: do you think Silas would feel happy to claim the relationship with his rich brother?

Line 138 He'd keep so still: Silas would rather not mention that relationship as he used to.

Line 141 just the kind that kinsfolk can't abide: just the kind of person whose relatives can't tolerate him.

Line 143 quite as good: be as successful as any others.

Line 146 Si: Silas. "Si" is the common nickname for "Silas."

Line 152 how much he's broken: how completely down and out he has become.

Line 153 His working days are done: He is unable to work for anybody any more.

Line 154 to say that: to say he can no longer work.

Line 162 there were three there: When Warren had left, Mary was left alone with the moon and the cloud, thus "the three."
making a dim row: the three of them—the moon, the cloud and Mary are making a straight line. That means Mary was looking up at the moon but the moon was covered by the cloud.
In this line, the moon might be taken as a symbol for Silas, cloud, a symbol for death. The moon's being covered by the cloud symbolizes Silas' death. Furthermore, the moonlight of this line, as well as the moonlight mentioned in Line 103, suggests Mary's kindness and her considerate nature.

Line 166: dead: Silas was dead already.

Comment on the poem

John Lynen, one of the prominent American critics of the last century, once classified the "dialogue verses" of Robert Frost into three categories: pastoral dialogues, philosophical dialogues, and dramatic dialogues. *The Death of the Hired Man* is the representative work of the dramatic dialogue: It has characters, plot, playlet-like scenes, actions, and a climax at the end.

The dialogue in this poem is set against a farmer's house. Mary, the hostess was trying to persuade her husband, Warren, to be kind to and accept Silas, their aged hired man who had just returned to them for a shelter.

In this poem, Silas did not really appear in person. All the characters and his sufferings are described in the conversation of the couple. Mary, a very considerate and sympathetic woman, knew well about how to leave quarters for the self-respect of others, no matter what condition she was in; while Warren, the husband, appeared more on the rational side. He is the character who makes changes in the poem. He changes from a firm denial to the returning of the hired man ("If he left then, I said, that ended it") (Line 14) to the mild wards "I know, that's Silas' one accomplishment" (Line 88) to the sincere praise of Silas "I can't think Si ever hurt anyone". Silas, though never appearing in person in the poem, is described as the one who is "worthless," who had "nothing to look backward to with pride / and nothing to look forward to with hope," is the person with proper self-respect, despite all his misfortunes and errors. It is just him, Silas, who provides the central theme of the poem: self-respect and independence of each. Subordinate to that, sympathy, rationality, and forgiveness are also what are highly praised in the poem. The climax of the poem arrives at the end when Silas had obtained understanding and had been forgiven by all, but was already dead.

雇 工 之 死

玛丽坐在桌旁，对着灯焰沉思，

Section Four
American Poetry of the Modernist Period

等待着沃伦。她听到他的脚步声，
就踮脚跑着穿过黑洞洞的走廊，
在门口迎接他，带给他一个
足以让他惊讶的消息。"赛拉斯回来了。"
她拥着丈夫进了门，
随后把门关上，"对他好点，"她说。
她从沃伦胳膊上取下市场买来的东西，
搁在门廊那，然后拽他坐下来，
坐在木阶上，坐在自己的身边。
"我何时亏待过他？
但我不要那家伙回来，"他说道，
"上次农忙时我对他说过这话，不是吗？
那个时候我就说过，如果他离开，那一切就完了。
他有什么优点？其他人谁会收留他？
他那把年纪，还能做什么？
没人对他还有什么指望。
他总是在我最需要他的时候走开
他觉得他应该挣些小钱，
至少足够买他的烟叶，
有这些钱他就不必乞求被怜悯。
'好啊，'我说。'我不能负担
任何固定的薪金，虽然我希望我能做到，'
'别人可以啊，''而别人会那么做的，'
我并不介意他改善他自己的生活，
如果真是那样一回事，这一点你可以相信我，
当他开始想入非非之际，有人在他身边
用几个零用钱哄他离开——
在农忙时，在那人手罕缺之际，
大冬天他回到我们身边，我早把所有活儿干完。"
"嘘，别那么大声，他会听到的，"玛丽说。
"但愿他能听到，他迟早必须听到。"
"他累坏了。在壁炉旁睡着了。
我从罗家回来时，发现他在这儿，
蜷缩着，靠着谷仓门睡得正熟，
悲惨的景象，还很吓人——
你别笑——我没认出他来——
我一直未曾留意过他——，他变了，
你等着看吧。"

"你说他去过哪里?"
"他没说。我把他拽进屋,
给他茶喝,还试图让他抽烟。
还试图让他讲讲他去过那里。
徒劳无益,他只是不停得打盹。"
"他说什么啦?他什么也没说?"
"只是一点。"
"什么?玛丽,告诉我
他说过他是回来帮我圈草场的。"
"沃伦!"
"但他是这么说得吗?我只想知道。"
"当然,他是说了。你还想让他说些什么?
千万别再怨恨那可怜的老人了,
用谦卑的态度去给他个面子吧。
他还说,如果你真想知道,
他还惦记着去清理坡上的牧场,
你以前听过这样的话吧?
沃伦,我希望你听过
他那嘟嘟囔囔说话的方式。我停下来看他,
有两三次——他,让我感觉很古怪——
我想知道他是不是在说梦话。
他一直在说哈罗德·威尔逊——你记得的——
那个四年来你在农忙时雇的男孩。
他已经完成了学业,留校教书。
赛拉斯说你必须让他回来。
他说他俩会结组工作。
有他们俩,会把农场安排得妥妥当当!
他的语气中掺杂着异样的东西。
他觉得威尔逊虽然学业不精,
是个招人喜欢的年轻人。"
——你知道他们是如何
在七月的骄阳下奋战,
赛拉斯站在车上堆草,
哈罗德在旁边搭草包。
"确实如此,我还得当心别被他们吵嚷干扰。"
"是,那些日子像梦一样笼罩着他。
你不会认为那些日子如何,一些琐事常驻心头!
哈罗德小孩子的狂傲激怒了他。

Section Four
American Poetry of the Modernist Period

很多年以后他还在找寻
他以为会用到的好论据。
我同情他,我只是知道那是一种怎样的感觉,
想着那事,说出来却太晚了。
哈罗德满脑子拉丁语。
赛拉斯问我对于哈罗德说的
他学习拉丁语正如他学习小提琴一样
是出于爱好作何想法——那只是个借口!
他说他没办法使那孩子相信
他能够用榛树杈取水——
这件事证明了受教育对他有多大好处。
他想要强调这一点。但更多的时候
他在想是否还有机会
教那孩子如何堆干草堆——"

"我知道,那是赛拉斯的一个成就。
他能把那些草团各归其位,
将它们标识以备来日参考之用,
因此他可以找到,并且在卸货时
轻易地移走它。他干这活干得很好。
他把干草弄出来像大鸟巢一样地排列起来。
你绝不会看到他站他试图举起的
草上,他凭自己竭力举起那些草团。"

他想如果他教会哈罗德那个技巧,
他就成为了对这世上的某些人有贡献的一个。
他憎恶看到被书本愚弄的孩子。
可怜的赛拉斯,他如此地关心别人,
却落得前无荣耀事,
后无希望光的地步,
现在事事如常,将来事事都一样。"

月亮向西方垂下,
整个天幕被拖近山巅。
月光轻轻地洒在她膝上。她看见月光,
迎着月光展开她的围裙。她伸出手,
穿梭于那如竖琴般沐浴在晨曦中的丝带间,
它们被遍布园中和屋檐的露珠沾染而绷紧。

她的姿势仿佛是在演奏那闻所未闻的优柔之音。
夜幕中,身边的沃伦被触动了。
"沃伦,"她说,"他是回家来等死的;
你不必害怕这次他会离开你。"
"家,"他微微有些嘲笑。
"是的,除了家还能是什么呢?"
这完全取决于你对家的理解。
确实如此对我们而言,他算不上什么,
甚至还不及从林中出来的一只在归途中
累得筋疲力尽的陌生的猎犬。
"家是一处当你不得不回去之时,
他们必须接纳你的地方。"
"我本应该称之为
你无论如何都不值得的东西。"

沃伦侧着身子踱了几步,
拾起一根小棍,拿了回来,
折断它,掷了出去。
"你认为赛拉斯更有权利要求我们
而不是他的兄弟? 只十三里
路程就可以通向他兄弟家的门口。
无疑赛拉斯今天已经走了那么远的路程。
为什么他不到那里去呢? 他兄弟有钱,
一个什么重要人物——,是个什么银行主任吧。"

"他从未告诉我们那些事,"
"尽管我们知道"
"我想他兄弟应该帮他,那是当然的。
我会留意是否有必要,他有义务
收留赛拉斯,他或许会乐于这么做的——
他可能比表面上好。
但是,可怜可怜赛拉斯吧,你以为
是否他会骄傲地去认亲戚
或是他惦记着从他兄弟那得到什么东西?
他到现在都没有提到过他兄弟。"
"我真想知道,他们之间发生了什么"
"我可以告诉你,
赛拉斯就是他这副样子——我们不会介意他——

但他的亲戚们不能忍受他这样的人，
他从未犯过什么弥天大错。
他不知道为什么他无法像其他人
那样好。虽然他毫无价值，
但他不会低头去取悦他的兄弟。"

"我认为赛拉斯没有伤害过谁。"
"不，但他躺着的姿势让我心痛，
他缩着脑袋靠在尖尖的椅背上。
他不让我扶他进休息室。
你必须进去看看，能干些什么。
今夜我为他在那里，铺好了床。
你看到他会惊讶的，——他垮成那个样子了。
我确信他不能再工作了。"

"我绝非妄下断言"
"我从来不会那样。去，看看他，你亲自去看。
但是，沃伦，请记住这些话，
他是来帮你围牧场的。
他已经计划好，你千万别嘲笑他。
他可能不会提，以后他会说的。
我会坐着，看那片浮云是否
会遮蔽月光。"

浮云遮住了月亮，
那里有三样东西，排成模糊的一列，
月亮，泛着银光的云，还有她，
沃伦回来了—— 对她来说，太快了，
他悄悄地坐在她身边，抓起她的手，等待着。
"沃伦，怎么样？"她问道，
"死了。"这是他全部的回答。

（田洁　杨丽译　李正栓校）

(8) Mending Wall

Something there is that doesn't love a wall,
That sends the frozen-ground-swell under it,
And spills the upper boulders in the sun;

And makes gaps even two can pass abreast.
5 The work of hunters is another thing:
I have come after them and made repair
Where they have left not one stone on a stone,
But they would have the rabbit out of hiding,
To please the yelping dogs. The gaps I mean,
10 No one has seen them made or heard them made,
But at spring mending-time we find them there.
I let my neighbor know beyond the hill;
And on a day we meet to walk the line
And set the wall between us again.
15 We keep the wall between us as we go.
To each the boulders that have fallen to each.
And some are loaves and some so nearly balls
We have to use a spell to make them balance:
"Stay where you are until our backs are turned!"
20 We wear our fingers rough with handling them.
Oh, just another kind of out-door game,
One on a side. It comes to little more:
There where it is we do not need the wall:
He is all pine and I am apple orchard.
25 My apple trees will never get across
And eat the cones under his pines, I tell him.
He only says, "Good fences make good neighbours."
Spring is the mischief in me, and I wonder
If I could put a notion in his head:
30 "Why do they make good neighbours? Isn't it
Where there are cows? But here there are no cows.

Before I built a wall I'd ask to know
What I was walling in or walling out,
And to whom I was like to give offence.
35 Something there is that doesn't love a wall,
That wants it down." I could say "Elves" to him,
But it's not elves exactly and I'd rather
He said it for himself. I see him there
Bringing a stone grasped firmly by the top
40 In each hand, like an old-stone savage armed.
He moves in darkness as it seems to me,
Not of woods only and the shade of trees.

Section Four
American Poetry of the Modernist Period

    He will not go behind his father's saying,
    And he likes having thought of it so well
45 He says again, "Good fences make good neighbours."

Notes

Line 1 Something...wall: There is something that doesn't love a wall;
    Something: something in nature.
Line 2 send: cause to become.
    the frozen-ground-swell: Freezing expands the damp earth, which causes the stone wall to crumble.
Line 3 boulders: large round stones.
Line 4 two: two persons.
    abreast: (move forward) side by side; shoulder by shoulder.
Lines 1-4 The poet is seeking the causes for the collapse of the wall.
    His first supposition is "something that doesn't love a wall."
Line 5 is another thing: maybe the other possible reason.
Line 6 them: the hunters.
    made repair: repaired the wall.
Line 7 have left not one stone on a stone: have turned over every piece of stone.
Line 8 But: by doing that (turning over the stones).
    would have the rabbit out of hiding: they would drive out the rabbits hiding under the stones.
Line 9 yelping dogs: excitingly barking dogs.
Line 10 them: gaps in the wall.
Line 11 spring mending-time: in spring when farmers traditionally repair their fences.
    them: the gaps.
Lines 5-11 The poets shows his second guess for the gap in the wall—the hunters' chasing of rabbits.
Line 12 beyond the hill: my neighbor on the other side of the hill.
Line 13 to walk the line: to measure, to walk along the fence together, repairing it as they go.
Line 15 keep the wall between us: (As we are measuring the length) we go along the wall on each side and keep the wall in between.
Line 16 To each...to each: Each takes up the boulders that have fallen on his side of the wall.
Line 17 loaves: boulders in a long, round shape.

so nearly balls: quite similar in shape to a ball.

Line 18 We: A "that" is needed before it to correspond with the "so" of the above line.

use a spell: use words with a magic power, make the effort (to keep the boulders in balance).

Line 19 Stay... are turned: (We are ordering the boulders to) stay at the right spot at least till the completion of our mending.

Line 20 wear our fingers rough: We got our fingers harmed when mending the wall.

Lines 12 – 20 The detailed description of our mending work.

Line 21 Oh, just... game: (our mending work is) just like another kind of outdoor game. The poet implies they don't necessarily need this job.

Line 22 One on a side: one works on each side of the wall (just as in playing tennis or other court games).

It comes to little more: It appears little more than an outdoor game.

Line 23 There where it is... wall: The wall stands at a spot where it is not really needed.

Line 24 He is... apple orchard: My neighbor has grown pine trees on his side and on my side, I have an apple orchard.

Line 25 get across: move across the wall.

Lines 21 – 27 The poet's arguments for denying the necessity of the wall and the neighbor's sincere believe that "Good fences make good neighbors." The poet rejects the wall not because of laziness: he takes this physical labor as a game though the stones "wear our fingers rough." What he really can't accept is the fact that the wall stands where people don't need it.

Line 28 Spring is... in me: Spring brings me a mischievous mood.

Line 29 put a notion in his head: have him enlightened; make him understand.

Line 31 (Isn't it) Where there are cows: Isn't it the fact that sometimes the fence makes good neighbors just because there are cows on one side?

Line 33 walling in: enclose with a wall; protect.

walling out: defend against; get rid of.

Line 34 give offense: attack or insult somebody.

Line 36 say "Elves" to him: I could explain to him that it must be the "Elves" who had knocked down the wall.

Line 37 But it's not elves exactly: Practically it could not be elves (who

Section Four
American Poetry of the Modernist Period

had knocked down the wall).
Line 38 He said it for himself: (I'd rather) he enables himself to explain the matter—what the force is which doesn't like a wall and wants it down.
Line 39 grasped firmly by the top: (My neighbor) is tightly holding a piece of stone by the top (of the stone).
Line 40 an old-stone savage armed: (like) an armed uncivilized man of the Old Stone Age.
Line 41 He moves in... to me: It seems to me as if he is roaming in darkness.
Line 42 Not of... of trees: (It seems to me he is roaming) not in the darkness of woods or in the darkness of tress; the darkness is not necessarily that of the woods or of the trees, what's worse, the neighbor, without any argument for his believe, sticks to the old saying firmly. He is actually quite in the darkness psychologically. His mind is in the darkness. His spirit is in the darkness. Therefore, the neighbor is too innocent to know the significance of a wall, to share the poet's comprehension of a wall.
Line 43 go behind: have a profound thinking about...
Line 44 likes having thought of it so well: So far, he just enjoys having kept the old saying in mind.
Lines 28 – 45 The poet's failure in persuading his neighbor to give up the unnecessary wall and the great pity he felt for the neighbor's stupidity of taking over the tradition without any further consideration over it.

Comment on the poem

The wall symbolizes the regulations made upon human beings in modern society. Living in the modern society, one is bound by many rules and laws, the establishment of which is to enforce the normal social order. A modern society without laws is hardly imaginable. Similarly, a society with too many rules is not desirable either.

Robert Frost intended to complain that in the modern world, when God is very indifferent to human beings, the natural links between individuals is, as well, collapsing. With the development of modern science and industry, more and more barriers, instead of freedom, had been, quite ironically, brought upon society, which, at most times, are rather unnecessary; however, they could not be all pulled down just for the instant obligation they would play at some ambiguous moments. In Frost's poem, the collapsing of the wall strongly suggests the human's wish to eliminate the estrangement, but the wish often results naturally in a new mending job. Sometimes people are exposed to the paradoxical fact that it is just due to the existence of these walls that human beings may possibly feel safely defended and, therefore, be calmed down to communicate just over the fence so as to, more or less, understand each other.

Some say the speaker symbolizes the younger generation who calls for a complete social change, whereas the neighbor represents the old generation who tries to keep the tradition and hates reform and change. Some agree that the wall prevents any two nations from understanding each other, hence the need to pull down this barrier so as to promote communication between two parties. Many regulations limit the imagination of human beings and make them unable to develop themselves. Therefore, this contradiction of ideas shows the dilemma of modern civilization. Human beings living in this society ought to waver between the two extremes.

参考译文

补　　墙

人们天性不喜欢墙，
它使得墙脚下的冻地膨胀，
把墙头圆石在阳光下鼓起，
　使墙裂了缝，二人并肩都走可以过去。
猎人行猎时又是另一番糟蹋：
我总是跟在他们后面去修补，
他们宁可把石头掀得乱七八糟
也要把兔子从隐处赶出来，
以讨好那群狂吠的狗。这墙上的缝
怎么出现的，谁也没看见，谁也没听见，
到了春季整修时，我们才发现。
我通知了住在山那边的邻居，
约好日子巡查地界，
在两家之间再把墙重新砌起。
我们走着，中间隔着一堵墙。
落在各边的石头，由各自去料理。
有些像长面包，有些几乎圆得像球，
费了半天劲才把它们放稳当：

Section Four
American Poetry of the Modernist Period

"老实呆在那里,等我们转过身!"
我们搬弄石头,把手磨出了茧。
哦!这不过又是一种户外游戏,
一人站在一边。比游戏没强多少。
在这地方,我们根本不需要墙:
他种的是松树,我种的是苹果树。
我的苹果树永远也不会越过去
吃掉他松树下的松球,我对他说。
他只是说:"篱笆牢,邻居好。"
春天在我心中里作祟,我在想
能不能让他明白一点:
"为什么说'篱笆牢,邻居好'?是否指的是
有牛的人家?可是我们又都没有牛啊。"

我在筑墙之前先要弄个明白,
把什么圈进来,把什么圈在外,
并且我可能得罪的是些什么人家。
人们天性不喜欢墙,
盼着墙倒塌。
我可以对他说这是"爱恶作剧的孩子",
但严格说也不是爱恶作剧的孩子。我希望
他自己能明白。我看见他在那里
搬一块石头,两手紧抓着石头的上端,
像一个旧石器时代野蛮人手执武器。
我觉得他好像走在黑暗里,
这黑暗不仅是来自深林与树阴。
他不肯探究他父亲传给他的格言,
他很满意自己一直都没有忘记,
于是再说一遍,"篱笆牢,邻居好。"
(魏慧哲 李正栓 译)

(9) Birches

When I see birches bend to left and right,
Across the lines of straighter darker trees,
I like to think some boy's been swinging them.
But swinging doesn't bend them down to stay
5   As ice storms do. Often you must have seen them

```
        Loaded with ice a sunny winter morning
        After a rain.  They click upon themselves
        As the breeze rises, and turn many-colored
        As the stir cracks and crazes their enamel.
   10   Soon the sun's warmth makes them shed crystal shells
        Shattering and avalanching on the snow crush—
        Such heaps of broken glass to sweep away
        You'd think the inner dome of heaven had fallen.
        They are dragged to the withered bracken by the load,
   15   And they seem not to break; though once they are bowed
        So low for long, they never right themselves:
        You may see their trunks arching in the woods
        Years afterwards, trailing their leaves on the ground
        Like girls on hands and knees that throw their hair
   20   Before them over their heads to dry in the sun.
        But I was going to say when Truth broke in
        With all her matter of fact about the ice storm,
        I should prefer to have some boy bend them
        As he went out and in to fetch the cows—
   25   Some boy too far from town to learn baseball,
        Whose only play was what he found himself,
        Summer or winter, and could play alone.
        Only by one he subdued his father's trees
        By riding them down over and over again
   30   Until he took the stiffness out of them,
        And not one but hung limp, not one was left
        For him to conquer.  He learned all there was
        To learn about not launching out too soon
        And so not carrying the tree away
   35   Clear to the ground.  He always kept his poise
        To the top branches, climbing carefully
        With the same pains you use to fill a cup
        Up to the brim, and even above the brim.
        Then he flung outward, feet first, with a swish,
   40   Kicking his way down through the air to the ground
        So was I once myself a swinger of birches.
        And so I dream of going back to be.
        It's when I'm weary of considerations,
        And life is too much like a pathless wood
   45   Where your face burns and tickles with the cobwebs
```

Section Four
American Poetry of the Modernist Period

Broken across it, and one eye is weeping
From a twig's having lashed across it open.
I'd like to get away from earth a while
And then come back to it and begin over.
50 May no fate willfully misunderstand me
And half grant what I wish and snatch me away
Not to return. Earth's the right place for love:
I don't know where it's likely to go better.
I'd like to go by climbing a birch tree,
55 And climb black branches up a snow-white trunk
Toward heaven, till the tree could bear no more,
But dipped its top and set me down again.
That would be good both going and coming back.
One could do worse than be a swinger of birches.

Notes

birch: a type of northern forest tree with smooth bark and thin branches.
Line 1 bend to left and right: (the branches of a birch) turn, curve or crook to left and right. The tree spreads widely but not always straightly.
Line 2 Across the lines of straighter darker trees: looking through some other trees which are straighter and darker than birches.
Line 3 I like to think: I prefer to imagine the scene.
　　　　some: a person who is unknown.
　　　　swinging them: shaking the trees (when the boys are gaming).
Lines 4 – 5 But swinging doesn't bend them down to stay as ice storms do: But the boy's shaking is not as forceful as the power of the ice storms to bend them down towards earth.
Lines 1 – 5 When I see some birches bending towards the ground, I suppose it results from a boy's mischief or from the ice storms.
Lines 7 – 8 click upon themselves as the breeze rises: After a rain, in the gentle breeze, the branches of the tree are likely to have a thin cover of ice and while they strike each other they give out the slight short sound.
Lines 8 – 9 and turn many-colored as the stir cracks and crazes their enamel: When the gentle wind blows, the icy coat of the branches cracks and crazes and that may turn the branches into very rich

colors.

Line 9 stir: the striking of the branches with each other in the gentle wind.

Line 10 makes them shed crystal shells: The warmth of the sun will melt the icy coat of the branches and cause them to fall from the tree like crystal shells.

Line 11 Shattering and avalanching on the snow crush: (the crystal shells will) break into pieces and will pile up on the snow-covered ground.

Line 12 heaps of broken glass: large amount of the fallen ice.

sweep away: sweep off one's sidewalks.

Line 13 You'd think: you may mistake it as...

the inner dome of heaven: In Frost's time, glass is much more precious than it is today. Here, the poet is supposing the heaven as a magnificent building, which must be decorated with precious materials. Therefore, the icy crust of the tree is described as "crystal shells" in Line 10 and appears in this line as the broken glass of the dome of heaven.

Line 14 They are dragged to the withered bracken: The branches of the birch have been weighed down (by the icy coat) towards the ground and have almost touched the dry bracken there.

Line 16 right themselves: return themselves to an upright position.

Line 17 their trunks arching in the woods: the trunks of birch tress cannot grow straight among the other trees.

Line 18 trailing their leaves on the ground: their stems are growing spreadingly and drooping to the ground.

Line 19 girls on hands and knees: girls in the posture with hands and knees on the ground (for showing respect).

In Lines 19 and 20, the poet used a simile, it presents a lovely picture of girls in the bright sunshine.

Lines 6 – 20 A detailed description of a birch in winter is presented.

Line 21 Truth: the truth which had been universally recognized. The poet had this word personified here, and thus, a "her" appears in the next line.

broke in: interrupted one's words (about the frozen birch).

Line 23 I should prefer to have some boy bend them: I would rather the branches were bent by some boys.

Line 24 went out and in: as (the boy) went out and in the woods.

Line 25 baseball: Baseball is a game played in a team with other boys. But when playing trees, the boy plays alone. He has to learn by

Section Four
American Poetry of the Modernist Period

himself and teach himself.
Line 28 subdued his father's trees: played with the trees planted by his father.
Line 30 Until he took the stiffness out of them: Until the trees are no longer stiff at all.
Line 31 not one but hung limp: (until) every branch is not firm any more.
Lines 32 – 33 He learned all there was to learn: (When riding a tree) the boy learned whatever he could from a tree.
Line 33 not launching out too soon: (The boy had learned when riding a tree) he should not let go off the tree too quickly.
Line 35 Clear to the ground: directly and very closely down to the ground.
Lines 35 – 36 kept his poise to the top branches: when the boy is high in the tree, he always tries to keep good balance there.
Line 37 pains: efforts; cares.
Line 38 and even above the brim: Scientifically, water in a cup can grow a bit above the brim just because of the surface tension, but this must be done gingerly.
Line 39 with a swish: (swing through the air) with a hissing sound.
Line 41 So was I once myself a swinger of birches: I myself was once a swinger of birches. Once when I was a boy I had the same experience of swinging on a birch tree too.
Line 42 And so now, though I am much older, I still hope to return to my childhood and play with trees again.
to be: to be a swinger of birches.
Lines 22 – 42 Despite the work of the storms, the poet still prefers to believe it is some boy's mischievous game that had bent the branches, and that reminds him of his boyhood experience.
Line 43 It: time when I wish I could return to boyhood.
I'm weary of considerations: I feel tired of the sophistications of the world.
Line 45 your face burns: your face may be marked or injured by the sun or by hard work.
tickles with the cobwebs: the cobwebs (in the pathless wood) may cause a tingling sensation when one wants to break across it.
Lines 46 – 47 and one eye is weeping from a twig's having lashed across it open: and there are tears in one of the eyes, for there had been a twig lashed across it when it was open.

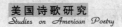

Line 48 I'd like to get away from earth a while: I'd like to leave this annoying human world for a short time.

Line 49 begin over: begin all over; start again.

Line 50 May no fate willfully misunderstand me: I don't hope any fate intentionally misunderstand me.

Line 51 And half grant what I wish: and (I don't hope the fate will) half agree or admit what I had wished.

snatch me away: seize or grab me away quickly.

Line 56 till the tree could bear no more: till the climber is too tall for the tree to bear his weight.

Line 57 dipped its top: (the tree) has bent until its top is close to the ground.

set me down again: brought me back to the ground again.

Line 58 That would be good both going and coming back: both going and coming back would be good.

Line 59 One could do worse than be a swinger of birches: Being a swinger may not be the best way of human life, it may be destructive to the trees. Anyway, it is close to nature. Somebody lived worse than that, for they are completely alien to nature.

Lines 43－59 The poet meditates on the matter of human life. Though life is "like a pathless wood" and he prefers to get away a while, he finally admits "Earth is the right place for love" and he would like to be set back to the world again for the whole enjoyment of life.

Comment on the poem

Birches are very common trees in Northern America. Robert Frost, as the poet good at exploring complexity through triviality, expressed in this poem, quite effortlessly, his comprehension of life through colloquial language and conversational rhythms. However, the poet did not praise the pastoral scenery to intend an escape from modern life; instead, he did it as a way to understand modern life.

The poem, composed of 59 lines, is in the form of blank verse. The first 5 lines can be taken as a brief introduction to the whole, a reminder for the poet of his boyhood. From the 6th line to the 20th, a vivid picture of birches under snow is presented: The slim twigs with ice, in the gentle breeze of the sunny winter morning, are "bending, swinging, clicking" in various colors; when the branches are "cracking" and "crazing", "shattering" and "avalanching" as though the "inner dome of heaven had fallen," the picture is added with contrasting colors and lively sounds. The simile of the trunks, "trailing their leaves on the ground like girls on hands and knees that throw their hair before them over their heads to dry in the sun" is so original and novel that it enhances the presentation in a great scale.

The words of Line 21 to Line 40 contribute to the description of the country boys' gaming at conquering the birches. The memory of a country boy's childhood may be the one of loneliness: He did not have the chance to learn baseball, a team game; his playmates are animals or trees; any pleasure, if he wants any, must be learned by himself. Juxtaposed with human kindness, the specific depicting of a birch swinger can often remind anyone of the pleasant time of childhood.

The recalling of a childhood game results in a meditation over reality. As a former swinger of birches, the poet felt "Life is too much like a pathless wood" where "your face burns and tickles with the cobwebs broken across it, and one eye is weeping from a twig's having lashed across it open." That leads to the inclination of the poet "to get away from earth a while." Fortunately, the poet remains an optimist as he believes in "Earth is the right place for love" and wishes to "come back to it and begin over." There is something miserable and cruel in this world, however, we cannot find anywhere better. As the boy's swinging of a birch, it may be destructive to the tree, it brings one, anyhow, close to nature. One can jump off the earth a while or escape from the reality for a time, but no one is able to stay completely away from earth. Consequently, any avoidance of reality is a temporary recession for inspiring greater confidence and ambition in life.

Frost believes that a poem begins in delight and ends in wisdom. This poem provides the best interpretation to this theory by starting with the description of winter scenery and ends with a philosophical argument.

参考译文

白 桦 树

我看见白桦树向左右两边弯下身子，
黑树直直的枝条下垂，
肯定是有孩子一直在上边打秋千。
可是荡悠一下不会叫它们再也起不来，
不像冰封一样。冬雨过后，
朝阳初照，
你准会看到白桦上挂满了冰。

微风轻扬,树枝就咯喇喇作响,
这一颤动,冰块就像瓷瓶,
裂成无数细纹,闪射出五彩缤纷。
很快阳光的温暖使那水晶般的硬壳
从树枝上崩落,倾泻在雪地上——
这么一大堆碎玻璃要打扫,
你还以为是天顶的华盖塌了下来。
不堪重负,枝条被冰压下去,
直到贴近地面的枯草,
但并没折断;虽然一度被压得
这么低、这么久。
他们再也没有直起来:
数年后,你会在森林里看到那些白桦树:
弓着树干,树叶在地面上拖拉着,
好像趴在地上的女孩子把一头长发
甩到头前,好让太阳把头发晒干。
我原是想说,(可是事实插开话题,
说起那雨后的冰柱,)
我宁愿是个孩子,
来回走过拉牛的时候把白桦弄弯了。
或这孩子离城太远,没人教棒球,
他只能自个儿想出玩意儿来玩,
不管夏天冬天,自个儿能玩的游戏,
只有征服他父亲的树,
一次又一次地把它们骑在胯下,
直到把树的倔强劲儿完全制服,
一株又一株都弯下来
直到他再没有用武之地。他掌握了
所有的技巧:不能立刻跳上去,
免得一下子把树干扳到了地面。
他始终保持平衡,一直到
那高高的顶枝上——小心翼翼地
往上爬,就像把一杯水倒满,
满到了杯口,甚至满过了边缘的那样谨慎。
然后,纵身一跳,
两脚先伸出去,在空中一登,
于是飕的一声,落到地面。
我自己也曾经是"荡桦树"的能手,

Section Four
American Poetry of the Modernist Period

还梦想着再去荡一回桦树，
那是每逢我厌倦于思考世事，
而人生太像一片没有小径的森林，
摸索中撞在蛛网上，你的脸又热辣、又刺痒，
一根嫩枝迎面打来，
睁着的眼睛一只被打中，疼得直掉泪。
我真想暂时离开人世一会儿，
然后再回来，重新开始。
但愿命运之神不要故意曲解我，
只成全我愿望的一半就把我卷走，
一去不返。人间是有爱的地方，
我想不出还有哪儿是更好的去处。
我真想去爬白桦树，
沿着雪白的树干爬上乌黑的树枝，
爬向那天堂，直到树身再也支撑不住，
树梢碰着地，把我放下来。
来来去去都很好。
"荡桦树"不是最好，可是更糟糕的比比皆是。
（魏慧哲 译 李正栓 校）

(10) Nothing Gold Can Stay

Nature's first green is gold,
Her hardest hue to hold.
Her early leaf's a flower;
But only so an hour.
5   Then leaf subsides to leaf.
So Eden sank to grief,
So dawn goes down to day.
Nothing gold can stay.

Notes

Line 1 Nature decorates its early stage with gold, the most precious color of all, thus nature was generous at the beginning of life.
green: In old English, "green" signified "growth" as well as a color. In addition to that, "green" also implies "unripe."

Line 2 hue: variety or shade of color.
Line 3 Her early leaf: the youth of human beings.
Line 4 only so an hour: very short.
Line 5 leaf subsides to leaf: leaves may quietly wither away one layer under the other.
Line 6 Eden sank to grief: the merriest garden as Eden may be turned into a sorrowful place. The Hebrew word "Eden" means "delight," and it is here contrasted with "grief." (*The American Tradition in Literature*, Perkins, p1285)
Line 7 dawn goes down to day: time moves forward inevitably.
Line 8 Nothing gold can stay: Nothing, however precious it may have been, can stand the wearing of time.

Comment on the poem

Time, youth, and flower are the most precious in human life. Nature has been so generous to human beings as to decorate the first half of life with gold. However, in the eternal nature, season changes, time fleets; confronting the constancy of nature, the human being's existence is so trivial and frail that it easily withers away just as "leaf subsides to leaf." The poet is sighing with sadness and helplessness. The helpless sigh will be taken as a warning or goad to motivate us to take good advantage of time and to appreciate life.

The poem is written with the typical features of Frost's work: easy vocabulary, plain structure, and very smooth style but also with profound meaning. The rhyme scheme, "aabbccdd," semi-modern and semi-traditional, is characteristic of Robert Frost, too.

参考译文

金贵之物难永垂

自然的初绿是金，
她这颜色最难存。
她早期叶子是花；
时间只是一刹那。
叶落又催新叶生，
伊甸园尽忧愁成，
黎明之后白日随。

Section Four
American Poetry of the Modernist Period

金贵之物难永垂。
（李正栓　译）

(11) Departmental

An ant on the tablecloth
Ran into a dormant moth
Of many times his size.
He showed not the least surprise.
5　His business wasn't with such.
He gave it scarcely a touch,
And was off on his duty run.
Yet if he encountered one
Of the hive's enquiry squad
10　Whose work is to find out God
And the nature of time and space,
He would put him unto the case.
Ants are a curious race;
One crossing with hurried tread
15　The body of one of their dead
Isn't given a moment's arrest—
Seems not even impressed.
But he no doubt reports to any
With whom he crosses antennae,
20　And they no doubt report
To the higher-up at court.
Then word goes forth in Formic:
"Death's come to Jerry McCormic,
Our selfless forager Jerry.
25　Will the special Janizary
Whose office it is to bury
The dead of the commissary
Go bring him home to his people.
Lay him in state on a sepal.
30　Wrap him for shroud in a petal.
Embalm him with ichor of nettle.
This is the word of your Queen."
And presently on the scene
Appears a solemn mortician;

35　And taking formal position,
　　With feelers calmly at widdle,
　　Seizes the dead by the middle,
　　And heaving him high in air,
　　Carries him out of there.
40　No one stands round to stare.
　　It is nobody else's affair.

　　It couldn't be called ungentle.
　　But how thoroughly departmental.

Notes

Line 2 Ran into: met with by chance.
　　　　dormant: temporarily inactive.
Line 4 He: the ant.
Line 5 with such: such things as to show surprise to the meeting of a moth.
Line 7 off on his duty run: ran off to do his duty.
Lines 8 – 9 one of the hive's enquiry squad: a group of ants coming out form the same hive for their duty of gathering information.
Line 12 He would put him unto the case: The ant would go up and make a brief inquiry of their duty.
Line 14 hurried tread: quick and heavy steps.
Line 15 The body of one of their dead: the dead of one of his folk ants.
Line 16 Isn't given a moment's arrest: the ant does not stop.
Line 17 Seems not even impressed: The ant seems not being impressed by the death of one of his folk at all.
Line 18 reports to any: reports the death of his folk to any other ant he meets on the way.
Line 19 whom: the any other ant meets on the way.
　　　　crosses antennae: touches each others' antennae, a sign of intimacy and recognition.
Line 20 they: those with whom he crosses antennae.
Line 21 the higher-up at court: the more important figures in high positions.
Line 22 word goes forth in Formic: word in the language of Formic may widely spread.

Section Four
American Poetry of the Modernist Period

Formic: the language of ants. The family of ants is called the Formicidae.

Line 23 Jerry McCormic: name of the dead ant. A typical name in Irish world.

Line 24 selfless forager: Jerry, whose duty is searching for food for all, is very selfless.

Line 25 the special Janizary: Janizary who are in the special duty of ... Janizary: A member of the special troops assigned to Turkish sovereigns. In this line, the word refers to the ant with the special duty of burying the dead; a mortician.

Lines 26 – 27 an attributive clause modifying "Janizary."

Line 27 commissary: those responsible for provision and supply.

Line 28 him: Jerry McCormic.

Line 29 Lay him in state on a sepal: Place our selfless Jerry on a sepal for the mourning from others.

sepal: the leaf-like part of a plant which lie under and support the petals of a flower.

Line 30 Wrap him for shroud in a petal: wrap Jerry McCormic in a petal as if it is the shroud.

Line 31 Embalm him with ichor of nettle: preserve his body from decay by daubing a thin film of the nasty liquid of rotten nettle.

nettle: wild plant with hairs on its leaves that sting and redden the skin when touched.

Line 32 the word of your Queen: the order of the Queen of ants.

Line 33 presently on the scene: immediately I can see it.

Line 34 mortician: one whose business is to prepare the dead for burial or cremation and arrange funerals; undertaker.

Line 35 taking formal position: began to work very normatively and professionally.

Line 36 With feelers calmly at widdle: the mortician is working with his antennae turning back and forth, but rather calmly (without showing the least of his passion).

Line 38 heaving him high in air: forcefully raising the corpse high in the air.

Line 40 to stare: to victim; to attend the funeral; to show their lament.

Line 42 ungentle: unkind; not sympathetic.

Line 43 departmental: canonical; indifferent to each other.

Comment on the poem

This poem, by depicting the regularity of ants' life, condemns the indifference of them, and consequently implies the indifference of the human world. Each ant has its duty and does not give "a moment's arrest" to any others' affairs. Quite similarly, human communication is obstructed by laws or regulations of the society. Departmentalizing affords society with good order. It, however, estranges one person from another to the extent that every job is done for the fulfillment of a duty without the least normal passions between the congeners.

The moral of the poem is educed by the description of a single ant's activity of carrying out its duty. The mortician ant in this poem, following the prescribed order in doing everything, just had the burying of one of its fellows professionally completed done, without the usual mourning from the family, nor with the bemoaning from the fellow workers. Each is busy in its duty but without communication, let alone the cooperation of any kind. A society like this, either the one of ants or that of humans, is perfect but cruel: the thorough departmentalization resulting from the perfection of the social order is sure to dehumanize and estrange social members into unsympathetic individuals. The world of ants is the miniature cosmos of human society.

The poem is structured in rhymed couplets without the division of stanzas. This contributes to the fluency of presentation and comprehension.

参考译文

本位主义

桌布上的一只蚂蚁，
偶然遇到一只比它自己
大好几倍的正在睡觉的飞蛾，
它丝毫没有惊愕。
它碰都不碰一下，
因为这不是在它的职责，
它离开飞蛾，继续履行自己的义务。
但如果看见同穴中的调查小组
来探寻上帝
还有时间与空间的性质，
它将上前问个究竟。
蚂蚁是一类奇特的物种：

它们会脚步迅疾,
越过同类的尸体,
一点也不予理睬,
似乎毫不挂怀。
但遇到深交的同类,
必将消息传兑。
必将把所见所闻,
向上一级汇报充分。
之后命令用蚁语颁布:
"杰瑞麦克考米命乌呼,
他是我们无私的搜粮者。
请专司埋葬死者
的殡葬官
把它带回来交给族人下葬。
把它体面地放在萼片上,
用花瓣寿衣给他裹身,
荨麻灵液把它泡浸。
这是蚁后的旨意。"
不久,现场出现一
肃穆的殡仪员:
一丝不苟地把活儿干,
他庄重就位
触角平静地转动来回,
抓住逝者的腰体,
高高地把他举起,
带它离开现场。
没有人驻足观看,
这事与任何人无关。
这不能被称作是不仁慈,
但确是彻头彻尾的本位主义。
(李正栓 魏慧哲 译)

II. Edwin Arlington Robinson
(1869 – 1935)

1. Life Story

When Robinson was born, American literature was flourishing with fictional works. Francis Harte, Mark Twain, and Henry James were all at the summit of their talent. It was the time when the novel had developed into full scale and poetry had entered an era confronted with crises: poets were no longer being honored as the King's respected guests. Because of the rapid development of industry, poets were forced to try any new themes or styles possible for their survival, to have a revolution of language so as to reconstruct poetry in a new literary form. This is why Robinson, as the transitional poet of the time, wasn't recognized as a poet of the first class until he won the Pulitzer Prize in 1922 for his *Collected Poems*.

Robinson, whose initials spell E. A. R. (ear), was ironically born deaf in one ear. He was born on December 22 in Head Tide, but grew up in Gardiner, Maine. He was a descendant of Anne Bradstreet. After a lonely childhood, Robinson managed to enter Harvard University for two years, which, though not enough for creating a prominent poet, widened his eyesight and brought him some new friends and new ideas.

Robinson grew up with no other ambitions but that of becoming a poet. However, being introspective by nature and poor in health, he was always lonely. While fond of his family, he felt himself an outsider among the other members; friendship seemed great favor, he always felt alienated from the society of his own. As a result, his life was often isolated and miserable.

Fortunately, Robinson, even in the darkest part of his time, did not give up his belief in man's highest duty that each one is to develop his best attributes as fully as possible. Being by nature introspective and conscious of psychological depth, Robinson, the one who was often at a loss as a social creature, was actually rather quick and accurate in catching and interpreting the spiritual world of human beings. With his wide reading of classic works and the influence of Thomas Hardy (1840 – 1928), Robinson succeeded in bringing his attributes to the summit by winning the Pulitzer Prize in 1922, in spite of the pessimistic mood in most of his works.

2. Major Works of Robinson

For Robinson, the year 1921 was a dividing line. Before 1921, several volumes of poems were published but attracted little public attention, though President Roosevelt helped him to get a better job after reading his poems. In 1921, his *Collected Poems*, poems about wasted, or impoverished life in American society, was published and brought him his first Pulitzer Prize.

From 1921, his career as a poet was smooth. *The Man Who Dies Twice* came out in 1924 and gained him a second Pulitzer Prize.

Three years later, a long narrative poem, *Tristram* (1927) won him the Pulitzer Prize for the third time.

3. Writing Features of Robinson

(1) Theme: The futility of human life is the very frequent theme of Robinson. He created out of the model of his hometown, a naturalistic world, Tilbury town, where life seems futile and meaningless.

(2) Style: traditional verse form on non-poetic subjects.
Robinson was skillful in staying content with the old way and calmly expressing his individual view of life and hence succeeded in evaluating the current society.

(3) Language: Robinson used non-poetic language for non-poetic subjects.
Robinson did not write in dialect, but he made the effort to use plain language, the language of the folk speech pattern, which he believed would best convey the emotion of people. He was not interested in the innovative or experimental writing of poetry of the time. On account of this, such traditional factors as beat, rhyme, rhythm, meter, foot, etc. can still be seen in his poems.

(4) Irony: Robinson's poems are characterized with a striking ironic tone. In his poems, the sense of humor is too often juxtaposed with a pervading sense of alienation or futility, that would quite likely result in a strong impression of irony. Since man is absolutely powerless in the destructive hand of time, all the joy, entertainment, love, friendship, is rather ironic, and is the laughter of the devil, in the face of death.

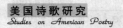

4. Selected Poems

(1) Richard Cory

Whenever Richard Cory went down town,
We people on the pavement looked at him:
He was a gentleman from sole to crown,
Clean favored, and imperially slim.

5   And he was always quietly arrayed,
And he was always human when he talked;
But still he fluttered pulses when he said
"Good-morning," and he glittered when he walked.

And he was rich—yes, richer than a king—
10 And admirably schooled in every grace:
In fine, we thought that he was everything
To make us wish that we were in his place.

So on we worked, and waited for the light,
And went without the meat, and cursed the bread;
15 And Richard Cory, one calm summer night,
Went home and put a bullet through his head.

Notes

Line 3 a gentleman from sole to crown: (he was) gentlemanlike from top to feet; (he was) a standard gentleman.
Line 4 Clean favored: clean and tidy; neat and elegant in appearance.
imperially slim: slim but not without the majestic air.

Stanza 1: An introduction of Richard Cory and a suspense about his popularity is intended.

Line 5 quietly arrayed: properly dressed.
Line 6 human: sympathetic and understanding others.
Lines 7 – 8 But he still causes people's pulses to beat irregularly or he still makes the passers-by feel extremely flattered when being greeted by him.

Line 8 glittered when he walked: wherever he goes, he appears very attractive and people's eyes focus on him.

Stanza 2: A further description of Richard Cory's character and the neighbors' impression of him.

Line 10 admirably schooled: well educated; strictly trained.
    in every grace: in all manners; in every aspects.
Line 11 In fine: to make a long story short; in short.

Stanza 3: A depiction of Richard Cory's family background, his education, his social status and his accomplishment which arose the admiration from us all.

Line 13 So on we worked: So we worked on and on after his model; we worked on and on by just following his example.
    waited for the light: waited for the opportunities to change our lives; waited for good fortune to fall upon us.
Line 14 went without the meat: (For the purpose of catching up with Richard Cory, we had to) live a thrifty life and eat meat at long intervals or none at all.
    cursed the bread: (we) grudged having bread everyday. This is the way for the ordinary people to save money so as to accumulate a large sum and become rich.
Line 16 put a bullet through his head: committed suicide.

Stanza 4: Out of the admiration for Richard Cory, we grudged ourselves for a dream of being like him, but, unexpectedly, he killed himself one calm summer night.

Comment on the poem

This poem was published in 1897.

The poem ends with an open ending by not telling why Richard Cory died which provides wider range for imagination. The possible reasons for it may be numerous but the absolute fact is that people in modern times, when God is quite indifferent to us, want sufficient opportunities to communicate and mutual understanding as well.

The poem does not tell why Richard Cory killed himself. That is left for the readers to think over. Robinson just wrote this like O. Henry's story-with a surprising ending.

Like Frost, Robinson gained great reputation in poetry for his experiments in various poetic forms. Moreover, the majority of his works are imagery and very symbolic, as we can see in *Richard Cory and Miniver Cheevy*, which are, as a matter of fact, character portraits written in perfect regular stanzas. However, Robinson wrote only these two in the same form. He devoted the late part of his life to the writing of long poems.

Many of Robinson's poems were written in a pessimistic tone. Being always with failures of various kinds, life seems unacceptable to him.

参考译文

理查·科里

理查·科里走在大街上，
人们驻足路旁把他看：
他绅士气派、无限风光，
他仪表堂堂身似仙。

他穿着朴素不彰显，
谈吐文而雅又达理；
他向人们问"早安"，
声音令人悦，步态光四溢。

家缠万贯胜国王——
学问美德令人羡：
人间一切唯他强
令人欲把其位换。

我们苦苦劳作盼荣光，
无肉可吃，诅咒面包坏；
一个宁静夏日夜，
他回家，枪推子弹穿脑袋。

（李正栓　译）

Section Four
American Poetry of the Modernist Period

(2) Miniver Cheevy

Miniver Cheevy, child of scorn,
    Grew lean while he assailed the seasons;
He wept that he was ever born;
    And he had reasons.

5   Miniver loved the days of old
    When swords were bright and steeds were prancing;
The vision of a warrior bold
    Would set him dancing

Miniver sighed for what was not,
10   And dreamed, and rested from his labors;
He dreamed of Thebes and Camelot,
    And Priam's neighbors.
Miniver mourned the ripe renown
    That made so many a name so fragrant;
15 He mourned Romance, now on the town,
    And Art, a vagrant.

Miniver loved the Medici,
    Albeit he had never seen one;
He would have sinned incessantly
20   Could he have been one.

Miniver cursed the commonplace
    And eyed a khaki suit with loathing;
He missed the medieval grace
    Of iron clothing.
25 Miniver scorned the gold he sought,
    But sore annoyed was he without it;
Miniver thought, and thought, and thought,
    And thought about it.

Miniver Cheevy, born too late,
30   Scratched his head and kept on thinking;
Miniver coughed, and called it fate,
    And kept on drinking.

Notes

Line 1 child of scorn: a scornful child; one who is apt to complain.
       scorn: strong usually angry feeling of disrespect, contempt.
Line 2 Grew lean: became very thin; become frail.
       assailed the seasons: killed the time.
Line 3 wept: cried regretfully.
Line 4 he had reasons: he had reasons to weep, to be regretful.

Stanza 1: Miniver Cheevy is a scornful child and he regrets he was ever born at his time.

Line 5 the days of old: ancient time; Middle Ages.
Line 6 steeds: horses.
       prancing: run quickly and proudly with a springing or dancing step.
Line 7 a warrior bold: a bold warrior; an adventurous soldier.
Line 8 set him dancing: excite him; cause him dance for joy.

Stanza 2: Miniver Cheevy deeply indulges himself in a dream of Middle Age soldiers. Any image of them would result in his enthusiasm.

Line 9 sighed for what was not: felt very sorry for the fact that he was unable to become an ancient warrior; longed for what did not exist.
Line 10 rested from his labor: (while he indulged himself in dreaming, he) stopped working.
Line 11 Thebes: capital city in Boeotia, rival of ancient Athens and Sparta.
       Camelot: the legendary court of King Arthur and the knights of the Round Table located close to the present Winchester.
Line 12 Priam: the last king of Troy, father of 50 sons including Hector and Paris, the latter stole Helen away from Sparta and thus aroused the Trojan War. "Priam's neighbors" refer to the neighboring countries of Troy. In this poem, together with Priam, they all indicate the embodiments of ancient heroes.

Stanza 3: Miniver Cheevy is so absorbed in his dreaming of the old city, old heroic kings and the ancient heroes that he had completely neglected his business.

Section Four
American Poetry of the Modernist Period

Line 13 mourned the ripe renown: grieve for the brilliant achievements (in literature and art) of the old time.
Line 14 That: the ripe renown.
　　　　so many a name: so many names (of the ancient heroes).
Line 15 Romance: literature.
Line 16 And Art: And he also mourned for Art.

Stanza 4: Miniver Cheevy was extremely sorrowful for the mistreatment to literature and art, which, in the modern world, have long been deserted, and which is now wandering in town like beggars.

Line 17 Medici: Family of wealthy merchants, statesmen and art patrons in Renaissance Florence. Many businessmen, politicians and literary men came from the family and some of them were notorious for ruthlessness and sinfulness.
Line 18 Albeit: Although.
　　　　one: a single member of the Medici family.
Line 19 incessantly: never stopping; continuously.
Lines 19 – 20 If he were a member of the Medici family, he would have been as ruthless and sinful just as some members of that family used to be.

Stanza 5: Miniver Cheevy longed to be a member of Medici family so as to live a ruthless life.

Line 21 commonplace: the plainness.
Line 22 eyed: looked at; regarded... as...
　　　　khaki suit: military uniform of a yellowish brown color; the military uniform of modern time.
　　　　loathing: a feeling of disgust; hatred.
Line 24 iron clothing: ancient military uniform made of iron; armor.

Stanza 6: Miniver Cheevy misses the ancient warriors but shows contempt for modern soldiers.

Line 25 the gold he sought: the money, wealth he obtained.
Line 26 sore annoyed was he without it: he became anxious if he was without money.
　　　　sore: sorely.
　　　　it: money; wealth.

Stanza 7: Miniver Cheevy scorns money but he was annoyed when he was without it.

Line 29 born too late: Miniver Cheevy regrets he was born too late.
Line 30 Scratched his head: Miniver Cheevy scratched his head.
Line 31 it: the fact that he was born too late.
Line 32 kept on drinking: He found solace nowhere else but in his cup.

Stanza 8: He was born late and he could not do anything for a change. Miniver Cheevy indulged himself in drinking.

Comment on the poem

　　Miniver Cheevy, sounding rather similar to "mini achieves," is the lively sketch of an ambitious and cynical young man who believes he would be successful in any other age but the present one. This kind of person is often too cynical to face reality. Their life is, therefore, a succession of windbaggary and complaints. They are used to imagining wild and far but resentful for any practical intentions. They feel that life is futile but still live with an optimistic desperation—attempting to search for excuses for all the failure in reality. However, due to the frailty in nature, the best resolution they result in is often "kept on drinking," which, instead of easing them from misery, plunges them deeper into suffering.

参考译文

弥尼沃·切维

弥尼沃·切维怨天又怨地，
他终日虚度，身材瘦削，
他常恨自己生不逢时，
他却哭的有理由。

弥尼沃喜欢遥远古日子：
那时候，宝剑锋利，战马奔腾，
想象着勇敢的战士
便会点燃他狂热的激情。

Section Four
American Poetry of the Modernist Period

他慨叹不是其中一员,
心神恍惚,荒废手中的活计,
梦见古城底比斯,又梦见亚瑟王的宫殿,
还梦见普里阿摩斯的古邻居。

弥尼沃悲痛那远扬的名声,
它使无数美名如此传世流芳;
他悲叹传奇文学遗废城,
他哀叹艺术沦落于丐帮。

弥尼沃热爱梅第奇这家族,
尽管家族风貌从未睹。
倘若真能成一员,
他也会罪孽累累不间断。

弥尼沃诅咒这平凡界,
看见黄色军装就生恨,
他盼望中世纪优雅永不灭,
他思念铁甲铠衣威风凛凛。

弥尼沃鄙视自己聚巨财,
无财富,他又忧恨心中生;
他思来想去又思来,
试图把这事想明白。

生不逢时的弥尼沃
骚首皱眉又思索;
他咳嗽完后认了命
杯复一杯酒不停。
(李正栓 韩志华 译)

(3) The House on the Hill

They are all gone away,
   The house is shut and still,
There is nothing more to say.

Through broken walls and gray

5   The winds blow bleak and shrill:
    They are all gone away.

    Nor is there one to-day
      To speak them good or ill:
    There is nothing more to say.

10   Why is it then we stray
      Around the sunken sill?
    They are all gone away.

    And our poor fancy-play
      For them is wasted skill:
15   There is nothing more to say.

    There is a ruin and decay
      In the House on the Hill:
    They are all gone away,
    There is nothing more to say.

Notes

Line 4 Through broken walls and gray: Through broken and gray walls. The inverted order aims at the regular rhyme scheme.

Line 5 The winds blows bleak and shrill: the winds are blowing bleakly and shrilly.

Line 7 Nor is there one to-day: no one is there at present in this house.

Line 8 To speak them good or ill: to praise, admire or execrate them.

Line 10 stray: wander; move away from one's proper place with no fixed destination or purpose.

Line 11 the sunken sill: the collapsed window.

Line 13 our poor fancy-play: the simple and plain games often played during our childhood.

Line 14 For them is wasted skill: Is wasted skill for them. Because the games are too easy and they are all adults now.

Comment on the poem

    This poem is written in strict Villanelle style, a popular verse style

Section Four
American Poetry of the Modernist Period

in 16th century France, with 6 stanzas, 3 lines for each of the first 5 stanzas, but 4 lines for the last. The first and the last lines of the first stanza appear alternatively at the end of the next 4 stanzas until in the last stanza, they meet to conclude the whole. The repetition and cycling structure contribute greatly to a nostalgic mood.

The house in the poem is the one in which the poet enjoyed his childhood. Now it is "broken and gray" with "sunken sill," all the old acquaintances had left. The memory of childhood games just makes the poet even more sentimental and sad. Robinson, as a naturalist poet, is accustomed to looking at the world on the pessimistic side and presenting the predestinate emotion. In this poem, he succeeds in these by concise words, exquisite structure, and very melodic rhythm.

参考译文

山上的房子

他们都走了，
房门紧闭无声息，
再也没什么可说的了。

寒风呼号尖叫
穿透破裂灰黑的墙：
他们都走了。

如今没有一人要
把他们评说：
再也没什么可说的了。

那么我们干吗要
在塌陷的基石旁流连？
再也没什么可说的了。

我们那些可怜欢腾的嬉闹
今天已成废弃的游戏：
再也没什么可说的了。

山上的房子里
一片废墟、万物枯凋：
他们都走了，
再也没什么可说的了。
（李正栓 译）

III. Stephen Crane
(1871 – 1900)

1. Life Story

In spite of the limitation of short life, Stephen Crane was well-known as the first American Naturalist novelist. However, another surprise is that, besides novels, Crane also contributed some valuable poems to the literary history of the State.

Crane was born in Newark, New Jersey, the 14th and the youngest child of a Methodist clergyman's family. Though sickly and frail in appearance from the very beginning, Crane was a rebel in the religious, conventional family. He attended the university but devoted more time to sports than to his studying of any curriculum and he, thus, left the school and started his writing career as a roving reporter. His first novel, *Maggie, a Girl in the Streets*, was published in 1893 at his own expense. The book, though it was later regarded as the first naturalist work in American literary history, was rejected by both the editors and the critics due to its stark description of the seamy side of the society. Crane's fame as a writer came to him in 1895 with the publication of his second novel, *The Red Badge of Courage*. The revealing, alarming honesty of the effects of war on a raw recruit won the appreciation of such prominent writers as Howells and Henry James, and what's more, it won the admiration of some veterans of the Civil War.

As a poet, Crane was recognized also in the same year with the publication of his first collection of poems, *The Black Riders and Other Lines*, which was, as a matter of fact, composed in very experimental form and with many startling images and appeared too unconventional to be widely accepted. His second volume of poetry came out in 1899 under the title of *War Is Kind*. Crane died of tuberculosis in Germany on June 5, 1900 at the age of 29. It is a pity he died too early; however, as a very diligent writer, Crane contributed to the world novels, short stories, and poetry of about 12 volumes.

2. Writing Features of Crane

Probably due to his poor health, Crane was by nature a pessimist. Influenced by Charles Darwin's Evolution Theory, Crane believed that when God died and people are left alone in an indifferent or even hostile world, and when a human's fate is completely decided by heredity and environment, where might is power, human beings are rather helpless and nothing like dignity or honor is able to exist before the crushing forces of nature. Consequently, as a person with social responsibility, Crane took up his pen to expose the cruelty of modern society by interpreting the naturalist ideas in various written forms and thus became a pioneer in the American naturalist tradition.

Whether as a novelist, short story teller, or a poet, Crane dwelt on the depiction of the truth of the harsher realities of American life.

Insisting in telling the truth at all costs, Crane made every effort to report reality, truthfully and objectively, to expose the darkness of the world. As a result, the tone of his works is often pessimistic and gloomy.

With the influence of the impressionistic painters, Crane was good at taking advantage from private symbols, namely picking an object from an experience and giving it a symbolic meaning. This exerted a significant influence on later imagist poetry and his poetic works were hence recognized as the earliest imagist poetry.

In his novels as well as in poetry, Crane tells everything directly but vividly. His syntax is usually on the simple side, however, he is very careful in choosing a narrative point of view. Most frequently, Crane would start from a scientific observer's view to present nature's indifference to man, or to record the physical, emotional, and intellectual response of man under extreme pressure.

3. Selected Poems

(1) Black Riders Came from the Sea

Black riders came from the sea.
There was clang and clang of spear and shield,
And clash and clash of hoof and heel,
Wild shouts and the wave of hair
5 In the rush upon the wind:
Thus the ride of Sin.

Section Four
American Poetry of the Modernist Period

Notes

Line 2 clang and clang: repeated loud ringing sound, such as when metal is struck.

Line 3 clash and clash: repeated loud confused noise.

Comment on the poem

This is the first poem in *Black Riders Came From the Sea* (1895).

Black riders are the heroes of this poem. They first appear exactly as real heroes: "Came from the sea" implies the distance and adventurous spirit; "clang and clang of spear and shield" and "clash and clash of hoof and heel" indicate they are armed warriors and thus rather violent; "Wild shouts" means they come recklessly; "the wave of hair" suggest their handsome appearance; "In the rush upon the wind" tells us the speed of their approaching; they are every piece a hero but who are they? The poet offers the real hero in the last word of the last line—Sin. The reader may be quite shocked to find a "Sin" is so honoured. However, with a sincere consideration, one has to boldly face the cruel reality of modern society that all the evils are malicious, destructive and impossible, which are, unfortunately, the most vigorous, most pervasive but disastrous elements in nature; as a striking contrast to this, the individuals, who had always been self-reliant and self-important since Emerson's Transcendentalist declaration, are now discovered to be rather frail and vulnerable. What's worse, evils are, as well as every other substance, parts of nature created by God! People were born to confront them and have to devote part of their precious life to resistance against them. This sounds cruel but it is the reality of the modern world. As a naturalist poet, Crane just revealed the true face of nature so as to warn the unrealistic optimists about the dangerous circumstances in this godless world.

This poem, despite the short size, is written with figurative speeches: the alliteration in "hoof and heel"; the repetition of "clang and clang," "clash and clash," which make the work read rhythmical though it is done without rhyme schemes. Besides, since the "Black riders" came from a distance, the poet first leads us to hear them by the words as "clangs," "clash," "shouts"; then we can use our eyesight to enjoy the waves of hair; finally, appears the whole figure of the impending catastrophe—the Sin.

美国诗歌研究
Studies on American Poetry

参考译文

黑色骑手来自海上

黑色骑手来自海上。
盾矛丁当响,
蹄跟闪闪亮,
匆忙赶来落狂风,
呼喊狂,发飞扬:
罪过骑来也这样。
(李正栓 译)

(2) A Man Said to the Universe

A man said to the universe:
"Sir, I exist!"
"However," replied the universe,
"The fact has not created in me
A sense of obligation."

Comment on the poem

When a pious person who believes in God joyfully declares his arrival in this world, he was unexpectedly responded to by God that his arrival didn't arouse any sense of responsibility within Him. Confronted by the human beings' desire for identification, God appears no longer a benevolent father of Puritans; instead, he behaves very indifferently as the mother of leisure who had left everything to the child himself. In other words, this world is now godless, such things as a Savior is nothing but a religious fantasy. Therefore a human being is brought into this world to make all the decisions completely by himself. Everybody is God to himself, otherwise, in this world where only "the fittest survives," a person is prone to meet with doom if he is too frail or doesn't strive for survival.

This poem was collected in *War Is Kind* (1899).

Section Four
American Poetry of the Modernist Period

参考译文

一个男人对宇宙说

一个男人对宇宙说:
"先生,我存在!"
宇宙回答说:"不过,
事实是,我还没有产生
责任的感觉。"
(李正栓 译)

IV. Ezra Pound
(1885 – 1972)

1. Life Story

Ezra Pound was one of the most influential American poets who decisively affected the course of 20th century American literature.

Although born in Hailey, Idaho, Pound was brought up in Pennsylvania. He was undoubtedly a genius of language—before graduating from the University of Pennsylvania, he had already mastered nine languages as well as English grammar and literature and become a professor of language at the age of 22. However, after 4 months of teaching and a lot of quarrels at college, Pound left the United States for Europe in 1908, first to Venice, and then resided in London from 1908 to 1920, where he associated with many writers, including William Butler Yeats, for whom he worked as a secretary, and T. S. Eliot, whose *Waste Land* he drastically edited and improved. Pound's first book of poetry, *A Lume Spento*, was published in Venice in 1908. From then on Pound began to lecture on romantic literature, published several volumes of verse and criticism, and translated medieval Italian poetry; what's more important, he spearheaded the new school of poetry known as the Imagist Movement.

The Imagist Movement refers to a trend of literature, especially in poetry writing, in England and the United States, which flourished from 1909 to 1917. The Imagist poets approved the use of free verse, direct common speech, creation of new rhythms, absolute freedom in choice of subject matter, and the evocation of precise imagery in hard, clear poetic works. In 1914, the first anthology of Imagist poems was edited by Pound, entitled *Des Imagistes*, including the works of 10 outstanding imagist poets, such as William Carlos Williams, H. D. (Hilda Doolittle), Amy Lowell and Ezra Pound.

After 1917, Imagism, as a literary genre, ebbed. With a terrific zest for experimentation, Pound championed various other poetic approaches and dedicated plenty of time to the composing of his life-work *The Cantos*, which was initiated two years before.

2. Pound's Major Works

During his long and, otherwise, politically controversial life — during the Second World War, Pound lectured over Radio Rome (he was in Italy then) against the Allies, claiming his approval for Mussolini's fascist totalitarianism and was sentenced to imprisonment after the war— Pound accomplished 70 books of his own. Moreover, he contributed, as an editor, to 70 books for struggling talents. Besides, he composed over 1500 critical essays as well as several volumes of translation work from widely divergent languages. In the long list of his achievements, *The Cantos* is the most outstanding.

The Cantos, begun in 1915 and completed in 1969 is Pound's lifework. Being well-known as "Pound's intellectual diary since 1915," the book culminates Pound's writing and has become an important landmark of modern poetry. This modern epic consists of 117 chapters. It is a long work, with neither a central theme, nor a complete plot; it is not composed in any systematic order, either. As a matter of fact, *The Cantos* is executed in various styles by applying various languages, including modern and ancient English, colloquial English, French, German, Greek, Italian, and Japanese. Strangely, in the book appeared about 100 Chinese words. The writing form of the book also varies widely: lyrical poems, prose poems, letters, even documents were juxtaposed and the content of the book covered nearly everything of human history and world civilization. Actually, it is a book that requires the readers' extremely profound academic level to comprehend the entire content.

Pound also translated the poems of Li Bai. Though the translation was not good enough in terms of faithfulness, his translation and creation of images from Chinese poetry helped a lot in the forming of imagism in the United States.

3. Selected Poems

(1) In a Station of the Metro

(*This poem is an observation of the poet of the human faces seen in a Paris subway station.*)

The apparition of these faces in the crowd;
Petal on a wet, black bough.

Notes

Metro: short form for metropolitan railway. It usually refers to the subway between London and its suburbs. Here it refers to that of Paris.

Line 1 apparition: a visible appearance of something not present, and especially of a dead person; the spirit of a dead person moving in bodily form; ghost.

The word "apparition," with its double meanings, binds the 2 aspects of the observation together:

a. "apparition" means "appearance," in the sense of something which appears or shows up; something which can be clearly observed.

b. "apparition" means something which seems real but perhaps is not; something ghostly which can't be clearly observed.

these faces: the human faces; the pretty and fresh faces of Paris women.

the crowd: the crowd of people in a Paris subway station.

Line 2 Petal: any of the coloured leaflike divisions of a flower.

Comment on the poem

This short poem, published in 1913, is the earliest and the best of Pound's work. When writing it, Pound adopted the Japanese haiku (はいく, a type of Japanese poem with 3 lines, consisting of 17 syllables, divided into a stanza of 5 - 7 - 5).

The poem, regarded as the classic specimen of Imagist poetry, was first written in more than a hundred lines but was later condensed into two lines to convey an accurate image by using the fewest possible words.

Pound was once so impressed by the pretty faces of some women and children hurrying out of the dim, damp and somber station that he attempted to record exactly the spectacle of the faces which reflected variously toward light and darkness, like flower petals which are half absorbed by half resisting, the wet, dark texture of a bough.

参考译文

在地铁车站

(本诗是诗人在巴黎地铁车站

Section Four
American Poetry of the Modernist Period

对他所看到的人群面孔进行
的描写。）

人群中幽灵般的一张张面孔；
黑色潮湿枝头上的一片片花瓣。
（李正栓 译）

(2) A Pact

I make a pact with you, Walt Whitman—
I have detested you long enough.
I come to you as a grown child
Who has had a pig-headed father;
5 I am old enough now to make friends.
It was you that broke the new wood,
Now is a time for carving.
We have one sap and one root—
Let there be commerce between us.

Notes

pact: agreement; treaty.
Line 2 detested: hated with very strong feeling.
     long enough: for rather a long time.
Line 3 I come to you as a grown child: now I have grown up and begun to understand you.
Line 4 has had a pig-headed father: I used to have a stubborn father. There is an old saying as "like father, like son"; I, as the son of a stubborn father, must have been rather obstinate. But now, fortunately, I have changed.
     pig-headed: stubborn;
Line 5 old enough to make friends: have grown up to understand others.
Line 6 broke the new wood: made experiments with the conventions of traditional poetry.
Line 7 time for carving: it is the proper time to cut "the new wood" into a significant shape—something new as imagist poetry.
Line 8 We: Whitman and Pound as poets of the same nation.
     have one sap and one root: share the same sap and same root; we

grew out of the same root by being fed with the same sap. Pound used a metaphor to imply that the two poets are like two branches of the same tree.

Line 9 Let there be commerce between us: Let us have a trade so that each can profit from the other.

commerce: exchange of views, attitudes, etc.

参考译文

合　约

沃尔特·惠特曼，我与你有约在先——
我以前一直把你讨厌。
我现在向你走近，
因为长大的孩子已离开愚蠢的父亲；
我已长大成人，能交友择朋。
是你砍下了新木，
现在已适合雕刻。
我们合一种树汁，合一条根，
我们有同种汁液同样根须——
愿你我之间存有流通和交易。
（李正栓　译）

(3) A Virginal

No, no! Go from me. I have left her lately.
I will not spoil my sheath with lesser brightness,
For my surrounding air hath a new lightness;
Slight are her arms, yet they have bound me straitly
5 And left me cloaked as with a gauze of aether;
As with sweet leaves; as with subtle clearness.
Oh, I have picked up magic in her nearness
To sheathe me half in half the things that sheathe her.
No, no! Go from me. I have still the flavour,
10 Soft as spring wind that's come from birchen bowers.
Green come the shoots, aye April in the branches,
As winter's wound with her sleight hand she staunches,
Hath of the trees a likeness of the savour:

Section Four
American Poetry of the Modernist Period

As white their bark, so white this lady's hours.

Notes

Virginal: a type of small square legless piano-like musical instrument popular in Europe in the 16th and 17th centuries, usually played by young girls—virgins.

Line 1 No, no! Go from me: The musical instrument, virginal, is personified and repelling a new player to get away from it.
 her: the former virginal player, who must have been a pretty girl, a virgin.

Line 2 I will not spoil my sheath: I would not be willing to uncover myself to a new player, for I am still missing the former player.
 with lesser brightness: in a less bright atmosphere.

Line 3 For my surrounding air hath a new lightness: For I feel I am still bathed in the bright air left by the former player.

Line 4 her: the former player's.
 they: the former player's arms.

Line 5 cloaked as with: I was covered as if with...
 a gauze of aether: a cover of pleasant air.
 aether: equivalence to ether. the upper air; a very fine substance, once believed to fill the whole of space, through which light waves were thought to travel.
 left me: with the embrace of that air, I felt...

Line 6 As with sweet leaves: I was covered as if with sweet leaves.
 as with subtle clearness: I was bathed as if in subtle clearness.
 subtle clearness: all the brightness around, which is not easy to describe in words.
 The poet implies the lady had been compared to a birch tree, which has leaves, branches (arms), bowers, shoots and white bark.

Line 7 have picked up magic: have gained a mysterious quality.
 in her nearness: with the fresh memory of my former player.

Line 8 To sheathe me: to influence me.
 half: almost in the way of...; She (the former player) influenced me almost in the way as that brightness had influenced her.

Line 9 I have still the flavour: I can still sense the special quality (of the former player).

Line 10 Soft as: (Her flavour) was as soft as.
 birchen bowers: shade of birch trees.

bowers: shady places under trees or climbing-plants in a wood or garden.

Line 11 Green come the shoots: (Her flavour is able to) change the shoots of plants into green — bringing new life to them.

aye April in the branches: (Her flavour) brings April, an image of spring, to the branches of all plants.

aye: yes; brings.

Line 12 As winter's wound with her sleight hand she staunches: Her hand is so gentle as to staunch the winter's wound.

her sleight hand: the gentle, delicate hand of her flavour. "Sleight" means "magic," or "magical."

staunch: =stanch. stop the flow of blood.

Line 13 Hath of the trees a likeness of the savour: (Her flavour) shares the charm of a birch tree.

savour: pleasant taste or flavour.

Line 14 As white their bark, so white this lady's hours: this lady's (the former player's) time has been bright and pure as the bark of birch trees.

Comment on the poem

This poem was written in the form of a sonnet but narrated by a personified musical instrument, a virginal. In the virginal's narration, either the beats or the rhymes vary from those of a traditional English sonnet. The poem can be divided into two sections.

In the first section—the first 8 lines: the brightness of the former player of the virginal is highly praised. That lady, with all her brightness, appears a perfect figure and thus the virginal cannot extricate itself from the light and missing of her.

The second section, the last six lines, suggest a presentation of the flavour of her ladyship. Soft as the spring wind, her flavour brings green shoots to the birch and cures the winter wounds with her sleight hand.

Obviously, the poet had compared the lady to a birch tree: white in colour, bright in appearance, graceful in shape, and cloaked with leaves. Besides, two minor images were offered: the brightness of a lady in the first 8 lines and the flavour of the lady in the latter 6 lines. The image of the birch tree is better interpreted by the two minor images: the brightness of it and the flavour of it, through the sense of sight and the sense of smelling.

What's more, the poet used similes in this poem: "left me cloaked

Section Four
American Poetry of the Modernist Period

as with a gauze of aether," "as with sweet leaves," "as with subtle clearness." In the last two lines, the lady's time is as bright as the bark of a birch.

All the images, comparison, as well as the similes contribute to the portraying of a noble woman with magnificent beauty.

参考译文

沃基诺歌

不！不！走开。我刚刚离开她。
我不会以更少的欢娱揭开琴套，
我周围仍有清新轻盈方向环绕；
她双臂不大却把我紧紧地缠匝，
双臂给我留下一层芳香的薄气，
似香叶缠绕，似明晰微妙。
啊，想起她，我品质玄奥
影响我，她好像欢娱影响她自己。
不！不！走开。她的味道我仍有，
柔香似春风来自桦树林。
四月催绿叶生，表现在枝叶中，
妙手回春，她把严冬的创伤治。
她的气息与白桦之魅力承联，
她的贞洁如永恒的白桦绵延。

（李正栓　韩志华　译）

Ⅴ. Hilda Doolittle
(1886 – 1961)

1. Life Story

As imagist poets, Ezra Pound's name is often closely followed by Hilda Doolittle, best known as H. D. Hilda Doolittle encountered Pound in Pennsylvania University at the age of 15. In 1911, when she arrived in London three years later than Pound, the acquaintance was developed into a passionate love between them, which concluded with an intimate friendship and the later well-known name of "H. D." to her, initiated by Pound.

Hilda Doolittle was born and brought up in Pennsylvania, her father an astronomer and mother a mathematician. Married in 1913 to Richard Aldington, a prominent English imagist poet, she resided in London until their separation in 1919. Afterwards, she kept on writing and traveling in Europe, America and Egypt until 1923, and settled in Switzerland thereafter.

In 1913, with the help of Pound, Hilda Doolittle, for the first time, published several of her poems in *Poetry*, a literary journal of Chicago, in the name of "H. D. Imagiste" and thus inaugurated the new poetic movement and remained an essential imagist therefore. For this newly sprung experimental poetic genre, Hilda Doolittle contributed a lot to illustrate the imagist principles by taking a specific image so as to present the momentary impression of the author, by direct diction, economical expression, and by taking advantage of the interrelationship between music and verse.

2. Major Works of Hilda Doolittle

As a poet, Hilda Doolittle's reputation lies mainly in the imagist poems. The major imagist works are *Sea Garden* (1916), the trilogy of poems—*Walls Do Not Fall*, *Tribute to Angels*, *The flowering of the Rod*, came out successively in 1944, 1945, and 1946, dealing with religion and myth in a series of discursive meditations.

Section Four
American Poetry of the Modernist Period

As a writer, Hilda Doolittle, however, did not remain constricted by imagist doctrines but tried writing in various forms such as *Hippolytus Temporized* (1927), a drama in classic form; *Bid Me to Live* (1960) a novel written in stream-of-consciousness style; *Tribute to Freud* (1956), a psychoanalytic prose fiction; she also translated into English some classical works of the prominent Greek writers.

Helen in Egypt, a collection of poems, was posthumously published in 1961. In this book, Hilda Doolittle tried a new way to present the Trojan War through a dramatic monologue spoken by Helen, the abducted woman.

3. Selected Poems

(1) Oread

Whirl up, sea—
whirl your pointed pines,
splash your great pines
on our rocks,
5   hurl your green over us,
cover us with your pools of fir.

Notes

Oread: the goddess of forests in Greek mythology.
Line 1 Whirl up: move upward quickly by turning round and round.
Line 2 pointed pines: in the poet's eyes, the high waves of the sea are like mountains and the sharp tops of the waves are the pointed pines.

Comment on the poem

This, as Pound's *In A Station of the Metro*, is another representative work of imagist poetry.

When looking at the whirling sea, the poet takes in her mind the image of a roaring forest. Yet, the forest is acting as water—it whirls up, splashes, hurls, and covers with pools of fir. Actually the poetess is presenting neither the sea nor the forest in a conventional way, instead, the sea and the forest combine into an image of the momentary eruption of human emotion. "We," the embodiment of land, appeals to experience every aspect of the sea: the shape, the color, the motions, until all is immersed in water.

Some critics believe this poem is metaphorically written with the Freudian theories about subconscious sexual ideas, with all the waves and motions of sea symbolizing the masculine vigor, and as well, the land and "covering of us" symbolizing the sexual impression of a woman.

参考译文

山 林 女 神

大海，旋翻吧，——
旋起你针松般细浪，
溅起你松树般巨浪
拍打我们的岩石，
把你的碧波绿浪向我们投来，
用你冷杉般漩涡把我们覆盖。
（李正栓　译）

(2) Helen

All Greece hates
the still eyes in the white face,
the lustre as of olives
where she stands,
5　　and the white hands.

All Greece reviles
the wan face when she smiles,
hating it deeper still
when it grows wan and white,
10　　remembering past enchantments
and past ills.

Greece sees, unmoved,
God's daughter, born of love,
the beauty of cool feet
15　　and slenderest knees,

Section Four
American Poetry of the Modernist Period

could love indeed the maid,
only if she were laid,
white ash amid funereal cypresses.

Notes

Helen: the beautiful daughter of Zeus and Leda and wife of Menelaus, king of Sparta. Her abduction by Paris was the cause of the Trojan War.

Line 1 All Greece: All Greek people.
Line 2 the still eyes in the white face: the calm and quiet eyes in the white face (of Helen). White here implies the beauty and purity of Helen.
Line 3 the lustre as of olives: (All Greece hates) the olive-like soft smooth colour (of Helen's complexion).
Line 4 where she stands: (All Greece hates) the place Helen had once stood on.
Line 5 and the white hands: (All Greece hates) the white hands (of Helen's).

Stanza 1: Because of the mythical tale about Helen's abduction, the Greek people had concentrated their hatred on this otherwise beautiful woman, Helen. However, the poet did not mention the name of Helen, instead, she used three images—the still eyes in the white face, the lustre as of olives, and the white hands to indicate the otherwise perfect goddess.

Line 6 reviles: criticizes somebody in angry and abusive language.
Line 7 wan: white; pale and looking ill or tired.
Line 8 hating it deeper still: (All Greece) still hates it (despite it is already white and wan)
  it: the wan face.
Line 10 remembering: (Whenever the Greece can) remember.
  enchantments: (Whenever the Greece) remind the abduction of Helen.
Line 11 past ills: the unfortunate past; implying the abduction of Helen by Paris.

Stanza 2: All Greek people took the abduction of Helen as a great shame. Whenever the event came into their mind, the Greek people would scold her, despite her face had already gone pale.

Line 12 Greece sees: The Greek people just looked at the pale face.
  unmoved: without any sympathy for Helen.
Line 13 God's daughter: Helen, who is believed daughter of Zeus and Leda.
Lines 14 - 15 the beauty of cool feet and slenderest knees: Helen's beauty can be seen by her graceful feet and slenderest knees. Actually with what was mentioned above about her appearance—the still eyes, white face, olive skin, white hands, the poet strongly implies that Helen owns all the beauty of a woman.
Line 16 could love indeed the maid: (All Greece) could only show their love to Helen only after her death.
Line 18 (she were laid) white ash: when Helen was dead and had turned into ashes.
  amid funereal cypresses: when Helen was dead and lying among the funereal cypresses.
  funereal cypresses: cypress, a kind of tall, thin cone-bearing evergreen tree with dark leaves and hard wood. It is taken as the symbol for lamenting the dead in the western custom.

Stanza 3: The Greeks were very indifferent people. They would not love or show any sympathy to Helen in spite of all her beauty and noble birth.

Comment on the poem

By condemning the indifference and cruelty of the Greek people, the poet expressed her sincere love and heart-felt sympathy to Helen, an innocent but unfortunate woman. Helen, together with all her beauty, has passed away for almost four thousand years. However, she has never been completely forgiven by her native people. Helen, the most beautiful woman in history, should be the least to blame for the war, but she was treated so and is treated like that now. The poet could not help worrying about the destiny of all the other women: How many of them had been wronged and how much injustice they had suffered, no one knows! This is history. This is the cruelty and injustice in human history.

参考译文

海 伦

所有的希腊人都恨
那白皙面孔上镇定的眼睛,
她站在那里,
肌肤闪耀橄榄油的光泽,
双手有美丽的白色。

所有的希腊人们都恨
她微笑时脸上的苍白,
当她脸色从苍白到惨白时,
人们对她恨更深,
因为还记得她曾被诱拐,
因为她过去还有其不清白。

出于爱,所有的希腊人
漠然望着这神的女儿,
她双脚很酷,很漂亮,
她双膝尽展柔情。
人们的确爱这姑娘,
即使她化作灰烬,
身躯也与常青柏树为伴。
（李正栓　韩志华　译）

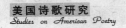

VI. William Carlos Williams
(1883 – 1963)

1. Life Story

William Carlos Williams, whose fame as a poet paralleled that of Ezra Pound and T. S. Eliot, was a physician factually all his adult life.

Dr. Williams was born in Rutherford, New Jersey, and studied medicine at the University of Pennsylvania, where he came into contact with two masters of imagism: Ezra Pound and Hilda Doolittle, whose imagist ideals had a tremendous impact on Williams' early poetic works. Nevertheless, as a professional physician, Williams derived from his practice of medicine the knowledge of people that inspired the best of his poems. With a special knowledge of humanity and a diagnostic reserve towards the frailty or strength of mankind, Williams soon distinguished himself as a poet who was able to illustrate a probing and clinical realism by seeking beauty and truth in plain reality.

As a poet, Williams, though overshadowed by Pound and T. S. Eliot all his life, had been experimenting to give up the conventional and metaphysical interest, and seek signs of permanence in the local and concrete by applying the natural American idiom and the variable rhythms and vocabulary, by concerning himself with the ordinary, the commonplace, and the specific American atmosphere.

2. Williams' Major Works

While busily occupied with his engrossing medical practice, Williams managed to compose more than 25 volumes of fictional and poetic works. Williams' first published work is *Poems*, a collection of his early works, coming out in 1909. It was very poorly accepted by the public. However, it started the composition of poems of a long list: the collection was followed up by a lot of others, among them, the most popular are *The Tempers* (1909), *Kora in Hell* (1920), *Sour Grapes* (1921), *Spring and All* (1922), *Complete Collected Poems* (1938), *The Desert Music* (1954), *Journey to Love* (1955), and *Pictures from*

Section Four
American Poetry of the Modernist Period

Brueghel (1963), which brought Williams the Pulitzer Prize of the year. Above all else, Williams accomplished Paterson, a tremendous epic of 5 volumes (1946, 1948, 1949, 1951, 1958). The poetic fragments Williams left were compiled into the 6th volume posthumously in 1963.

3. Selected Poems

(1) The Red Wheelbarrow

So much depends
upon

a red wheel
barrow

5   glazed with rain
water

beside the white
chickens.

Notes

Wheelbarrow: an open container for moving small loads in, with a wheel at one end, and two legs and two handles at the other.
Line 1 So much: so much of importance.
Line 5 glazed: covered with a thin shiny transparent surface.

Comment on the poem

    This poem is the representative expression of Williams' poetic theory about "No ideas but in things!"
    The poet conveys to the reader a common sight of the farmyard: a heavy loaded red wheelbarrow is glazing in rain beside some white chickens. However, in the glazing transparent rain, a red wheelbarrow and white chickens promise a sharp contrast of bright colors. By contrasting the colors, the poet actually merges some images into the descriptions of the concrete objects. The wheelbarrow, as a farm tool, stands for human labor; rain and chickens are obviously symbols of natural exist-

ence. In the first 4 lines, the wheelbarrow, in the thick color of red and with "so much depends on" it, looks dignified and solemn; while in the next two lines, when the heavy loaded barrow is glazing with rain water, the solemnity is weakened into a bright scene. Finally, when the wheelbarrow appears beside white chickens, the serious mood of the poem is completely lightened into a fresh and vivid picture of words.

Yet, when a picture is composed of words, it is presented as if seeing a film, one frame after another, with few differences to each but changes distinguish themselves gradually from solemnity to liveliness. Williams, as one of the representative imagist poets, through very fresh image, conveys to the reader imagist ideas in "things."

参考译文

红色手推车

几多沉重
压在

一辆红色
手推车上

推车上雨水
闪亮

停放在几只白色
小鸡旁
（李正栓 译）

(2) This Is Just to Say

I have eaten
the plums
that were in
the icebox

and which
you were probably

saving for breakfast

Forgive me
they were delicious
so sweet
and so cold

Comment on the poem

This poem is quite similar to an apologizing letter, leaving to a sweetheart for having eaten the delicious plums which might have been saved for a breakfast.

What the speaker wants to express is that he loves his sweetheart so much just as he simply could not resist the temptation of the delicious plums. Therefore, what he just wants to say, though not directly told in the poem, should be the apology for what he had done, and for more love from her.

参考译文

也就是说

我吃掉了
那些李子
他们原本放在
冰箱里

这些
可能是你准备
早餐要吃的美食

原谅我
真好吃
真甜
真凉

（李正栓 译）

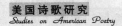

(3) Spring and All

By the road to the contagious hospital
under the surge of the blue
mottled clouds driven from the
northeast—a cold wind. Beyond, the
5   waste of broad, muddy fields.
brown with dried weeds, standing and fallen

patches of standing water
the scattering of tall trees

All along the road the reddish
10 purplish, forked, upstanding, twiggy
stuff of bushes and small trees
with dead, brown leaves under them
leafless vines—

Lifeless in appearance, sluggish
15 dazed spring approaches—

They enter the new world naked,
cold, uncertain of all
save that they enter. All about them
the cold, familiar wind—

20. Now the grass, tomorrow
the stiff curl of windcarrot leaf
one by one objects are defined—
It quickens: clarity, outline of leaf

But now the stark dignity of
25 Entrance—still, the profound change
has come upon them: rooted, they
grip down and begin to awaken.

Section Four
American Poetry of the Modernist Period

Notes

Line 1 contagious: disease that can be spread by contact.
   The contagious hospital refers to an image of death.
Lines 2 – 4 under the surge of... a cold wind: under the surge of the blue mottled clouds which were driven by a cold wind from the northeast.
Line 5 waste: wasteland.
Line 6 brown with dried weeds: (the broad, muddy fields) look brown with dried weeds.
   standing and fallen: (the weeds) are standing and fallen; in a random state.
Line 7 standing water: not flowing, stagnant water.
Line 8 the scattering of tall trees: there are but a few tall trees dotted among the patches of standing water.

Stanza 1: When the poet is presenting the arrival of spring, he began with what he saw far in the sky—the blue clouds, what he felt in the air—the cold wind from northeast. Then his view shifted to the ground and fell on the patches of melted water and the trees dotted there.

Lines 9 – 13 Words in these lines are what the poet can see under the sky, beside the road.
Lines 14 – 15 Lifeless in appearance, ... approaches—: spring is approaching though rather reluctantly, in a lifeless appearance.

Stanza 2: In spite of all the decadent scene of the bushes, the trees, the vines, the approaching of spring is felt.

Line 16 They: bushes, trees, vines mentioned in above stanza.
Line 17 cold, uncertain of all: "they" feel cold and know very little about this world.
Line 18 save that they enter: except the fact that "they" have arrived in spring.
Line 19 the cold, familiar wind—: though in spring, all around "them" are still the cold, familiar winds of winter.

Stanza 3: The plants know they have entered the spring; however, they fail to catch the least hint of the season.

Line 22 one by one objects are defined—: one after another, the leaves take shape.
Line 23 It quickens: the pace of spring quickens.

<u>Stanza 4</u>: Grass and leaves now can feel the quickened pace of spring.

Line 24 But now the stark dignity of: Now the leaves are entering spring with great dignity.
Line 26 them: leaves, trees, plants.
Line 27 grip down: takes a firm hold of soil and root in it.
         begin to awaken: begin to sprout for a new life.

<u>Stanza 5</u>: The arrival of spring has been felt and the leaves entered the new season with dignity.

Comment on the poem

  With the coming of spring, the sky turns blue but the mottled clouds are driven by cold wind, the ground is still brown with dried weeds. Through the visual images, a scene of the severe fight between winter and spring can be easily caught. In the first three stanzas, the power of winter predominates and the pace of spring appears slow and hard. However, the quickened pace of spring in the third stanza brings quicker rhythm to the poem. The change is profound; the leafless vines, the reddish purplish forked bushes, the trees with dead brown leaves all begin to awake and grip down in earth. The revival of life comes slowly but surely. There is nothing in the world is so able as to stop the pace of it.

参考译文

春天和全部

在去传染病院途中，
抬望蓝天：
云彩斑驳飘自
东北方——冷风吹来。眺望远处：
广阔泥泞的荒田，
枯叶棕黄，像宁静倒落的

Section Four
American Poetry of the Modernist Period

一片一片的死水潭
树木参天处处现。

一路上,那红色的、
紫色的、劈了叉的、挺直而上的、多枝的
灌木丛和小树,
树下枯叶棕红,
藤蔓裸枝——

春天来了:
面无生机、慵懒疲惫,行动迟缓。

这一切景物也进入春天,赤裸裸,
冷冰冰,对一切无把握,
只知他们进来了。周围尽是
野风凄寒,司空见惯——

现在,是草,明天,
僵僵的卷叶,就像萝卜叶,
一件一件,清晰可辨——
春天催发:叶有轮廓,形状可见

现在,这样进入春天,
十足的尊严——还有,深刻的变化
已发生在它们身上:根深扎,它们
紧抓着大地,生机勃发。
(李正栓 韩志华 译)

VII. T. S. Eliot
(1888 – 1965)

1. Life Story

T. S. Eliot (Thomas Stearns Eliot) was the descendant of a well-to-do but religious family in St. Louis, Missouri. His grandfather went west as a Unitarian minister and founded the Washington University; his father was a successful businessman and his mother, a prominent poetess of the time. The family afforded Eliot the best education, respectively at Harvard, the University of Paris, and Oxford. As a student and then a scholar, Eliot's study profoundly covered language, belles-lettres, metaphysical poetry, literature of Italian Renaissance, Western and Oriental philosophy, and Sanskrit. Consequently, Eliot came out a poet of the first class, a critic with original ideas, and an outstanding dramatist of his time. After his marriage in 1915, Eliot settled down in London, and in 1928 he became a British subject and converted to Roman Catholicism to prove what he describes himself as "a classicist in art, a royalist in politics, and an Anglo-Catholic in religion." In 1948, Eliot was honored with the Nobel Prize for Literature due to the progressive refinement and illustration of the aesthetic theory displayed in his works.

In poetry writing, Eliot was rebellious, experimental and radical. In addition to the profound knowledge of various language, Eliot's poems, with all the copious quotations, metaphors, and images, are often difficult to understand to readers of any level. He was capable of writing with circumstantial evidences, without the least attention to the limitation of space and time but combining the memory of the past with that of the present to record the movement of human consciousness. In his mind, any tradition was temporal; every writer, instead of merely taking advantage of the classics, should add to history. Rather firmly, Eliot insisted on a writer's contributing to the tradition and becoming a part of the tradition.

Meanwhile, Eliot, through his critical essays, headed an intellectual reaction against the romantic poetry of the 19th century by strongly advocating the English metaphysical poets of the 17th century, which resulted in the reevaluation of such important English poets as Shakespeare, John Donne, Milton, and Dryden in the 20th century.

Fascinated by the theater, Eliot composed several "verse dramas" including *Sweeney Agonistes* (1932), *Murder in the Cathedral* (1935), *The Cocktail Party* (1949) and *The Confidential Clerk* (1953), all religious in theme and monologue in technique.

2. Eliot's Major Works

As a poet with greater reputation than any others of the century, Eliot was prolific. However, Eliot, different from Whitman who designed to praise American dreams to express the common aspirations of Americans, wrote with pessimistic ideas and with a purpose to criticize society. Because of the obscurity of his poems, Eliot's audience used to be small, but he enjoyed being appreciated by a few elitists and withdrawing from mass culture. Now there are more and more scholars studying his works.

Eliot's career as a poet of international reputation began with the publication of *The Love Song of J. Alfred Prufrock* in 1915 and the appearance of *Prufrock and Other Observations* in 1917. His other well-known poetic works are *The Waste Land* (1922), *The Hollow Men* (1925), *Ash-Wednesday* (1930), and *Four Quartets* (written during 1936, 1942, published in 1943).

Among his principal dramatic works, besides what is mentioned above, *The Family Reunion* (1939), and *The Elder Statesman* (1959) enjoy almost the same fame.

Eliot's important critical essays have been collected into books. Among them, the most popular are *The Sacred Wood* (1920), in it *Tradition and the Individual Talent* is found; *The Use of Poetry and the Use of Criticism* (1933), *Elizabethan Essays* (1934), *On Poetry and Poets* (1957), and *To Criticize the Critic* (1965).

3. Selected Poem

The Love Song of J. Alfred Prufrock[1]

S'io credessi che mia risposta fosse
a persona che mai tornasse al mondo,
questa fiamma staria senza piu scosse.
Ma per cio che giammai di questo fondo
non torno vivo alcun, s'i' odo il vero,

senza tema d'infamia ti rispondo[2]

1

  Let us go then, you and I,
  When the evening is spread out against the sky
  Like a patient etherised upon a table;
  Let us go, through certain half-deserted streets,
5 The muttering retreats
  Of restless nights in one-night cheap hotels
  And sawdust restaurants with oyster-shells:
  Streets that follow like a tedious argument
  Of insidious intent
10 To lead you to an overwhelming question...
  Oh, do not ask, 'what is it?'
  Let us go and make our visit.

  In the room the women come and go
  Talking of Michelangelo.

2

15 The yellow fog that rubs its back upon the window-panes,
  The yellow smoke that rubs its muzzle on the window-panes.
  Licked its tongue into the corners of the evening,
  Lingered upon the pools that stand in drains,
  Let fall upon its back the soot that falls from chimneys,
20 Slipped by the terrace, made a sudden leap,
  And seeing that it was a soft October night,
  Curled once about the house, and fell asleep.

3

  And indeed there will be time
  For the yellow smoke that slides along the street
25 Rubbing its back upon the window-panes:
  There will be time, there will be time
  To prepare a face to meet the faces that you meet;
  There will be time to murder and create,
  And time for all the works and days of hands
30 That lift and drop a question on your plate;
  Time for you and time for me,
  And time yet for a hundred indecisions,

And for a hundred visions and revisions,
Before the taking of a toast and tea.
35 In the room the women come and go
Talking of Michelangelo.

4

And indeed there will be time
To wonder, 'Do I dare?' and, 'Do I dare?'
Time to turn back and descend the stair,
40 With a bald spot in the middle of my hair—
(They will say: 'How his hair is growing thin!')
My morning coat, my collar mounting firmly to the chin,
My necktie rich and modest, but asserted by a simple pin—
(They will say: 'but how his arms and legs are thin!')
45 Do I dare
Disturb the universe?
In a minute there is time
For decisions and revisions which a minute will reverse.

5

For I have known them all already, known them all—
50 Have known the evenings, mornings, afternoons,
I have measured out my life with coffee spoons;
I know the voices dying with a dying fall
Beneath the music from a farther room.
So how should I presume?

6

55 And I have known the eyes already, known them all—
The eyes that fix you in a formulated phrase,
And when I am formulate, sprawling on a pin,
When I am pinned and wriggling on the wall,
Then how should I begin
60 To spit out all the butt-ends of my days and ways?
And how should I presume?

7

And I have known the arms already, known them all—
Arms that are braceleted and white and bare
(But in the lamplight, downed with light brown hair!)

65 Is it perfume from a dress
That makes me so digress?
Arms that lie along a table, or wrap about a shawl.
And should I then presume?
And how should I begin?

8

70 Shall I say, I have gone at dusk through narrow streets
And watched the smoke that rises from the pipes
Of lonely men in shirt-sleeves, leaning out of windows?...

I should have been a pair of ragged claws
Scuttling across the floors of silent seas.

9

75 And the afternoon, the evening, sleeps so peacefully!
Smoothed by long fingers,
Asleep...tired...or it malingers,
Stretched on the floor, here beside you and me.
Should I, after tea and cakes and ices,
80 Have the strength to force the moment to its crisis?
But though I have wept and fasted, wept and prayed,
Though I have seen my head (grown slightly bald) brought in upon a platter,
I am no prophet—and here's no great-matter;
I have seen the moment of my greatness flicker,
85 And I have seen the eternal Footman hold my coat, and snicker,
And in short, I was afraid.
And would it have been worth it, after all,
After the cups, the marmalade, the tea,
Among the porcelain, among some talk of you and me,
90 Would it have been worth while,
To have bitten off the matter with a smile,
To have squeezed the universe into a ball
To roll it towards some overwhelming question,
To say: 'I am Lazarus, come from the dead,
95 Come back to tell you all, I shall tell you all'—
If one, setting a pillow by her head,
Should say: 'That is not what I meant at all.
That is not it, at all.'

10

And would it have been worth it, after all,
100 Would it have been worth while,
After the sunsets and the dooryards and the sprinkled streets,
After the novels, after the teacups, after the skirts that trail along the floor—
And this, and so much more? —
It is impossible to say just what I mean!
105 But as if a magic lantern threw the nerves in patterns on a screen.
Would it have been worth while
If one, settling a pillow or throwing off a shawl,
And turning toward the window, should say:
'That is not it at all,
110 That is not what I meant, at all.'

11

No! I am not Prince Hamlet, nor was meant to be;
Am an attendant lord, one that will do.
To swell a progress, start a scene or two,
Advise the prince; no doubt, an easy tool,
115 Deferential, glad to be of use,
Politic, cautious, and meticulous;
Full of high sentence, but a bit obtuse;
At times, indeed, almost ridiculous—
Almost, at times, the Fool.

12

120 I grow old... I grow old...
I shall wear the bottoms of my trousers rolled.

13

Shall I part my hair behind? Do I dare to eat a peach?
I shall wear white flannel trousers, and walk upon the beach.
I have heard the mermaids singing, each to each.

125 I do not think that they will sing to me.

I have seen them riding seaward on the waves
Combing the white hair of the waves blown back
When the wind blows the water white and black.

We have lingered in the chambers of the sea
130 By sea-girls wreathed with seaweed red and brown
Till human voices wake us, and we drown.

Notes

1. J. Alfred Prufrock: an invented name for the narrator of the story, a disillusioned aesthete.
2. This is taken from Lines 61–66, Inferno, chapter XXVII of Dante's *Devine Comedy*. It's Italian. The English version runs as follows:

   If I believed my answer were being mae
   to one who could ever return
   to the world, this flame would gleam no more;
   but since, if what I hear is true,
   never from this abyss did living man return,
   I answer thee without fear of infamy.

   (*The American Tradition in Literature*, the Seven Edition)

   Line 2 one that might return to view the world: the person who might revive from death and return to the human world.
   Line 5 abyss: hole so deep that it seems to have no bottom; hell.
   Line 6 infamy: infamous behavior; wickedness.

   This is the introductory section of the whole poem. It provides the supposed situation of the background: J. Alfred Prufrock, narrator of the story, like Guido de Montefeltro, is suffering from the inner conflict in the inferno. Since no one "might return to view the world," the narrator is free to expose his self-conflict.

   Line 1 you: The explanation of "you" greatly diverges. The poet himself declared that "you" indicates an "unidentified male companion"; while some critics prefer to believe "you" to be the other psychic self of Prufrock. Some others regard "you" simply as a general reference to the reader.
   Line 3 The hospital images happen in this poem from time to time. The poet must be indicating by the hospital image that the world is like an etherized patient.

Section Four
American Poetry of the Modernist Period

etherised: (= etherized) Ether is a light colorless liquid made from alcohol, which burns and is easily changed into gas. It is often used in industry or as an anaesthetic to put people to sleep before an operation. In this line, the past participle implies while they were walking, the streets were all quiet, pervaded with a sense of stillness and numbness which, as was felt by the poet, was the state quite similar to a stagnant and spiritless patient.
table: the operating table.

Line 4 Prufrock is imagining he is walking through a street.

Line 5 muttering retreats: the isolated places where people are gossiping in a low unclear voice.

Line 6 Of restless nights: go through the certain half-deserted streets of the restless nights.
one-night cheap hotels: hotels of very poor condition where one would stay for only one night.

Line 7 sawdust restaurants with oyster-shells: Cheap restaurants where food tastes as sawdust and the floors are always dirty with oyster shells.

Lines 4 – 7 The poet reveals the state of his mind by an image of the streets which are half-deserted, filled with cheap hotels and dirty restaurants. Hotels and restaurants are images for the human's basic necessities, which are irresistible for life; however, they are dull and boring as well.

Line 8 Streets: go through the streets that...; "Streets" in this poem symbolizes the flowing of thinking—the stream of consciousness—in Prufrock's mind.

Lines 8 – 9 follow like a tedious argument of insidious intent: A simile is used here to compare the meandering streets to a tiresome but maliciously plotted argument.

Line 10 overwhelming question: very important question.

Lines 13 – 14 These two lines repeat themselves several times in the poem, paralleling Prufrock's going in the streets. With the interruption of these two lines, the poet implies a striking contrast that on the one hand, through Prufrock's eyes, we catch sight of the etherized people and a spiritless world; one the other hand, some women dilettantes are actively "Talking of Michelangelo" just to show their gentility; which was, doubtlessly, as tedious as sawdust food. However, this is the fashion of modern society.
Michelangelo (Buonarroti ~, 1475 – 1564), the world famous

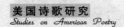

Italian sculptor, painter and poet of the Renaissance period, is mentioned here as an embodiment of fine arts. The poet wrote ironically with a sincere belief that fine art is not something that can be thoroughly understood by plain people, let alone by the genteel women gathered in a salon. Yet in this world, there are always those who are apt to the "talking" about fine art. Their gossip, as well as the cheap hotels and the dirty restaurants, is obviously just an unavoidable section of society. They are talking not because they really know, understand or are interested in fine art; instead, they just talk to show off. The phrase "come and go" adds, more or less, a bit of vigor to the line, but when mingled with their gossip, it represents another kind of very tedious life.

<u>Stanza 1</u>: As the prelude to the narration, the poet presents the modern world as he is presenting the tedious and dirty streets and thus leads the reader to the innermost part of Prufock's mind.

Line 15 The yellow fog (and "The yellow smoke" in the next line): Yellow fog or smoke of the sordid city was a familiar detail in French symbolism. Yellow is the colour of barrenness and timidity, which, in this line, intensifies the sense of the city as a wasteland.

Lines 15 – 22 The fog and smoke are animated as something like a yellow cat, which rubs its back, rubs its muzzle, licks its tongue, lingered upon the pools, slipped, leapt, curled and fell asleep, which roams down the lanes and houses, indicating the density and movement.

<u>Stanza 2</u>: The description of the farther background of the streets, where everything is dull except the fog and smoke, which seem active but are also in a color of decay; which appear vigorous but vanish easily.

Line 23 there will be time: The repetition of these words indirectly refers to "Ecclesiastes" of the *Old Testament*: For everything there is an appointed season, and there is a proper time for every project under heaven: a time to be born, and a time to die; a time to plant, and a time to root up what is planted; a time to kill, and a time to heal; a time to wreck, and a time to build; a time to weep, and a time to laugh; a time to mourn, and a time to dance; a time to cast away stones, and a time to gather stones; a time to embrace, and a time to refrain from embracing; a time to seek, and a time to lose; a time to retain, and a time to throw away; a time to rend, and a time to sew; a time to be silent, and a time to speak; a time to love, and a time to hate; a time for war, and a time for peace.

(Chen Jia, *Selected Readings in English Literature*, vol. 3, p79)

Line 27 To prepare a face: to make up before meeting his lady.
    face: Prufrock's face.
    faces: women's faces.
Line 29 works and days: "Works and Days" is a poetic work of Hesiod, a Greek poet of 8th century B. C. Here the phrase means there is enough time for what one wants to do.
Line 30 on one's plate: to occupy one's time or energy.
Line 32 indecisions: state of being unable to decide; hesitation.
Line 33 visions and revisions: thinking imaginatively again and again; again and again you have pictures of this kind.
Line 34 the taking of a toast and tea: image of trivial but absolutely necessary things of human life.

Stanza 3: With the allusion of "there will be time for..." the poet depicts Prufrock as an indecisive character and exposes the intention of modern people to idle away their life.

Line 38 Do I dare: Do I dare to propose to the lady?
Line 39 Time to turn back and descend the stair: There will be time to turn back and go down the stairs. The narrator is still hesitating and is almost going to retreat.
Line 40 a bald spot in the middle of my hair: That indicates that Prufrock is, if not old, at least a middle-aged man.
Line 41 They: the women.
    his: Prufrock's. Prufrock is imagining that if he dares to propose, he would be laughed at by those women.
Line 42 My morning coat... to the chin: the collar of my morning coat stands firmly against my chin.
Line 43 My necktie... a simple pin: My necktie is luxurious but not expensive; it is fixed to the shirt by a plain pin.
    Judging from his clothes, Prufrock is not very rich, probably a petty banker or clerk.
Lines 45 – 46 Prufrock imagines his question (proposal to one of those

genteel women) might be such a shocking one that the universe would be disturbed by it.

Lines 47 – 48 Prufrock has a timid mind which may make a quick decision and a revision, and a prompt change of it soon after.

Stanza 4: Prufrock is still hesitating and imagining that he will be laughed at if he dares to propose to any of those women.

Line 49 them all: the various life styles of all those ladies.

Line 51 measured out my life with coffee spoons: (I have been) killing time by drinking much coffee; (I have) wasted my life in such boring, superficial things. People usually use a spoon to stir in coffee cups. You may stir round and round without ending, for the coffee spoons are usually in the tiny size, with it, one is able to measure life with extraordinary leisure.

Line 52 a dying fall: a tone which begins with a high pitch and then steadily falls. This tone is commonly used in upper society when speaking. T. S. Eliot may have borrowed this expression from Shakespeare who, in his *Twelfth Night*, through a lovesick duke's mouth, says, "That strain again! It had a dying fall." (1.1.4)

Lines 52 – 53 I recognized that the voices of those women were characterized with a falling tone and was fading in the music from a distant room.

Line 54 presume: venture to do something; be so bold as to do something. Here and in the next two stanzas, this word appears to imply Prufrock's venturous prospect for disturbing those women or having sexual acts with them.

Stanza 5: Prufrock knew something about those women but as a timid man, he is doubting his ability to propose to any of them.

Line 56 The eyes that fix you in a formulated phrase: those women stare at you may be impolite and greet you with clichés.
formulated phrase: clichés; boring words. This simply shows the women's contempt for him.

Line 57 sprawling on a pin: Prufrock used a "pin" to imply that, once he heard the boring word from those women, he feels like a small insect, being lifeless and pinned on the wall to be studied by others.

Section Four
American Poetry of the Modernist Period

Line 58 wriggling: making quick, short, twisting and turning movements. Despite I was trapped in the boredom, I attempt to escape.

Line 60 butt-ends: stub; short piece at the end of a cigar or cigarette that is left when it has been smoked. In this line, Prufrock compares the rest part of his life to butt-ends and is doubting how he could get out of futility.

<u>Stanza 6</u>: In front of the arrogant women, Prufrock felt inferior and wants to escape from them but doesn't know how to.

Line 63 Arms that are braceleted: arms wearing bracelets.
Line 64 downed with light brown hair: (those arms are) shown, covered with light brown hair.
Line 66 digress: turn away or wander from the topic in speech. In this line it indicates Prufrock's failure to have sexual impulse in his wild imagination. This implies Prufrock, as a man, is not only timid by nature, but also sexually impotent.
Line 68 should I then presume?: This time Prufrock is doubting the necessity of venturing his life on a proposal to one of those women.

<u>Stanza 7</u>: Prufrock had an imagined sexual act with those women but failed, so he began to doubt about the necessity of the venture.

From Line 48 to Line 68, we have actually three paralleled stanzas, all beginning with "I have known them all already, known them all," and "I have known the eyes already, known them all," and "I have known the arms already, known them all." What is more, each of the first two stanzas is with the similar ending: "How should I presume?" but the third ends with "how should I begin?" The change suggests that if Prufrock could not quite understand how he should presume at the beginning, his doubting had shifted to a negative idea at the end of this section: He was inclined to deny the necessity "to presume."

Lines 73 – 74 a pair of ragged claws: a crab; crab is a relatively primitive thing. Prufrock is tired of the human world and is likely to be a crab which "scuttling across the floors of silent seas" rather than venturing in this world to make various decisions.

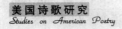

Stanza 8: Prufrock felt himself too weak to face the world and he, as a result, intends to escape by living a crab's life.

Line 77 malingers: pretends to be ill in order to avoid work or duty.

Line 79 after tea and cakes and ices: the time late in the afternoon. The mentioning of "tea and cakes and ices" strengthens Prufrock's sense of hesitating.

Line 80 to force the moment to its crisis: to regard the moment as the crisis time; to have his crucial question asked.

Line 81 I have wept and fasted, wept and prayed: Eliot here makes an allusion to the words from Samuel of the *Old Testament*, it runs as "And they mourned, and wept and fasted..." (II, 1 – 12) That means in order to obtain the lady's love for him, he has made every effort.

Line 82 seen my head brought in upon a platter: another allusion to the story of John, the Baptist from Matthew of the *New Testament*. The head of John the Baptist was brought to Queen Herodias by the King, Herod by name, on a "charger" to please her step-daughter Salome, whose dances the Queen enjoys very much. (XIV, 3 – 1) Therefore, John is mentioned here as the image of sacrifice to show Prufrock's determination for his love, which includes the sacrifice of his life.

Line 83 I am no prophet: I can't predict the consequence of the matter; I can't tell whether that lady will accept me or not. Despite all his will of sacrifice, Prufrock is a weak person by nature, he hesitates once more.

Matthew xiv: 3 – 11. The head of John the Baptist was brought to Queen Herodias on a "charger." Prufrock is "bald," quite unlike John the Baptist as represented in Richard Strauss's opera *Salome* (1905) or Oscar Wilde's play (1894) on which it was based, both emphasizing the passion of Herodias for the prophet.

here's no great-matter: (my death) is not a crucial thing. I'd like to have my love be accepted at the cost of my life.

Line 84 flicker: (light or flame) burn or shine unsteadily; be felt or seen briefly. For a short while, I felt my confidence.

Line 85 And: but; meanwhile.

the eternal Footman hold my coat, and snicker: Prufrock imagines a frequent scene of upper-class social life: while he is enjoying himself at a luxurious party, the male servant is holding his coat motionlessly but sniggering at him, which greatly lowered his dignity.

Line 86 I was afraid: I was afraid of being rejected.

Stanza 9: Prufrock was determined to express his love even at the cost of life. However, he was too timid to accomplish that purpose and so once more he shrank.

Line 86 When Prufrock, after hesitating, doubted "would have been..." in this stanza, it implies that he had probably made up his mind not to ask, or it is no longer possible for him to ask his question.

Lines 88 – 89 "the cups, the marmalade, the tea, the porcelain, some talk of you and me" are symbols of the trifles of upper society daily life.

Line 91 To have bitten off the matter with a smile: to solve the problem peacefully. "The matter" indicates Prufrock's proposal to the lady.

Line 92 squeezed the universe into a ball: This expression originates from *To His Coy Mistress* by Andrew Marvell (1621 – 1678). It runs as, "Let us roll all our strength and all / Our Sweetness up into one ball."

  The line is adopted here to indicate Prufrock's concentration of attention on one point or his determination to gather enough courage to fulfill the difficult task—proposal to a lady.

Line 93 some overwhelming question: one of the crucial problems—Prufrock's proposal to the lady.

Lines 94 – 95 The story of the resurrection of Lazarus is adopted from the New Testament, John XI, 1 – 44 or from the 16th chapter of *Luke*. Lazarus was a student and friend of Jesus Christ. He was poor and seriously ill with scabies. He was restored to life 4 days after his death. As a matter of fact, during that 4 days, he lived in the Afterworld quite leisurely but he saw the rich suffering in Hell. At his leaving, he was begged by the rich to pass the word to their families that they must be kind to the inferior and behave themselves as to avoid all the sufferings after death. Prufrock doesn't appreciate the life style of the upper class, yet he felt quite unable to make any change, for he was aware that he was no Lazarus who had a friend as Jesus Christ ready for the revival of all. This simply implies that in Prufrock's mind, the genteel upper class is actually going downhill and is thoroughly irrecoverable. When doubting "would it have been worth it to ..." Prufrock showed disappointment with modern society and had already made the negative decision.

Lines 96 – 98 the "one" refers to a lady. The three lines convey Prufrock's fear of being rejected by a lady.

Stanza 10: Prufrock doubts whether it is worthwhile to ask his question if he is supposed to be rejected and thus he is inclined to make a negative decision.

Lines 101 – 102 "sunsets, dooryards, the sprinkled streets, the novels, the teacups, skirts trail along the floor" are, like those mentioned in Lines 88 – 89, symbols of the trifles of upper society's everyday life.

Lines 104 – 105 Prufrock seems unable to expose his inner world or to make his proposal, that would be like showing one's nerves in patterns against the light of a magic lantern.

Lines 106 – 110 Prufrock's supposition of being refused. Eliot doesn't directly mention the rejection, instead, he mentioned the actions of refusing: "turning toward the window," "That is not what I meant."

Line 107 one: a woman.

Stanza 11: This stanza parallels the structure of the one above. Again, Prufrock doubted the necessity of asking his question and tried to persuade himself not to do so.

Line 111 Prince Hamlet: the hero in Shakespeare's tragedy *Hamlet*, well-known for his hesitating and melancholy character. Prufrock believed he is not as important as a Prince, nor did he want to be as hesitating and melancholy as Hamlet.

Line 112 an attendant lord: a minor figure.

Lines 112 – 114 one that will do. To swell a progress, start a scene or two, advise the prince; ... an easy tool: Prufrock realized that he was just a trivial person, whose function is to walk in a file in a ceremonial parade (while figures such as Hamlet would be on the stage). "A progress" refers to the ceremonial royal parade, the rank and file.

Line 113 start a scene or two: as a minor role, one is supposed to appear

Section Four
American Poetry of the Modernist Period

in just one or two scenes in society, without the possibility of those major heroes, who are dominant figures everywhere and who are able to make scenes whenever.

Line 114 Advise the prince: Prufrock implies he is playing the role of Polonius, the lord chamberlain, father of Ophelia and Laertes in *Hamlet*. Polonius is knowledgeable and eloquent, well remembered for his worldly advice to his son.

no doubt, an easy tool: Prufrock was aware that he is, doubtlessly, not a decisive person but a tool easily taken by a master.

Line 116 Politic: (Prufrock thought he was) wise; prudent.

Line 117 Full of high sentence: be filled with boasting. The expression is adopted from the *Canterbury Tales*, II. 303 – 306, when Chaucer describes the speech of the Clerk as terse, and "full of high sentence."

Line 119 the Fool: Prufrock considered his role in this world as no better than a court Fool, a conventional fixture in Elizabethan dramas who ridicules and is ridiculed, similar to a clown.

<u>Stanza 12</u>: Prufrock indicates his own futility by comparing himself with a number of literary characters.

Line 120 After the realization of the insignificance of life, Prufrock is confronted by another cruel fact—His youth is no longer with him.

Line 121 wear the bottoms of my trousers rolled: Old people always become thrifty and shorter in stature, thus when wearing the old trousers he had to roll up the bottoms of them.

Line 122 part my hair behind: change my hair to a new fashionable style.

eat a peach: an allusive phrase for Adam and Eve's eating of apple. It therefore means to venture a new experience.

Line 123 wear white flannel trousers: Flannel is the soft loosely woven woolen cloth usually for making fashionable dresses. To wear flannel trousers means to keep up with the fashion.

walk upon the beach: another symbol of fashionable life.

Line 124 I have heard the mermaids singing: I'd like to be very much indulged in the fashion as able to hear the mermaids singing to each other.

mermaids: symbol of beauty. It is a mythical creature having the body of a woman, but a fish's tail instead of legs, who sat on rocks and lured the sailors by her beautiful songs. It may also be an allusive image from "Go and Catch a Falling Star" by John Donne, "Teach me to hear mermaids singing," when the poet was actually paralleling something impossible as "catch the falling star" and "hear the mermaid singing."

each to each: In Greek mythology, there are eight mermaids (Sirens) in all. I heard each of them singing to the other.

<u>Stanza 13</u>: Though Prufrock has to face the reality, his youth has gone and his old trousers are loose to wear, he is still wildly imagining the possibility of keeping up with time.

Line 125 Prufrock was not confident enough to be lured by the mermaids.
Line 126 them: the mermaids.
Line 129 Eliot changed "I" into "we."
the chambers of the sea: the imagined palace at the bottom of the sea.
Line 130 sea-girls wreathed with seaweed red and brown: Sirens in the sea wearing wreathes made from red and brown seaweed.
Line 131 In Western legends, the sirens had the power to lure men to visit them in caves beneath the sea; but when their singing stopped the spell was broken, and the men would drown. Therefore, when "human voices wake us," the singing of mermaids is stopped and "we drown."

Human beings will be drowned if they are in water for too long. However, Prufrock thinks his life is with him when he is in water, or, among women. When he comes back to reality, he feels frustrated and is drowned.

Comment on the poem

This poem is a typical monologue in line with John Donne's tradition, seeming like a dialogue with one mock listener in the poem.

In the title of the poem, "Alfred" is the name of the first English King, which implies the social status of the major character or may remind the reader of somebody of a heroic figure. However, "Prufrock," with striking Germanic features, is said to be the name of a furniture dealer in Eliot's hometown (*A Survey of American Literature*, Chang Yaoxin, Nankai University Press, the 4th Edition. p245), a name without the least hint of a hero or any romantic event at all. The contrast between the names suggests one irony.

In addition, this poem is entitled as a "love song." However, no one can expect any of the beautiful feelings of a love song appearing in the true sense throughout the poem. Although the character of Prufrock is probably that of a middle-aged man of the upper-middle class, he is haunted by a constant fear of almost everything—communicating, rejection, misunderstanding, women, death and other things. What he dares to do in this modern age is to imagine the journey through the streets, or to imagine the love affair he may have with a lady of the upper class, or to measure out life with coffee spoons. He allows his imagination to run wildly but is without the courage to leave his room to put any of his ideas into practice. Prufrock is a little arrogant, but very self-conscious and rather overcautious. Therefore, nothing he does has deep consequence. Prufrock, as the representative figure of modern time and with the typical character of modern people, provides to the readers the second irony: This is a love song without any evidence for the passion of love.

By understanding this as a love song without love, a reader can easily discover the theme of this poem and also find the characteristic of modern intellectuals: they are harassed with self-doubts, psychological conflicts and a sense of frustration, and thus they have been split between passion and timidity, between desire and impotence. With the development of science, they know more about the world, but they fear more and are able to do less and less to prove their ability. Modern society is a world of conflicts, of emptiness, but not that of love.

This poem begins with an imitation of dramatic monologue: an ineffectual, sorrowful, middle-aged dandy was narrating his imagined love affair with a rich woman. However, the dramatic monologue is presented when exploring the internal world of Prufrock rather than directly told in the first person.

When exploring the character of the major figure and dissecting modern society, the poet presents many striking contrasts: the contrast between Prufrock's names: Alfred, name of the first king; while Prufrock, a name of a plain furniture dealer; the contrast between the title and the contents; the contrast between Prufrock's imagination and his real ability; the contrast between Prufrock's arrogance and his lack of courage; the contrast between Michelangelo and the gossiping noble women; the contrast between Prufrock's internal world and his appearance.

Modern literature becomes more complex. There isn't much time sequence in it. This poem is written in free verse, because Eliot thought different meters are needed for the different parts. By putting his thought into Prufrock's mind, Eliot is able to express the internal ideas of a person. Eliot, like James Joyce, Virginia Woolf, William Faulkner, etc, is deeply engaged in the writing skill of Stream of Consciousness—not everyone's thinking is logical. People do not think with capital letters or periods. As a matter of fact, when we are thinking, we forget, or something may suddenly emerge to us. People's thinking consists of an uninterrupted, uneven, and endless flow of the events, while modern literature is often the scientific record of these flows. So is *The Love Song* of J. Alfred Prufrock.

Some critics say Eliot displayed his knowledge for his own sake. Anyway, it is a fact few can deny that Eliot's poems cannot be easily followed and understood. His poem is totally nihilistic or simply negative, which expresses the momentary passions of the poet himself.

This poem was published in 1915 and soon brought fame to the poet. When the Imagist movement was at its summit, Eliot, though not a representative figure, somewhat juxtaposed his first prominent work with those of the imagist poets by using no fewer images than the latter ones while expressing Prufrock's psychological experience.

At the very beginning of the poem, Eliot described the evening as "Like a patient etherized upon a table." This strongly suggests the fundamental atmosphere for the whole work: the psychological experience of a frail man in an obscure situation.

As we can see in lines from 15 to 22, the "yellow smoke" is presented rather in the image of a yellow cat which "rubs its back," "rubs its muzzle," "licked its tongue," "lingered upon the pools," "slipped by the terrace," "make a sudden leap" and "curled and fell asleep."

The "talking of Michelangelo" indicates an image of fine arts' being misused by the upper-class women. However, the repetition of their "coming and going" implies the tediousness of the upper class society.

The endless, winding streets can be taken as an image for a human's insidious intent.

The "the voices dying with a dying fall beneath the music" is an image for the depressing tone of upper-class people.

On the whole, T. S. Eliot does no less than any imagist poet in taking advantage of images when writing his first piece of prominent work.

参考译文

阿尔弗莱德·普罗夫洛克的情歌

如果我认为我的答案是为
为一个要重返世界的人而作,
那么这火焰将不再熠熠生辉,
如果我听到的是真的
真的没有一个人能活着从这个深渊逃离
那我就回答他们,不惧任何邪恶!

1

那么,咱们走吧,我和你,
黄昏正在伸展倚天际,
像手术台上麻醉过的病人;
咱们走吧,穿过一些半荒废的街道,
街旁临时过夜的简易旅馆里
女人们唠叨个
不眠之夜,
街旁小饭庄,满地都是锯屑和牡蛎壳:
这些街道像冗长争论,
用心险恶,
引导问出难以抵抗的问题……
哦,别问:"那是什么?"
咱们走吧,看看去再说。

房间里,女人们来往穿梭,
谈论米开朗琪罗。

2

黄色的雾霭在窗棂上蹭背,
黄色的烟也在窗棂上蹭鼻和嘴。
用舌头舔着夜的各个角落,
在阴沟里小水潭流连延拖,
让烟囱里飞落的烟灰落在自己的背上,
烟灰从台阶上滑落,突然一跃,
见是一个柔和的十月夜晚

绕房子飞转一圈便入睡乡。

    3
肯定会有足够的时间
让黄色烟雾沿街道滑行
并在窗棂上蹭背：
会有足够的时间,会有足够的时间
准备一幅去见别人面孔的面容；
会有足够的时间去谋杀和创造,
会有足够的时间让那些在你的餐桌上
提问和休问的人们干活、过节；
你有你的时间,我有我的时间,
有时间犹豫上百次,
有时间上百次地看了又看,
之后才饮酒与喝茶。
房间里,女人们来往穿梭,
谈论米开朗琪罗。

    4
肯定会有足够的时间
反复问,"我敢吗？我真敢？"
会有时间转身下楼离去,
头顶中央秃头一片——
（她们会说,"瞧他头发多么少！"）
我的早礼服,我的领子紧顶着下巴,
我的领带贵重得体,
但只简单地别着一个别针——
（但她们会说,"瞧他胳膊腿儿多细！"）
我敢吗？
一分钟就足够
犹豫不决、考虑再三、反复修正。

    5
因为她们的一切我都知道,我都知道——
熟悉这黄昏、早晨和下午,
我用咖啡勺把生命分配；
我知道那些声音渐消,远处那房间
的音乐也在消减。

Section Four
American Poetry of the Modernist Period

所以我怎么敢猜测?

　　　　　6
还有,那些眼睛我早就知道,早就知道——
那些你说一句礼貌话就盯视你的眼睛,
当我语言规矩,跌趴在一根别针上,
当我扎在别针上,当在墙上痛苦扭动,
我怎么能开始
把我的生活与方式和盘托出、吐个干净?
就这样,我怎样去猜测?

　　　　　7
还有,那些胳膊我早就知道,我早就知道——
那些胳膊戴着手镯,白皙,赤裸,
(但是在灯下,显出棕黄色软毛!)
是衣裙上的香水味?
引诱我如此离题?
那些放在桌子上或者裹着披肩的胳膊。
那么,我应当去猜测?
我该怎么去猜测?

……

　　　　　8
我是否可以说我在黄昏时分走遍了大街小巷,
观看了穿着衬衫、身子探出窗外的孤独男人
的烟斗里冒出的烟?

我真该变成一对粗糙的蟹爪
急匆匆地在寂静的海底爬动。

　　　　　9
这下午,这夜晚,睡得多安详!
让修长的手指抚慰,
　入睡……疲倦……或装病,
　平躺在地板上,就在这儿,在你我身边。
喝过茶,吃过糕点和冰淇淋,我会
有力量逼这一瞬间到一个极端?

323

但是尽管我哭过,斋戒过,哭过,又祈祷过,
尽管我看见了我的头(有点秃顶)被放在盘中,
但我并非先知——这也无关紧要;
我看到我伟大的那一刻扑朔迷离,
我还看到我那永恒的仆人拿着我的衣服窃笑,
简之,我害怕。

那么,到底值不值得
在喝过酒、吃过果酱、喝过茶后,
在杯盘之间,在你我对谈之间,
到底值不值得
微笑着把这事情咬掉,
把宇宙挤成一个小球,
把它滚动挤出那个重要的问题,
说,"我是拉洒路,从阴界复活,
我回来告诉你们大家,告诉你们一切"——
如果有人在她头边放个枕头
并说,"我根本不是那个意思,
不是那意思,根本不是。"

　　　　　10
那么,到底值不值得
值不值得如此下工夫,
日落后,庭院中,洒过水的街道,
小说读毕,茶水喝完,多少扫地而过的长裙——
就这些,还有更多的吗?
要想说出我想说的,不可能!
但好像一盏魔灯把神经
在屏幕上组成一种模式,
这值不值得?
如果有人放下一个枕头,或甩掉一个披肩,
转身朝向窗户,竟然说:
"根本就不是,
我不是这意思,根本就不是。"

……

Section Four
American Poetry of the Modernist Period

11
不！我不是哈姆雷特王子，也不想是；
我是一个侍臣，一个可以
国王出巡时位于其列，捧一两次场，
给王子出点注意的人；毫无疑问，是个好用的工具而已，
是个配角，有人用就高兴，
讲究策略，为人小心，处事谨慎，
满腹韬略却略显愚钝，
有时还近乎荒谬，
有时就是白痴。

12
我老喽……我老喽……
我要穿裤腿脚往上卷翻的裤子。

13
我要不要把我的头发在脑后分开？
我敢吃桃子吗？
我要穿白色法兰绒裤子，在海滩上漫步。
我曾听到美人鱼歌唱，它们为彼此歌唱。

我认为他们不会为我歌唱。

我看见它们乘风破浪向海里奔去，
海风把水吹成黑白两色，
它们梳理被吹回的海浪的白发。

我们在海底的闺房流连，
海姑娘头带红棕色海草做成的花环，
直到人声把我们唤醒，于是我们溺水而终。

（李正栓　韩志华　译）

Ⅷ. Carl Sandburg
(1878 – 1967)

1. Life Story

　　Sandburg was born into a poor but affectionate family of Swedish immigrants in Galesburg, Illinois. The family failed to afford him a proper formal education and thus he was obliged to give up school and learn from experience. At the age of 13, he began to move from job to job as a migratory laborer in the southeastern states in various professions, including once enlisting in the army to participate in the Spanish-American War in 1898, and working as a correspondent for the Galesburg Evening Mail in Puerto Rico for 8 months. Afterwards Sandburg settled down in his home town and was accepted by Lombard College, where he studied diligently, made a serious beginning with his writing, and obtained fame as an excellent basketball player. However, Sandburg disappeared from college a few weeks before the graduation ceremony, and very eagerly began his career as a roving reporter until 1908, when he secured a position as political organizer for the Social Democrats in Wisconsin. Feeling uninterested in politics, Sandburg gave up that position 2 years later and returned to his trade as a journalist. In 1937, Sandburg moved to Chicago on an editorial engagement. There he settled down and the history of his illustrious poems started.

　　In 1944, Sandburg published his first poem, "Chicago," in *Poetry*, a magazine of verse. The work soon aroused dispute among the critics: some showed admiration for the passions it expressed, the straightforward style it used, and the contempt it implied for old conventions; some others bitterly denounced the work just for its vulgar language and insolent tone. Despite all the debates, Sandburg went on with his composing and 2 years later, his first book of poetry, *Chicago Poems*, came out, by which his stable reputation as a poet ranking with Frost and Robinson was largely recognized.

Section Four
American Poetry of the Modernist Period

2. Characteristics of Sandburg's Poems

As a poet, Sandburg was an active member of the imagist group in the early part of the century: either "Fog" or "Lost—" is illustrated with vivid images. However, most critics considered Sandburg to be a close follower of Whitman. Imitating and experimenting, Sandburg reached the maturity. Having succeeded with his optimistic spirit and freedom in dealing with rhythm, Sandburg was also able to take advantage of Emily Dickinson's epigrammatic style. What's more important, he insisted on innovation in American poetry, not only by invention of new ways of expression, but also by shifting the subject matter from traditional rural landscapes to modern industrial city life. In addition, Sandburg tried to keep up with time in praising modern mechanical culture and adopting colloquial diction into versification.

The early works of Sandburg refer to those concerned with his settling in Chicago, the *Chicago Poems*, *Cornhusker* (1918), *Smoke and Steel* (1920); the later works include those which appeared thereafter: *Good Morning America* (1928), *The People*, *Yes* (1936) *Complete Poems* (1950), and *Honey and Salt* (1963). "Fog" and "Chicago" can be found in the early *Chicago Poems*.

3. Selected Poems

(1) Chicago

Hog butcher for the world,
Tool Maker, Stacker of wheat,
Player with railroads and the Nation's
    Freight Handler;
Stormy, husky, brawling,
5 City of the big shoulders:

They tell me you are wicked and I believed them,
    for I have seen your painted women under the
    gas lamps luring the farm boys.
And they tell me you are crooked and I answer:
    Yes, it is true I have seen the gunman kill
    and go free to kill again.
And they tell me you are brutal and my reply is:
    On the faces of women and children I have seen

     the marks of wanton hunger.
And having answered so I turn once more to those
     who sneer at this my city, and I give them
     back the sneer and say to them:
10 Come and show me another city with lifted head
     singing so proud to be alive and coarse and
     strong and cunning.
Flinging magnetic curses amid the toil of piling
     job on job, here is a tall bold slugger set
     vivid against the little soft cities;
Fierce as a dog with tongue lapping for action,
     cunning as a savage pitted against the wilderness,
         Bareheaded,
         Shoveling,
15   Wrecking,
         Planning,
         Building, breaking, rebuilding,
Under the smoke, dust all over his mouth, laughing
     with white teeth,
Under the terrible burden of destiny laughing
     as a young man laughs,
20 Laughing even as an ignorant fighter laughs
     who has never lost a battle,
Bragging and laughing that under his wrist is the
     pulse, and under his ribs the heart of the people,
         Laughing!
Laughing the stormy, husky, brawling laughter of
     Youth, half-naked, sweating, proud to be Hog
     Butcher, Tool Maker, Stacker of Wheat, Player
     with Railroads and Freight Handler to the Nation.

Notes

Line 1 Hog butcher for the world: (Chicago, as an industrial city) runs as a butcher providing meat for the world. Chicago for most of its history has been the center of the meat-producing industry in the United States.

Line 2 Stacker: person who put things into or formed a neat pile. In this line it refers to the dealer of wheat.

Section Four
American Poetry of the Modernist Period

Line 3 Player with railroads: runner of the railway.
       the Nation's Freight Handler: people who handle the railway transportation of the country.
Line 4 Stormy: noisy fierce expressions of feeling.
       husky: of a person or voice which is difficult to hear, as if the throat were dry; a big and strong person.
       brawling: always ready for a noisy quarrel, often in a public place, includes fighting.

  In the first 5 lines, Chicago is personified as the one who shoulders much responsibility: a butcher, a tool maker, a grain dealer, a manager of railroad; on the whole, the backbone of the country.

Line 6 you: Chicago.
       painted women: prostitutes.
Line 7 crooked: dishonest; illegal.
       gunman: murderer.
       go free: without being punished.
Line 8 wanton hunger: reckless hunger.
Line 9 sneer at: laugh scornfully at; smile contemptuously at.
Lines 6 – 9 The seamy side of the city is exposed: wickedness, crookedness, brutality, prostitutes luring boys, gunmen killing and going free, and women and children going hungry; nevertheless, despite all these, the poet speaks in defense of the city.
Line 10 You can't find another city which is as lively as Chicago, which is as coarse, strong and cunning as Chicago.
Line 11 Flinging: speaking, expressing in a violent way.
       magnetic curses: violent words with powerful attraction.
       amid: in the middle of...; among.
       toil of piling job on job: doing hard work day and night.
       a tall bold slugger: a tall and strong boxer.
       set vivid against: appear quite different from...; contrasting.
Line 12 Fierce as a dog: (Chicago is as) fierce as a dog.
       with tongue lapping for action: with the tongue reaching out to lap for an attack.
       cunning as a savage: (Chicago is as) clever and ingenious as savage people.
       pitted: test somebody or something in a struggle or competition with...
Line 13 Bareheaded: Chicago is like a toiler who is working bareheaded-

ly, but diligently.
Line 14 Shoveling: Chicago is toiling with shoveling.
Line 15 Wrecking: dismantling, tearing down.
Line 16 Planning: After destruction, Chicago revived to make another plan for a brighter future.
Lines 13 – 17 Chicago is like a diligent and persistent worker trying to improve its image.
Line 18 When it (Chicago) is under the smoke and with dust all over its mouth, it still laughs merrily.
Line 19 Despite the heavy burden and bad luck, Chicago is energetic, vigorous and hopeful.
Line 20 Chicago is optimistic as a fighter who has never lost a battle.
Line 21 under his wrist is the pulse: Chicago is laughing in the rhythm of the pulse of its people. Chicago is a giant, under its ribs throbs the heart of its people.
Line 22 Chicago is proud to be "the big shoulders" of the country; it is proud to take all the responsibility.

Comment on the poem

When Chicago was condemned for all its defects, the poet rose up to speak in defense of the city by making use of personification and metaphor. First he compares the city to various fierce figures. Then he expresses his respect for them despite the seamy side. Finally, as a conclusion, the poet shows his pride in the city, he is proud of its diligence, its persistence, its vigor and its hopeful future.

This poem was published in *Poetry* in 1914 and later collected in his *Chicago Poems* (1916).

参考译文

芝 加 哥

向全世界供肉的屠夫,
粮食储藏者,工具制造商,
铁路玩弄者,国家运输王;
你脾气暴怒,声音嘶哑,喧哗不止,
是个膀大肩阔的城市。

Section Four
AMERICAN POETRY OF THE MODERNIST PERIOD

有人说你邪恶,我相信,
因为我见过你城内浓妆艳抹的妇女
站在汽灯下引诱农家小伙子。
有人说你畸形,我就说:
是的,是真的!我见过有人持枪杀人,
逍遥法外又杀人!
有人说你残暴,我的回答是:
在城内妇女和儿童的脸上
我能读出极端饥饿的痕迹。
答完这些问题,我又一次转问那些
蔑视我们城市的人,我对他们
回报以蔑视,并且告诉他们:
来,给我展示另外一个城市,哪一城能昂首挺胸
富有活力地傲唱,唱得粗犷,
可爱又响亮?
在粗重的体力劳动中夹杂的极富魅力的咒骂,
这是一个勇敢的大个子拳击手
与娇小的城市形成鲜明的对照;
凶猛得像狗伸舌要行动,
机灵得像野兽面对荒野要谋生,
光着头,
挥着锹,
拆旧物,
想新景,
建了拆,拆了建,
在烟雾之下,满嘴泥土,大笑露齿
露着白白的牙齿,
在命运重压下,大笑
像个青年人那样大笑,
笑得像一个从未战败过的
斗士天真地大笑,
又是夸口又是大笑,说他腕下
跳动着脉搏,在他肋下是人们的心脏,
他大笑!
笑得粗犷、嘶哑、响亮,那是青年人的
大笑,半裸着身子,大汗淋漓,自豪地担当屠夫、
工具制造商、粮食储藏者、
铁路玩弄者、国家运输王。

Studies on American Poetry

（李正栓　韩志华　译）

(2) Fog

The fog comes
on little cat feet.
It sits looking
over harbor and city
5　on silent haunches
and then moves on.

Notes

Lines 1 – 2 comes on little cat feet: comes soundlessly and very softly.
Line 5 on silent haunches: sitting there quietly.
Line 6 then moves on: (After sitting and looking for a while, the fog) leaves quietly without being noticed.

Comment on the poem

　　The poem is pervaded with a tranquil atmosphere. The shapeless fog is embodied as a cat, an image of softness and tranquility. The cat is quiet, but it is not without curiosity. It sits, looks; it searches into every part of the city and then it leaves by itself. Therefore, the tranquility of the picture is rather set off by all the motions of a cat. Everything is quiet, everything is moving: the cat, the fog, the harbor, and the city.

　　This short poem is written in "Free verse," of course it is without any feet or rhyme scheme. Yet it is written in colloquial words and is structurally quite similar to Japanese Haiku（はいく）. The similarity is understandable because this poem was done in 1916 when American imagist poets led by Ezra Pound was experimenting to imitate the form of Japanese Haiiku and Sandburg, more or less, was involved in the latest trend of fashion.

Section Four
American Poetry of the Modernist Period

参考译文

雾

雾来了
迈着碎小猫步。

它坐下来张望
港口与城市
悄悄地蹲息
之后又继续前行。
（李正栓 译）

(3) Grass

Pile the bodies high at Austerlitz and Waterloo.
Shovel them under and let me work—
    I am the grass; I cover all.
And pile them high at Gettysburg
5 And pile them high at Ypres and Verdun.
Shovel them under and let me work.

Two years, ten years, and passengers ask the conductor:
    What place is this?
    Where are we now?

10   I am the grass.
    Let me work.

Notes

Line 1 the bodies: the corpses of soldiers off the battlefield.
    Austerlitz: a town in south Moravia, in central Czechoslovakia; it was the battlefield for Napoleon I to defeat Russian and Austrian armies in 1805, a decisive battle for Napoleon to establish himself as emperor of Europe.
    Waterloo: a village in central Belgium, south of Brussels; Napo-

leon was decisively defeated here on June 18, 1815.

Line 2 Shovel them under: bury the bodies in the ground by using shovels.

let me work: save me (the grass) the space to grow, let me do my work.

Line 4 Gettysburg: a borough in south Pennsylvania. The Confederate forces were defeated in a Civil War battle fought near here on July 1 to 3, 1863, a decisive point for the triumph of the Northern army, and the place was soon dedicated as a national cemetery. It is also famous for President Lincoln's *Gettysburg Address* on November 19, 1863.

Line 5 Ypres: a town in western Belgium. During the WWI, it was one of the major battlefields.

Verdun: a fortress city in northeast France, on the Meuse River. In 1916, a fierce battle was fought there.

Line 7 passengers: people of later generations, riding on trains.

Comment on the poem

Austerlitz, Waterloo, Gettysburg, Ypres and Verdun are all well-known battlefields in world history, where a lot of heroes were created and more lives killed. This poem, published in 1918, appeals to eliminate disastrous wars and return the world to peace through the mouth of grass. The irony is that battlefields and their events are so quickly forgotten.

参考译文

草

让尸首在奥斯特里兹和滑铁卢堆积成山,
把它们铲下去,然后交给我来处理——
我是草,我能把一切覆盖掉。

让尸首在葛底斯堡堆高成山,
让尸首在伊普勒斯和凡尔登高高堆起,
把它们铲下去,然后交给我来处理。
两年后,十年后,游客们便会问导游:
这是什么地方?

Section Four
American Poetry of the Modernist Period

我们现在什么处?

我是草。
交给我来处理。
(李正栓 译)

Ⅸ. Wallace Stevens
(1879 – 1955)

1. Life Story

As a poet, Stevens had a stronger passion for perfecting what he wrote than for his literary fame; for all his life, he was well-known as a lawyer, and later, a successful businessman.

Stevens was born in Reading, Pennsylvania, into a prosperous attorney's family of Dutch stock. With the encouragement of his father, Stevens studies at Harvard and New York University Law School, preparing for a career to the bar. In 1916, after practicing law for many years, he was engaged by the Hartford Accident and Indemnity Company and secured the position of vice-president of this insurance company until 1955, the year of his retirement and his death.

Stevens began his writing of poems during his time at Harvard. When he was busily associated with business, he never gave up his interests in poetry. As a matter of fact, Stevens made great efforts to bridge the world of reality with the world of imagination. Consequently, he was recognized as a successful businessman, and an outstanding poet as well.

2. Characteristics of Stevens' Poems

Most of Stevens' important poems were composed during the time of the Great Depression and the two World Wars. Yet he showed little concern with the sufferings and frustrations of the time, for he believed that, as a poet, what he should and could do is not to heal or reform society, but help his people to become more happily aware of the beauty and pleasure and excitement and meaning in the sordidness of reality.

However, Stevens was not blindly optimistic, nor was he the one who escaped from reality. Instead, he was interested in the "ideas of order," that is, true ideas correspond with an innate order in the universe. He was interested in the relationship of chaos and order, the reconciliation of reality and imagination, by insisting that an artist should observe reality and create reality out of his imagination, and that the order and faith we have lost in modern society can be recreated in artistic work through imagination.

Having been regarded as a poet of the imagist group, Stevens was good at applying metaphors and symbols. As with all the other imagists, he experimented a lot with styles, sound, and rules of rhymes.

3. Stevens' Major Poems

The earliest poetic work of Stevens came out in 1914, but he did not have his poems collected into a book *Harmonium* until 1923. After it, more and more poems poured out over the next 20 years, including *Ideas of Order* (1935), *Owl's Clover* (1936), *The Man with the Blue Guitar* (1937), *Parts of a World* (1942), *The Auroras of Autumn* (1950), *The Necessary Angel: Essays on Reality and the Imagination* (1951), and *The Collected Poems of Wallace Stevens* (1954).

4. Selected Poems

(1) Thirteen Ways of Looking at a Blackbird

I

Among twenty snowy mountains,
The only moving thing
Was the eye of the blackbird.

II

I was of three minds,
Like a tree
In which there are three blackbirds

III

The blackbird whirled in the autumn winds.
It was a small part of the pantomime.

IV

A man and a woman
Are one.
A man and a woman and a blackbird

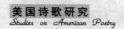

Are one.

V

I do not know which to prefer,
The beauty of inflections
Or the beauty of innuendoes,
The blackbird whistling
Or just after.

VI

Icicles filled the long window
With barbaric glass.
The shadow of the blackbird
Crossed it, to and fro.
The mood
Traced in the shadow
An indecipherable cause.

VII

O thin men of Haddam,
Why do you imagine golden birds?
Do you not see how the blackbird
Walks around the feet
Of the women about you?

VIII

I know noble accents
And lucid, inescapable rhythms;
But I know, too,
That the blackbird is involved
In what I know.

IX

When the blackbird flew out of sight,
It marked the edge
Of one of many circles.

X

At the sight of blackbirds
Flying in a green light,

Even the bawds of euphony
Would cry out sharply.

XI

He rode over Connecticut
In a glass coach.
Once, a fear pierced him,
In that he mistook
The shadow of his equipage
For blackbirds.

XII

The river is moving.
The blackbird must be flying.

XIII

It was evening all afternoon.
It was snowing
And it was going to snow,
The blackbird sat
In the cedar-limbs.

Notes

Stanza I : The blackbird and the 20 snowy mountains suggest a striking contrast of color, and a striking contrast of size—a tiny blackbird against the huge background of 20 white mountains.

Stanza II : Tree and blackbirds symbolize human and soul.

Stanza III : pantomime: a type of play with music, dancing and clowning, based on a traditional story or fairy-tale; expressive movements of the face and body used to tell a story.

As man and woman, a blackbird is a part of nature; it is in harmony with the human world and the natural world. A blackbird enables a man to imagine he is a woman, or a human being to be a bird.

Stanza V : inflections: the changes of the ending or form of a word to show its grammatical function in a sentence, the qualities of one's speaking voice.

innuendoes: indirect reference usually suggesting something bad or discreditable about somebody; implication.

The blackbird whistling or just after: (I do not know which bird I did prefer. Do I prefer) the bird when it was whistling or the one just after its whistling—a whistling bird or a silent bird?

This section can be understood as I just can't say which is better: a whistling bird or a bird in silence, since each is as pretty as the other.

Stanza Ⅵ: Icicles: a pointed stick of ice formed when water freezes as it runs down.

the long window with barbaric glass: the window which is long but with coarse, rough icicles, which look like glass.

Crossed it: (The shadow of the blackbird flew) across the window.

Traced in the shadow: followed the vague shadow of the blackbird.

An indecipherable cause: The cause for the mood's tracing in the shadow of the blackbird is not quite understandable.

indecipherable: unable to understand; unable to interpret.

Rather willingly my mood follows the shadow of the bird.

Stanza Ⅶ: Haddam: a small town by the sea in Connecticut. However, Stevens claims the name is accidentally given out of his imagination, which indicates just any plain area.

golden birds: expensive, luxurious things.

The blackbird becomes the image of plain but valuable things.

Stanza Ⅷ: noble accents and lucid, inescapable rhythms: speech of noble people, the fine arts.

I know, too, that the blackbird is involved in what I know: I am clear that besides a lot of other fine things, I also know the blackbird well.

The blackbird has become a part of my knowledge.

Stanza Ⅸ: The blackbird is impressive to people.

Stanza Ⅹ: the bawds of euphony: the dealer of sound and rhyme; the professional poets who wrote scholastically attached too much importance to the style, rhythm, feet or word choice in versification. A bawd is a prostitute or procurer, hence Stevens expresses his low opinion of such poets.

A blackbird flying in a green light may provide such a beauti-

Stanza XI: He: one person.
　　　　　a glass coach: a coach with a glass window.
　　　　　a fear pierced him: to be suddenly controlled by a fear.
　　　　　A blackbird sometimes may be frightening.
Stanza XII: The blackbird is active.
Stanza XIII: It was evening all afternoon: it was very dark that afternoon.
　　　　　In the cedar-limbs: in the small branches of a cedar tree.
　　　　　As a harmonious part of nature, the blackbird keeps up with weather.

Comment on the poem

　　Taking a blackbird as the central figure, the poet presents pictures of more than thirteen images. Wherever the blackbird appears, it enlivens—mountains, trees, autumn wind, man, woman, icicles, green light, carriage, river and snow. The poet, instead of describing the bird, actually put much of his attention on the black color so as to reveal the striking contrast between the bird and the others. Thus, the blackbird, on the one hand, indicates a common bird which surveys mountains from the sky, which whirls in the autumn winds, which flies to and fro across the icy windows, which sits in the branches of a tree. On the other hand, a blackbird is the embodiment of imagination. Led by this blackbird, the reader is able to imagine everything in nature: mountains, trees, autumn wind, winter windows, happiness, fears, or anything, since "the blackbird is involved in what I know." Consequently, the thirteen ways of looking at a blackbird could have implied to readers thirteen ways to apply imagination.

　　This poem may have inspired Kenneth Patchen's noted poem, "The Little Green Blackbird," at least in part.

参考译文

对山鸟的十三种看法

1
在二十座雪山中，
唯一的活物，

是山鸟的眼睛。

2

我有三种意念，
就像一棵树，
上面有三只山鸟。

3

山鸟在秋风中盘旋，
是哑剧的一个场面。

4

一个男人和一个女人
是一体。
男人、女人和山鸟，
是一体。

5

我不知道更喜欢哪一个，
变化之美？
还是影射之美？
鸣叫时的山鸟？
还是鸣叫后的山鸟？

6

冰溜充盈了长长的窗棂，
玻璃面变得粗糙。
山鸟的身影，
飞来又飞去，
一种情绪
融在这影子里，
莫可名状。

7

哦，海达姆瘦弱的男人们，
为什么想象金色的鸟？
你看不见这山鸟
是怎么在你身边女人的

脚周围盘旋?

8
我懂得贵族的声调,
节奏流畅、动人,
但我也知道,
这山鸟之美
容纳于我知道的内容。

9
当这山鸟飞出视野,
标志着一种边缘,
一种圈的边缘。

10
当山鸟飞入视野,
在绿光之下飞翔,
即使是声音悦耳的鸨母,
也会发出尖叫的声响。

11
他穿过康涅狄格州,
乘坐玻璃马车。
一次,他感到恐惧,
因为他错把
马车的影子看作
了山鸟。

12
河水在流动。
山鸟肯定在飞翔。

13
整个下午如同黑夜
天在下着雪,
并且还要下,
山鸟栖息在
雪松树枝里。

美国诗歌研究
Studies on American Poetry

(李正栓 韩志华 译)

(2) The Snow Man

One must have a mind of winter
To regard the frost and the boughs
Of the pine-trees crusted with snow.

And have been cold a long time
5 To behold the junipers shagged with ice,
The spruces rough in the distant glitter

Of the January sun; and not to think
Of any misery in the sound of the wind,
In the sound of a few leaves,

10 Which is the sound of the land,
Full of the same wind
That is blowing in the sane bare place

For the listener, who listens in the snow,
And, nothing himself, beholds,
15 Nothing that is not there and the nothing that is.

Notes

Line 1 mind of winter: the state of mind harmonious with the atmosphere of winter.
Line 3 crusted with snow: covered with a hard outer surface of snow.

Stanza 1: In order to appreciate the scenery of winter, one must first adjust his mind proper to the season.

Line 5 junipers shagged with ice: trees roughly covered with ice.
Line 6 The spruces: a type of evergreen tree with dense foliage.

Stanza 2: Only those who have experienced the harshness of winter can enjoy the picture of junipers shagged with ice and that of spruces rough but glittering in distance (in the January sun).

Section Four
American Poetry of the Modernist Period

<u>Stanza 3</u>: Only those people who have the mind of winter can enjoy themselves in winter without imagining the misery existing in the sound of wind which may appear in the sound of leaves. In the first three stanzas, the poet applied three verbs: "regard," "behold," and "think" to indicate the cognitive activity of human beings. However, these otherwise synonymies have trivial differences. The word "regard" refers to the activity of both mind and body; "behold" emphasizes a person's physical behavior; while "think" simply means the activity of one's mind.

Line 10 Which: the sound of wind in the sound of leaves.
Line 14 nothing himself: forget everything of himself; in a self-denial condition; as a snow man which does not originate from nature.
Lines 14 – 15 beholds nothing that is not there: beholds nothing that does not exist there;
  nothing that is not there: nothing substantial.
  nothing that is: the nothingness exists there; the state of emptiness there.

<u>Stanza 4</u>: The snow man, as nothing a part of the world, would behold only something that exists before it and would behold nothing else which does not exist to it; however, not as a natural figure of the world, what it can really behold at present is the nothingness in front.

Comment on the poem

In this poem titled "Snow Man," the snow man does not appear in lines. What the poet intends to discuss is each's appreciation of the other between the snow and man.

The winter picture is presented first by a description of distant trees, covered with snow; then the leaves are rolled up in winter winds; thereafter, the land under the trees appeared, until to the end, everything returned to nothingness, the objective and the subjective worlds are united into one.

参考译文

雪 人

人若喜看冬严霜，

心怡冬雪披青松。
他心必与冬相通。

严寒时节已久长,
刺柏树上冰狼卧,
云杉挂冰熠熠光。

那是一月寒太阳;
莫忌风声多凄厉,
莫忌疏叶好凄凉。

此乃大地恒声音,
相同寒风总充盈,
那是空地神智音。

听者站在雪中听,
忘掉自我独自看
原本无物万事空。
(李正栓 韩志华 译)

(3) The Emperor of Ice-cream

  Call the roller of big cigars,
  The muscular one, and bid him whip
  In kitchen cups concupiscent curds.
  Let the wenches dawdle in such dress
5 As they are used to wear, and let the boys
  Bring flowers in last month's newspapers.
  Let be be finale of seem.
  The only emperor is the emperor of ice-cream.

  Take from the dresser of deal,
10 Lacking the three glass knobs, that sheet
  On which she embroidered fantails once
  And spread it so as to cover her face.
  If her horny feet protrude, they come
  To show how cold she is, and dumb.
15 Let the lamp affix its beam.

Section Four
American Poetry of the Modernist Period

The only emperor is the emperor of ice-cream.

Notes

Line 1 the roller of big cigars: the one who rolls big cigars; god or the unknown power controlling life and death.
Line 2 The muscular one: a strong man; the roller of cigars.
Line 3 concupiscent curds: lustful or sensual curds.
Line 4 wenches: mature girls or young women; maiden girls; it is a pejorative term.
    dawdle: loaf around; be slow; waste time.
Line 7 Let be be finale of seem: Let "be" be turned into "seem" by the end; let the possibility become less possible or impossible.
Line 8 emperor: an image for the most powerful being.

<u>Stanza 1</u>: Every one is a part of the world; every one enjoys his life in his own way. In this world, nothing is really powerful; except the god of death.

Line 9 the dresser of deal: the cupboard made of cheap pine or fir planks.
Line 11 fantails: fan-shaped designs.
Line 12 it: the embroidered sheet.
Line 13 horny feet: feet made hard and rough by the diligent toil of her life
    protrude: jut or stick out from under the surface (the sheet)
Line 15 affix: stick; fasten or attach something.

<u>Stanza 2</u>: Let's take, from the cupboard of deal, a sheet with an embroidered pattern to cover her face. If the sheet is not large enough to cover her body, the exposed feet show that she is cold and dumb.

Comment on the poem

    The god of death is compared to the ice-cream which is hard, cold, and stiff, wearing everything of the appearance of death. Moreover, like ice-cream, which melts easily and quickly, human life is short and burdened with empty reputation.
    The two extremes of life—reality and imagination, interweaved in the work. When a woman died, she was covered with a sheet embroi-

dered by herself while the others still live in their own ways: the girls were dressing in the usual way and the boys made use of the old newspaper. The world is cold. God is indifferent. The power of death is so fierce that it controls everything in the world. Thus in reality, "the only emperor is the emperor of ice-cream."

参考译文

冰淇淋大帝

让那卷大雪茄的人,那雄健的人
过来,让他去厨房
弄几杯淫欲的冰淇淋,
让少女穿上惯常的服装
来悠闲鬼混,让男孩们
用上个月的旧报纸把花儿包装好送来,
让看起来像的东西成为实实在在的东西。
唯一的王是冰淇淋大帝。

从缺三个玻璃把手的妆台
取出那床单,
在上面她曾刺绣扇尾鸽图案
铺开它,盖住她的脸。
如果她角状双脚伸出单子外,它们
是显示她尸骨已寒,再也不能说话,
让那盏灯光亮闪闪。
唯一的王是冰淇淋大帝。

(李正栓　韩志华　译)

Section Four
American Poetry of the Modernist Period

X. E. E. Cummings
(1894 – 1962)

1. Life Story

In the first half of the 20th century, E. E. Cummings remained a controversial figure for all the dexterous novelty of his versification and for his daring experimentation.

E. E. Cummings (Edward Estlin Cummings) was born in Cambridge, Massachusetts, the town in which Harvard University is located. Cummings' father was a professor at Harvard, and in 1915 Cummings himself graduated from Harvard with a master's degree. The next year, Cummings was recruited by the Red Cross for World War I and was sent to France. But he was soon, very unfortunately, charged with treason because of a censor's mistake, and stayed in a French detention camp for three months. This experience, fortunately, provided the raw material for his first literary work, *The Enormous Room* published in 1922. After the war, Cummings went to Paris to study painting, with all the fascination for such post-Impressionist and Cubist painters as Cezanne and Picasso. His genius in art, harmoniously combined with his talent in language, freed him from the bondage of conventional style and distinguished him as one of the most outstanding poets of the 20th century.

2. Characteristics of Cummings' Poems

All his life, Cummings was absorbed in the pursuit of perfection in art and literature. He was not like most writers in history, who toiled to add something of novelty to enlarge the content of the treasure house of art; nor was he like those who arrogantly spurned convention and started anew. Cummings was a poet who defined independently his own universe by expressing conventional ideas through employing modern techniques.

As a poet, Cummings was famous for the experiments he executed. His experimental techniques are evident first in the defying or complete rejection of the capitalization. He deliberately ignored the conventional capitalization of the proper names "god" and "america" and even refused to capitalize the word "i."

Then there is the violation of regular grammar by freely splitting or combining words, purposeful underpunctuation, and breaking phrases by cadence to the advantage of the melody. Sometimes Cummings would arrange the letters of a word or lengthen the space between letters or words, all for the same aim to convey the vividness of life and present the power of rhythm. Besides, Cummings, as a master of the stream-of-consciousness technique, often employed words and phrases symbolically or simply as an image to display something meaningful in mind but probably illogical in appearance. Whereas, compared with the works of other poets in this group, Cummings' works are shorter and more flexible.

The experimental poet in Cummings was very traditional in mind. Science, industry, and machines are often the object of condemnation in his works. Instead, love for nature, children, normal family life, and artistic work are the frequent themes of his poems. What's more, as a professional painter, he was much more concerned than other poets with the typographical order of words: the arrangement of them into a picture. Some of his poems are virtually unreadable because of his experimental skills—Cummings deliberately presented them as "picture-poems" to please the reader's eye with all the beauty contained in a pattern.

3. Major Works of Cummings

Immediately after the publication of his first book in 1922, Cummings' first collection of poems, *Tulips and Chimneys*, came out the next year. His other works include: *&* (1923), *is* 5 (1926), *Viva* (1931), *No Thanks* (1935), and 50 *poems* (1940).

4. Selected Poems

(1) L(a

    L(a
    le
    af
    fa

    ll

Section Four
American Poetry of the Modernist Period

```
s)
one
l
iness
```

Notes

This is an example of Cummings' "picture poem," which is not directly readable.

It consists of two parts—the major part appears inside of the brackets; it can be read as: a leaf falls; the rest of the poem, the material outside the brackets, though separated by the major part, forms one word: loneliness.

The poem is deliberately arranged in this form as if the poet wants the reader to experience directly the process of the leaves' falling from their mother tree to the ground.

The arrangement and choice of letters suggest that leaves are leaving their mother in different ways: some are falling vertically as being suggested by "le," "ll," and "l"; some others are falling horizontally as suggested by "one." The last line, though not a whole word, provides the longest line of the work, as if all the fallen leaves have gathered here to cover the autumn ground.

In the brackets "a leaf falls" strongly suggests the scenery of autumn, the time, and the story.

Outside the brackets, the connotation of "loneliness" diverges: It may indicate that each leaf feels lonely when it leaves its mother (the tree) and the warmth of family; or that the tree feels lonely when it sees her children are leaving; what's more, the poet may feel lonely when he is watching the bleak autumn scene. If he had experienced the spring and summer, the flowering period of life, he could not help feeling lonely when he is old and fading, and when he is helplessly falling.

参考译文

```
孤(一
  片
  树
  叶
```

美国诗歌研究
Studies on American Poetry

飘
落）
孤
单单
（陈岩 译）

(2) [R-P-O-P-H-E-S-S-A-G-R]

r-p-o-p-h-e-s-s-a-g-r
who
a)s w(e loo)k
upnowgath
5　PPEGORHRASS
eringint(o-
a The):l
eA
!P:
10　a
(r
rIvInGgRrEaPsPhOs)
to
rea(be)rran(com)gi(e)ngly
15　,grasshopper;

Notes

    If you have never seen any grasshoppers jumping in poetic lines, if you have never heard the grasshoppers singing in chorus, just read this poem. Here we are exposed to a vivid and natural picture of the jumping and singing of grasshoppers by random, unreadable but living words.

    When he was writing, E. E. Cummings not only broke the proper word order, but also rearranged the capital letters, small letters, punctuations, brackets and lines in a random order with the only exception of the last line, which offers a normal word "grasshoppers."

    Following the cue of the last line, we can comprehend the part above:

    The first line is actually "grasshopper"; the random order of letters indicates the grasshopper in general, which is that kind of insect that constantly jumps, backward and forward. The random order of the word enlivens the plain word "grasshopper" into a vivid picture of a group of active insects.

Lines 2 to 9 read like "who, as we look up now, gathering into a leap." However, the sentence has been freely interrupted by "grasshoppers" in random order which are believed to have made great noise before leaping.

Lines 1 to 6 suggest a scene: the grasshoppers are chirping while gathering strength, preparing for a high jump.

Line 12 The word "riving" means "break into pieces." This word implies the grasshoppers jump and shriek so fiercely that they almost tear themselves into pieces.

Lines 7 to 12, in the shape of stairs, these words strongly suggest the grasshoppers' leaps and the scene of their continuous leaping forward.

Line 14 The letters in the brackets form "become" and letters outside the brackets can be read as "rearrangingly."

Comment on the poem

This poem provides a vivid picture of grasshoppers: they are singing, dancing, and leaping without exhaustion. The activity of them just reveals the motion of nature and the sound of nature as well; the mixed use of capital letters and small letters is simply the implication of the stronger or weaker sound of the noise. This is the work which calls for the use of both the physical eyes and the mental eyes for a thorough enjoyment.

参考译文

蚂蚂蚂蚂蚂蚱蚱蚱蚱蚱

蚂蚂蚂蚂蚂蚱蚱蚱蚱蚱，

就像我们所寻找的，
　　蚂蚂蚂蚂蚂
　　　　蚱蚱蚱蚱蚱

　　起　　群　　　　　起　　群
群　　　　落　群　　　　　　落

（韩志华　译　李正栓　校）

(3) In Just—

    in just—
    spring when the world is mud—
    luscious the little
    lame balloonman

5   whistles far and wee

    and eddieandbill come
    running from marbles and
    piracies and it's
    spring

10   when the world is puddle-wonderful

    the queer
    old balloonman whistles
    far and wee
    and bettyandisbel come dancing

15   from hop-scotch and jump-rope and
    it's
    spring
    and
    the
20   goat-footed

    balloonman whistles
    far
    and
    wee

Notes

Line 3 luscious: rich and sweet in taste or smell.
Line 5 wee: little; very small; to stay a little longer and in vibrating sound.

Section Four
American Poetry of the Modernist Period

Lines 1 – 5 When spring comes and the air is fresh and sweet, a lame balloonman is whistling and coming.
Line 6 eddieandbill: the combination of two boys' name, Eddie and Bill.
Line 8 piracies: a game usually played by boys when each of them pretends to be a pirate, a robber over sea.
Line 10 puddle-wonderful: puddles by the melting mud which symbolizing the appearance of spring.
Lines 6 – 10 The boys stop their games (marbles and piracies) and run to the balloonman.
Line 14 bettyandisbel: the combination of two girls' names, Betty and Isbel.
Lines 11 – 14 The girls are also attracted by the balloonman's whistles and merrily run to him.
Line 15 hop-scotch and jump-rope: two games girls like in particular.
Line 20 goat-footed: lame. The character of the "goat-footed" balloonman with his whistle strongly suggests the god of shepherds, Pan, who is half-man, half-animal and carries the sense of spring to the world with a pipe.

Comment on the poem

This is a poem presenting a vivid picture of childhood in spring. The structure of this poem is obviously in great violation of English grammar: neither the punctuation, nor the capitalization is orthodox; the division of paragraphs and lines don't conform to traditional grammar either. However, a close examination of the poem enables us to notice that beneath the loose structure there exists a striking inner harmony between children and nature: when it is warm, children are happily playing outside; a balloonman comes with the message of spring and children stop their games and run toward him; the balloonman leaves but his message stays down. The poet purposely breaks the lines and scatters the words to remind the reader of a childhood world; "eddieandbill" and "bettyanddisbel" are typed together to indicate these are just common names for boys and girls and thus the scene of this picture is generalized.

In the poem, "whistles far and wee" is repeated three times. When it appears for the first time in the fifth line, there are pauses between words which remind us of a peddler's whistles sound now and then and from a long distance. When "whistles far and wee" appears for the second time, the pauses come out regularly between "far" and "wee" just to imply that the balloonman is now surrounded by children and can be heard clearly. By the end each word takes the space of a whole line just to show the gradual disappearance of the peddler and his whistle. As an eye-poem, the shape of the poem, as well as its words, contributes greatly to the presenting of a particular childhood world of playfulness and innocence.

参考译文

正　好

正好在——
春天,当大地散发泥香——
味道甘美,那个跛脚的
卖气球的小老头
从远处　吹着口哨　哨音微弱,
艾迪和比尔从跑过来
本来丢石子和
抓海盗,原来
春天到了。

当大地冰雪消融,一展魅力,

那个卖气球的
古怪的老头吹着哨子
从远处走来　哨音微弱,
贝蒂和伊莎贝尔跳着过来

她们正在跳房子,跳绳子,
原来是
春天到了,
还有,
那
山羊脚的
卖气球的人　吹找哨子
来自远处
还有
哨音微弱。
（李正栓　韩志华　译）

Section Five

American Poetry of Contemporary Time

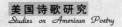

Ⅰ. Theodore Roethke
(1908 – 1963)

1. Life Story

Theodore Roethke was one of the most important poets during the middle decants of the 20th century. As the son of the most successful florist in Saginaw, Michigan, Roethke was able to further his education at Harvard after obtaining the A. B. (1929) and M. B. (1936) at the University of Michigan.

Roethke was a genius in writing poetry, but a reserved person in manner. His talent was first inspired by the beauty of his father's greenhouse, where every leaf and petal appeared significant to the boy as the embodiment of life, and meanwhile, as the symbol for something delicate and pleasant in this world. Nevertheless, outside the greenhouse, he found himself in torturing conflict with the ingrained values of conventional society. He had to make himself occupied in teaching and reading voraciously the books of the masters he admired: William Blake, William Butler Yeats, Walt Whitman, and Emerson. His first book of poetry, *Open House*, appeared in public in 1941 with controversial comments. However, he did not give up but became a Pulitzer Prize winner for the poems of 8 volumes.

2. Characteristics of Roethke's Poems

As a poet, the family greenhouse experience enabled Roethke to be a close observer of natural beauty. When composing, he was good at depicting the specific details of life and displaying the momentary aspiration of people. In his poems, metaphysical tension expresses itself in varied metaphors and fractured syntax, but he was, unlike most poets of his time, always optimistic in discussing such themes as life and death. He worked diligently to write poems in simple words and easy structure. As everyone can see, his early poems were written in a traditional style, while in the latter ones, some modern experimental skills can be largely traced.

3. Major Works of Roethke

Since the publication of his first book, Roethke succeeded through the publication of a chain of collections, until in 1963 his life was surprisingly interrupted by his accidental drowning in a friend's swimming pool. *The Lost Son*, a book in memory of his father and the greenhouse childhood, was published in 1948. Two years later, the same theme was continued in another book *Praise to the End* (1951). The sincere pathos and affection carried in these two books were widely shared by his readers. Consequently, two years later, when Roethke's new collection of poems, *The Waking*, came out, the Pulitzer Prize was awarded to the writer. In 1957, *Words for the Wind* obtained the Bollingen Prize.

In his honor, the Theodore Roethke Memorial Poetry Prize was established in 1967, and is awarded every three years. It is one of the most prestigious literary prizes in America.

4. Selected Poems

(1) In a Dark Time

In a dark time, the eye begins to see;
I meet my shadow in the deepening shade;
I hear my echo in the echoing wood—
A lord of nature weeping to a tree.
5   I live between the heron and the wren,
Beasts of the hill and serpents of the den.

What's madness but nobility of soul
At odds with circumstance? The day's on fire!
I know the purity of pure despair,
10 My shadow pinned against a sweating wall.
That place among the rocks—is it a cave
Or winding path? The edge is what I have.

A steady storm of correspondences!
A night flowing with birds, a ragged moon,
15 And in broad day the midnight come again!
A man goes far to find out what he is—
death of the self in a long tearless night,
All natural shapes blazing unnatural light.

Dark, dark my light, and darker my desire.
20 My soul, like some heat-maddened fly,
Keeps buzzing at the sill, Which I is I?
A fallen man, I climb out of my fear.
The mind enters itself, and God the mind,
And one is One, free in the tearing wind.

Notes

Line 1 dark time: It doesn't refer to the darkness of a certain sequence; instead, it indicates the darkness, blindness of the human soul in the modern world.

Line 4 A lord of nature: a master of nature; here it refers to "my echo." My echo is like a lord of nature which is weeping to a tree.

Line 5 live between the heron and the wren: live a quite natural life; live close to nature.

heron: a water-bird with a long neck and long legs that lives in marshy places. （苍鹭）

wren: a type of very small brown songbird with short wings. （鹪鹩）

Line 6 Beasts of the hill and serpents of the den: (I live between) beasts of the hill and the serpents of the den. Beasts and serpents are also parts of nature, though often supposed on the evil side.

Stanza 1: I find the eyes begin to see in dark time, I hear my echo in the echoing wood; these all sound paradoxical, but very philosophical as well.

Line 7 nobility of soul: the noble state of human soul.

Line 8 At odds with: be disagreeing or quarrelling with somebody about something.

In the first two lines of the stanza, the poet was requiring: Is the connotation of "madness" simply the disagreement between a human's noble soul and circumstance?

The day's on fire: When the noble soul is at odds with circumstance, one's time is burning—it must be very difficult for any one to keep the psychological peace then.

Section Five
American Poetry of Contemporary Time

Line 9 I know the purity of pure despair: I understand exactly the state of being extremely despair.

Line 10 My shadow: my soul.
  pinned against a sweating wall: fixed or attached to the wall by a pin or pins.
  a sweating wall: the dirty place one is reluctant to stay in.

Line 12 winding path: the curving, twisting or spiral course.
  The edge is what I have: "The edge" refers to that of the "cave" or that of the "winding path," the image of dangerous circumstances. In modern society, a person is often trapped in dangers.

Stanza 2: The poet intends to find out the connotation of "madness" but just resulted in a fact that human beings in modern society are confronting a dangerous existence.

Line 13 A steady storm: a strong sense.
  A steady storm of correspondences: I had a strong sense of being corresponding with nature; I had the interaction with nature as follows.

Line 14 A night flowing with birds: During annual migration, great numbs of birds fly across the face of the full moon at night—a "flowing river" of bird.
  a ragged moon: (under) a new moon.

Line 15 in broad day: in the full light of day.

Line 16 A man goes far....: A man may search everywhere in the universe to prove his existence.

Line 17 death... night: But the discovery of the man is probably just the death of himself in a long tearless night.

Line 18 All natural shapes....: The research may just result in that all natural shapes blazing unnatural light.
  natural shapes: normal human beings.
  blazing unnatural light: burning fiercely with all the absurdities of society.

Stanza 3: The poet shows that when the world is in a random order, the soul expects to strive out of body and fly freely so as to prove its existence, but fails.

Line 19 darker my desire: my desire is darker (than the night).

Line 20 heat-maddened fly: fly which is maddened by the heat of the season.
Line 21 Which I is I?: the soul is too confused to recognize itself; it feels quite lost in the modern world.
Line 22 A fallen man: When I fell down and was awoken.
Line 23 God the mind: God enters the mind, and when I was thoroughly awoken.
Line 24 one is One: When I was quite awoken, I finally discovered the truth that in the universe, one is all, and all is one. My soul is thus able to fly freely in the wind that tears everything.

Stanza 4: The poet finally realized the truth of human existence—one exists in all and all exists in one.

Comment on the poem

In the absurd, chaotic and mysterious world, the poet's soul is striving for a self-evidence. It searches through the echoing wood, through the birds and beasts, through caves and winding paths, through the storm, the flowing night and the broad day, yet, it fails to see "Which I is I." When he was rather disappointed with the modern society, he suddenly falls and becomes awoken to the reality that one soul exists in everything of nature and so it can fly freely in the tearing wind.

The poem, with all its obscure, absurd or paradoxical images, with its wild imagination, is rather written in a conventional form with six lines in each of the four stanzas. Each stanza is also done with an almost regular rhyme scheme of "abcadd."

参考译文

在昏暗的时刻

在昏暗的时刻,视线开始清晰:
渐昏渐暗的林荫中,我遇见自己的身影;
余音缭绕的树林里,我听见自己的回音——
一个自然之主对树哭泣叹息。
我与苍鹭和鸫鹩为伍,
我和山中兽与洞中蛇同住。

Section Five
American Poetry of Contemporary Time

疯狂是什么？难道是灵魂的崇高
与环境的格格不入？日子在火中煎熬！
我了解那彻底绝望的绝望，
汗渍渍的墙把我的影子钉牢。
那淹没在岩石间的地方——是洞穴隐现
还是小径蜿蜒？我拥有的只是外围边缘。

万千契合宛若狂风暴雨，猛烈如常！
群鸟飞舞，残月当空，夜在流逝，
天仍大亮，午夜却再次不期而至！
为寻找自我，有人觅寻远方——
却在漫漫无泪的黑夜发现自我的消亡，
所有那常态之物闪耀着非常的光芒。

昏暗，我的光昏暗，我的欲更昏暗。
我的灵魂犹如一只热疯了的苍蝇，
往窗栏门槛上嗡嗡乱撞，哪个我才是真我？
我失足跌落，从恐惧中向外爬攀。
心智归于其位，上帝进入心间，
在厉风中我心自由自在，原来万物皆唯一。
（李海云 译 李正栓 校）

（2） My Papa's Waltz

  The whisky on your breath
  Could make a small boy dizzy;
  But I hung on like death:
  Such waltzing was not easy.

5 We romped until the pans
  Slid from the kitchen shelf;
  My mother's countenance
  Could not unfrown itself

  The hand that held my wrist
10 Was battered on one knuckle;
  At every step you missed
  My right ear scraped a buckle.

You beat time on my head
With a palm caked hard by dirt,
15 Then waltzed me off to bed
Still clinging to your shirt.

Notes

Line 1 whisky on your breath: I could smell the whisky in your breath; I am aware that you are drunk.
Line 3 hung on like death: keep hold of you (the father) tightly.
Line 4 Such waltzing was not easy: it is not easy to waltz with a boy hanging tightly on you, nor easy for a boy to waltz with a drunken man.

Stanza 1: When father was a little drunk and felt everything turning around him, he insisted on me dancing a waltz with him. It is difficult for them, but still pleasurable.

Line 5 romped: play together in a lively way; running; jumping.
Lines 7 – 8 mother's countenance could not unfrown itself: mother could not help frowning at us; mother could not but feel angry with our destructive behaviors.

Stanza 2: Father and I danced crazily and bumped the pans which slid from the kitchen shelf. That caused mother to frown at us.

Line 10 battered on one knuckle: one knuckle of father's hands had been damaged to lose shape.
Line 11 step you missed: the dance step the father failed to accomplish.
Line 12 buckle: metal or plastic clasp with a hinged spike for fastening a belt or straps.
　　The boy was very young and his ear could just reach the father's waist. When dancing with father and a step failed, the boy's ear would scrape the buckle of the father's belt. The father, a physical laborer, was rather clumsy in dancing but was filled with kindness toward children.

Stanza 3: The father and son are waltzing, though clumsily, but really happily.

Line 13 beat time on my head: lightly knocked at my head so as to produce or keep with the rhythm of the music.
Line 14 a palm caked hard by dirt: a palm covered thickly with dirt (due to the hard toil for years), due to his work with plants and soil in his greenhouse.
Line 16 clinging to your shirt: holding tightly to your shirt; this line responses to the "hung on like death."

<u>Stanza 4</u>: The father's hand is hard and rough, the boy, however, enjoys it and feels quite reluctant to leave it.

Comment on the poem

This poem was selected from *The Lost Son* (1948), a collection of the autobiographical poems about his childhood days together with his father. After a whole day's labor and drinking of some whisky, the father was dancing with his little son. Although the father's steps were clumsy and the son was too short, they all enjoyed the crazy waltz round the house in spite of the mother's frowning. The rough hand touched the boy with all the affection a father can afford; while the boy was so attached to that until he was too tired to go on. The poem presented a living scene of a happy family of the laboring class.

参考译文

爸爸的华尔兹

你呼出来的威士忌酒气
足以使小男孩目眩头昏；
我却死抓着你紧紧偎依
这样跳华尔兹可不轻松。

我们又蹦又跳直嬉闹到
厨房搁板的锅盆掉下来；
妈妈的脸色可是不太妙
她额头紧蹙双眉展不开。

美国诗歌研究

那只紧握着我手腕的手
有一根砸坏关节的指头；
每当你踏错一个舞步后
我右耳就蹭蹭你皮带扣。

你沾满泥土硬块的手掌
在我脑袋上敲打着节拍；
跳着华尔兹送我去上床
我仍抓着你衬衣不松开。

(李海云 译 李正栓 校)

Section Five
American Poetry of Contemporary Time

II. Langston Hughes
(1902 – 1967)

1. Life Story

Langston Hughes was the first prominent Black writer in American literary history. He contributed to the treasure house of literature over 60 books, out of them 12 are collections of poems. Besides, he was also a master in novel writing and composer of plays for children.

Hughes was born in a black family in Joplin, Missouri. From a very young age, he was not without racial pride and dignity: being proud of the music, history, and legend of black culture. In 1921, Hughes enrolled at Columbia University and published his first poem "The Negro Speaks of Rivers." Nevertheless, bored by formal education, Hughes left the university one year later for Africa and Europe, first as a sailor, then as a cook and busboy. The story is always told that one day in 1926, when Hughes, who'd returned to the States years before, was waiting a table in a restaurant, he served a guest, instead of the menu, with several poems, for he had recognized the man to be a very popular poet of the time, Vachel Lindsay. As a result, encouragement fell on his prepared head and Hughes got the good fortune to collect his poems into a book, *The Wearing Blues*, and had it published in the same year. Good fortune was continued in the next year when another book, *Fine Clothes to the Jew*, followed suit. After finishing college education in 1929, Hughes began to support himself by his pen. He worked diligently and tried nearly every literary form and style: poetry, fiction, drama, and essays for newspapers.

2. Characteristics of Hughes' Works

Hughes was the first writer who brought the stories of Black people in the Harlem area into American literature and initiated a new trend in Black literature. This resulted in the later famous literary and artistic movement known as the "Harlem Renaissance" of the 1920's and Hughes became the spokesman of Black writers.

As a Black lyric poet, Hughes took great advantage of the rhythms of jazz and the blues and, in addition, developed subjects from Black life and racial themes. In his poems readers of the 1920s were satisfied to find primitivism combined with classical technique. Hughes reached the summit of his achievements when he was honored with the informal title of "Poet Laureate of Harlem."

Hughes' poems were characterized by short lines and simple stanza patterns, but with strong rhythms of jazz and strict rhyme schemes derived from blues songs. Two principal themes of the poetry are constantly passionate presentation of Black life by applying rhythms and refrains from jazz and blues, and poems of racial protest.

3. Major Poems of Hughes

Besides what are mentioned above, the other collections of Hughes include *Dear Lovely Death* (1931), *The Negro Mother* (1931), *Dream Keeper* (1932), *The New Song* (1938), *Shakespeare in Harlem* (1942), *and Ask Your Mama* (1961).

4. Selected Poems

(1) The Negro Speaks of Rivers

I've known rivers:
I've known rivers ancient as the world and older than
    The flow of human blood in human veins.

My soul has grown deep like the rivers.
I bathed in the Euphrates when dawns were young.
I built my hut near the Congo and it lulled me to sleep.
I looked upon the Nile and raised the pyramids above it.
I heard the singing of the Mississippi when Abe Lincoln
    Went down to New Orleans, and I've seen its
    Muddy bosom turn all golden in the sunset.

I've known rivers:
Ancient, dusky rivers.

My soul has grown deep like the rivers.

Section Five
American Poetry of Contemporary Time

Notes

Line 5 the Euphrates: the river runs through Turkey, Syria and Iraq into the Persian Gulf; the Euphrates is often believed to be one of the cradles of world civilization.

when dawns were young: at the dawn, the very early stage of world civilization.

Line 6 the Congo: the second longest river in Africa. It runs through west central Africa into the Atlantic and is believed to be the original area of Black culture.

lulled me to sleep: caused me to sleep and rest.

Line 7 the Nile: the longest river in Africa, often considered as the cradle of human civilization.

Line 8 the Mississippi: the longest river in the North American continent. It flows from its northern source in Minnesota to the Gulf of Mexico, and used to be the most important artery of transportation in the United States and the one that nourished the American nation.

Abe Lincoln: Abraham Lincoln (1809 – 1865), the 16th president of the United States. Lincoln is always remembered as the one who issued the Emancipation Proclamation which liberated some four million Black slaves in the South.

Line 9 its: the Mississippi's.

Comment on the poem

In the long line of human history, each civilization flourishes along a river. In this poem, "I" is the symbol of human beings, who have shared very much with the development of the four great river valleys. By mentioning his involvement with rivers, the poet expresses his passionate love for world civilization.

参考译文

黑人说河

我了解河：
我了解那像世界一样古老的河，

那比人类血脉里流淌的血液还古老的河。

我的灵魂已变得像河一样深沉。
我在曙色微现时分畅游于幼发拉底河中。
我搭小屋在刚果河畔,
河水诱我沉沉入梦。
我仰望尼罗河水,
视野中金字塔高于尼罗河。
我听到密西西比河在歌唱,
伴着亚伯·林肯
顺流而下到新奥尔良,我看到
她泥泞的胸膛在落日里金光闪耀。

我了解河:
那古老,朦胧的河。

我的灵魂已变得像河一样深沉。
(李海云 译 李正栓 校)

(2) Dreams

Hold fast to dreams
For if dreams die
Life is a broken-winged bird
That cannot fly.

5 Hold fast to dreams
For when dreams go
Life is a barren field
Frozen with snow.

Notes

Line 1 Hold fast to: firmly fixed or attached to.
Line 7 barren field: land not good enough to produce crops.

    This well-structured and well-rhymed short poem is popular in the United States.

Section Five
American Poetry of Contemporary Time

Comment on the poem

Dream symbolizes hope or imagination; with it, a human being is like a bird, which can freely fly far and high and fly everywhere.

When writing, the poet makes use of two metaphors: First when life is regarded as a lively bird, dream is compared to the wings which enable a bird to fly; when life is considered as a piece of warm rich land, dream is the timely rainfall which enlivens everything on earth. The poet's imagination is energetic and it runs wildly once high into the sky and then falls steadily on the ground. It has become the dynamic power for human life.

参考译文

梦

紧紧抓住梦想
如果梦想消逝
生命就像鸟儿断了翅膀
再也不能飞翔。

紧紧抓住梦想
如果梦想消失
生命就像
冰冻雪封的贫瘠土地。
（李海云 译 李正栓 校）

(3) Words like Freedom

There are word like Freedom
Sweet and wonderful to say.
On my heartstrings freedom sings
All day every day.
There are words like Liberty
that almost make me cry.
If you had known what I know
You would know why.

Notes

As a Black, the speaker was inclined to cry when he heard words like "liberty," because he has really suffered a lot for the gaining of Liberty. That word sounds sweet and wonderful, however, it takes hardships to take a real hold of it.

参考译文

有些词像"自由"

有些词像"自由"
说起来亲切甜美妙不可言。
它在歌唱,动我心弦
分分秒秒,日日年年。
有些词像"自由"
却让我悲伤难过泪水涟涟。
你若知道我的一切
就会懂得我为何这样神伤哀怨。
（李海云　译　李正栓　校）

(4) Warning

Negroes,
Sweet and docile,
Meek, humble, and kind:
Beware the day
5　　They change their mind!
Wind
In the cotton fields,
Gentle breeze:
Beware the hour
it uproots trees!

Section Five
American Poetry of Contemporary Time

Notes

Lines 1 – 5 Blacks are usually sweet, docile, meek, humble, and kind. Yet one should be cautious of the time when they have to revolt. change their mind: When Blacks have been too cruelly treated and they have to revolt.

Line 7 cotton fields: The southern states of the country used to be famous for their cotton plantations and black slaves working there.

Lines 6 – 8 The breeze in the cotton fields is often tender; but one should still be cautious of the fact once the tender breeze is gathered, it is quite able to uproot the huge trees.

In the first stanza the poet directly warns the people who approve of racial discrimination, while in the second stanza, Hughes made use of a metaphor for a further emphasis of the warning.

参考译文

警 告

黑人们
可爱、听话，
温顺、谦逊、善良：
当心有一天
他们会改变主意！
棉田里的
风，
和煦的微风：
当心有一刻
它会把树连根拔起。
（李正栓 译）

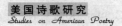

III. Robert Lowell
(1917 – 1977)

1. Life Story

Robert Lowell, related through his father to the poets James Russell Lowell (his great-grand-uncle) and Amy Lowell (his cousin), was born in Boston and grew up there as a rebel in the family tradition. He enlisted at Harvard College in 1935, but after a unsatisfied freshman year there, he completed his formal education at Kenyon College in Ohio in 1940. After graduation, Lowell secured a position at Louisiana State University, where he worked with some New Critics, developed a Southern accent, and converted to Catholicism, though, he retained an earlier interest in Puritan philosophy.

When World War II broke out, Lowell's offer to enlist in the American navy was twice rejected because of his poor eyesight. But in 1943, when he was called by the army, he declared himself a conscientious objector to the country's participation in the war and was thus sentenced to one year in jail. Next year, his first volume of poems, *Land of Unlikeness*, was published and he was well accepted as one of the important poets of the time.

For a long time, Lowell suffered from severe mental disease. With the suggestion of a doctor, he attempted to relieve the symptoms through writing about his inner feelings and succeeded. This resulted in more original poems.

2. Characteristics of Lowell's Writings

Lowell contributed most of his early poems to the rebelling against the social conventions of New England and to the description of his conversion to Catholicism. Poems of this period were scrupulously created with ironies, symbols and obscurity. With the publication of *Life Studies* in 1959, Lowell became more inclined for meditation and self-examination, which inaugurated an autobiographical project later called "confessional." Themes of this period also shifted from trivial private affairs

Section Five
American Poetry of Contemporary Time

to social problems as nihilist youth, to the deterioration of social morality, and to the spiritual sufferings of modern people. As a matter of fact, Lowell was once so radical in social activities that he was arrested for participating in a Pentagon March to protest against the Vietnam War.

As a poet, his style varied rapidly but the subjects were tended more and more towards a steady description of human internal world.

3. Major Works of Lowell

The complete works of Lowell's contains more than the works talked above. His first book was closely followed by another volume of poems, *Lord Weary's Castle* (1946), which brought him the Pulitzer Prize. Then the honor was succeeded by the publication of *The Mills of the Kavanaughs* (1951). His masterpiece, *Life Studies*, appeared in 1959, after that the major achievements of the 1960s and 1970s include *For the Union Dead* (1964), *History* (1973), and *Day by Day* in 1977.

4. Selected Poem

Katherine's Dream

(From Lord Weary's Castle)
It must have been a Friday. I could hear
the top-floor typist's thunder and the beer
That you had brought in cases hurt my head;
I'd sent the pillows flying from my bed,
5 I hugged my knees together and I gasped.
The dangling telephone receiver rasped
Like someone in a dream who cannot stop
For breath or logic till his victim drop
to darkness and the sheets. I must have slept,
10 But still could hear my father who had kept
Your guilty presents but cut off my hair.
He whispers that he really doesn't care
If I am your kept woman all my life,
Or ruin your two children and your wife;
15 But my dishonor makes him drink. Of course
I'll tell the court the truth for his divorce.
I walk through snow into St. Patrick's yard.

Black nuns with glasses smile and stand on guard
Before a bulkhead in a bank of snow,
20 Whose charred doors open, as good people go
Inside by twos to the confessor. One
Must have a friend to enter there, but none
Is friendless in this crowd, and the nuns smile.
I stand aside and marvel; for a while
25 The winter sun is pleasant and it warms
My heart with love for others, but the swarms
Of penitents have dwindled. I begin
To cry and ask God's pardon for our sin.
Where are you? You were with me and are gone.
30 All the forgiven couples hurry on
To dinner and their nights, and none will stop.
I run about in circles till I drop
Against a padlocked bulkhead in a yard
Where faces redden and the snow is hard.

Notes

Line 1 Friday: It indicates the time: a weekend, the frequent occasion for a mistress girl to meet her lover.

Line 2 thunder: the loud noise of a typewriter. The exaggeration suggests that the girl was quite annoyed by something.

Line 3 hurt my head: made my head feel slow because of drinking the beer.

Line 4 sent the pillows flying from my bed: throw the pillows away from bed to show my anger to that man.

Line 5 hugged my knees together and I gasped: (After throwing the pillows I began to calm down by) tightly holding my knees and taking quick deep breaths with open mouth.

Line 6 The dangling telephone receiver: the telephone receiver is hanging there and swinging loosely. This implies the receiver has just been thrown away by me because of disagreement with what was said from the other end. This also explains why I threw pillows to show my anger or the origin of my fury.

rasped: made unpleasant grating sound. My receiver had been thrown away, yet, the speaking of the other end is going on through the line.

Line 8 For breath or logic: (the speech in the phone did not stop) to take a breath or to add some logic to it.
his victim: the girl who had received the telephone call.
This "his" exposes to the readers that on the other end of the line, a man is speaking.
That must be the married man who had trapped the girl into being his mistress, but now he seems in a new trouble and will fail to meet the girl at the weekend.
Line 9 I must have slept: I want to fall asleep (but failed).
Lines 10 – 11 kept your guilty presents: (My father) kept the gifts you gave me out of your sense of guilt.
Line 12 he really doesn't care: he pretends not to think much about my unlawful relationship with that man.
Line 13 kept woman: mistress; an unlawful sexual partner of a married man.
Line 14 Or ruin your two children and your wife: Or my father pretends not to take it serious about the destruction I might bring to the man's family.
Line 15 my dishonor makes him drink: "my dishonour" refers to my illicit relationship with that married man. In spite of all his surface indifference, my father was rather ashamed of my illicit relationship with that married man and he thus had to try to escape from the reality through alcohol.
Line 16 the court: court of law, where divorces are obtained.
his divorce: my father's divorce from my mother just because of my behaviour.

The first 16 lines consist of the first section of the poem which, by probing into the heroine's present internal world, describes to the readers the girl's illicit love affair, her anger, her inner conflict and her feelings of guilt to her parents.

Line 17 St. Patrick's yard: the yard of St. Patrick's church.
Line 18 Black nuns: nuns in black dresses.
stand on guard: stand by.
Line 19 a bulkhead: a wall at the end of a building; the upright watertight partition or wall between compartments in a ship or aircraft; any of several walls which divide a ship into separate parts, so that, if one part is damaged, water will not fill the whole ship.

a bank of snow: the flat-topped mass of snow formed by the wind.

Line 20 Whose charred doors: the church's black doors.

good people: common people; people without a feeling of guilt.

Line 21 by twos: with the others' companies.

the confessor: the priest to whom one regularly makes his confession.

Line 22 to enter there: to enter the church.

Line 24 stand aside and marvel: stand by the side and wonder about.

Line 27 penitents: people who feel or show sorrow for having done wrong with the intention not to do so again; persons who are willingly suffering from a self-punishment to show that they are sorry for having done wrong.

dwindled: became gradually less or smaller; (The penitents are leaving.)

Line 28 cry and ask God's pardon for our sin: Much to my regret, I feel eager to enter the church to confess before God. However, I am such a timid girl that I dare not to go in alone. While I am admiring the "good people," I am rather helpless outside the church. That's why I cried and wondered.

Line 29 you: the lover who has abandoned her. She has no one to accomany her to confession.

Line 30 the forgiven couples: people who came in twos and now after the confession they have obtained the forgiveness of God.

Line 31 their nights: their entertainment during the evening.

none will stop: no one of the penitents was hesitating when leaving the church.

Line 32 run about in circles: I wandered around the church again and again, but was not courageous enough to go in by myself.

drop: give up (my trying to enter the church) and fall to the ground.

Line 33 padlocked: locked.

Line 34 faces: faces of the nuns', or any others.

the snow is hard: the snow is white and frozen and looks quite indifferent.

Comment on the poem

The second section, from Line 17 to the end, describes what the girl had imagined or probably just what she had dreamed for her penance. With a feeling of regret, she dreamed to have a confession in church. However, she was not courageous enough to enter the solemn site without company. She just admired the "good people" who, no matter how heavy their burdens were, were brave enough to relieve themselves. After winning forgiveness, people were able to enjoy the new life, but she was found the only one who was left outside the church door and regretting.

The poem is written in the first person. The first section presents to the reader the real trouble the girl is in while the second section provides an imagined world of the girl's journey for confession. She tried, but unfortunately, she failed. She is regretful, but the world doesn't know that, nor does God. The girl had to go on with her suffering from a sense of guilt, go on with her penance.

What the poet wants to show is that since human beings were all born with the original sin, a sin, or a wrong doing during life, is quite pardonable. What is rather unpardonable in the human world is a person without a mind of penance. God helps those who help themselves, but God would abandon those who offend others or the nature of themselves.

参考译文

凯瑟琳之梦

（从韦利勋爵的城堡）
那一定是星期五。我能听到
楼顶打字机的轰鸣，还有
你用箱子装来的啤酒弄伤了我的头；
我把枕头扔下床，
紧抱双膝喘着气，
悬摆着的电话听筒里传来的刺耳声
像是有人梦呓般地喋喋不休
不停下喘口气或顾不上推敲直说得他的牺牲品跌进
黑暗和床单之间。我一定是睡着了，
可仍听得见父亲的数落声，他留着
你罪孽的礼物却剪去了我的头发。
他低声说他真的不在乎
是否我一辈子的你的情妇
或毁掉你的两个孩子和太太，

但我丢人的行为却让他开始酗酒。当然
我会向法庭说明他离婚的真相。
我踏着积雪走进圣帕特立克教堂的庭院,
戴眼镜的黑衣修女们微笑着守卫在
白雪堆积的防水壁前,
它烧焦的门全都开着,那些好人们
成双结队走进去向神父忏悔。每人
要有一个朋友作陪,但大家
个个都有朋友陪。修女们在微笑。
我站在一旁惊讶不已;有一阵子
冬日的阳光令人愉悦,像对别人一样
它用爱温暖了我的心,可是
忏悔的人越来越少。我开始
哭着恳求上帝饶恕我们的罪孽。
可上帝,你在哪里?你本来与我同在现在却走了。
所有被宽恕的伴侣们匆匆前去
吃晚餐度夜晚,没人停下来。
我一圈圈地奔跑直到
跌倒在院中一面挂锁的防水壁门前
那里有一张张发红的脸和已变硬的雪。

(李海云 译 李正栓 校)

Bibliography

Abrams, M. H. Greneral Editor. *The Norton Anthology of English Literature* (5th ed). New York: W. W. Norton & Company, 1986.

Armand, Barton Levist. *Emily Dickinson and Her Culture*. New York: Cambridge University Press, 1984.

Booz, Elisabeth B. *A Brief Introduction to Modern American Literature, 1919 - 1980*. Shanghai: Shanghai Foreign Language Education Press, 1982.

Brooks, Cleanth, et al. *American Literature: The Makers and the Making*. New York: St. Martin's Press, 1973.

Chang, Yaoxin. *A Survey of American Literature*. Tianjin: Nankai University Press, 1990.

Chen, Jia. *A History of English Literature*. Beijing: The Commercial Press, 1984.

Chen, Jia. *Selected Readings in English Literature*. Beijing: The Commercial Press, 1983.

Cohen, Hennig. *Landmarks of American Writing*. Voice of America Forum Lectures, 1970.

Friebert, Stuart, and David Young. *The Longman Anthology of Contermporary American Poetry, 1950 - 1980*. New York & London Inc., 1983.

Gu, Zhengkun. *English Poetry*. Tianjin: Tianjin People's Publishing House, 2000.

Gui, Yangqing. *Selected Readings in English and American Literature*. Beijing: The Publishing Company for Translations, 1985.

Hart, James D. *The Oxford Companion to American Literature*. New York: Oxford University Press, 1965.

Lews, R. W. B. *The American Adam: Innocence, Tragedy, and Tradition in the Nineteenth Century*. Chicago and London: The University of Chicago Press, 1955.

Li, Gongzhao. *An Introduction to 20th Century American Literature*. Xi'an: Xi'an Transportation Institute Press, 2000.

Li, Weiping. *A Survey of English and American Modernist Literature*. Shanghai: Shanghai Foreign Languages Teaching Press, 1998.
Li, Yixie, and Chang, Yaoxin. *Selected Readings in American Literature*. Nankai University Press, 1991.
Perkins, Bradley Beatty Long. *The American Tradition in Literature* (7th ed) New York: Mcgraw-Hill Publishing Company, 1990.
Perrine, Laurence. *Sound and Sense: An Introduction to Poetry*. Princeton University. Harcourt Brace Jovanovich, Inc., 1973.
Rubinstein, Annette T. *American Literature: Root and Flower*. Beijing: Foreign Language Teaching and Research Press, 1988.
Shi, Zhikang. *An Outline of Backgrounds of American Literature*. Shanghai: Shanghai Foreign Languages Teaching Press, 1998.
Spiller, Robert E. *The Cycle of American Literature: An Essay in Historical Criticism*. London: Collier-Macmillan Limited, 1967.

常耀信等编著:《美国文学研究评论选》,南开大学出版社,1992年。
狄更生著:《狄更生诗选》,王晋华译,北岳文艺出版社,2000年。
胡荫桐等主编:《美国文学教程》,南开大学出版社,1995年。
惠特曼:《惠特曼诗选》,刘唤群等译,花山文艺出版社,1995年。
辜正坤主编:《英文名篇鉴赏金库》(诗歌卷),天津人民出版社,2000年。
江冰华译:《英美名诗选译》,陕西人民出版社,1984年。
刘岩编著:《英国诗歌导读》,北京语言文化大学出版社,2000年。
诗刊社编:《世界抒情诗选》,春风文艺出版社,1983年。
徐荣街等主编:《古今中外朦胧诗鉴赏辞典》,中州古籍出版社,1990年。
庄锡昌著:《二十世纪的美国文化》,浙江人民出版社,1996年。

剑桥美国小说新论·1-33

★ THE AMERICAN NOVEL ★

GENERAL EDITOR
Emory Elliott
University of California, Riverside

《剑桥美国小说新论》由英国剑桥大学出版社在上世纪80年代中期开始陆续出书，至今仍在发行并出版新书，目前已有五十多种……

每本书针对一部美国文学历史上有名望的大作家的一本经典小说，论述者都是研究这位作家的知名学者。开篇是一位权威专家的论述，主要论及作品的创作过程、出版历史、当年的评价以及小说发表以来不同时期的主要评论和阅读倾向。随后是四到五篇论述，从不同角度用不同的批评方法对作品进行分析和阐释。这些文章并非信手拈来，而是专门为这套丛书撰写的，运用的理论都比较新，其中不乏颇有新意的真知灼见。书的最后是为学生进一步学习和研究而提供的参考书目。由此可见，编书的学者们为了帮助学生确实煞费苦心，努力做到尽善尽美。

北京大学英语系教授　陶洁

CAMBRIDGE UNIVERSITY PRESS

北京大学出版社
PEKING UNIVERSITY PRESS

邮购部电话：010-62534449
市场营销部电话：010-62750672
外语编辑部电话：010-62765014

书名	定价(元)	ISBN
1.《嘉莉妹妹》新论	20.00	978-7-301-11430-8
2.《兔子，跑吧！》新论	20.00	978-7-301-11431-5
3.《向苍天呼吁》新论	20.00	978-7-301-11385-1
4.《就说是睡着了》新论	25.00	978-7-301-11444-5
5.《我的安冬尼亚》新论	20.00	978-7-301-11379-0
6.《漂亮水手》新论	20.00	978-7-301-11386-8
7.《白鲸》新论	24.00	978-7-301-11457-5
8.《所罗门之歌》新论	20.00	978-7-301-11364-6
9.《慧血》新论	20.00	978-7-301-11380-6
10.《小镇畸人》新论	20.00	978-7-301-11389-9
11.《白噪音》新论	20.00	978-7-301-11366-0
12.《瓦尔登湖》新论	20.00	978-7-301-11381-3
13.《太阳照样升起》新论	20.00	978-7-301-11357-8
14.《喧哗与骚动》新论	25.00	978-7-301-11436-0
15.《了不起的盖茨比》新论	20.00	978-7-301-11358-5
16.《尖枞树之乡》新论	20.00	978-7-301-11410-0
17.《麦田里的守望者》新论	20.00	978-7-301-11462-9
18.《永别了，武器》新论	20.00	978-7-301-11377-6
19.《只争朝夕》新论	20.00	978-7-301-11359-2
20.《八月之光》新论	22.00	978-7-301-11412-4
21.《海明威短篇小说》新论	20.00	978-7-301-11411-7
22.《汤姆叔叔的小屋》新论	26.00	978-7-301-11472-8
23.《他们眼望上苍》新论	20.00	978-7-301-11461-2
24.《红色英勇勋章》新论	20.00	978-7-301-11395-0
25.《贵妇画像》新论	22.00	978-7-301-11433-8
26.《土生子》新论	20.00	978-7-301-11437-7
27.《去吧，摩西》新论	22.00	978-7-301-11409-4
28.《美国人》新论	22.00	978-7-301-11378-3
29.《最后的莫希干人》新论	20.00	978-7-301-11367-7
30.《豪门春秋》新论	22.00	978-7-301-11388-2
31.《亨利·亚当斯的教育》新论	22.00	978-7-301-11093-5
32.《拍卖第49号》新论	22.00	978-7-301-11382-0
33.《觉醒》新论	20.00	978-7-301-11435-3